P9-DMW-753

ALSO BY MELINDA HAYNES

Mother of Pearl

Chalktown

WILLEM'S FIELD

A Novel

MELINDA HAYNES

FREE PRESS

New York London Toronto
Sydney Singapore

*f*P

FREE PRESS
A Division of Simon & Schuster, Inc.
1230 Avenue of the Americas
New York, NY 10020

This book is a work of fiction. Names, characters, places, and incidents either are products of the author's imagination or are used fictitiously. Any resemblance to actual events or locales or persons, living or dead, is entirely coincidental.

Copyright © 2003 by Melinda Haynes
All rights reserved, including the right of reproduction in whole or in part in any form.

FREE PRESS and colophon are trademarks of Simon & Schuster, Inc.

For information regarding special discounts for bulk purchases, please contact Simon & Schuster Special Sales at 1-800-456-6798 or business@simonandschuster.com

Designed by Jeanette Olender
Manufactured in the United States of America

1 3 5 7 9 10 8 6 4 2

Library of Congress Cataloging-in-Publication Data
Haynes, Melinda.
Willem's field : a novel / Melinda Haynes.
p. cm.
1. Men—Texas—Fiction. 2. Texas—Fiction. I. Title.
PS3558.A862 W5 2003 2002192796
ISBN 0-7432-3849-4

ACKNOWLEDGMENTS

The writing of this book would have been impossible without the support of certain individuals. Mary Gerhardt, a woman who never reminds me that a ten-thirty phone call on a weekday night from Alabama is really an eleven-thirty phone call in Massachusetts. Traci deLorge, who somehow manages to balance a manuscript on one knee and her new baby on the other. Neal and Kristin, Kevin and Spring, Shiloh and Christina: your gifts of encouragement have always been delivered with perfect timing. Sue Walker, who stood beside me during one of the hardest times of my life. Tommy Franklin and Beth Ann Fennelly, your gifts of friendship are as excellent as your writing. William Gay, whose work continues to inspire. Wendy Weil, my agent and friend, who without fail has always managed to jump-start a writer's timid heart. Martha Levin, my publisher at Free Press, also my friend, thank you for your excellent advice and your love of words. My husband Ray, who knows the toll it will take, yet still encourages me to write. And finally—not because the two of you are the last people on my mind; quite the opposite—to Ted and Cindy Haynes, I want you to know that the lessons in courage you've taught me are priceless and will never be forgotten.

For the boys, Benjamin, Nate, and George

The heart knows its deprivation;
and takes its own measures.

— NELSON ALGREN —

WILLEM'S FIELD

{CHAPTER 1}

1974

Ten o'clock in the morning and already the wind was busy. A king-size wind as big as the state itself rolling across the bottom shelf of Oklahoma and into Grayson County, Texas, crossing the border with a low, chaotic cloud of highway trash carried in its wake. Empty cigarette packs and crinkled cellophane. Rattling drink cans and tattered bits of rain-stained paper. The stuff of chaos. Willem Fremont sat watching the two young girls with waist-length hair as they stood on the lip of the old highway. The wind gathering along the backside of their blue jeans and sending their shirts away from their bodies like sails. At their feet the manic plunder of wind-driven waste. The highway was an old one, with cracked blacktop that buckled and sheared and pitched upward near the western horizon before sinking low in the vicinity of the truck stop, a perpetually downward ribbon of lane that made thoughts of going any direction other than east seem tiring. But west was where the girls wanted to go. A cardboard sign near their feet spelled out SAN FRANCISCO. Willem watched them from the red Naugahyde booth of RUBY'S REGAL TRUCK STOP where he sat, one hand flattened over his hometown paper, folded neatly in half; his other hand closing around the ribbed sugar dispenser with a grip that whitened his knuckles and forced old blue veins to bulge across the top of his hand like worms. He glanced around.

There was nothing regal about Ruby's, in his opinion. Unless one counted the regaleze references to food, or the construction-paper crowns that randomly decorated the place. (*Crowns*? he thought, momentarily sliding into the blinding red-light district of alarm.) One topped the menu blackboard, heralding the "Fit for a King Meal" of chopped steak and mashed potatoes and bacon-laced pole beans, *ALL* FOR *ONLY* $3.98! Another crown sat atop the cash register, next to a plastic toothpick dispenser filled with toothpicks the color of Easter eggs. Each time the drawer was slammed, the kingdom chanced being overthrown, for the crown jostled another half inch toward the metal edge of disaster, where the possibility of being trampled and ruined by collective serfdom seemed likely. The last paper crown hung from a wire over the single glass door, within direct line of Willem's sight. It hung like a flogged victim, forced to swing and spin upon the advent of customers escaping the dust-flat Texan winds. Once the doors were shut, it would begin to correct itself inside this airborne vortex until it moved with catastrophic slowness to a position static and dead.

It was this crown that worried Willem more than the other crowns, and as with most things that worried him, he felt responsible for the reason behind the worry. He just couldn't remember what that reason might be. Perhaps it had to do with the absoluteness of gravity or the snobbishness of British royalty, but he couldn't really be sure. His fingers twitched across the top of the newspaper and he shut his eyes. On a scale of one to ten, with ten the red-level mark of extreme fear and one the uncomfortable blush of moderate anxiety, Willem felt sevenish. It was like knowing there was something inside a bedroom closet that was bad. All he hoped at this point was that he could sit quietly and finish his meal before the door flew open and whatever was in there escaped.

There were squeals out by the highway where the girls were, and though the window was grease-fogged and plastered with various church revival and stock sale notices along its perimeter, he could see them clearly enough to ignore for a moment his nagging anxiety. They were bent at the waist, adjusting their San Francisco sign, which wouldn't stay put because of the occasional cattle truck that thundered by.

Willem took a deep, steadying breath and read the revival notice that was closest to his face, a beige pamphlet announcing "Sister Moxilianna Sánchez up from Waco Texas to Share Her Amazing Soul-Saving Deliverance from the Satanic Life of Palm Reading." Her picture had been printed on the notice, and in Willem's opinion, she seemed fiercely unhappy with her rescue. Next to that notice was an announcement concerning Black Angus cattle for sale by a man named Robert Gerhardt who lived 4.7 miles *exactly* from the Old Cutter Bridge in Pottsboro. There were no pictures on that flyer, and Willem was quickly bored. Through the narrow margin left between the two notices, he could see the two girls as they leaned into the wind.

Looking away from them, he turned to the menu fastened on the wall above a bank of heat lamps, those words written in chalk boasting a three-dollar panfried steak complete with the promise of hash-browned potatoes. He felt sure the words held a temporary cure, if only he studied them long enough: The Royal Steak and Potatos—cooked the way you like it. The unskilled cursive writing. The uneven loops of the L's. The improper spelling of "potatoes." Anything to stem the worry, since Willem Fremont's worry of late escalated to panic and manifested itself in ways the general population found unseemly.

He tightened his grip on the sugar dispenser and peered across the roomful of strangers, looking for the one familiar person with whom he might converse. The nondescript face that he knew beyond a shadow of a doubt would settle him and point toward the menu and talk to him about it, maybe bring him back where he needed to be, which was sitting in a booth with good manners and midwestern patience, waiting to order something to eat. The *Womanwhobroughtmecoffee* was the woman he was looking for, and while he couldn't remember the necessary details of her physical appearance—the color of her eyes, her height, an approximation of her weight—he could remember her smell.

Minutes earlier Willem had smelled her before he had seen her, and the smell was a puzzle in itself, since it was both pleasant and unpleasant. The odor of her unwashed armpits had migrated into the fragrance of fresh hot coffee and confused him, the coffee canceling out the harshest elements of armpit acidity and, in so doing, reducing its own appeal by at least fifty percent. The limbic portion of his brain had overfired then—he was already overtired and overstimulated and somewhat addled from twenty-four hours of driving—as he tried to register and place those mutated smells, and his eyes were shut because he had found through the years that if he shut his eyes and concentrated it helped break open riddles, so when he felt her arm brush the back of his shoulder, he had jerked to the side and things spilled. Coffee. A small glass pitcher of cream (real cream, not a powdered substitute, which would have been self-contained and much easier to clean up), the menu entombed in yellowed plastic she was holding in her hand. The time spent mopping up and fetching what was scattered came to his rescue and gave him the necessary seconds required to register patience and remorse.

He remembered how she had dabbed at his arm with genuine concern, taking care to get a clean cloth from behind the counter and work it against his sleeve, dipping the end of the cloth in a glass of ice water that had somehow appeared on his table. "I'm so sorry," she said. "I didn't mean to scare you." Willem, feeling the brunt of responsibility for the entire debacle, had hurried to excuse her and say, "Don't worry about it, I'm fine," while sliding nearer to the window to escape her ministrations, relieved she wasn't aware that her lack of hygiene and his love of coffee were coconspirators bent on his discomfort.

But now he needed her, because the crown was swinging and the vagueness of his worry was dissipating, and studying the letters on the menu wasn't working (the L's were amazingly well done for a group of people writing from the disadvantaged side of education, which, judging by the limited vocabulary of the short-order cooks and waitresses, had to be a fact). To add insult to injury, the girls outside were standing perilously close to an uneven highway, and the wind was picking up, beating their cardboard sign against their blue-jeaned legs.

He studied the faces inside Ruby's Regal Truck Stop. Most of the customers were involved with cattle. Willem could smell the shit on their shoes. A family that included a young boy ripping paper napkins to shreds and a baby sitting in a wooden high chair was in the corner. The baby's father fanned at its face with a folded courtesy map while he sipped his coffee. The mother, a brunette with slumped shoulders and out-of-date cat's-eye glasses held together on one side by Scotch tape, was fishing in her purse for some other child-distraction device. Keys, maybe.

A man sitting at the counter (which was too close to Willem for his comfort; he needed at least five feet of separation to feel fully operational and competent, and he had been afforded only three) leaned across and laid a meaty hand on the waitress's arm and said, "Sweet pea. Listen to me. If we just sit back and wait and see, he'll settle down. Boys are gone be boys. I knew his daddy and his daddy was the same way. Took years to get used to the idea of settling down."

"There's no 'we' to this. It's 'me.' I have to put up with it, not you."

"All I'm sayin is it takes some boys years—"

"I've not got years to wait," the waitress said.

"I knew his mama, too. She waited years and—"

"Well, I'm not his mama."

Willem didn't have years to wait, either. As inevitable as a sunset, the yellow caution light inside his mind was slowly beginning to turn to red. Glancing around the room, his blue eyes looking desperately for a diversion, he leaned toward the floor and noticed the irregular patterns of the black-and-white linoleum. It had been patched in places with blue replacement squares the color of Play-Doh, and to make matters worse, pollutants collected in the spaces where the squares didn't meet: bits of nondescript dirt, a clump of waxed-over organic material, and what seemed to be a small bristly wad of nonhuman hair. The bar stool nearest him was worse. Where its stainless-steel tube met the floor was a casement of black rubber that was torn and floppy, and when the customer put his shit-covered boot to it, the rubber slipped down the pole like skin off a bone. Willem looked to the warming tray for help, the fixed metal cones of radiant orange heat actively mummifying french fries and apple pies alike. It made him think of roadkill roasting in the sun. Wild-eyed and frantic, he jerked to the side, rattling the silverware on the table, pinging his spoon against his glass of water, frantic for the attention of someone, anyone.

His smelly less-than-regal waitress was nowhere to be found.

At this realization, his heart rate increased to such an alarming tempo that he was sure its galloping could be seen clearly by the person behind him eating her Fit for a Queen sausage and pancakes. He was sure his heart was pounding so ferociously that his booth inside Ruby's Regal Truck Stop was beginning to vibrate and shimmy and any minute now this seismic activity would shatter the glass and those handwritten notices concerning salvation and stock auctions would commingle out on a stricken landscape until plastered to the earth by eighteen-wheelers hell-bent on California. Willem knew that if he allowed his gaze to travel to the paper crown hanging over the glass-front door, it would be spinning with tornadic intensity.

The affliction had been happening for so many years that Willem no longer thought of it as a condition separate from waking and breathing and eating and shitting. It could not be fooled or cajoled or intimidated. But it could be delayed. Turning to the window, he said to his slack-jawed reflection, "Look." It was a command he always gave himself, as though the sanity to which he clung could be reinforced a little by self-examination. Seeing his face peering back at him only moderately distorted, he noticed that his thick white hair, no longer brown, was not receding as severely as he had imagined. His teeth were still good. Evenly spaced with a sufficient bite that had been tearing at meat for seven decades. He grinned at himself. The muscles along his face had relaxed, and there were ridges alongside his mouth, but his eyes were still bright and clear, not rheumy or wizened or weak or failing. He took in a deep breath through his nose. He had already figured out that his sense of smell was working at its optimum. These observations were good. They slowed down his heart, and he felt strong enough to chance looking at the front door.

The crown was not spinning like a tornado. It was aloft in a quiet, easy, rocking turn. Willem nodded. Relaxed his shoulders a little. Began to think of other things that hung: piñatas, wet flags, a noose. "Wait," he said to his reflection in the window, trying to backpedal to the least harmful item on the list (the piñata) and feeling that inevitable engaging of gears as his mind skipped over the innocuous vision of a parrot-colored swinging container of candy and headed straight to the hangman's noose. At this point he mentally slammed shut the door by physically slamming his hand on the table and lurching to his feet. Suddenly upright in the aisle of the restaurant, he felt the instantaneous jolt that comes from knowing you've done something stupid. To his surprise, he seemed the only one aware of it; whatever acknowledgment registered on the faces of the diners, surprise was not a part of it. They were bored with him. They saw him for what he was: one more crazy old man in saggy pants and wrinkled shirt given to jumping to his feet at the least provocation. Insulted, he stood as tall he was able and stumbled to the counter and said in a voice that was a little too loud: "Sir, I need a menu, please."

"Looks like you got one right there on your table," the short-order cook said with a point of his spatula. And there it was, grease-spattered but adequate, the words printed on paper trapped within a plastic binder bordered in red. His Majesty's Ham and Eggs. A complete family of Royal Waffles. The Duchess Omelette.

Beaten, Willem shuffled back to his booth and sat, his fingers running up the edge of his water glass. Early on he had decided he was crazy, and he had read every book he could find on mental illnesses. Studied the various aspects of psychosis. His bewilderment had grown. As far as he could tell, people who were crazy were not *aware* that they were crazy, and Willem Fremont was very aware that he was crazy.

The beelike drone of conversation ebbed and flowed around him. Sentences ran like water and lapped at his feet and the cuffs of his shirt and moved steadily across his shoulders as he sat in his booth listening to references concerning the weather, and the proper way to fence forty acres, and the stupidity of President Nixon. Drifting along on the current was the understanding that everything around him was normal, and if he would act normal, it might *be* normal. All he had to do was ignore what he was feeling and respond to his immediate surroundings. The salt and pepper shakers needed wiping off, and there was still a drop of coffee pooled on the table. Once these activities were completed, he noticed the stained menu and where it was placed in relation to his person, and he measured out the distance in inches and then converted the sum over to the metric system. He momentarily gave up on the metric system and forced an unworkable algebraic equation to the surface: *Coffee Puddle is to Menu what "A" is to "X."* There was also a backup should math lose its power to charm: he would get up and go into the small, nasty hovel of a rest room and study the circumference of the princely turd floating in a serfishly neglected toilet. And if *that* didn't do it, he would leave the rest room and go outside and feed some coins into the mouth of a metal box and reach inside and grope for a newspaper, remembering the whole while to slow down his breathing to steady his hands. And if, once he returned to his red Naugahyde booth in Ruby's Regal Truck Stop, his heartbeat was still threatening expulsion of his eyeballs, he could look out the grease-smeared window until he found those two young girls with waist-length hair, dreaming of San Francisco.

Realizing there was a plan helped him. Willem squeezed his eyes shut, and when he opened them again, his heart rate had slowed to an almost reasonable rhythm. There were no more trucks on the highway that he could see and the sun had broken through the clouds and the sky was that incredible blue that heralds the advent of autumn and the short-order cook, an untidy boy with thick sausage lips, had managed to scramble an egg to a customer's satisfaction and was whooping it up next to the glass-front refrigerator. For the moment all seemed right with the world. Willem looked outside toward the girls, so relieved the spell had passed and all his clothes were intact and on his body that he felt limp and grateful and strangely close to tears. The sad truth was that he couldn't even remember what it was he was worried about.

The taller of the two girls had dark brown hair with a portion pulled back into a long braid that was tied at its end with colored beads; the other girl's hair was blond and wavy, and when she'd lift her arms, she seemed mostly hair and very little else. Thin as waifs they were, so thin in fact that their ribs caught the light and became ivory crescents that disappeared underneath their sheer tops when they lowered their arms to bend to their cardboard sign. They both wore low-cut bell-bottomed jeans that hugged their hips, and wide leather belts that were tasseled. Braless, their breasts were evident because of the pressing wind, and on their feet were leather sandals.

He was sifting for some other aspect of their bodies to study because the wind pressing against their shirts had set it loose again. That large thing that had tried to escape earlier. He sat, rigid as a metal beam, and looked at their feet where dust and debris whirled. He watched the low clouds curl along scuffed leather and smooth ankles and fresh skin and pink toes. He noticed as the dust kicked higher and higher, brushing their thighs now, until, in a final fit of ejaculation, it spat a mouthful of loose gravel across the buckling asphalt. His heart pounding, Willem looked at the crown over the door and saw that it was swinging.

"Honey, you need more coffee?" the waitress said.

He realized he was panting when he turned to the voice and he hoped that she would attribute his irregular breathing to age. He hoped the panic had not traveled to his eyes. The voice belonged to the same one as before, the *Womanwhobroughtmecoffee,* but either she had washed and applied deodorant or she was standing too far away for him to smell.

"Yes." He paused and put his hand to his chest. "Please."

"You have time to think about what you might want to eat?"

Willem wondered why she was minus her odor now. He wondered why he was worried about her smell at all. Fixating on one thing was dangerous. It made him say things he didn't want to say.

"If you need more time to think, it's okay. I got nowhere to go."

Her voice rode on a musical note of shyness, and he figured she might be new here. Maybe her first job, even. Maybe she was so nervous about starting this new job that she couldn't sleep much the night before and woke up late and didn't have time to wash properly. His throat was tight because he didn't want to blurt out anything about her bathing habits. He wanted to eliminate the possibility of making a statement olfactory in nature, so he thought about the menu; he had decided on the Royal Knight Ham and Eggs for $3.98.

"I smell a pig," he said and instantly wondered if the fork might be clean enough to stab in his neck.

"Honey, don't we all." She pointed with a pencil toward the counter where two men sat. "They raise pigs. Got forty acres of nothin *but* pigs." She paused and then lowered her voice in a conspiratorial whisper and pointed with her head to a loner eating toast at the far side of the room. "And that one there left his wife and four kids for a piano teacher over in Bonham. I say he's a pig, too." Her laugh was a little bit mean, and Willem decided she must know the rejected wife and abandoned kids personally.

Willem looked toward his coffee cup, at its lukewarm liquid, and tried to remember all the great cups of coffee he'd had in his lifetime. He wondered, if it was somehow possible to collect all those great cups of coffee, whether they would fill a ditch, or a pond, or a lake. "No. I mean I want . . ."

He wanted to tell her about the Ham and Eggs for $3.98, he did not want to insult her, he absolutely would not be able to *bear* it if he insulted her. "I want . . . something," he said.

"You want something from the menu?"

He nodded a little too forcefully.

"You want something to eat?"

He nodded again.

With a kindness reserved for the old and infirmed, for vintage priests as well as withering librarians, the waitress did what good waitresses do: she waited.

"I . . . want."

"Yes?"

"I want." He paused and swallowed.

"You want."

"I want . . . to smell a pig!"

Willem made himself grin like an idiot. If she thought he was making a joke, she wouldn't be insulted. Sheer inspiration made him point to the menu. He prayed his finger landed on the Royal Knight helping of Ham and Eggs.

"Oh. *I* get it." The tiny truck-stop pad was being written on. "You old guys. I swear. Always cracking a joke."

And then she turned and ripped the sheet off the pad and tossed it to the thick-lipped boy searing meat on the grill. "Oink and eggs. Over easy. Two racks." She was finally gone, moving with a mean set to her shoulders toward the man who left his wife and four kids for a piano teacher over in Bonham. Willem bowed his head and wanted to cry.

It is a misconception that the elderly grow beyond the grasp of shame's fingers. That they become so ensconced inside maturity's arms, they remain untouched. Willem sat, recalling his words, his gaze trained on the girls out by the road. For a long while he watched them. They were playing with each other's hair. It was an innocent moment.

⇢⇠

"Here you go."

Crockery slid in front of him. Steam rose off his eggs. Turning his head to tell her thank you, he saw it wasn't necessary. She had already moved away and was busy handing menus to two new customers who had just entered. Willem picked up his fork and cut into the ham.

It is probably a good thing that the elderly, for the most part, go ignored. This is what he was thinking while he ate. Glancing down at his newspaper, he noticed *The Colorado Mountain Gazette* had spelled his name wrong. William, not Willem. Shrugging, he reasoned it was an easy enough mistake to make. They got most of it right. He *had* established Fremont Renovation Millworks and run it successfully for close to thirty years. It *had* been bought out by the suits in Chicago. The part that was a mistake in *The Colorado Mountain Gazette* was the business about Willem's being a missing person. He *wasn't* a missing person. He knew exactly where he was going. Shoving his plate away, he wiped at a droplet of grease on the table. He thought he saw a hair floating in his ice water, so he looked away.

"You from there?"

The *Womanwhobroughtmecoffee* was back and pointing with her shoulder and head toward the newspaper he had folded on top of the table. A glass coffeepot was in her hand, steam was escaping its metal-banded mouth. She seemed to be avoiding his eyes. "I wasn't trying to pry. Just noticed the word 'Colorado.'"

Willem didn't want to have a conversation with her, because conversing was too hard. He was too likely to ask her point-blank when she had bathed last. Keeping his lips sealed, he looked up at her with his old man's smile and tapped a finger along his coffee cup and waited quietly while she poured. She did such a good job of filling his cup that he nudged judgment aside and decided to answer her.

"I used to live there," he said.

"I've lived here for*ever*." She blew at her bangs.

He took it she was unhappy about this.

"Born here, in fact."

He wondered if she meant she had been born inside Ruby's Regal Truck Stop. Maybe in that back cubicle where they cooked. If so, she was in direct lineage for the crown.

And there it was again, the swinging crown. Right in front of him. Merging with his fear of saying the wrong thing, doing the wrong thing. (*Swinging Crown* is to *Comments About Hygiene* what "*Y*" is to "*Z*.") Scrambling and desperate, he averted his eyes toward the destruction in the seat across from him. A rip began at its upper corner and traveled down until it disappeared from view. Yellowed foam rubber bled out like fat around a wound.

"You're still young. You might leave one day," he said, finally looking at her, fully aware that his hands were shaking.

"You better believe it. There's no way I'm gonna stay here and serve pig farmers all day long. No way."

Move away from me, he thought. *Move away from me now.* Willem rubbed at the buttons of his shirt, his fingers catching on the third one and slipping it free of its hole. He lowered the offending hand to the sugar dispenser again.

"There are worse places, I would guess."

"If there are, I'd hate to see them." She shifted on her feet until her stomach was resting on the table edge. It was a poochy stomach, an I've-had-a-baby stomach. The hand was minus a wedding band, and Willem prayed she was Pentecostal, the sect that refused jewelry of any type.

"How long'd you live in Colorado?" Her smile was honest and bright, and he could smell her now.

"A long time."

"A really long time?"

"Seems like."

She slid a plate of apple pie across to him. He couldn't remember ordering it and wondered if, earlier, when he said he wanted to smell a pig, she had relied on her insider knowledge of pig farming, remembered how some of the better farmers fed their pigs apples, and made the leap. Shaking his head, he looked up at her.

"No, sweetheart, you didn't ask for this. This is on the house." She tapped on the table with her finger. Her fingernails were painted red and uneven. She looked across the room toward the man in the white apron and nodded in his direction.

"I spilt coffee on you. He just thought— "

"That wasn't your fault."

"It *felt* like my fault. That one over there thought it *looked* like it was my fault. But hey, if you don't want it—"

"No. This is fine."

There was a moment when he thought she might be seeing him as he wished she was seeing him, a man who had looked at one time an awful lot like Gary Cooper. (The older, Technicolor *Friendly Persuasion* one.) A tall man who filled his clothes in such a way that there was no pair of pants cheap enough to cheapen his appearance. Willem hoped she might be seeing the shadow of that person sitting there trembling in yellow light, and he entertained the foolish notion that if he could foster an image of his younger self in this woman's eyes, he might *become* his younger self and be more able to cope with what he was feeling. Foolishness was foolishness at any age. There was nothing left of that young man and he knew it. This being the case, he prayed that she was at least seeing the image he so carefully perpetuated: an old, elfinesque man with a head of white hair, a blue-eyed man blessed with the sensibility and manners required to sit at a shitty truck stop and eat a meal.

He began to feel a little better about the situation. He was not noticing the paper crown spinning over the door. He did not feel inclined to overanalyze odors of any type. Best of all, the girls out by the highway seemed a little older now, a little more able to take care of themselves; having shed, through some form of magic, that tender skin of helplessness. Willem relaxed a little, and his hand slid off the newspaper.

"My God. Is that you?"

Willem saw where she was looking. The folded newspaper. In a glance he saw the words *EL PASO COUNTY* peeping out from underneath his thumb. *Today officials at the Colorado Springs Police Department issued a missing-person report for William Frem* was covered by his palm. Too bad his hand wasn't big enough to cover his picture.

"Is that you in that paper?"

He looked up at her and saw open curiosity that lacked the intellect to go much deeper. He wished he were younger and still remembered how to flirt a little, but the best he could do was "You think it looks like me?" He was genuinely curious about this. The picture was over twenty years old, and in his opinion, he still looked a lot like Gary Cooper in it.

"Yeah. Well, sorta."

"Then I guess it's me."

"My God, you're in the paper." She was beaming. Her teeth were uneven and needed brushing. Her free hand was resting on her hip.

Willem shrugged. Watched the black coffee slosh around in its pot.

Guessed it was hot enough to peel off at least two layers of tough skin.

"Holy cow. I've not *ever* been in the newspaper."

Well, good for you, he thought, watching her move away from him. He noticed she refilled all the coffee cups at all the occupied tables in less than two minutes, all except one. He thought it was a testament to her capacity to hold a grudge that she was still ignoring the loner at the counter who had abandoned his wife.

Kitchen crockery was steaming in the back cubicle, sending rising drifts that muted faces and stainless steel and ceramic tile in a sweeping coverage of cloud, creating a surrealistic indoor-weather system birthed by seared meat and boiling water, a not so bad thing to witness. Willem settled a little bit in his booth, felt overwhelmed by the sadness that was always with him, realized the sadness had its origin in the basic alchemy of fear: extortion. In order to alleviate fear, one has to give up certain things, so with the infinite care of a man who has messed up time and time again while doing routine, uncomplicated chores, he removed his wallet and lifted a five-dollar bill from its hiding place. His fingers closed around a single and he removed it as well. (The waitress deserved a little extra for being shackled by prevailing body odor.) He folded both bills in half and set his water glass on George Washington's face and leaned back in his booth with a sigh. It would have been nice to relax and wait for the woman to bring him a ticket.

Looking back on it, he realized even then that he had known something was about to happen. Known that his composure, wobbling and inexcusable, would suffer a small chip or ping along its surface, like a windshield greeting a rock, and begin to crack. How to stop the sun? Or the climatic heat of an afternoon that sends a tiny abrasion nicked into hardened silicates into a yawning vein of distress? It can't be done. And so, with a sense of accustomed dread, Willem studied the bills under the glass and waited. Something was about to happen. Something always did.

He was right.

A station wagon pulled up outside and parked on the far side of the lot, partially blocking Willem's view of the two girls. As the family disembarked (four large people, complete with lumbering father, waddling mother, hulking son, and rotund daughter whose general appearance was as far from the two girls as China was from Tyler, Texas), their steps on

3008 09

TANITA
BODY COMPOSITION
ANALYZER
TBF-310

BODY TYPE	STANDARD
GENDER	FEMALE
AGE	47
HEIGHT	5ft 7.5in
WEIGHT	173.0lb
BMI	26.7
BMR	6299 kJ
	1506kcal
IMPEDANCE	533 Ω
FAT%	39.1%
FAT MASS	67.5lb
FFM	105.5lb
TBW	77.0lb
DESIRABLE RANGE	
FAT%	23-34%
FAT MASS	[illegible]1.5-54.5lb

TARGET BF% is:
34%

Predicted weight:
159.5lb

Predicted fat mass:
54.0lb

FAT TO LOSE
13.5lb

Consult your physician before beginning any weight management program. Tanita is not responsible for determining your target BF%.

TANITA
BODY COMPOSITION
ANALYZER
TBF-310

the gravel made as much noise as the car's tires had, and Willem felt pity for them as he watched. His pity evaporated once they reached the door and decided to try and enter all at once.

The father took the mother's arm. The teenage son attached himself to his sibling. The mother swatted at her children the way a person would swat at worrisome flies. All told, they stood there, a wall of genetic obesity, the door open to every gust of wind.

Move.

Move now, Willem thought.

The paper crown was whirling over their midwestern heads like a dervish, and still they stood there, the sullen daughter glancing over her shoulder toward the highway where those girls stood, the father making a game of it and laughing, elbowing his son with faux parental aggression. The crown was not only spinning, it was being sucked toward the opening. Its wire tether stretched to its limit.

"Ah, Christ," Willem said, pushing away from the booth and lunging to his feet. His plan was a reasonable one that involved bodily escorting the family in and shutting the door behind them, and then, if the crown was still swinging, he would get a broom from one of the waitresses and manually stop it. His plan was so simple, so cloaked in the seeming sensibilities of an elderly man, it was fail-proof. The plan might have worked if a rogue cattle truck ferrying cows to the slaughterhouse had not roared by, sucking the girls' cardboard San Francisco sign up into its grillework, sending great hurricane gusts across the parking lot and straight into Ruby's Regal Truck Stop (*Fat Family* is to *Crown* what *Truck* is to *Girls*). The girls were knocked to their rears and sandblasted, their ankles bleeding. Willem stood like the old man he was, in the center of the aisle, one shaking hand on the table, the other pointing to the crown that had been ripped from its wire and was sailing through the internal cloud system of Ruby's. He watched in horror as it caught a blast of oatmeal steam and rode its current before settling on the grill, where it caught fire and blazed.

It was at this point that Willem Fremont began to scream.

He was all the way to the Arkansas border before he could think about what came next, and even then he was so steeped in embarrassment he could think about only certain parts of what he'd done. Certain moments when his behavior could have been worse but hadn't been.

He remembered how he had climbed up into the booth and beaten at the glass, and torn at his hair, and fumbled at his belt. He remembered people staring and jumping to their feet, and the two waitresses and how they rushed from behind the counter to his side and stood gazing up at him. Willem remembered standing with his shoulder pressed to the window, his arm knocking free a revival flyer that floated to the floor.

"Come on, now, honey. Come on down," the *Womanwhobroughtmecoffee* said, her voice cooing like a dove.

"Get away from me!" he had yelled, watching the thick-lipped cook pick up a large knife from the sink and slide it like a mug of beer down the counter to the white-aproned king of Ruby's Royal Truck Stop. As a response to what he saw, Willem kicked the sugar dispenser across the room, where it shattered against a red padded bar stool.

"I'd get away from him," the thick-lipped cook said, his thick lips curled in a thick-lipped grin.

Willem *had* yelled, but the words were benign in that they made no sense. No sense at all. One mark against him was that the decibel level of all the yelling had been piercing enough to cause the white-aproned owner to drop his utensil, as well as the knife, but the words themselves were innocent and would make sense only to an equally crazy old man occupying the exact level of Willem's mind.

Episodes from the not so distant past rose up in his face: the time he had become so worried about shouting in church that he had screamed during the benediction; the evening of his secretary's funeral, when he had gotten so anxious about his appearance that he stood inside a restroom stall and undressed and redressed over and over again, missing the eulogy as well as the cemetery burial; that time in the shipping room when he couldn't quit taking off his shoes and rinsing them under the faucet, sure he had stepped in dog shit on his way in. Willem had done all these things and more.

As far as this particular day was concerned, losing Gary Cooper was the worst: the process through which that final dusty shadow of his former self had slipped away while his back was pressed to the greasy window of Ruby's Regal Truck Stop. It was enough to break his heart. He had heard a faint tapping, and the sound was so different from the internal bedlam that he had turned to find its source and seen those innocent girls (those sweet, innocent girls!) who wanted to go to San Francisco, standing with their hands cupping their faces. Their feet were bleeding. They didn't seem to care. The blond one was doubled over laughing at him, and the other one was falling to the ground, overcome by hilarity. That Willem had harbored tenderness in his heart for such heartless females was cataloged in a part of his brain that was still registering insults.

It could have been worse, he thought. *It could have been much worse.*

The fact that he had to be thrown bodily out of the truck stop while screaming at the top of his lungs knocked him out of the gold-star category. There *had* been a measure of redemption, though. Not for Willem Fremont but for a stranger he'd not had the pleasure of meeting face-to-face: the man who'd left his wife and kids for that piano teacher over in Bonham. That man came to the rescue by lifting Willem off the table and carrying him outside and depositing him on his ass in the parking lot. Willem had been stiff as a board and busy pounding on this stranger's shoulder the whole while, an act made all the more degrading because of its level of childishness. Rising to his feet and brushing the grit and dust off his legs, Willem opened the door to his truck and climbed inside, his hands shaking so badly he could barely manage the keys. The last thing he saw of Ruby's Regal Truck Stop was his smelly waitress pouring that adulterous man a congratulatory cup of hot coffee.

Willem took Highway 82 and drove steadily east, taking special care to maintain the proper speed limit, goading his mind to remember not to veer across the center line into oncoming traffic, and summoning up a heightened awareness of those treacherous long stretches of nothingness where half-asleep drivers were abruptly and often fatally bushwhacked by creeping tractors that appeared from the tall corn to cross the highway. Direction. Speed. Turn signals. The pressure of his foot against the brake pedal. He was careful of everything. If there was one lesson he had learned through seven decades of living, it was this: if an accident was going to happen, it was going to happen somewhere in the vicinity of Willem Fremont. The mileage signs changed numerically as he navigated away from the Lone Star State toward Purvis, Mississippi, the place where he had done most of his growing up. Close to a stupor, he kept trying to disengage from the wreckage of the day, disassembling piece by piece the moves and countermoves of all the participants, stepping back until he no longer felt like the star fool in a long-running farce but an unobtrusive production hand. The prop master, perhaps. After all, the only thing he had wanted back in Sherman, Texas, was a really good cup of coffee—

"—wood's trying to drum up their own brand of support. You got a whole nation of pinhead moviegoers who think Vietnam's terrain is similar to what Patton faced. And it's Hollywood's fault."

"Patton?"

"George C. Scott. Hollywood. The Academy Awards."

"I see."

"I say let them make a movie about our own war. About what's going in these United States. The Angela Davis story. She was a professor, you know."

"The University of California."

"Yes. Or the William Calley story. The Kent State story. There's a crew set to take those cameras to Attica in New York. It says right here that they've received a grant from the National Endowment for the Arts. And the strange thing is that they aren't interested in the causative force behind the riots, or the changing face of the American landscape. All they want is a documentary showing the damage. And do you know why they need it?"

"No." (the rustle of papers being shuffled)

"Because they need the evidence that we're no longer sitting around our perennial holiday turkey—"

"That reminds me of a Norman Rockwell painting."

"Exactly! Now imagine a Norman Rockwell painting on drugs. A Thanksgiving turkey smashed against a wall. A bong on the table instead of a glass of tea."

"Would you want to see that?"

"Not necessarily. But other people will. It's the car-wreck syndrome—"

Willem was reaching to turn the knob of his radio in search of Patsy Cline when the tires of his truck drifted to the shoulder and hit a smudge pot left by a field crew. It went flying like a cannon ball through a billboard advertising Coppertone suntan lotion. The missile was unlit, which was good, he supposed, but the impact of the unexpected ordnance reacting to his truck's bumper tore a hole clean through the small grinning child's bathing suit. It was enough to make him pull off the road and sit, his hands gripping the steering wheel, his face drenched in sweat, his knees, as well as some other deeper, previously unknown bone in his ass, quaking. A leather-clad hoodlum on a motorcycle slowed as he passed and yelled, "Dude! I bet that really burned that baby's ass!" before roaring off down the highway, his right hand up in a peace sign, a tattered American flag unfurling off his motorcycle's rear framework.

Willem leaned his head on the steering wheel and waited, the truck idling, the noise soothing, the wind off the passing eighteen-wheelers rocking his truck with a motion that came close to putting him to sleep. Fourteen songs played on the local bluegrass radio station while he sat there, his head frozen against the steering wheel, and he couldn't recall a single chorus, or word, or metered line. Should someone put a gun to his head and demand that he forfeit a phrase for his life, he still could not do it. When he looked into his rearview mirror, he saw that the sun was a huge circle low in the sky, and all around him dark was being summoned.

{CHAPTER 2}

A feathery nimbus of light illuminates the far field where the cows graze. It is always this way at this particular hour. Pink as a new pearl, the light is, fashioning halos around dried nettles and leaning posts and elements of nature previously deemed unremarkable. Leah watched the spread of light from her darkened kitchen, her hand pulling on a leather glove even as it reached to free the spring latch on the back door. The kitchen was small but warm, the wainscoting around all its walls painted a pale, earthy green, the floor highly varnished, as were the door frames and the window frames and the mahogany arch separating kitchen and parlor, the ceiling staged in the standard country way, twelve feet throughout. Against the far wall stood the pie safe, and next to it a window that opened to the best side of the homestead.

The window was tall and wide and exposed the far fields and the pecan grove, and on clear spring nights, once she turned off all the lights in the house, Leah was able to sit in a kitchen chair and smoke a cigarette and look up over the trees and study the face of the night sky, a view so constant and absolute she could spend hours looking and looking and still find something never seen. The kitchen window was her portal to a bigger place, and once the season of cows was done, she intended to ask Bruno if she might widen it.

Breakfast had been cooked, and she stood next to the back door smelling it. Not much these days, just a tray of biscuits set out beside a jar of honey, a pot of coffee perked, a tray of dry toast for Bruno. Her cup and saucer had been put in the sink to soak. Bruno's cup and saucer were sitting on the cloth-covered arm of the chair.

"I'm goin now," she said to him, seeing his back shape squared off in his chair that faced the bookcase, his brace riding up behind his head, where a beige pad of rubber cushioned his neck. His feet were crossed at the ankles and resting on the hooked rug her grandmother made back in El Dorado, Arkansas. But for Bruno's low and steady breathing, the man could be counted a monument, a piece whose place was forever fixed in a park, or a specimen of life-size taxidermy destined for a den. "Kate's started to bag up," she said, catching up her hair and fixing it in a low ponytail. "I expect a calf is waitin for me."

"She bagged up for two weeks last time," he said. "That cow's no good at signals."

"I know that. I'm just tellin you in case I'm gone awhile."

"How's her hips look?"

"She's close."

"I'd guess next week," he said.

"Maybe."

A magazine was spread open across his lap, and she studied the yellow spine and wondered at the month, for the subscription had lapsed and all his choices now consisted of previously viewed mountains and buried mammoths and hordes of Amazonian bats. It was still dark on that side of the house, and he sat immersed in it, stoically. She wondered if he had been given some compensatory gift in exchange for the use of his neck. Perhaps the ability to decipher words in the semidarkness. She watched him, her back resting against the door frame, remembering the shape of his lips, how incredibly soft they could be. She wondered if he'd stir and want to go with her. Maybe sit beside her on the truck seat while she rode along the fence line of the far plat. She waited inside the doorway and watched him; if he was aware of it, this awareness had moved beyond the irritation one feels upon being watched. He was immune to it, to her, to their life, to her body. Leah finally stepped out the door and onto the porch.

The air was unnaturally cool, evocative of October, which she knew to be a lie, for it was late May and the day would turn white-hot and devious in the blink of an eye. She was already set for the wet-heat noon that would try its best to smother her while she worked. But still she stood there, her head cocked slightly, her ear toward the interior of the house, waiting to see if Bruno might call her back. Maybe ask her for a second cup of coffee. Maybe ask her to rub his head. But there was nothing, just the huge container of quiet she had lived in for some time now.

To the east a delicate shifting then. The sky turning up a notch to the color of some lone river stone. Gray as old wet alabaster inside this moment. She crossed her arms and watched while the trunks of the trees along the far plat stepped out from their nondescript mass and gained clarity to become spruce and pecan and dogwood and oak. All gray fellows. All shoed in mist. *If a tombstone could sing, it would sing that color,* she thought, and then she ran a hand over her eyes and felt the stiff touch of the glove.

The wringer washer was to her left, and next to it a stack of milk crates, the cat sleeping atop its bed of croaker sacks. The sacks no longer ocher in color, no longer rough in texture, but yellow now and silky, cushioned with the shed hair of the tom. Leah reached out and patted its back and belly with her leather fingers and watched it stretch its legs in a lazy feline preen. When she stepped off the porch, the cat commenced a vigorous licking where her hand had touched, replacing the intruder smell of leather with its own fish-breath familiar.

She worked her fingers while she walked toward the pump shed. Rubbing the rough leather seams, bending the joints, first the little finger and then the one that wore the ring, loosening up the stiff leather to a more pliable condition. Low beggar's-lice clutched the tops of her leather boots, and dew soaked the hems of her jeans and the white caps of meadow mushrooms dotting the lawn. She noticed how thick the grass had grown around the shed's base, the clover that used to be there, buried, and how the constant slow leak from the faucet had spread a soggy border all around where cinnamon fern had taken hold in emerald clusters, all those pinnate fronds covered in orange woolly hairs.

Pulling open the door to the shed, she watched a garden spider scurry across its laced web and then huddle down near the trap's center, growing still while the web swung easily in the breeze. Hugely black with yellow markings, it seemed the size of a large man's palm, and Leah leaned in and searched its egg-shaped middle for a spider breath and couldn't find one. The four pairs of eyes seemed still as beads, black as India ink, wise as any of Earth's creatures. Leah watched the tiny drops of moisture captured inside the sticky webbed geometry sway gently in the wind before she looked away.

The tractor key was hanging on a nail, and she reached and took it. Her hat was there, too, resting on the metal water tank, and she took it as well and then slapped it against her jeans to ward off mud daubers or ticks before putting it on.

Off to the west, a single light blinked on and harsh yellow spilled out her mother-in-law's kitchen window. Leah saw it in passing and ducked her head out of habit, her hands rammed to her pockets while she walked the distance to the barn.

Spied upon. Tested publicly. This was how the kitchen light made her feel. *You must change your drawers inside this great plate-glassed window while the whole world watches. And if not the whole world, then one reed-thin woman who arises before the night is done in order to judge the quality of a marriage.* Because Leah Till's marriage was failing. Failing in ways that felt gargantuan and of Leah's own making. Close proximity to one's in-laws was commonplace in a rural community. Land never changed hands, it just got parceled out and fenced in, autonomy fading to the category of failed myth. Having to live under the scrutiny of a strong-willed woman whose favorite son seemed hopelessly miserable was the price Leah paid when she said "I do." A part of her would always know that it wasn't her fault, that she had tried to make the best of a sad situation, but that part fell silent under the perusal of Eilene Till.

Leah looked down at her boots, watched her feet walk across the vapored ground. *Go ahead, step out of them drawers, girl. First one leg, then the other . . .*

The silo was between the two farms. An indignant-looking tower with a galvanized dome painted red. Empty of grain for years now, it served a new purpose, a gaudy advertisement blazoned around its middle, and in the early fog she could see a "P" and a "D." Neat white fencing ran to the north as well as to the south before disappearing into a grove of pecan trees standing in neat rows.

Fourteen more steps and the eyes from that far kitchen window would have to strain to see. Elbows pressed to a kitchen counter would have to shift. The woman would have to go up on her toes, or perhaps pull over a chair and climb up on it in order to search for her.

"Well, go ahead and look, then," Leah said. "You'll not find me."

The woman was short and thin, not much larger than a seamstress's dress form. A moderate chest to match equally moderate hips. A slight vibratory stillness to her, indicating neatly compressed rage. Most saw her as easygoing and congenial and attributed her slight trembling to boundless energy, unaware that inside her gray-headed, sensibly dressed figure was a woman so angry she stood poised on the verge of spontaneous human combustion.

The source of this anger was her children, both grown men who had long since fled the boundaries of such description and would argue to the death that it was a demented woman's illusionary keepsake, a widow woman's ivory cameo, a folded fan of Chinese silk. But children they remained inside Eilene's mind: the child of her youth who wanted to work but couldn't; the child of her menopausal waltz, who was fully capable of working, yet refused. Eilene was chronically irritated, eternally frustrated, enormously weary of her boys. Like bad viruses they invaded her heart, wreaked havoc with her brain, stole the strength from her muscles, wore her fingers to the bone. To admit any of this (even to herself) would smear the work she'd done on her presentation of motherhood, a painting carefully orchestrated from the moment she put the first child to her leaking breast, a composite rendering that grew grayer and grayer with each passing year. There were trade-offs, though. Ways to get even.

Eilene had discovered one such way five years earlier, on the drive back from Vicksburg, where she'd hurriedly gone to sell her mother's silver in order to buy Sonny's way back home from Australia. She began to pretend she was growing deaf. Eilene (who could hear perfectly fine) made this claim in order to shout, because shouting at her sons kept her sane. Kept her from grabbing the gasoline can and burning down the place, or standing outside and breaking the windows of her house with rocks, one by one. She shouted on the phone, from the bathroom, at the ironing board, in the car. She gauged the level of the shout according to the proximity of whichever son was closest to her, preferring to increase the noise level the closer that son stood.

She also used the kitchen. Pots could be banged. Plates could be thrown. Pretending to be absentminded, she could burn the corn bread that Sonny was craving, or scorch the lima beans he was nearly starved for. She could put too much sugar in the tea and not enough mayonnaise in the potato salad. She could claim to have forgotten Sonny's allergic reaction to cream and load up the macaroni and cheese with an entire crock of it. She could slam the refrigerator door and hear the crash of the milk bottle and smile. She could stand next to the sink and watch for that veinish trickle of white to appear in front of the Kelvinator's door. She could jerk a dishcloth out of the drawer, bang the drawer shut, sling the rag to the floor, and stomp on it with her feet. She could wait until a week went by to clean the broken glass out of the stick of butter.

Eilene did all these things, always careful to spare the less fortunate of her sons from the extent of her wrath. Bruno no longer made her itch with nervousness. Now he made her cringe with pity.

Sonny wasn't so fortunate. Eilene's temper was just as likely to spring up over a peaceful Sunday dinner, while he sat at the table slurping his gravy with a spoon, as it was to erupt while she sat under low lamplight doing the monthly paperwork. The son who was able to ignored her. The son living under her roof was not that lucky.

Eilene leaned her elbows on the kitchen countertop and watched her daughter-in-law walk across an expanse of yard, headed for the barn. Early light filtered up through the trees, for it was nearly five o'clock in the morning. A shallow fog mist floated above the dew-wet grass, haphazard and surreal. It seemed for a brief moment that the woman being watched might be traveling across a low cloud, her feet buried up to the middle shafts of her legs inside a swirling mist that trailed behind her in a wake. Eilene shuffled to the side and leaned against the sink while Leah pulled open the heavy barn doors one at a time and disappeared into the dark. There was no sound. No light. A long minute passed, and the early morning aura shifted slightly and fog began to dissipate. A fresh crop of jays dipped noisily across the side yard, integrating with a mated pair of thrush calling out *whit whit heep heep.*

Eilene took the coffeepot and rinsed it (loudly) in the sink and measured the coffee and then banged the pot to the stove. She did all this work automatically, the level of loudness constant, her eyes watching out the kitchen window the whole while. The doors to the barn were standing open, agape in the dust, and still there was no noise; no movement. She struck a match to the gas and once it was lit, she coughed (loudly) into her hand. Minutes passed and the coffee began to boil.

Tiptoeing down the hall, she peered into the dark of Sonny's room and found him in the center of the iron bed, snoring. It had been a new mattress a year earlier, but now its edges curled upward like drying cheese, and she wondered just how many more mattresses she was destined to purchase to support the back of her younger son. On the far wall hung his horse-collar mirror, and below it, on her grandmother's prize cherry table, were his television set, four bags of potato chips (two of them empty), three snuff jars, and a rusted boat propeller. She had told him to put down newspaper before he unloaded it, but he had refused to listen to her. A fresh gouge ran diagonally across the entire width of its hand-rubbed top.

Shaking with rage, she tiptoed back up the hall to the kitchen and searched for a weapon, picking up the closest thing she could find: the bent metal spatula she would use for his eggs. With a somewhat lighter heart, she went back down the hall.

Moving until she stood at the foot of the bed, she studied him, the way his hand was tucked under his cheek like a child's, his opened mouth, his gray stubble of beard. His hair needed washing as well as cutting, and with that thought, she reared back and began to bang on the iron bed frame with the utensil, yelling, "SHE CAIN'T GET IT GOING!" rewarded instantly by the sight of her son throwing off the quilt and four pillows and sitting upright in the bed. She saw that he was sleeping in his underwear and socks.

Eilene went back to the kitchen and waited, and while she stood at the sink, she trembled with the anticipation of Sonny's drifting back off to sleep and the larger, louder kitchen pot she would use to bang against the wall.

"Do you *hear* me? Sonny? SONNY!" Eilene called toward the back of the house, reaching to the windowsill and taking up her hair net and spreading it with her fingers and putting it over her hair. The elastic formed a bead of skin around the perimeter of her face and flattened the tops of her ears against her head. Her hair was cut short, and she didn't need the net, but the thin mesh made her feel helmeted.

"DID YOU HEAR WHAT I SAID?"

There was silence from out the bedroom, then, "Hell. It ain't my tractor," Sonny said, his voice muffled.

She waited. Because she was pretending to be deaf, she was required to wait. To answer immediately would give her away. She also was required to ignore the countless times Sonny mumbled under his breath "Bitch" and "Fuck you" and "Why don't you try and make me, you old lady."

"Sonny? SONNY!" Eilene moved closer to the stove. "Sonny? Are you talking to me? Did you say something?"

"I *said* it *ain't* my tractor!"

"Well, I certainly know that!" Eilene yelled.

"I didn't take her to raise, neither!"

"I'm not saying you did!"

The tall silo was to the west, and Eilene looked at it, the cylindrical shape capped in red. Her garden should be resting in its shadow, experiencing the evolving sequence of the sun.

"Mama!"

Eilene bowed her head and waited. She knew what he wanted.

"I'm about to do it!" Sonny said. "Get over there by it just in case!"

Eilene stepped over the steel tubing, which originated in the back bedroom next to Sonny's bed and fed down the hall into her kitchen. It had been taped in place with brown freezer tape that she swept and mopped around, and she followed it to its course and stood watching where it ran up the wall until it connected with a switch. She tilted back her head and peered through her glasses, holding vigil over three white toggles braced by a small metal bar. She heard a loud click from the bedroom and watched the bar in front of her slide down, switching on the huge mechanics' fans in the backyard, around his latest project: the boat. She had to hand it to him: he never even had to leave the center of his bed.

From the bedroom he yelled, "Hot damn. I knew it would work!"

"Get up!"

"Didn't I tell you it would work?"

She went to the stove and turned the flame to low. From the window she could see those open doors to her daughter-in-law's barn. The overhead light had been turned on, and shadowy movements cut through the illumination. She knew Leah was moving around. Trying to do something.

Sonny clapped his hands. "What'd I tell you!" he said.

Eilene tied an apron around her middle and refused to answer. She put her hands to her temples and pressed at her skull with tiny rotating movements.

"Didn't I tell you?" He was shouting.

"I wish you'd hush!"

"Them switches workin?"

"You hear the fans running, don't you?"

Eilene placed her hands on the countertop, feeling the vibration while she watched small swirls of loose debris ferreting across the grass, sucked there by giant gin fans big as propellers. Sonny was painting his boat for the third time, and even though it was spring, he needed the fans on his backside while he painted because he got hot and sweated down his legs, and the sweat made his ass itch. The boat stood where Eilene's garden used to, and she was still not over her resentment. "This is damn foolishness!" she yelled.

"There are worse things than a couple of fans blowing in your backyard!" Sonny yelled back.

Yeah, rabbits, she thought to herself. Rabbits in Australia that needed killing to collect a bounty. Rabbits that wouldn't be killed unless you were standing in New South Wales holding a rifle in your hand . . . She kept quiet about it, though. The boat had cost her only four hundred dollars so far; the episode with the rabbits had come close to costing her a house.

"That boat's where my tomatoes need to be!" Eilene was so resentful she felt she might explode.

"I told you it'd work!" Sonny repeated, pleased. "There's not a problem in the world cain't be cured by cleverness. Give me a pencil and I'll work it out every time!"

Eilene looked at the proof where it was thumbtacked to the wall, ornate detailing on brown butcher paper that required the complete rearranging of her dining room for accommodation. And this was just the drawing. Once it was done, her son had spent hours hand-coloring the whole business with pastel chalk he had to send to Vicksburg for, then fixed it to the kitchen wall with red tacks, where he worshiped it with a zeal she found embarrassing. She had wanted a good print of Blue Boy or Pinky or maybe those bulldogs playing cards, and instead she had this thing that seemed more kin to a child's imagined pirate's map. Tiny stick men ran along what she supposed was an electric current. Circles for their primitive heads. Smiles on their faces. The view was from overhead, and every other one was looking up with a stick-fingered wave. The diagram shouted Sonny's true intentions: the stove drawn with expert proportions in accordance with his healthy appetite, the sink too small, his reluctance to wash a dish evident. The table and four chairs were satisfactory, and she leaned forward in amazement, realizing he had penciled in the sugar bowl and salt and pepper shakers. Tiny footprints were drawn where they were supposed to walk, allowing for the tubing that veined the floors.

"Please hush," he'd said to her that November night. "I'll fix it so you're not about to trip and bump your head. I'll draw you a map, even." And he damn sure had.

The paper showed the hall and the kitchen, the footprints side by side, a bizarre dance in consideration of eggs and bacon and the washing of a dish, a figure eight encompassing the stove and sink area. Female feet, she noted. Finally, a border of lightning bolts formed an intricate pattern around its edges. She was of a mind to take it over to Hattiesburg and have it framed as proof positive her younger son was a fool.

Sonny rolled over in the bed, and she heard the groan of bed slats.

Taking a butter knife in hand, she began to slip the tacks out of the wall. They dropped to the table with tiny sounds of industry. She picked up one and moved over to the doorway and set it on the floor, where, with any luck, he might step on it. Once the paper was free, it floated down to the tabletop. She took it by the edges and folded it to a good-size square and stood it behind the napkin holder. "Time to GET UP!" she said.

"There're likely be others who'll want to see that piece a paper you just taken down!"

She ignored him.

"Likely this very day somebody'll want to come in and look!"

Boxes of bolts and electrical wire and switches of all makes and models were still scattered around her kitchen in boxes she had tripped over for weeks.

"Somebody might a wanted it, and now it's creased!"

Eilene went to his bedroom and caught him sitting by the side of the bed scratching at his balls. His shape was like that of a hulking bear in the zoo.

"You give them the plan, they'll build it on their own! ON THEIR OWN! NO NEED FOR YOU!" she yelled, remembering to inject the enticement of paying work into the conversation.

There was silence while he mulled it over, realizing he was treading into hostile territory, where job-bearing sentries stood waiting to heave him out of bed. It was a land Sonny wanted no part of, so he said, "Leah out the barn yet?"

Studying him blankly, Eilene just stood there. "What'd you say?"

"What I *said* was"—he peered up at her, then looked down at his socked feet, at the highly polished wood of the bedroom floor—"God-amercy. You fix one thing and another crops up."

Point taken, Eilene moved back to the kitchen, where she listened to the noise of Sonny shifting himself up out of bed. Habitual sounds. Hands fumbling in the not-so-dark. The thud a boot makes when stumbled upon. The slight clang of metal grabs hitting the floor. He was mumbling his simmering diatribe: "I told Bruno she don't know shit about it. I told him the woman's not fit to do farmin, but what does he do? He ignores me. And now who has to go and clean up the mess? I guess you know good and well who . . ."

There was more, but Eilene quit listening.

There was silence but for the noise of the fans. Behind her, the floorboards creaked, and she followed the sound of her son's progress up the hall. Sonny sidestepped the tack in the doorway, tipped the lid off the sugar jar, and popped a cube in his mouth. When she turned to him he extended his hand and said, "Mornin, Mama."

"Mornin, yourself," she said, shaking his hand.

"Where's the coffee at?" he said, running a hand through his gray hair, his face close to hers to avoid shouting.

She pointed toward the stove.

Lifting the cast-iron skillet from the oven, she banged it to the eye and then took a slab of bacon and sliced it and set it to frying. Eggs were in a wire basket next to the sink, and she set out four of them and then went to the fridge and pulled out the pan of biscuits she'd made the night before. Moving to the cabinet, she found his cup and filled it with hot coffee and put it on the table. Once these things were done, she sat down in the chair, pulled it close to his, and faced him, her glasses pushed up on her nose.

"What're you goin to do?"

"Why, I think I'll just sit here and wait on breakfast," Sonny said. "It's smellin good, too."

Eilene nodded and looked at her son, at this hulk of a man she had little use for. She pursed her lips a little. "She cain't git it runnin!" she said, her head giving a nod in her daughter-in-law's direction.

Sonny leaned his head to his hand and scratched at his eyebrows with his fingers. "I guess you ain't gonna stop about it."

"Those biscuits got fourteen, fifteen minutes to bake."

"And?"

"I think that's time enough to help out your kin."

"Bruno don't like—"

"FOURTEEN MINUTES!" Eilene screamed.

"Hell. I guess it won't hurt to check," he said, rising to his feet. "There'll be no hushin you till I go."

"Just do what you can!" she shouted. "I'll have breakfast ready time you git back. I'll even make gravy."

He opened his mouth to tell her how lumpy her gravy had been of late, how it lacked the proper amount of salt, how it had taken on a mustardy color as well as a bitter taste, but then he saw the look to her eyes and decided he would be better served by holding his peace and doing what she asked.

Sonny spent an inordinate amount of time out on the back porch petting the dog's head, lavishing affection on a blue tick hound that, in his heart of hearts, he hated, puzzling the dog with this exhibition because it was a smart one and knew it was despised. Once this overt act was played out, Sonny reached into his pockets and pulled out his shoelaces and sat down on the top step and began to string up his boots. He glanced across the way to the opened barn doors and saw movement. He glanced down again while he fed a string through a metal boot eye. Upon completion, he held up the laces in measurement and saw how the left one had ends that failed to meet equally. With a sigh, he began to undo and relace all over again.

He could see the sky all around was lighting up the place, and he sat there watching shadows disappear. Leah appeared to be lifting hay off the trailer that was hitched to the tractor, and dragging it bale by bale to a spot closer to the barn door. Now that the light was fairly good, he could see three stacks, two bales high, and two more stacks to go. He stood to his feet and headed her way.

Near his mother's clothesline, he stumbled and stopped in his tracks and kicked at the dirt, bending at the waist in an effort to find what had tripped him up. He couldn't find the durn culprit and walked on. It was right about then that he felt the loose dirt that had migrated down the inside of his boot due to all that kicking, and he was forced to stop and unlace his boot and remove it from his foot and hold up the boot and shake out the vagrant. When he bent to put it on again, Leah was done with rearranging her hay and was headed to the side of the house where the truck sat.

Sonny stood to his feet and yawned mightily and set to walking again. He could already smell those biscuits.

He stomped his foot every few steps, in expectation of more dirt hiding inside the top of his boot waiting to slide down, but didn't feel any. When he walked past the old silo, he patted its side as one would the shoulder of a friend.

He was near the mid-gate now, with its weighted chain, and he slipped the noose and watched it swing inward with a clicking grace he found beautiful. The hinge was loose, though, and careful man that he was, he intended to fix it before he went a step farther. He glanced up and saw the hay waiting there, and he could hear the noise of Bruno's old Ford and then he searched around in his pockets for his Swiss Army knife and pulled it out and found the proper blade and went to work on the loose screw. Once it was done, he decided he needed to scrape a bit of rust off the hinge and went to it, filing and tapping and brushing away the red with his finger, watching Leah pull the truck around in a three-point turn and back it toward the barn.

He finally walked on. But then he thought of the dog and how, though the hound had never done it before, it might be liable to stray, so he turned around and went to the gate and pulled it shut. Remarked to himself that it was a good thing he had found that loose screw when he did, he'd not like it much to come out and see the gate resting off its proper plumb.

Leah was heaving bales onto the back of the truck, making small grunts, and Sonny stopped to inspect his mother's fig prospects. The trees were as old as Davy Crockett, with gnarled limbs big as a man's leg, and he thought it'd be a good season for preserving jellies and jams, and he meant to tell her about this prediction as soon as he made it back to the house.

He looked at his watch and, though it seemed impossible, slowed his pace.

He had fifty feet to go when Leah put the truck in gear and drove around the side of the barn and headed toward the back plat.

Sonny raised his arms to mid-waist, his palms upward to the sky, his mouth opened wide in what he hoped was an expression of disbelief. The truck was missing its side mirror, and he couldn't tell if she might be watching him or not, so he held his hands up for a second longer and then lowered them and looked around the place.

She had not shut the barn doors, and he could see the brown flash of mice quickening around the old barrels of feed and, in the center space, the tractor with its trailer attached. Sonny bent and studied those big tires and the tatting of spiderwebs that connected them.

Going to the tractor, he raised its hood and checked the cables and saw that they were sound. He leaned around and looked at the switch and put a hand to the horn and pressed and heard nothing.

"I bet my good eye she didn't turn that switch far enough," he said, shaking his head. He noted a sturdy ladder leading to the loft, calculated how he would rearrange things should it be his barn and not his brother's, and then he pulled the heavy doors shut and went out into the yard. He could hear the Ford making its way across the pasture, just an echo now, a coughing, sputtering one.

"Them truck axles ain't gonna like that back field," Sonny said. And then he turned to the porch along the backside of his brother's house. The cat was there atop its crate, licking itself, the washer was rusted out a little at the bottom, Leah's plants needed a good watering. With only a moment's hesitation, he walked toward the steps, his hands to the pockets of his overalls.

→←

The draperies are pulled together in the living room, but not all the way, and a small needle of light finds its way to the floor, hitting the legs of the coffee table and the magazine rack set to the side of his chair. Bruno Till sits still as a statue and watches it spread up and across Leah's ceramic knickknacks, blazing against a trumpeting swan, and then the porcelain cow, and then stretching to the far wall, brightening up the room by slow, piercing degrees. The trunk stored in the hallway he can see now, as well as the bookshelf built into the wall. He can see the titles, mostly farming periodicals and old *National Geographics*. His hand is open on the thrice-read pages of the magazine, and his coffee cup is sitting on the cloth-covered arm of the chair as other items come into view. A basket holding mending. An ashtray. A cup.

The cup is decorated all around with tiny pink flowers, and the rim is ribboned in gold, but the cup itself is crackled in places and worn, with a tiny chip above its handle. The saucer is not the one it belongs to. This bothers him, and he glances through the opening to the kitchen. In the cool morning, Leah is out in the barn, but there is silence and the silence is forcing him to listen, even more so than the ribbon of light through the draperies is forcing him to watch. The tractor won't start for some strange reason, and she will have to use the truck to carry morning feed, and even in the midst of her predicament, he thinks about calling her back inside to see if she can find the matching saucer. Similitude. This is the concept that leads him down the path to this place concerning commonality and matched sets. He is similar to every other thing in the world, and just as every other thing in the world has its accompanying set of rules and guidelines, so does Bruno Till. A cup should sit its saucer. Socks should match. A tractor, not a truck, should pull a hay wagon out into the field.

He had noticed her hair when she walked through the house. He couldn't keep his eyes off it, in fact. Even as she pulled on her work gloves and tucked her shirt into her jeans, he was watching. It was its true color now, honeyed brown, the color of her eyes, though her eyes held a slight blush of renegade green. Her hair was longer these days, and she wore it pulled back and fastened at her neck with a gold-tone clip. He knew that once she was outside, she would find her cap and put it to her head and pull the ponytail through the hole in back, and it would swing against her shoulders while she worked.

He heard the truck start and saw a blur of movement as the truck reversed across the yard to position itself in front of the barn. She had left her overshirt on the back of the kitchen chair, and if the heat held true, she would need it later on in the day. Folks who thought stripping down was the key to coolness were fools. The actuality of it was sweat, good and honest, dampening layers of cloth, and then a sweet breeze wafting up against that cloth. That was how it had always been done. Try telling that to a city boy stripped down to his jeans, a damn bandanna tied around his head, leaning against a lamppost.

Her shirt was dirty from yesterday's work. Yesterday's jeans were on the bed frame. He had seen them when he rose to dress. She had turned thin on him, too, losing her roundness in accordance with the seasons, and it was the spring birthing time, and she was loose in her jeans, and the shirts that used to snug across her front seemed different these days, though they weren't. She was like a half-empty bag of sweetfeed instead of a full, and while the comparison might seem uncaring, or perhaps limited as an endearment, Bruno didn't mean it that way. It was a mere comparison made by a man who framed his life in ordinary terms. Sweetfeed was sweetfeed, and all "half-empty" meant was that his wife was losing weight doing man-work that should be falling to the man, and Bruno grieved over it.

The words blurred on the pages. He had been reading about a lost tribe discovered in New Guinea and wondering why in the world a seemingly scientific journal had ascribed the words "lost tribe" to a tribe that was no longer lost but found when he'd seen movement across the rear of the house. His line of vision was better than most thought, and from where he sat, he could see all the way through the house and out into the yard. Leah had left the back door open, and he watched his brother shuffle into view and then stand peering into the room, or at least trying to. The two men stared at each other, and Bruno felt his face blush, weaker for the moment, his guard down.

"How come that tractor ain't runnin!" Sonny shouted.

"I ain't Mama. Lower your voice."

"What's wrong with the tractor?"

"You know she's not deaf, don't you?"

Sonny stared at him. "I don't know if she is or not."

"You live with her. You ought to know." Bruno shut the magazine and watched his brother fidget behind the screen door. He reasoned he weighed over three hundred pounds these days, with the weight still climbing.

"What's wrong with the tractor?"

"Cain't say."

"I bet she didn't turn the switch all the way off."

"Could be."

"Could be, my ass. It's a fact. I looked, and it weren't turned off all the way. I went on and turned it all the way off, in case you're wondering." Sonny reached for the handle to the door, then hesitated and put his hand back to his pocket.

"I'm not wondering," Bruno said.

"Well. If you were."

"I'm not."

"I come over to see if I could help," Sonny said. "Mama seen the barn doors left open, and no tractor and sent me over. You know how she is."

"Leah's headed to the fields. I'm sitting here reading." Bruno put his hand around his coffee cup, steadying it. He could feel sweat collecting underneath his brace, tickling his neck.

"You gonna have to jump it off."

"I got the cables."

"Yeah, but who's—"

"Get the fuck off my porch," Bruno said.

"Hell. All I said was—"

"Sonny." It was more than a word. It was a warning.

Sonny blinked a few times and then reached out to scratch the tomcat and said, "You need anything before I leave?"

"Do I look like I need anything?"

Sonny stared at him, then cupped his hand around his eyes as he leaned in to the screen. "Nope. You seem fine to me."

"Fine." Bruno snorted quietly. "I'm fine, all right." And then he wanted to kick himself in the ass because it sounded pitiful, and that was not his intention.

"Well, maybe not fine. But the same. You seem the same."

"I am the same. Now git the hell off my porch."

Sonny turned to leave and then called back over his shoulder, "Should Mama ask if I come over here to check on you, tell her I did. She sent me over here, and I done what she said. And if Leah cain't git them cables on right to jump it off and recharge that battery, you know where I'm at."

Bruno was silent, watching his brother put a hand to the porch post and ease down the steps and then hurry across the yard with a marvelous economy of movement for a man his size.

➻➻

The terrain was sensible, and Leah Till drove out through the middle of it with quiet confidence, a quilt of wildflowers to her left, the tops of yellow star grass and bluets and orange milkweed undulating, casting scarves of brilliance over the low brown sedge. She was not old, nor was she young. This is what she was thinking while the truck bounced across the middle pasture and her hair brushed against the back of her neck. And this thought, too: *This is how we live our lives—so caught up in work, our self-awareness drifts away.*

She stopped the truck at the first gate and got out and pulled it open, drove through, stopped and shut the gate behind her, then climbed back in the truck and drove on toward the next. It was May, and the air still had an edge to it, and across the way, above the ridge of trees, the sky had turned its prominent color, a shade she had come to associate only with men, more gray than blue, holding inside itself the promise of a storm or some other turbulence. Leah looked away.

She was nearing her destination and could see the huge not-quite-toppled pine, the thick tip of it webbed with cones pointing toward the west, its weight a marvelous thing to consider, how it danced on the currents and refused to fall. How, year after year, it refused to fall.

The tree was the first thing she had noticed about the land when Bruno first brought her here, straight from Meridian, where she had lived too close to the city to be considered rural and too far away from the county courthouse to be considered urban. The size of Bruno's acreage had stunned her, for she had grown up in a house that sat on a small lot, and had spent all of her twenty-two years looking out on a backyard that was crowded with a toolshed and carport and two gnarled pear trees. Close to two hundred acres, his place was, at least in the beginning. Small portions had been sold off through the years to satisfy taxes, or to buffer a lean season full of unproductive crops, but the portion that held the pine was still theirs, and while she wished it had been held on to for sentimental reasons, she knew this wasn't true. It was a wild portion thick with trees that would've been hell to work, and the two of them had never even walked it, just stood near its margin and acknowledged its beauty.

"I think that tree points west for a reason," Leah had told him, her arm tucked inside his, the feel of flannel comforting. She was in love with cowboys and horses and men with scuffed-up boots and large hands. It was a Hollywood love drummed up on a sound stage, but it was still love, and Bruno, with his German name and stocky build, settled all around her like a Wild West sun. The toppling tree reminded her of him in a way she found embarrassingly erotic, and the great red orb, setting behind a ring of crimson clouds, made her feel complete in a way she found baffling.

"Don't go and change to a girl on me," he had said. "Only reason it points that way is because the land wants it to," but he was laughing when he said it, and Leah had looked up at him, still wondering how the two of them had gotten on, seeing as they were polar opposites. What common ground there happened to be was purely physical, which had made a lie of her mother's words: "There's not enough time spent between the sheets to compensate the breach." But there had been, at least for a while there. Leah refused to throw out his beat-up work boots as proof of what had been. She was just that sentimental. But she kept them hidden away underneath a rollaway bed in the front bedroom. She was just that smart.

"That taproot's thick as a barrel, I bet," Bruno had said that day, grinning at her. And that had been the end of it. He would ship out five years later and everything would change, but on that particular day the moment seemed permanent, carved in stone, and they had stood there watching quietly before spreading a cloth down to the ground and sitting and eating a lunch of cold baked chicken and potato salad while field grass waved all around. A half hour later, while Bruno took his own sweet time unbuttoning her shirt and peeling it off her shoulders and running his work-worn hand across her belly, the tree was watching over them, its tip bouncing in the wind while birds surfed the branches.

The cows were kneeling on front wrists like old penitents stricken and arthritic, and then they began to rise, heaving back finally, straightening forelegs in calm deliberation. Once this was done, they wandered toward the truck. Thirty or so cows. All accounted for but Kate, the one Leah was looking for. Cows are social creatures and seldom stray, and she knew this, knew the reasons for isolation were all ominous.

Leah turned off the motor and opened the door and climbed to the bed for a better look. To the east a thick wood bordered the fence line, and behind her, to the north, was the open pastureland she had already driven through. The only questionable area was in the direction of the pine, and while she could see its tip and where it pointed, the surrounding land was thick with bracken and shrub and tangling vines and deadfall shapes of impassable geometry. No path for a cow. Even a determined one.

"Shit, then," she said, climbing back into the cab and lifting down the .30/.06 from the rack. The truck had turned into a true country truck, which meant it was more traveling toolshed than vehicle. Cigarette empties littered the floor, as well as oil cans and thick shanks of rope and clotted rags and boxes of shells and calf pullers and salve. A case of liniment rode shoved under the seat and stuck in the springs was a pair of shears heavy enough to lay to the bone, should the need arise. The only peculiarity was a bent harmonica standing upright in the ashtray. For the life of her, Leah couldn't remember who had put it there; all she knew was it had been there for as long as the truck had been. That Bruno had played the instrument seemed incongruous to everything she knew to be true concerning her husband.

"Fuck it, then." She slammed the door and backed away, holding the gun under her arm, noticing how the wind was up and whistling through the sedge, and how the cows all seemed agitated and restless, the way they got before a storm. Brown eyes moved across Leah's torso and then shifted to the western section, where the land was so thick it had never been trod. There were twenty or so cows milling about, all moving in her direction.

"Shoo, then," she said, throwing up an arm and waving. "Git." One bumped her hip, and she hit it with the palm of her hand, watching dust fly up. The cows stumbled away from her, all of them moving together until their flanks touched, forming a restless bovine pond with a shifting nervous wake.

I'll make it up to you later, she thought, moving out into the field. Behind her the cows stood watching, some beginning to settle, some grazing. She noticed the new quiet and stood there listening, and then she bent and began to make her way through the brush, the gun under her arm, a box of shells tucked in the pocket of her shirt.

The woods were full of life, or so it seemed. Overlooked life, quiet, teeming, pulsing life. Mushrooms were scattered about where she walked, a crop of Old Man of the Woods, their umbrella tops freckled and scaled, and the smaller, green-gilled Lepiota, wearing braceletlike rings along their stalks. Near the base of a rotting tree felled so long ago that its appearance as tree seemed questionable, a Stinkhorn stood upright, its olive tip slightly open and greasy-looking, and she stopped in her tracks, a heaviness settling around her heart. The mushroom resembled a penis, an organ thoroughly aroused by its surrounding decay, and she stood there taking note of all its intricate details. It grew upright out of a thatch of gray twigs, its stalk whitish pink, and try as she might to see it for what it was, it stood as a reminder of what Bruno kept to himself. She kicked at it with her boot when she went past, her eyes to the ground, sweeping side to side for cow tracks. The lump in her throat was for something else, not that, she told herself. *I don't miss* that. *Besides, it's a mushroom, not a man, and I got one of those back at home.*

The area was crowded with longleaf pines, trees ignored by man, with towering tops that seemed to stretch forever. Leah put out her hand and brushed against the small saplings that stood three feet tall in all directions, for the forest floor was covered with them, and when the wind caught, a wave of pale green seemed to funnel toward her before washing away. There were hardwood trees as well, their opaque leaves creating a cover as dense as a roof, their trunks covered in lichen conveying the appearance of trees dipped in chalk. It was dark underneath the trees, and cooler, and she wished for her overshirt as protection against the unexpected chill. Looking back, she saw a small opening of light blinking off the hood of the truck, and the image of rust and paint conjured up warmth in a way she found remedial.

Repositioning her hat, she took the gun and used it to press against the wild privet that was springing up all around, pushing the growth forward, and then, once it was held down, stepping on it with her foot. She thought better of this a few seconds later, not wishing to stumble, the gun in hand, and shoot off an arm or possibly a foot, since she was walking up a small hill, the incline so slight its presence was accounted for only by the increased effort at breathing. The cow had been this way, there was proof everywhere: broken limbs, sedge grass pressed down, a not so fresh pile of manure.

The path had thinned a bit, and she walked forward, seeing the tip of the toppled pine appear occasionally between a break in the treetops, its crown sheared by the elements to a shape resembling an arrowhead, and it really did seem to be pointing west. It was larger than first imagined, for no matter how many steps she took, it still appeared a distant apparition, a thing both real and unreal. Like a pot at the end of a rainbow. Illusionary yet absolute. Leah was remembering her effort as a child to find such a pot, alongside her father, who took great pains to make it a lesson of sorts, recalling how he had pointed up to the sky while they stood out in some broad field, and urged her to squint her eyes. "There's more than three colors there. More than just red, yellow, and blue." "Where?" she asked. "Up in the sky," he said. "Look now and squint like I told you." And she had done what he'd asked and seen the slight variations of spectrum, more bands of color than she ever envisioned. Purple and alizarin graduating to fiery orange. A lemony green shimmered into blue. Undulating colors carrying a life of their own. The remembrance so vibrant and surreal that here, in her thirty-fifth year while seeking a wayward cow, she looked up through the limbs of the trees in search of what she had viewed so long ago. She had one hand to her hair, brushing back a shank that had come loose from its clasp, her eyes still up to the sky, when she took a step forward through low cutty brush and fell off the edge of the world.

Falling down a cavernous shoot was how it felt, and between her legs she saw the open spaces below, speckled by sun and shade, and a distant green she supposed was the ground floor. Converging into the dilemma, a picture of her life segmented by no particular time or event, just parcels and refrains called up to flash before her eyes while she fell to her death. *So it's true* was her thought. *You see it all. Every last second.* And then her back touched a wall of earth, and her arms flew open and the gun flew outward toward the sky, sun glinting off gunmetal gray as it pinwheeled through the air before tumbling against a clay embankment and on down into a gully that had been hidden from sight.

Her slide was stopped short by something that reached out and grabbed her and jerked her so hard she bit through her tongue. Liquid, bitter and metallic, filled her mouth while she swung back and forth against a wall of clay, her legs dangling, her boots touching the lush leaves of a sycamore crown, her arm numb from shoulder to hand. Her immediate thought was that she was dead and just didn't know it, that whatever death was, its handiwork was not easily accepted by the one actually dying. That a person could actually stare death in the face and say *No thank you, not now.* Her next thought was that if she was dead, she wouldn't feel as though she'd been run over by a truck. Stretching out the one arm that worked, Leah felt the shifting of dirt behind her as it separated in huge slabs that dropped into the trees. When she looked up, soft sand funneled down into her hair and eyes, and she spit out a mixture of blood and dirt, finding more in her mouth than she'd realized. She was caught against a gully wall, midways down, or so it seemed.

"God*dammit*," she said.

Her arm was pinned inside the root of a tree, and this was what had saved her. Reaching around carefully, which was hard to do because all of the earth seemed intent on loosening, she put her free hand to her mouth and began to remove the leather glove with her teeth, working one finger at a time. Once this was done, she spat the glove free and reached across her body and moved her fingers up and down her arm, then around behind her back and up and down her arm again. Her shirt was torn off above the elbow, and she was bleeding at a spot on her forearm, but sensory response met each touch, and when she flexed the fingers of the trapped arm, she could feel the tingle of nerve, with very little accompanying pain.

The root that held her was the size of a man's leg, a leg bent at the knee, with its foot buried in the earth, and Leah thought of Bruno stretched out on his back in the far pasture, his hands folded across his chest, a can of beer propped between his bent legs, and she wanted to cry but didn't.

As considerable as it was, she wondered at the root's original size, its hidden, buried mass, for it measured the length of her torso, and she supposed that from a distance she would appear to be a part of it, a figurehead in the making: it held her that securely. A great portion of it had been hewn away, exposing red root brindled by mildew, and from this wound seeped a whitish fluid.

"It's bleeding milk," she said. Her nose was running, and her voice was thick and scared-sounding, and rough dirt was in her eyes and eyebrows and the wells of her ears. Another shelf of clay broke away behind her, and she reached behind and felt the small cave forming behind her back, out of which she was being thrust before the world by a renegade root, her eyes a treat for wild crows or the hawks, the flesh of her neck a meal for whatever feral creature might be willing to crawl down the side of a cliff to feast. She shut her eyes against the rain of dirt.

"Jesus," she said. "Don't let me die like this."

When all settled around her, she opened her eyes and looked down and saw light winking off something on the gully floor. The wind stirred, and shade interfered with what she was seeing, and it would be there one minute and gone the next. The latest shifting of dirt had exposed other things as well. All the way down the face of this cliff were knobbed portions of root, twisted and looped in places, perfect hand- and footholds for any fool wishing to make a day of it. The nearest one was two inches from her left foot, and when she moved her leg, she could touch it with the toe of her boot and it seemed at once close and far, far away, like that rainbow she never saw the end of. The wind picked up and the shade skated away and the light blinked and Leah saw the gun down below. The wooden stock was shattered into three pieces. The long barrel, half the distance away, was blinking in the light. And this wasn't all, for the cow was there, a broke-open mass of black and brown and red, and next to it the calf, still in its sac, its umbilical cord coiled across the legs of its dead mother.

As she held to the root with her free hand and pressed her body against the dirt wall behind her, Leah began to free her arm, feeling her body begin its slide downward even as her elbow left the clutch, her foot catching on the nearest outcropping of root. Reaching out, she caught at the next exposure of root with her hand and swung to face the wall, tasting dirt, still seeing what was below all broken and ruined and dead. She could glimpse the carnage as she worked her way down, and it was at this point that Leah began to cry.

{CHAPTER 3}

It was as worrisome as a mosquito, Bruno's failure to remember the feel of his wife's hair.

The memory lapse came up behind him as he was sitting quietly in the living room amid all her belongings—the table holding her knickknacks, her shoes by the couch—and hovered behind his head while he watched thin blades of sunlight make their way up the far wall. He reached behind his head and felt the cushion of the chair against his neck. Thick fingers stroking the attached doily. His neck brace was bothering him, and he stuck one finger down alongside and pressed at the skin, hearing the releasing suck of flesh against padding. He imagined a remora, greasy-filmed and dishwater gray, its small lidless eyes. He imagined himself a tired shark, sick to death of being sucked on. Sweat coated the inside of the pad, and when he leaned to the side, as far as the brace would allow, the coolness of the room filtered down to a spot along his collarbone. The respite was brief, and he couldn't quite figure out the worst of it: dealing with the heat of the moment or trying to lay hold of a memory that would tiptoe in and stand not quite there before dancing away. Of all her features, her hair was the most sensuous, and while he wasn't aware he was thinking of sexual trigger points, he was. He was also becoming erect, in spite of that being the last thing in the world he wanted.

Some nights when he couldn't sleep (and there were many of those), he would reach out and lift her hair from her shoulder or her pillow and sweep it against the palm of his hand, carefully, so she wouldn't wake. He would bring it up to his face and smell it, preferring the smell of hard work over shampoo, and then he would feather it along the metalwork of his brace, across his nose and eyes, and after several minutes of this, he would make braids of it against the pillow. If she stirred, he would stop. If he began to notice the curvature of her waist underneath the sheet, he would not stop. If he became erect (and most times he did), he would begin to stroke the braids one at a time until he brought himself off, a shameful wad of spunk he would catch in his hand.

All he wanted was the hair, for reasons that were vague and elusive and related to being very young and healthy. At best, he reasoned the hair to be harmless, without expectations, obliging. The hair was perfect, almost magical in the way it changed colors in the moonlight. The way it refused to be captured, for it was wayward hair, hating all clasps and barrettes, its obedience limited to minutes instead of hours. That morning before she left, when she reached behind her to pull it through its fastener, tiny tendrils escaped, and he wanted to applaud.

Outside, the cat jumped off its roost and arched its back up against the screen door and lifted a paw to scratch at the wood. Bruno eyed it, waiting. After a moment the feline sauntered away, its shadow shifting across the yard, elongating and warping until it morphed with the shadow of a cloud drifting overhead and lost its identity.

Reaching behind his head, he began to work at the leather straps of the brace, pulling each through its buckle until it was free. The brace was customized and followed the shape of his body from his neck to the shelf of his shoulders, with a curved hinge down its front to his breastbone. Once the straps were free, the brace could be broken open. Bruno used both hands to do this, feeling his head spring back against the cushion of the chair in a wayward arc that struggled for completion. A bowhunter since the age of six, he gave up the sport after the accident, unable to tolerate watching or feeling the physics of the activity. He felt it every day. That pulling and relentless pressure. Felt it in a way one would never think possible.

Reaching behind, he lifted the brace off and held it up in his hands and worked the hinge until it spread open like a broken bird. There was the slight odor of his body against the padding, a thing not all that unpleasant, and near the core of the brace, the padding was bleached white, the color of a trematode. He removed the brace only twice a day: in the mornings while he showered, once he was sure Leah was out in the fields and not likely to return; and at night, so he could wipe it clean and powder his neck. Each process took about fifteen minutes, and every time he did them, he went a little faster, for the muscles along the back were more determined than ever to pull inward to complete that arc, and it interfered with his breathing. Resting his head against the chair bought him a little more time, and he used it to wipe the inside of the brace clean with his handkerchief, and then he felt along the floor for the tin of talc he kept hidden underneath the skirt of the chair. Pulling it out, he aligned the pinprick openings and dusted the padding, noticing how pink the rubber seemed these days. How it had taken on the color of flesh to the point that it seemed some perverse appendage. Closing the tin, he rested it in his lap and looked up at the ceiling. Not by choice but because the muscles along his back were forcing him to do so.

There were days, more and more of them, when he thought he might just sit without the brace and let nature take its course, do what it would with him. Tighten and tighten until the butt of his head was pressed against his backbone and his windpipe was flattened against his spinal column and he suffocated. There were days, and this was one of them, when the weight of living seemed a frivolous option, one he could do without. He wondered how long it would take. Twenty minutes? A half hour? A breeze from the open windows held a captured feather in its wake, and he watched it dance across the top of the bookcase and disappear behind the mahogany crown.

Long minutes passed, and his breath became a whistle, then a teapot's scream. Gray dots were forming in his vision and his heart was thundering inside his neck and he could feel his body being propelled toward a place that was unrelenting as stone. And all he wished as a final thought was that he could remember her hair. Just her hair.

He sensed he was about to lose consciousness and moved slightly to the left, the movement infuriating and telling and a crowing gamecock that shouted Bruno's true intentions, and once his breathing was easier, he wanted to kill the world and embrace it at the same time. Unbidden, a tear welled in the corner of his eye, and he clawed at it with his fist. Movement of a small child. A wounded baby. A weakling who would never be anything but.

Outside, shadows latticed across the draperies of the house. A tall shadow and two smaller ones. Shadows Bruno failed to notice, for he was in the process of putting the brace back to his neck, and when the knocking sounded, he was so startled he jerked and the *National Geographic* slid off the arm of the chair and the talc rolled off his lap and clattered across the floor, coming to a stop near Leah's shoes. White powder trailed behind, and however the day might end, Leah would come back from the fields and see the floor and know that something had happened. Everything was bundled together like dirty laundry. Those masturbatory thoughts. His lame suicide attempt. The powder on the floor. He could stand and walk and move around, but getting down on his hands and knees to clean up a spill was all but impossible, and she would know.

Again the knocking. Insistent and strong. A stranger's knock.

"Hold your goddamn horses!" he yelled.

There was silence, and he worked at the brace, slipping the leather back into its buckle, buttoning up his shirt as high as was allowed. Once it was done, he pushed himself up at the arms of the chair and knocked the teacup to the floor, where it crashed and spilled the last dregs of morning coffee.

"Oh, for Christ's sake," he said, looking down at the mess. In less than a minute he had fucked up everything in general.

He went to the door and pulled it open and blinked against the light. A young woman was standing on his porch, a big, strapping woman, with two small boys by her side. A satchel of some sort was on the step behind her. While he watched, she wiped at the cheek of the smallest child, using her spit to moisten her handkerchief. Bruno cleared his throat, and the woman jumped.

"Oh. You're here now."

"Where else would I be?"

She frowned. "Here. I mean, I know you'd be here. You live here. But I heard you yell for me to hold my blankety-blank horses. But I never heard you open the door . . ."

She trailed off, embarrassed, and looked down at the smallest child, who was looking up at her with something akin to worship. The boy smiled, and she smiled back and brushed his blond hair from his forehead, smudging away a bead of sweat with her thumb. Bruno guessed the boy to be three or four. The other boy was older, perhaps six, and he was looking up at the roof of the house as though something of extraordinary interest might be living in the gutters. Both boys were dressed in clean clothes, denim shorts and matching red T-shirts and clean socks and fresh tennis shoes, and their mother was equally clean, though dressed in a swingy skirt that was too short and a paisley top that was too modern for this neck of the woods and sandals that would be better suited for California. A small bandanna hid most of her brown hair.

"Blankety-blank horses," Bruno said, trying to shake his head in amusement. The woman looked up at him, startled. "You said 'blankety-blank.' I said 'goddamn'—"

The woman, who was more girl than woman, covered the little boy's ears and looked at the older boy and frowned.

Bruno put his hands to his pockets and sighed. "Can I help you?"

She seemed to recover and pounced on his words. "Maybe I could help you, sir."

She appeared to be working at her speech. Trying her damnedest to sound sophisticated.

"How so?" he said.

"If I could take just a moment of your time—"

"No," he said and began to shut the door.

Her hand shot out and pressed against the wood, stopping its movement. "Sir?"

Bruno just stared at her, noticing the beads of sweat across her upper lip and the color of her eyes, blue and clear, with tiny flecks of gold.

"Look, mister," she said. "You're the first one I tried this on, and if I walk away from here without followin through, I ain't never gonna be able to do this again."

Her speech had lapsed backward into true Mississippi country, and he shook his head.

"Mama," the older boy said, reaching for her hand.

"Not now," she said.

"But Mama," he said, pulling at her skirt.

Bruno watched them, the tug-of-war going on across the woman's face, the child's determination. He saw the moment of surrender, and then she knelt on the porch and pulled the boy to her side, and her skirt slid up another two inches. "What'd we talk about, Joe?" she said.

"I know," he said. "But —"

She kissed him and turned him to his younger brother, who was standing on the porch sucking his thumb. "We're gonna be just fine. Just watch Ben for a minute. He's not as big and grown-up as you are. If you watch him careful, we'll get on home in a little while."

Her movements were so full of something Bruno failed to have a name for, he felt he might smother if he had to watch much more of it. "Listen, what is it you're trying to do?"

"I got these two little boys here, and —"

"I ain't blind," he said.

"No, you're not blind. But you are rude." She stood up and whispered this, leaning forward to peer up into his face. "I'm tryin to make a living sellin to folks."

"What is it you're tryin to sell?"

"I sell a couple things. Vacuum cleaners and cosmetics." She turned and made a show of her beat-up truck where, he figured, she kept the vacuum cleaners. The case, he supposed, held cosmetics.

"We don't need anything," he said, not in an unkind way, just an honest way.

"Your shirt's unbuttoned," she said, reaching as though she meant to remedy his oversight.

He stepped away and watched her, his eyes narrowing while his hand groped up the front, stumbling for buttons. It was buttoned as high as his shirts always were, so his hands stopped their movement. She was watching his fingers, where they stopped and what was above those fingers, and said, "Oh." Then, "Lord."

"Yes," he said.

"I didn't mean—"

"I know you didn't. Now I need you to leave."

"What kind?" she asked, reaching behind her head and tightening her bandanna.

"What kind of what?"

"You said you didn't need what I had to sell. I was just wonderin what kind a vacuum you had."

"Oh, for God's sake." He looked around the room, noticing the spill on the floor, wondering exactly what type of machinery the wife used for cleaning the floors. He never noticed these days. Hadn't noticed for a very long time.

"I sell Electrolux," she said.

"It might be one a those," he said.

"Don't you know?"

The younger boy said, "Mama," and she ignored him and continued, "Electrolux ain't just any vacuum cleaner. It's an investment."

"That cain't be good," Bruno said. He might as well have said "Mama" like that small boy of hers, for she ignored him and kept on talking.

"It costs more than others, but you never have to buy another one."

She reached down and scratched at her knee, and he saw down her blouse and how she wasn't wearing a bra, and this new information seemed at odds with her face, which beamed out a steady beacon of innocence. He looked away from her toward the bookcases that lined the wall.

"Never's a long time," he said, wondering how she could bear to stand outside in the sun. He was sweating, and he was resting in a shadow.

"Well, it's true. I bought one myself, and it cleans like a dream. I run the Rocky Creek Inn, and I use it every day. Well, almost every day. Some days I'm too tired to vacuum." She watched him while rubbing her son's head. The boy swatted her hand away and stepped to the side and sat down on the concrete with a sigh, pulling his younger brother down beside him. A piece of pine straw was there, and he lifted it and teased at a roly-poly. The bug curled and then crawled. Curled and crawled.

"If you run that motel, how come you got this other job?" It seemed like a mild question, something a gentleman might ask. Bruno was intrigued by the word "motel," the thought of all those beds, the way the thought resonated against his backbone.

"I don't just run it. We live there. Me and my husband and my two little boys. Not just in one little room. Lord, no. We tore down some walls and fixed it up real nice. I use most of it for that. There's about six rooms still open for business. There's not a lot of people who actually want to stop in Purvis, though."

She seemed to sense that the conversation was getting away from where it needed to be. "Listen, if you'll just let me come in and demonstrate it, I'll leave. That's all I'm askin." The boys' backs were to him, huddled and still, their heads tucked down near their bellies, their unpredictable hands hidden from sight.

"I'm not about to buy a vacuum cleaner," he said.

"Sir, just let me show you how it works, and if you don't start beggin me to sell you one, I promise I'll leave. I really will."

"I'm still not about to buy a vacuum cleaner."

She held up a hand and backed away from him, pointing a finger at her children, whose heads popped up as she was moving away. "Stay put," she said, and then she hurried to the truck, where she hauled a rectangular box from its bed and pulled open the cardboard and lifted out a gray tube machine with attached hose. Bruno watched it all, feeling the sweat trickling down behind his neck.

When she made it back to the porch, the boys didn't want to come inside and she looked down at them and paused before she spoke. "Remember what I said?"

"We remember," the older one answered.

"You ain't put ant poison out recent, have you?" she asked Bruno while she looked around the yard.

"No."

"Stay out of the yard anyhow," she told them, as though he had lied about the poison. "Stay right there on that porch and don't you move."

The boys didn't answer, just looked up at her with their obedient blue eyes. Bruno had the feeling they had never disobeyed a single command that had come from the woman, not out of fear but because they trusted her completely, they adored her absolutely. If she had told them to stop breathing, they would have obeyed without question.

Once inside, she took a few minutes to figure out the attachments, and she was whispering under her breath and sweating, and at one point she pulled out the instruction sheet from the box and studied it. Bruno took a seat on the couch and watched. His chair was empty, and he could have sat there, but for some reason he didn't want her to see him sitting where he always sat. He felt the chair bore the visible residue of a cripple, and if not a cripple, then a person terribly clumsy. He wanted her to think that the chair was Leah's and she had been the one who made the mess of the powder and the busted cup. He put his arm across the back of the sofa, even though it was awkward and pinched his neck to do so.

"You end up with several tools with this particular model. A thing for cleaning corners. One for draperies. A brush for couches and chairs. One with soft brushes so it cleans like a feather duster. A molded plastic one that cleans along the baseboards, and a heavy motorized head that cleans carpet." The whole while, she was bending and pulling out tubes and ripping off plastic.

Once all the pieces were arranged across the floor according to size, she wiped her hands down the front of her skirt and turned to him. She seemed to mentally pull out a notecard, and her words became rote. "My name is Alyce Benson, and I want to introduce you to a marvel of technology."

Bruno held up a hand. "Wait—"

"No, you wait. Please. Just let me do this."

She blinked hard, and he worried that she might be about to cry, so he lowered his hand and shut his mouth.

Pulling out the electrical cord, she looked around the room for an outlet. He pointed to a spot near the bookcase, and she went there, stretching the cord as she went. "It's got a spring attached. Watch this." She gave it a tug, and the cord fed back up into the canister, which meant she had to retrace her steps and start all over again. "Just wanted to show you that before I forgot."

Bruno was silent.

When it was plugged into the wall, she bent to the canister and attached the tube and the small narrow brush. Stepping out of her sandals, she pushed the on/off button with her toe, and the machine hummed to life. While he watched, she vacuumed the whole room, the talc being the first dust to disappear. She was humming while she worked, her back to him. He was watching her feet and her hips underneath her skirt. The material moved over them like music. Music without words. Healthy music coming from another life.

With the motor still running, she bent and removed the attachment and replaced it with the smaller brush and began to run it across the bookshelves, stretching as high as she could. Turning, she said, "You got a small ladder or a stepstool?"

"No!" he yelled, since the machine was loud.

"If you did, I'd do up here, where I know there's a pile of dust."

"Just leave it alone. I seen enough," he said.

"Okay, then," she said.

She moved to the chair and began to vacuum across its padding and down along its seat. "You got no idea about dust mites, do you?" Her eyes were wide and innocent. His were not.

He just stared at her.

"Dust mites are the leading cause of allergy fits." She attacked the crack of the chair with the nozzle. Her arm disappeared up to the elbow, and he thought of how he had to check the cows twice a year to see if they took. He cleared his throat.

"I use the machine I got at home to clean the mattress. I put a little white filter right there in the canister just to prove to myself they were real, 'cause I didn't believe what the man told me. I mean, how in the world are you gonna see something so small as a mite? Well, you should a seen what come off my mattress. All sorts a things showed up. Dirt. Hair. You could eat off my mattress now."

Bruno wished she would stop talking about her bed and what could be done there.

"This thing has power. Ben out there dumped his marbles all over the floor, and they rolled under the bed. I used it to suck them out to where I could reach them. I used the number two nozzle so none a the marbles would go up into the machine, and it pulled out ever single one of them. You ain't never seen a machine that can suck like this one."

"You don't say?" He was locked on the word "suck" and found himself short of breath. "Just leave that," he said, for she had begun to pick up the broken pieces of his coffee cup. She ignored him and walked into the kitchen. He heard the sound of the water running, and when she came back out, there was a dishrag in her hand, and she knelt and wiped at the floor. "Now we got to wait a minute for the floor to dry. You cain't vacuum wet places. Might get a shock if you try it."

All he heard was the word "wet," and it had conjoined with her speech about her mattress and how it was clean as a whistle, absent of hair and dirt and whatever else might lodge there. He suddenly thought of his own mattress and Alyce on top of it and the depository dross of sweat and sweetness, the wrinkle of a sheet. He'd even settle for a dust mite or two.

The floor seemed to take an unusually long time to dry and the vacuum cleaner was running and the noise was white and soothing. She stood tapping her naked toes against the floor.

"Joe?" she yelled.

The older boy pressed his face against the screen. "Ma'am?"

"What's Ben doin?"

"Just sittin here."

"Well. Okay, then."

"Mama?"

"I'm almost done. Sit back down on the steps." She smiled at the face in the screen and the face disappeared and she picked up the hose and worked at the floor all the way to the kitchen. Finished finally, she turned off the machine with her toe and jerked at the cord and they both watched it feed back into the canister.

"If you'll show me where your vacuum's at, I'll take out the bag and we can compare the results. I wasn't here but ten minutes, but I bet you a ten-dollar bill I sucked up more dirt than a month's worth of work in yours."

"That's okay," he said. Truthfully, he wasn't sure if they even had a vacuum cleaner anymore. He seemed to remember Leah using a dust mop across the floors, but even that memory was hazy.

"This company's been around a real long time. Long enough not to be some fly-by-night organization who don't back up their products. There's real easy payment plans, too. Not much of a deposit required, either. I could fill out the paperwork for you—"

"I can hold a pencil good enough," he said.

"I didn't mean that. I just meant I could—"

Bruno sighed. "I know what you meant."

She knelt and began to put the pieces back into the box. Her movements were slow and childlike, and he felt like a playground bully, one who had kicked a pile of painstakingly built blocks into the dirt. He had liked her better when her hips were dancing underneath her skirt as she struggled to clean the dust off the spines of his *National Geographics*.

"Alyce?"

She looked at him.

"How many a these you sold?" he said.

She sat back on her feet. "None."

"How come?"

"Oh, I don't know. I guess it's because they're expensive and folks around here don't have a lot a money. I keep tellin them how good a machine it is, and how reasonable the company is about payin for it. But most won't let me git out of the truck. You're the first person to actually let me inside the house." She brushed her hands across her skirt and stood. "Thank you for lettin me in. If nothing else, it was good practice."

"Well, you cleaned up the mess the wife made." He nodded at where the powder had been, and she cut her eyes to him and seemed to see straight through the lie.

"If you ever change your mind about owning one a these, just call me," she said.

"How would I do that?"

It seemed to be a question she had not considered. One built on the expectation that no one would ever want to call her back.

"I could give you my phone number," she said, and then she blushed and Bruno wondered why.

"Where does all the dirt go?" he asked, clearing his throat.

"It goes right in here." She stood the canister on end and pressed a button. The top popped open, and she lifted out a paper bag and handed it to him. "Feel how heavy it is," she said.

He did. It was heavy at the bottom and loose at top, and he immediately thought of a scrotum.

"It comes with five more bags, and once they're full, all you have to do is call me and I'll hand-deliver some more to you. That's part of the Electrolux package. You don't never have to leave the house to buy replacements."

He was watching her, the way she had sweated into the thin fabric of her shirt, her wrinkled skirt that was creased across her hips, her bare feet on the floor. Tendrils of hair had worked free from her bandanna, and she lifted a shank and tucked it behind her ear, where it curled outward like a shiny horn.

"All I have to do is call and you'll be here?"

"Just pick up that phone and dial," she said, and then she smiled. "Holy cow, you're gonna buy one, ain't you?"

"Where do I sign," he told her, sighing, wondering how he was going to explain to his wife that he had bought an expensive vacuum cleaner they didn't need just because the woman who did the demonstration had tucked her wayward hair behind her ear.

→←

Leah stood on the floor of the gully and peered up toward the cloudless sky and turned in a slow circle, her immediate sensation that of being vertical inside a grave the size of a football field. Leaning trees seemed all about, some growing out of the cleft in the wall, their trunks horizontal, their rack and crowns curving toward the sky so that the trees looked hooked, or hobbled by some event that defied naming. And then she looked to her feet. Blood was on her boots. The cow's blood, not her own, and she kicked dirt across each boot until the blood was covered, and then she put her hands to her hips and looked around again.

It was as though some force of nature had undermined a section of land and the undermining had shifted eternal Earth itself, for she stood in a section that was neatly squared off at its corners, and above was the sky and clay walls surrounded her, and she could hear water falling somewhere close at hand, but the trees, longleaf pine and sycamore, were thickly branched, and while the water sent out a signal that it was near, she failed to see evidence of it. She guessed she was fifty feet down, on a patch of planet that had been hidden for years, a desolate trap waiting for a dumb cow to stumble upon and fall to her death. Green flies were buzzing, and dark shadows soared across the ground in front of her, and she knew the buzzards were watching and waiting, and while she had not been born a country girl, she had been one long enough to know they were not known for their patience.

Walking through the first stand of trees, she found dried limbs of varying lengths and dragged them to the cow and covered her. Nettles were clinging to Leah's pants and shirt. A small pinecone cradled in a shirt pocket. She made three more trips until a pyre was neatly arranged, all gore hidden underneath last season's deadfall. The thought of a fire was not with her then, she had meant to cover the cow from predators was all, but motive mutated to cremation once the last limb was laid, and she patted her shirt pocket, realizing her matches were back in the truck. She would have to climb back up and then back down again, but now that she was free of her fear of dying, she thought the task seemed possible. But first she needed some water.

Following the sound of it, she parted the low shrubs along the clay wall near the north side and felt her way along the brittleness of a nature that was ignored, passing a cluster of colicroot, white flowers atop, bordered by blue-eyed grass, the combined palette like that of a faded quilt—a strange living and breathing one. All around her, wind was whistling through the trees and playing forlorn notes that echoed against the walls. It reminded her of music blown out of a bottle, music somehow reduced and hollow-sounding, and she looked up, one hand shielding against the sun, and realized the sounds would be lost to anyone walking on higher earth. The sounds were hers alone to hear.

She smelled the water before she saw it. The sulfur and iron smell that goes along with an artesian well, water good enough to drink if one could bear the odor of it. Parting low mimosa, she saw it funneling down the cliff wall from a pipe twenty feet above her head, a border of white on either side and a green pool at its base, where the floor had been washed free of its sand and found limestone. The pool was ten feet in diameter, small as a font, and she bent to it, sniffing first, and then tasted, tentatively, to make sure it was clean. Scooping up water in her hands, she drank and then bathed her face and neck while she leaned back to study its source. An ancient pipe protruding from a wall of dirt was a strange thing, in her opinion, and she wondered if she might actually be dead and viewing surreal life through spirit eyes. Reinventing elements to suit current circumstances. And then she looked up at the sun, wondering over the time, realizing a corpse would not be inclined to worry about the time of day.

She had left the house around six that morning. The sun was not quite overhead, and she guessed the hour to be around eleven o'clock. Bruno would not be concerned. Yet. He knew the cows were dropping their calves and would probably believe she was neck-deep in it, and she was glad. It had become very important to her that he not find out about the dead cow, and it was this worry that brought her up short about burning the remains. A fire would result in smoke, and smoke would be seen, and before she knew it, Sonny, who had a habit of noticing things he shouldn't, would wander over to the house and warn Bruno, and the two of them, or possibly just the big, nosy one—Sonny—would head to the fields to see what was going on.

"Well, shit."

She sat back on her heels to think about it, focusing on the mechanics of carcass disposal. There would be decomposition, which had already begun, and once she left the place, the carrion birds would do their part. She could just leave it alone and keep her mouth shut about the whole business. Or she could bury the cow. There was a shovel in the truck. But digging a hole the size necessary would take hours, hours she wouldn't be able to explain. She began to wonder how many days it would take for the cow to disappear, and what would be left of her. A sheet of hide? A broken bone? A skull?

Scooting back against the wall, glancing up first to make sure it was stable, she stretched out her legs and trailed one hand in the water and marveled at her sense of peace. Her shoulder ached where she had been caught in the root, and there was still blood on her boots, but she felt as though a vise that had been clamped on her chest sometime back had suddenly been released and she could breathe again.

"Hey," she said, out loud to nothing in particular.

"Hey," returned her echo, softer and with a slight reverberation, like notes off a saw.

"My cow died," she said.

"My cow died," came her voice, whispered and surreal.

And here I sit doing nothing, she thought, and with that she rose and brushed off the seat of her pants and was about to head back when she heard a low, drumming noise. Like wind beating on a barrel. Stepping over the water, she worked her way along the gully wall, turning a small corner, where she was blocked by a fallen sycamore, its trunk so ghastly white that she saw blinding bars when she looked away from it. Jimson and nightshade grew all around, and at a distance of ten feet, gray planking was stacked and rotting. Beyond the planking was a large piece of collapsed tin that had rusted out. Holes constructed by the elements appeared as a grinning face with obloid eyes, and she grimaced and moved beyond it, seeing a hulked shape riddled by vines.

The section of vines was as tall as Leah and it appeared to be growing in a flattened sheet, rigid and disciplined. When she reached through the green, those whippery cords of honeysuckle wrapping her wrist in a living bracelet, she felt a hardness, a man-made resistance. A shake shingle came off in her hand. Taking up a stick, she poked until she found the corner of the wall and walked around it, seeing a darkness beyond the green like that of a doorway or a cave. She thought at first it might be an entrance to a mine, but when she squatted on her heels and looked through, she saw signs of somebody's past life: a bench, a window that had collapsed on itself, shards of glass peppered with mold, an old door that had fallen off its hinge next to a crockery piece the size of a pickling urn.

What she was seeing was the backside of a house, a house that had been crushed for the most part by falling dirt. Getting down on all fours, she fastened the wall of vines back with a limb and crawled through the opening to the doorway and saw light checkerboarding through the roof slats in irregular patterns. Old varnish peeled up off the floor in tiny whitecaps of decay. Scrolling was carved in the wood over the fallen fireplace, a relief of vines and fruit, beautifully done, at least the work that was evident, for it appeared to have been interrupted mid–grape cluster. Hornets had made nests inside blackened corners, and dried husks of corn from some disappeared age were fluttering in the wind. Old sections of mortar clay lay scattered along the floor. Feeling her way, she stood up, her head bumping a low ceiling that angled down until it collapsed into the hearth, where old ironwork for holding logs still stood and ancient bundles of kindling were netted by spiderwebs. A barrel was turned on its side, and when she tried to lift it to sit, its girdle ring snapped in two and she was left holding slats of wood she knew were older than her mother. A hornet flew in and out of the mottled darkness. Leah swatted it away.

An old bed frame stood next to a window. The gray ticking had rotted away, and she could see that at one time the mattress had rested on ropes. An old gun was buried in the dirt, and next to it was some type of clothing, or maybe a blanket. She couldn't tell.

As old as it was, the place had the curious feel of being recently abandoned, and she backed out of the doorway and crawled off the porch into sunlight and again was met with a sense of tranquility. The sound she had been hearing was wind against what was left of the roof, and now that she had worked her way through the wall of vines, more wind gained entry, and with each gust, the dirt and grime of decades past skated across the shattered flooring like thrown rice at a wedding.

Leah left the area and headed back toward the wall to begin her ascent, barely noticing the cow underneath its funeral pyre, barely noticing the swarming flies and the smell that was already permeating the air.

"I'll just say the cows were calving and it took longer than expected," she said, for it seemed she had stumbled across a place where disappointments could be hidden, or stored, or placed out in the sunshine for examination. A place where she could think about where her life had been and where it was going. A private place where she would make her decision about whether or not to be a part of its eventual tide. She didn't know how or when. She just knew that she would.

{CHAPTER 4}

Willem Fremont crossed the Lamar County line a little after two in the afternoon, relieved the trip had been uneventful, though slightly bored by the void of scenic appeal. While driving through Natchez, he had temporarily entertained the notion of stopping at the Homochitto National Forest in nearby Franklin County. A lookout was built there, in the middle of the wildlife sanctuary. The sight-seeing brochure he had picked up at the Mississippi welcome station had mentioned this, and went on to proclaim the area beautiful and serene, with a picture of an all-blond family paddling a canoe across a tea-colored ribbon of water on the front of the pamphlet and, on the back page, children wearing gift-shop Indian headdresses squatted next to a small orange campfire roasting marshmallows. At first glance, it seemed like a wonderful place for an old man to take a break from driving and get out and stretch his legs before beginning the final push toward Purvis. It was the picture of the campfire that made him change his mind. He was already dragging ass, taking the long, meandering route, not because he wanted to see the lay of the land but because he didn't really want to get where he was going, and while an afternoon spent swatting mosquitoes through a forest of pine trees would kill a few hours, this benefit would be offset by the reality that while Willem strolled through the woods, he would be sniffing the air for the hint of a campfire whipped out of control by renegade wind. A dilemma that would do little more than weaken his bladder and increase the hefty card catalog of his memory, where ideas for fresh nightmares were stored. The park's beauty was undeniable, but he passed on it, driving down County Road 84 toward Brookhaven, the shade of ancient pine trees falling across the hood of his truck.

Once the national forest was behind him, and the string of Indian-themed gift shops had disappeared from his rearview mirror, he settled into the routine of driving, forming a mental note that the population of lower Mississippi seemed divided on the business of spirituality. Half had apparently found Jesus, while the other half was busy running away. Honky-tonks and religious signs were scattered along the two-lane highway in what seemed to be equal groupings. All religion indicators—billboards announcing the soon-coming Jesus; barns with platitudes painted on their sides; even the series of Burma Shave–type notices bearing scripture verses—were positioned on the right side of the road, and directly across from most of these iconic messages stood a Cimarron Club, or a Top Cat Lounge, or a Ruby Lee's, or the generic concrete-block dive with a front door that looked as though it had been kicked in at least a dozen times.

Willem had been to a dive or two, all of them out in Colorado, and they always made his nervousness worse, alcohol feeding his imagination, which was already a glutton. He wondered how it would feel to sit in a booth and look across the street and see a message about the wages of sin leading to death while sipping Scotch and soda. More than likely, one would end up standing on the table and screaming one's lungs out, and instead of some coffee-drinking, toast-eating adulterer's picking him up and escorting him bodily from the premises, the more logical scenario included a maniacal bartender pulling out his sawed-off shotgun and blowing Willem's brains out. He shuddered at the thought of it, passing his favorite sign yet: THE DEVIL WALKS ABOUT LIKE A ROARING LION SEEKING WHOM HE MAY DEVOUR.

It was a sentiment Willem agreed with, though in all fairness to Satan, who got blamed far too many times for human shortcomings, he would have to exchange "devil" for "calamity." He thought about it and realized the sentence, if revised, wouldn't read correctly. "The Calamity Walks About Like a Hungry Lion Seeking Whom He May Devour" sounded ridiculous, especially for the counties he was driving through. Case in point: the old shoeless black woman draping wet laundry across a fence line. Willem studied her as he passed. If a cross section of the general population were polled, he reasoned, "calamity" would do little more than summon to mind the western character Calamity Jane. He could almost see the broad spectrum of pollees scratching at their heads. No harm there, they would say. Just a gal with a gun and a nice set of tits.

Turning south in Collins, he connected with Highway 59 and drove through the outskirts of Hattiesburg. Purvis was fifteen miles south of the city, and he glanced at his wristwatch, dismayed to see that in spite of his ass-dragging speed, he had somehow managed to make excellent time. He took his foot off the accelerator and coasted along at twenty miles an hour. A car passed him on the wrong side of the road, fantailing onto the gravel shoulder, honking for a humiliatingly long minute. Hunkered over the steering wheel, Willem glared at the rear window, where faces were trained in his direction. He knew how he looked: feeble and senile and worst of all, silly. Smiling and waving—responses he had discovered further enraged already livid drivers—he watched with a form of amusement as the car righted itself and its driver reestablished control not only of the car but also the road, and managed to fly Willem the finger in the process.

One day you'll be old and someone will do the same to you, he thought. It gave Willem a small measure of comfort to imagine the driver of the car hunkered down over a steering wheel while teenagers screamed obscenities out the windows of their cars. He could only pray that one of the tormentors be a female and have on her chest a rack the size of Jane Russell's, in order to heighten the humiliation. He tried to remember if one of the faces shining in the back window had been female, but he couldn't and accelerated to forty miles an hour, toying with the idea of trying to catch up with the car and check it out. Passing a pecan grove and a fruit stand where jars of honey were lined up across the counter and golden combs gleamed in the sun, he watched the car disappear across the top of a hill and quickly gave up the chase.

Willem wiped his hand on his pants and fiddled with the radio, being especially careful to keep his truck on the road. He found a station that boasted "the country's best country!" and left it there, a bead of sweat dotting his upper lip, his eyes squinted against the light, his left hand tapping on the meat of his thigh, two taps per second, a hundred and twenty taps per minute.

{CHAPTER 5}

Willem found that Purvis was as spartan as he remembered. Where Hattiesburg seemed an actual city with businesses set close to the rail hub, Purvis was spread in a broad arena all over the county. Turning off Highway 11 and crossing Shelby Street and then the railroad tracks, he veered north and entered the rural area, which bore a resemblance to the urban area, and miles were traveled, and it seemed Willem was going nowhere at all. He found the Purvis–Columbia Road and drove down it and turned around where it intersected with a road running north, then he drove back the way he had come. He had thought the property was eight miles from town, near a waterway named Rocky Creek, but he saw no proof of a creek, rocky or otherwise.

Willem gave up the search in the middle of the afternoon because he couldn't find anything that remotely resembled what he had left fifty-six years earlier, and he drove around until he stumbled across a motel. ROCKY CREEK INN was painted on the sign out front, though the place seemed more domesticated than commercial, with ruffly curtains in all the windows and potted plants arranged along the concrete path and used tires that had been cut in half and painted white and arranged in a circular pattern around daylilies waving in the wind.

He parked the truck and got out and walked to the front door and peered in. The place was empty. BACK AT 4:00 was printed on a piece of paper taped to the window. Willem looked at his wristwatch, realizing he would have an hour of sitting and waiting, but given his nature, he would probably need the time to adjust to his surroundings, to check out all the paths in search of uneven bricks that might make him stumble, to look for rot in the awnings, to tuck in his shirt and comb his hair so that he might be presentable, which was not going to be easy since he smelled like a goat and his shirt looked like he had rolled around in it for a month.

Feeding coins into a Coke box, he lifted out a Dr Pepper and headed back to his truck, where he cranked down the window a bit and leaned back against the seat and looked at the sky. The wind drew what air there was in the rear of the truck through a small screened panel over the seat, and Willem could smell the tung oil and spirits and old wood yet to be re-finished and new wood yet to be stained, all remnants of something yet to be reconciled. He drank deeply from his soda and set the bottle on the floor next to his empty thermos and lifted his arm over his head and turned his head away from his reeking armpit, and while a part of him thought he was still studying the sky through the windshield, his head fell to the side and lodged against the window panel and *it is another sky he is seeing, a black night sky full of southern stars. Centaurus and Hydra. Ursa Major. Leo. Shining over the small house out in the middle of a clearing where a giant pine tree grows. A curl of smoke hangs suspended over the cabin, and there's a small paddock where a horse stands splay-legged and pissing and lowering its head as it snorts against the ground, blowing dried stubble and dirt and bits of gravel that continue to move even after the horse lifts its head and tosses it to the side. And the moonlight catches in the galvanized tub beneath the artesian spring and the water ripples and the moon becomes obloid and looks like some other thing, not like a moon. And through the magic of a dream, he is standing away from it and safe and sees it all. The crevice that begins near the outhouse and runs like a seam all around the place, as though it's been cut or chiseled out from below, and the walls of the cabin as they bend at impossible angles and finally crack with the explosive sound of lightning. The rear of the house as it disappears first and the chimney that rocks to the left and then the right, sending smoke in a lazy circle like a smoke ring off a cigar. And a young man clawing his way out the door and running for the open field that's disappeared. Running as he wipes the red dirt from his face, spitting out a tooth that's been knocked loose in the fall . . .*

Willem sat up with a start and tried to still his flopping hands; they were fluttering around his face like night moths engaged in activities turned incomprehensible in daylight hours. He thought he had dirt on his face, or perhaps dross from a half-eaten bag of pretzels, but he couldn't concentrate long enough to be sure because a small blond head was bobbing up and down by the truck window, appearing one second, disappearing the next. Another small boy had his nose to the glass, nostrils forced upward like a pig's. He saw down a woman's blouse to her breasts as she tapped at the glass with a slender finger. Wiping at his chin for fear he had drooled, Willem reached for the steering wheel and pulled himself up, smelling his own sour breath and unwashed body, a combination of road grime and dust and the suspicious smell of old-man urine that apparently had dribbled and then dried on his pants.

She tapped at the window again.

"You need a room?" Her voice was muted somewhat by the window.

He was aware how he must look: old and unkempt, a three-day stubble on his face, a man who, in order to be recognized as a man and not some decrepit oddball, would have to move his body out of the truck and into their presence; but to open the door would free the odor out into the courteous atmosphere of small-town America, where a small American Family stood waiting. To do this was unspeakable. He may have left the last blush of Gary Cooperism back at Ruby's Regal Truck Stop, but there was still the memory of his former self to deal with, the old belief of his that a first impression was the most important one. His first impression of his waitress back in Texas had led to disaster, and the part of his brain that acknowledged life's ironic symmetries believed he was about to be on the receiving end of a woman's scorn.

Nodding, he solved the problem with a lie: he slid away from them to the passenger side and opened the door.

"That driver-side door's been jammed for a while now," he said over the hood of his truck, walking toward the rear where his suitcase was.

They all stood and watched him. The ticking of the cooling engine as persistent as a metronome, a subtle musical score for a movie in which an awkward man gets caught in a senseless awkward lie that leads to a climactic moment of awkwardness. The older boy raised his eyebrows at the opportunity to prove to his mother that he was a natural-born problem solver and stepped forward and tested the door handle Willem had just lied about. The betrayer door didn't just swing open, it hurled itself open as though on a coiled spring. It opened so easily a baby could have done it. The boy peered up at his mother with a question in his eyes.

"It's harder to open from the inside, I guess," Willem said, watching their faces. Sweet air brushed through the truck. He was downwind and thanked God for that small mercy.

"You here for a room?"

"Yes, ma'am. If you got one."

"I got six right now. You can take your pick." Reaching out to the older boy, she smoothed down his hair. The boy studied Willem Fremont from eyebrows to shoes.

"I seen you here earlier, but you were sleeping," Alyce said.

"I been driving for a while."

"You got any luggage?"

He nodded and took the key and unlocked the rear of the truck and pulled open the doors and lifted out his large suitcase. All the way from Colorado Springs with only two things: a suitcase and that folded-up newspaper . . . he stopped cold, blinking in the sunlight. The last time he'd seen his hometown newspaper, it had been underneath his shoes as he stood screaming on top of a table.

"You okay?"

"Yes." Looking at his feet, he commanded them to immediately keep walking, even though an alarm bell was clanging in his chest. Anyone could pick up that newspaper and read about him. Maybe call the officials of the Colorado Springs police department and offer fresh information. There were probably more than half a dozen roads leading out of Sherman, Texas, to points north, south, east, and west, but inside his heightened state of anxiety, he saw one road only, and it was labeled in red and segmented with arrows that pointed toward Purvis, Mississippi.

"The room's right down there. Room six. It's clean and it's quiet. Far enough away from the rest of us so that you can get good sleep. I thought you might appreciate not having to listen to two little boys thump around and bang into the walls before breakfast—"

"Mama," Joe said.

"Well, you do."

"Not all the time."

"Most of the time," she said. "Mister, are you feelin okay?"

Willem realized she was looking at him, that his feet had disobeyed and were boycotting walking. That this was one more object in a menagerie of misfires set in motion because he had lost his newspaper. If he had known her name, he would have used the lull in movement to comment on her small motel. Perhaps saying, ——— (Lola? Christine? Mary Lou?), how'd you turn such a plain cinder-bricked series of cold boxes into a home? But he was flying blind where her name was concerned, so he put down his suitcase and scratched at his palm as though freshly bitten by a swarm of invisible but irritating insects. He stood in the shade of the oak tree studying his fingers.

"Mom," the older boy said.

"It's okay, Joe. Mister?"

Alyce thought she knew the type: a freshly dead wife who had done all his thinking for him, who washed his socks and ironed his clothes and then was inconsiderate enough to up and die on him, leaving him standing in her parking lot, no one left to tend him. She sighed. He smelled of travel and needed to shave but was still too clean to be crazy. Too courteous to be dangerous.

"I'm fine," Willem said, rubbing his forehead and glancing around. Geraniums stood in ancient pots next to the doors of the motel. Old geraniums with papery stalks that fed out of their containers, drooping in loopy avenues along the concrete walkway. He imagined small insects hiding inside a vermilion shade and wondered how it would feel to live constantly in red. As soon as he saw himself through an aphid's eyes—gargantuan and capable, completely able to stroll across a parking lot and sign his name in a ledger book—he had the courage to try it again. *Walk!*, he told his feet, and miraculously they obeyed.

"Guess I got bit by something," he said, watching the older boy, whose eyes told him he was on to him, that he knew good and well there wasn't a biting bug for ten miles around.

She waved toward the yard. "There's not that many mosquitoes this time of day. But we got all these old oak trees that nobody's got the heart to cut down, and even if they did have the heart, I'd not want them to. The only bad thing about the trees is that roaches breed nonstop in their leaves. But the man come out last week and sprayed. Room six was sprayed first, so there's not likely to be much of an odor."

He stumbled momentarily at her use of the word "odor" but the sound of their feet walking across the oyster shells was soothing, and he began to calm down. She stopped by her truck and lifted out a large empty box and folded it once across her knee and handed it to the older boy and said, "Joe, go put this in the trash for me."

The boy said, "But Mom, it's big."

And she said, "I know it's big. Now go throw it away."

"But Mom, it would make a great boat."

Willem had judged the box as exceptional and had to agree with him. Good cardboard of that particular size and weight was not an everyday occurrence.

"What did I say?" she said.

"But Mom, I promise to use it."

She looked at her son, and Willem found himself hoping she'd let the kid have the box. He was already seeing how the cardboard could be shaped to make a fine-looking hull.

"The first time I find it in the middle of the living room, it's going in the burn pile."

Going through double glass doors, Willem stepped inside a small room where a window unit was humming and dripping condensation down the pane. There was a desk with a black swivel chair and a low bench where newspapers were stacked. A ficus with waxy green leaves shaped like spoons towered in the corner. A child's red wagon was in the other corner, piled high with blocks and books and one of those bumblebees you pull along with a string. The concrete floor had been painted a deep green.

Alyce stood in the center of the room and looked out toward his truck. "You a businessman?"

"Was one. I'm recently retired," Willem said, rubbing his forehead again.

Moving to the chair behind the desk, the woman sat and crossed her legs, pulling the smaller child up to her lap, sending her clinging skirt up to midthigh.

"Sit here, Ben, and be still." She kissed his neck while he leaned his head against her and began sucking his thumb. "Now. You know how long you want to stay?"

Until I die was his thought. But he knew that level of truth would scare her. "I don't know yet. At least a couple of weeks."

"It's ten dollars a night. You can pay now or pay later. Since you're going to be here awhile, I'd appreciate it if you go ahead and pay me at least a part of it, so I can pay the woman who'll do your laundry. Thirty dollars would do it. I'll trust you for the rest. You can sign right here." She pushed the book toward him, and he patted his shirt pocket for a pen, fully aware that there was a perfectly good pen on the desk. He was fishing for a name. Something other than Willem Fremont.

She studied him and then extended her hand across the desk. "My name's Alyce Benson. And this little boy here is Benjamin. That one over there is Joe."

Taking her hand was like signing a contract. An agreement passed between them. He thought her fingers were kind and honest. His were scared and undependable. He wondered briefly which current might be stronger, the question meshing in his mind where gears of mindless trivia turned. Her face was turned away from him, as though to give him time to consider what he was about to do, whether or not he was going to sling the agreement to the dirt and trample it. She knew he had lied about the truck door and being bitten by an insect. She had known these things and still offered him a room. She was a good mother. One who set up rules based on the knowledge that children (and old men) fail; children (and old men) fall short and forget to put down the lid on the toilet, or to feed the dog, or they say "shit" or "dammit" in front of the preacher when he pays them a visit, or they whisper "You smell like a pig" into a working woman's ear. Children and old men were more human than most and merited a broader latitude of grace. They deserved that second chance to make things right.

Her handshake was firm, and he missed the warm feel of it once they were done, and though her face was turned away from him, light from the side window washed over her, and Willem saw the pale cheek and red lips, the wheat color of her hair as it curled out from behind her bandanna. There was a wholesomeness to her that forbade any further lying on his part, and with a heavy heart he decided to come clean, at least about his name, and signed "Willem Fremont" on a faded blue line.

"Willem," he said. "My name's Willem Fremont."

"Nice to meet you, Willem. I hope you enjoy your stay. If you need anything, just walk down here and let me know. We don't have phones in the rooms, but that there's what most folks use." She pointed to the wall and its large black pay phone. Then she pulled open a drawer and handed him a key with a red plastic tag that had the number six printed on it. "You need any help with your bags?"

"No, Alyce. I'm fine." He tucked the key in his pocket and headed for the door. It was only a little past four o'clock, but he felt weighed down by fatigue. Forty pounds heavier than he had felt that morning. Walking past the geraniums, his suitcase in hand, he noticed the quality of the potting soil, dark and moist, how it seemed to have just the right amount of vermiculite added in order to drain properly and postpone the rotting of the plant's roots. It was a wise choice, he reasoned, that bag of lightweight white granules. A dollar at a gardening center. But there was only so much a product could do when it came to delaying the inevitable. Plants flourish, and then they die, and all the added ingredients in the world can't stop it. Unlocking the door, he stepped inside a musty room and went to the air-conditioning unit set in the window and clicked it to high. The curtains were made of dotted Swiss material and hung on a metal rod with metal rings; underneath the decorative set were light-blocking draperies that felt like rubber. Pulling them almost closed, he sat on the side of the bed and untied his shoelaces and removed his shoes and placed them underneath the nearest chair. He unbuttoned his shirt and removed it and folded it by his side and stretched out on the bed and fell instantly to sleep while, through the partial opening in the window, Alyce's older boy had his hands cupped around his face and watched.

{CHAPTER 6}

It was late evening when Ben followed his brother across the parking lot and down into the weedy ditch where the sweetleaf grew and the two of them walked along the sheared clay wall watching for rattlers, because their mother had seen one once and they trusted her.

"Lookathere," Joe said.

"Loo ah whah?"

"If you don't take your thumb out of your mouth, you're goin back," Joe said to him, and Ben removed his thumb from his mouth and walked to where his brother was and squatted down beside him and stared with severe concentration at the spot where his brother was pointing. He stared for a long time, looking at rocks and empty cans and tatters of paper thrown from the windows of passing cars.

"Whatcha lookin at, Joe?"

Joe was in front of the moldy mouth of the culvert, with its metal grid and its dam of sticks and trash and bent cans and wrappers, where beyond, on the far side of the road, there was a tiny crescent of daylight. He took a stick and poked around and then leaned back out again and wiped his face on his sleeve.

"Stop it," Ben said.

"Why?"

"'Cause Mama's gone whip you," Ben said.

"Hush or you're goin home."

"But whatcha lookin at?"

"Hold your blankety-blank horses and you'll see." He put a hand to the concrete pipe and leaned his head in, and since this wasn't far enough, he stretched out and began to enter the pipe, crawling along on his belly until only his legs showed.

"Joe, don't."

"I almost got it," he said, and his voice was an under-the-bed voice, and Ben became scared and looked over the crest of the ditch for his mother, who was nowhere to be seen.

"Here. Look," Joe said, backing out of the pipe. A pale thing was hanging off the end of his stick.

"What's that?"

"Snakeskin. It ain't a big one, but it shore is off a snake. Hand me that other stick."

Ben did as he was told, and Joe used it to catch at the dangling end and stretched it between the two sticks and held it up to the light.

"I bet it's off a radlur," Joe said.

"You don't know."

"I do *too* know."

Joe laid it on a flat piece of shale and they both sat back on their heels and stared at it as it lay twisted and wrinkled and odd-looking. They stared at it for a long time and poked once or twice at it with the stick and then they heard a car coming down the road and Joe put his hand to Ben's arm and said, "Be still, it's only a car." They both ducked their heads and the car approached at high speed and its tires went *ka-whop ka-whop ka-whop* on the asphalt and then the sound went away until all the boys could hear was the white noise of cicadas interrupted just once by the shrill call of the crow. The sun was lower in the sky now, and yellow was turning to red beyond the shafts of the trees.

"Can I touch it?" Ben asked.

"Do you wanna touch it?"

"If you do," Ben said.

"I get to do it first, though."

"How come you get to go first?"

" 'Cause I'm older than you. Here. Hold my stick." Joe reached out and placed his finger on the skin, running down its length with his forefinger.

"Lemme do it now."

"Okay. But don't mess it up."

Ben rubbed it and pressed his finger down on the other end of it, the end that was gray, and said, "There's somethin in there, Joe."

"Where at?"

"Right there." Ben pointed.

Joe took it by one end and lifted it and saw that it was stretchy like a balloon, and there was something in the end of it, like lint caught in the toe of a sock.

"This ain't a snakeskin after all," Joe said.

"How come?"

" 'Cause it looks too much like a balloon."

"It *might* be a snakeskin," Ben said, and both boys squatted and studied it and wondered if it was a snakeskin or not, and neither could decide. Ben said it don't look like no balloon, and Joe said yes it does, too.

"You reckon Daddy'll know?" Ben asked.

Joe shrugged.

"You think that ole man'll know?" Ben pointed toward the motel where the green truck was parked.

"He don't know nothin."

"He might."

"No, he don't."

"Mom'll know. We could ask her."

"She's cookin supper, and we ain't supposed to be out here by the road."

Joe worked at it with the stick until it was hanging off the end of it and went to the culvert and reached as far inside as he could, and this still wasn't far enough.

"Joe. Don't," Ben said.

"Just a minute," Joe said, and again it was the under-the-bed voice and Ben was frightened.

When Joe crawled back out, he stood and brushed off his clothes and said, "There. It's back where it belongs."

"How come you put it back?"

" 'Cause."

" 'Cause why?"

" 'Cause it ain't a snakeskin."

"It *might* be a snakeskin," Ben said.

"No it ain't. Now, let's go eat," Joe said, and pushed his way through the dense white flowers of the sweetleaf and waited for his brother, who was slow to follow and kept turning back to look at the place on the rock where the unknown thing had lain.

Across the parking lot, the old man had taken a chair out of the room and set it beside the door and was sitting there stubble-faced and wrinkled, holding a Dr Pepper bottle in his hand. It was tilted to the side as though he planned on watering the plants with it.

Joe ducked his head and walked on, but Ben called out, "They's a snakeskin down there," pointing to the ditch and its culvert that seemed so dark. The sky was losing its red color and fading to purple. "It's ours, so don't touch it."

The old man didn't say anything. Just looked at them like he wasn't seeing them at all, or even listening, and even Ben noticed his strangeness and hurried to catch up with his brother, who always looked at him the same way and had scared him only twice, and that was when he had crawled into the drainpipe.

"It might a been a snakeskin," Ben said.

Joe didn't say anything. Just opened the door for his brother and then shut it behind them. Turned the OPEN sign to CLOSED and pulled the string that lowered the venetian blinds. This way, if his daddy came home, he would think they were closed and go away, and maybe then his mother wouldn't cry.

{CHAPTER 7}

From inside the onyx shade of an ancient oak, Willem put his hands in his pockets and looked at the sedan that was parked next to the entrance to the motel. Blue light from the neon VACANCY sign shone down on its hood in reverse, and the word looked Russian: for it spelled out YCNACAV. The driver-side door was ajar, and Willem could see its side panel and whispered, "White," its conservative factory color before the car was painted lotus green. The reflection made Willem's eyes water, and he pulled his handkerchief from his rear pocket and wiped at them and then folded the cloth back into his pocket. There was an overabundance of chrome on the car. Bumpers. Hood ornament. Mag wheels. Wind spoiler across the top of the trunk. Narrow bands below the door panels. Even the grillework that stretched between the headlights. The overall image was that of a wide-mouthed, grinning frog. Fake leopard fur covered the seats, and a huge pair of dice hung from the rearview mirror. Willem shook his head. He was standing unnoticed, the only witness to his rumination a gnarled oak root blasted open by the day-to-day hazards of its old life. No one could see him. Not even the couple involved in the fight. The man had his hand on the door frame and was arguing with Alyce, who had her arms across her chest and her head down. Sidelit by the car's interior beam, the man appeared blond-headed and young as he climbed into the car and pulled shut the door. He reached through the open window to Alyce, and Willem watched her pull away from his touch.

"What should I tell the boys?"

"Whatever you feel like."

"But you've been gone for week. They'd like to see their daddy once in a while."

"I'll see them tomorrow mornin when they wake."

He cranked the car and began to reverse across the lot, the red brake lights shining across the broken oyster shells. "How about you, Alyce? You don't seem to miss me much these days."

Now that the side of the car was parallel with the road, Willem could see an elongated chrome ahoogah horn on the side of the door.

"Even when you're here, you ain't here," she said as she stood underneath the blue light of the vacancy sign. Moths batted around her head, and she swatted at them.

The husband honked, and the awful-sounding *ahoogah!* blasted through the quiet, and Willem jumped and reached out to the tree to steady himself. Alyce didn't even flinch. All she did was lower her head and turn and walk back indoors. After a moment the light in the front office went off, followed by the lights in the heart of the house, until all that was left was the blue neon VACANCY sign that blinked on and off and on and off. A sign more true than anyone realized. Willem watched it for a moment and then headed across the oyster shells toward his room.

→←

Three miles away, Sonny Till was close to being worn out from the effort it was taking to sneak out of his mother's house.

For fifteen minutes he had burrowed through the leather dop kit he kept in the third drawer of his dresser, searching for his outback necktie. He didn't really want to wear the tie but was using the time as a means of stalling. Nervous and sweating, he stood before his horse-collar mirror and slid the black nylon rope over his head and settled it under the collar of his white shirt and pushed the silver kangaroo up as high as it would go. Once he was sure it was fixed right, he went to the closet and got his Australian bush hat and slapped it against his leg before putting it on. And still he stood in his room, worried about his timing. Finally he moved toward the door.

The hallway stretched between jail time and free time, hard time and easy time, and he put one hand up to the wall and crept along, stopping every few seconds to listen for the sounds of his mother's sighs.

Sonny could hear the needles as they clicked along and knew Eilene was engaged in her latest brainstorm: knitting. A light was next to her chair, and he could see her cast shadow as it stretched out into the hall, and he thought of the painting *Whistler's Mother.* All she needed was one of them stiff white hats.

His mother sat in the overstuffed chair every evening after she had done the supper dishes and swept down the whole house and rearranged all of Sonny's working diagrams that he liked to keep spread out on the dining room table. She claimed to be knitting, but he was yet to see a scarf, and he was beginning to suspect the only reason she sat there was so she could spy across the field on her older son and his wife, charting the varying patterns of lights flickering on and then off, murmuring to herself, "They're in the kitchen, I guess" and "Now they've gone to bed," each declaration served up with a breast-heaving sigh. Sonny hated those breast-heaving sighs. They made him crazy. He had counted forty-seven sighs one night, each louder than the one previous, and, fed up to the teeth with it, he stomped into the living room and threw down his *Reader's Digest* and demanded she put down her knitting and go to bed. Of course, Eilene couldn't hear what he was saying because the poor old bag was deaf, and he had to squat in front of her and shout three times before she turned from the window and looked at him. There were times, though, when her habits suited him, and this was one of those times.

He stood in the darkened hallway and watched as he tried to time his getaway, but his timing, as usual, was off. Caught inside his mother's ragged, heaving shadow, he hesitated just long enough to start feeling sorry for her. *Jesus! Look at her! The way she's breathing!* He knew better than to do this. The last time he'd felt sorry for her, he had caved in and promised he would quit drinking beer, which led to an exhausting month of covert drinking out in the field behind the silo, where he smashed beer cans to the size of jar lids and packed them tight as turds in every single gopher hole he could find. Feeling sorry for Eilene made his stomach hurt, and he had just about decided that the only way he was going to feel better would be to stand in the shadows while somebody knocked her upside the head with a board.

His shoes were in his hand, and he was tiptoeing across the dark kitchen, taking special care not to walk near the sink, where the floor squeaked, not stopping to realize that his mother was deaf and wouldn't hear it even if he stood there and did a sweat-churning clog dance. His hand was on the doorknob, and he was wondering where in the hell he had put the car keys when she stuck her head through the doorway and screamed at the top of her lungs, "WHERE IN THE WORLD ARE YOU GOING!"

He froze and shut his eyes and felt the hairs stand up on the back of his neck, the pressed shirt collar digging into his flesh and reminding him of the oversight of wearing something freshly starched. She would want to know why he couldn't wear the shirt he'd worn all day long. Add to that the dug-out-of-the-closet Sunday shoes he was holding in his hands and the Australian bush hat on his head. Because his mother was forever losing her keys, he had made her a key holder out of fishhooks and fastened it to the wall. Now he stared at it, aware that he was hooked in the gills just as solidly as the mounted bass hanging over the fireplace mantel.

"Do you HEAR ME, SONNY?"

"I hear you, you old hag." He whispered this as he leaned his head against the door frame.

"What'd you say?"

Turning, he yelled, "Nothing! I didn't say a damn thing!"

Sonny thought about pretending he had a girlfriend, but that would lead to countermeasures more difficult than hiding smashed beer cans in a gopher hole. Eilene would not be satisfied until this made-up girlfriend was sitting at Sunday dinner eating lumpy gravy and undercooked roast.

Since he was caught and there was nothing he could do about it, he moved to a chair and began to put on his shoes. It gave him time to dredge up a clear thought from the mire of his brain. Her shadow found him, and he looked up at her and yelled, "I'm goin to the lodge!"

There was a lot to be said for a well-thought-out lie that had already been used.

The lodge lie was perfect. There was not a lodge, but if there *had* been one in Purvis, the place would have been off limits to women and Sonny knew this. Plus, he was taking the keys to the Pontiac with him, so Eilene would have to stroll over to Bruno's and wake them up in order to track him down. And even then, since he'd lied to her about the formation of this lodge and how it was yet to find a regular meeting place, just a caravan of sorts complete with fezzes and high ideals and secrecy, she'd never know where to go to look. The lodge story was much better than a fake girlfriend. He'd drink his beer, eat some peanuts, meet with the son of a bitch, and Eilene would never be the wiser. He couldn't bear to think what she might do to him if she caught him in a strip joint.

"I heard of a traveling circus, but never a traveling lodge!" she shouted.

"It's not a traveling lodge."

"Seems to be a traveling lodge, since you drift from place to place like the Pilgrim Virgin. How long before you boys get a regular meeting place?"

Sonny looked up at her, searching for a trace of sarcasm. He didn't see any. "I don't know."

"What'd you say?"

"I said, 'I DON'T KNOW'!"

"Hattiesburg has their own place. More than one place, now that I think about it. There's the Elk Lodge on Elk's Lake Road, and then there's that Scottish Rite place—"

"Look!" he yelled.

"Don't you 'look' me! I'm only CURIOUS! CAIN'T I BE CURIOUS?" She was holding her knitting in her hand, the recently attached arms stretching behind her like tentacles of an octopus, so large it seemed she was fashioning a sweater for some giant creature of the sea.

"I ain't wearin that!" he yelled, pointing at it, horrified.

"What'd you say?"

"I said, 'THERE'S NO WAY IN HELL I'M WEARING THAT THING'!"

Eilene caught a smile and stopped it before he saw it. Knitting had been added to shouting and cooking as her third line of defense. She had been working on the sweater for over a month, wondering when he would notice its perversity. Four men Sonny's size would fit into it.

"But it's your favorite color!"

"I'm still not about to wear it!"

"Baby blue to match your eyes!"

"No!" he shouted.

There was a pause and then she whispered, "I'm on to you," in such a low voice he felt his scrotum constrict. "You think I don't know what's goin on? You think I'm so dumb I cain't add two and two and get four? Sneaking out at night to go meet at the lodge. Well, I talked to Velma Dinkins, and she said there IS NO NEW LODGE!"

"Now, Mama," he said, holding up a hand in appeasement.

"LIAR!" she screamed, reaching out and knocking his bush hat off his head.

That didn't seem to be satisfying enough. Her next move sent the knitting sailing to the kitchen table. To Sonny's amazement, it covered the table entirely, the arms drooping to the floor and curling around the chair legs with an alarming amount of surplus.

"I guess you got me," he said, shaking his head and looking at his sock feet, at his upside-down hat resting next to the back door.

"I knew it!" she shouted.

"Yep. You're too smart for me."

Eilene was quiet. This was a new tone her son was taking: a new path of resistance. She was glad she had the pretense of deafness to hide behind, at least until she figured where the trail might lead.

"I'm not going to the lodge." Sonny slapped his legs and looked up at her, the shifting look in his eyes settling a little and gaining a new foothold. He opened his mouth and said, "I've got a date." This was an untried lie and would need some greasing, but he was running behind schedule, and if he didn't escape soon, he might be forced to try on the blue thing she was knitting.

Eilene stood still and trembled, the slight variation of the trembling recognized only by the woman experiencing it. *So,* she thought. *At last.*

"I think you're telling me a story!"

"Think what you want. I've said all I'm gone say about it."

Eilene changed her course and pulled up a chair with great anticipation. Her face cracked open in a smile. Her eyes twinkled like a damn Christmas tree. "Why, Sonny, this is wonderful news. Tell me about her!"

"No."

"Where'd you meet her?"

He couldn't say church, since he'd stopped going years ago, and because church was the only acceptable place to meet a woman as far as Eilene was concerned, he felt screwed by the lie. Lies usually took a while to come on the sheets. One day, at least. This one had shot off in record time: the speed of light.

"Sonny? Why cain't you answer me?" She reached out to his leg and picked a piece of lint off his overalls. Her fingers trembled.

"Mama. I'm late."

"Where'd you meet this girl?"

"I don't want to talk about it."

"What's wrong with her?"

"Nothin's wrong with her."

"You've never been able to keep your mouth shut longer than two minutes your whole life. If nothin's wrong with her, you'd be telling me all about her!"

"I'm just not ready to talk about it." He made an effort to keep his back straight against the chair. Eilene seemed tuned in to this and pulled her chair forward until their knees touched. Sonny began to sweat, because his mother's knee felt electric.

"When do you think you'll be ready to talk about it?"

"I don't know when."

"Is she nice?"

Sonny stared at his mother, bending his body to peer into her wide blue eyes, which appeared larger than female eyes had the right to be, like moons with shimmery pools of liquid catching against her lower lids. He stood to his feet in a rush. The sweater slid off the table and onto the floor. "She's nice right now, but she won't be if I'm late to pick her up!"

And with that, he scooped up his hat and left the house in a dead run.

⇢⇠

"You see. Here's the gist of it—"

"The what of it?"

"The gist. It means the crux—"

"The what?"

"Hell. Forget it," Sonny said.

There's a lot to be said for a crop of little red-shaded lanterns that nobody but a strip-club owner wants to buy. This is what Sonny was thinking as he watched Joe Benson clean his nails with a bent butter knife. A curl of black beaded up on the knife's edge and dropped to the table like a solitary mouse turd. Red light didn't carry far enough to expose the small growing pile, and Sonny, who was as fastidious about cleanliness as he was lazy, sure was glad. Other than his fingernails, Joe was spotless. Blond. Clean-cut. Groomed to the point that he seemed to glow. The man was slight of build, almost childlike, with tiny bird-boned shoulder blades that forever gave him the appearance of a man half starved. The white of his shirt caught the red cast of the tiny table lamps and sent a crimson stain up under his neck and across his high cheekbones and the tips of his ears. A bloody child, then. Or a pale bloody bird. Take your pick. He was in direct contrast to Sonny Till, who, no matter his habit of dress, looked hugely swollen about his extremities and packed to the eyeteeth with food.

Sonny had not wanted to meet at the Li'l Miss Roustabout, but Joe had insisted. The transfer of stolen property by way of exchanged monies called for dark alleyways and flashlights, and this was the way they had done it in the past, rummaging in the back of his decked-out Chevrolet's trunk, or along the train tracks, where a flatbed trailer sat mostly hidden behind an abandoned warehouse. Sonny had to wonder why Joe had changed his routine.

The table was a corner one, and the place buzzed with old whores who used to be dancers and young dancers just now turning to whores and men too poor to do little more than stand around and gawk. One tall fellow tried to stick a fifty-cent piece up the ass of a young Mexican dancer, and she slapped him hard across the face and sent the coin tinkling across the concrete floor, where it tinkled to death under the legs of a pinball machine. The slap did little harm, for he turned around and shook frenzied hands with every man within his range, a huge grin splitting his face. This very same behavior was repeated two minutes later.

"Listen," Joe said, raking the dross into the palm of his hand and dumping it to the floor. His voice was tenor-pitched and grated on Sonny's nerves; it was like talking to a man high on helium. "You think acting dumb is the same as being dumb, and that's where I got you."

Sonny glanced around. Noticed that Clayborne seemed to have plans for enlarging the place. A corpse-colored stack of cinder bricks sat covered in plastic over by the jukebox.

Sonny watched the Mexican gal across the room and said, "I never said you were dumb. It was a dumb word, now that I think of it. Mama uses that word. Look at that."

Joe looked over to the bar. "Him? That's Sparechange Dinkins."

"He's back? Lord. I thought he got killed in a lightning strike."

"He did. Well, technically, he died," Joe said. "A nigger found him and took him to the hospital, and they worked on him awhile and brought him back. He ain't the same, though."

"How so?"

"Well, dumb-ass. Look at him. He shakes hands with folks ever two minutes. Don't matter if you just shook hands with him or not. Don't matter if you just slapped him in the face or fucked him up the ass. The fool acts like he's never seen you before in his life and needs to get acquainted."

Dumb-ass watched, and sure enough, Joe was right. Sparechange tried to shake hands with a sleeping facedown drunk, the drunk's hand flopping with dead-weight and no resistance regardless of the pumping action. This done, he scrambled to his knees on the floor, searching the concrete for his lost half dollar. What he came up with wasn't it: a lone nickel appeared in the center of his palm like a metallic stigma.

"How bad'd it burn him?"

"About as bad as a lightning strike can." Joe sighed. "If he'd been standing on the train tracks instead of in the dirt, he'd still be dead, no matter how many niggers drug him to the hospital. You cain't really pity a man who's been told not to do a thing. Picked up at least three times by the sheriff for salvaging around the rail yard. And how much you think he brings in from them empty bottles?"

"Enough to stick a coin up a whore's ass," Sonny said, looking over at the girl dancing; he was uneasy with the naked gymnastics. There was a small triangle of gold cloth between her legs, covering something so foreign to Sonny that he felt drawn to examine it over and over again, calling up husbandry clues based on watched bulls and birthing sows, of sexless chickens and multiplying rabbits. Nothing came close to explaining what might be under there. "Some men might think that's all a body needs to get by."

"Not me."

"No. I realize that. You'd expect more."

A drunk bumped into the table on his way to the bar, and the tiny red light blinked on and off, and Sonny put a hand to the shade and steadied it. He would have liked to reach under the table and rip the plug out of the wall, but his girth prevented it. The room was aglow in hellish light, and the Mexican gal's ass glowed like a plump cherry, but that was all there was that was good about her. Sonny couldn't bear to look at her face, where her buck teeth made her look like a human bottle opener. He watched as she tried to hide her bad grillework with her hand as she twirled around the pole. The gal lost her balance and came close to falling off her heels, and Sonny hid his face behind his hand and peered through his fingers until she made her recovery.

"You're ab-so-fucking-lutely right I'd expect more."

Sonny pushed at the table, which was crowding his stomach, and glanced around, searching for familiar faces, people who might recognize him and go running to his mother with the truth about where he was. He didn't see anybody he knew.

"I know. But I cain't ask her for any more money right now," Sonny said, folding his hands on the table. He was chasing his six beers with an RC cola and feeling light-headed and overly sentimental. Joe Benson, experienced thief and die-hard whore chaser, seemed like a stand-up guy under these circumstances.

"I cain't operate on credit forever, Sonny. And the way it's lookin, that's what you got in mind. I got obligations just like everbody else. I got a wife and kids."

"I know that."

"I owe the hospital two bills for her damn miscarriage."

"I didn't know she had one a them."

"Well, she did." Joe paused and looked at a blond whore who spread her legs for him from a bar stool. Grinning, he shook his head and turned back to Sonny. "They said it was another boy, too."

"How much do I owe you, anyhow?"

"Last count, twelve hundred and seventy."

"Shit. I had no idea."

"You got a memory block, then," Joe squeaked. "I reminded you day before yesterday and the day before that. I think even last month I whispered it in your ear. It was them booms that did it. All that metal that won't do nothing but sink that boat in the middle of the Mississippi Sound."

Sonny's boat was a twenty-five-foot Grady-White inboard, with a cutty cabin in the front and huge bait wells built into the back. A good boat, just as it was. A sturdy fishing boat that would have at least twenty more years left in its life, if left alone. Sonny had other plans for it, though. *Sonny's Gal* was going to be a shrimp boat, rigged with all the necessary equipment, if it killed him.

"You ought to see them booms. They sure look good," Sonny said.

"Like I said, I owe the hospital money and if I don't walk out of here tonight with something from you, I cain't go home. Not with folks dunning me right and left. Not with the wife still in bed tryin to recover. You got no idea how much a woman bleeds when she loses a baby. I swear, it's enough to make a man sick."

"How much for a decent set of trawl boards?" Sonny said, hating the thought of Joe's wife being sick. The thought of a woman being sick made him uneasy. Unless it was his mother. He'd like to see her sick for a while.

"Moron, it's time to take some stuff *off* the checkout counter. I been sittin here explaining to you how things are—"

"What's a good set of Bosarge trawl boards gonna cost me?" Sonny asked.

Joe sighed and reached into his pocket and pulled out a handkerchief and mopped at his forehead. "How big?"

"The kind them big boats use."

"They won't work."

"I'll make 'em work."

"Your credit's topped out. You ain't got enough for that."

"What can you get, then?"

"Maybe a couple a oars."

"I'm serious."

Joe looked at him, put the knife down on the table. "I can get maybe some good used ones."

"How much, Joe. I ain't got all night."

"Say seventy-five."

"How about this. You get me two used sets, and I'll pay it. And see if you got any parts layin around belongin to a wrecked car. That inboard's on its last leg—"

Joe held up his hands and shook his head. "Sonny, you owe me money. A lotta money. We're here to work out how you're gone pay me what you owe me. I—"

"Look. I'm only askin you to check. I got money in the pocket to pay you part a what I owe you. I'd pay it all, but here's the deal. I owe Lewis Geigan for that net crank he made me, and I got to pay him this week or he's comin to take it back. I met him at the front gate last time. He swore if he had to come back, he was comin straight up into the yard. You and me both know what that means—"

"You idiot. Lewis is not gonna take that motor back. Especially a miniaturized motor that won't work anywhere except in a rowboat."

"He said he would take it back," Sonny mumbled.

"And you believe him?"

"He seemed real firm on it."

"How come Lewis seems more of a threat to you than me? How come I have to call you up and drag your ass out of your house to talk business?"

"I think you know that answer the same as me."

Joe was silent for a moment, and then he said, "I need my money."

"I know you do. But I need them trawl boards."

"I see," Joe said. "What if I knew a way to get you what you need, maybe even more than you need; a new set of shrimp nets, even? What if I knew a way for you to wipe the slate clean?"

Sonny looked at him, suddenly suspicious, his uneasiness battling with the thought of having a clean slate. "You're not a man known for his generosity, Joe."

"This has nothing to do with being generous. This has to do with you doing something for me that needs doing."

"I ain't a thief."

"I'm not askin you to be one. All I need is a lookout. A guard."

"No."

"How come?"

Of all the reasons in the world, there was only one that counted. "She'd kill me."

"So, it's your mama you're worried about," Joe Benson said.

"Joe, there's not a female alive that cain't make a man squirm," Sonny said, watching the Mexican girl as she dipped her head to the stage and wound a leg up around the pole in a feat of wonderment that came close to defying description. Her face was hidden underneath a tangled shock of hair, and her crotch was exposed by the neon blaze of a Pabst Blue Ribbon beer sign. At the sight of the small covered triangle kissing the pole, some signal fired in the moose organ of Sonny's brain, and he decided that if he could figure out a way of doing it without going near her bottle-opener mouth, he would kiss her. He began to wonder how she might look wearing actual clothes and if she would be presentable enough to sit around the dinner table come Sunday, completely unaware that Joe Benson had counted on this bankable weakness: the pliable nature of a middle-aged man who was yet to be laid.

{CHAPTER 8}

Leah went to her kitchen window, where the wooden farm table stood, and stared out at her world, wondering where the sun had gone. What meager light there was seemed diluted and weak, as though the sun were bleeding out, for its only evidence was little more than a pale representation of its truest form. A half-light haze covered everything in sight. Every blade of grass. Every fence post. Even the silo seemed wrapped in gauze. *I suppose Canada is covered,* Leah thought, realizing how one's immediate environment robbed the imagination of any other vision, any other place. On this particular day, it was hard to visualize a sun shining brightly anywhere at all.

She put a biscuit on a saucer and walked into the living room and sat down on the couch and slipped out of her house shoes. The vacuum cleaner was in the center of the room, and she looked at it and thought it looked more like an overfed dachshund than a motorized appliance. Plaid tubing coiled around its base like a tail, and a gray plastic nozzle lay nose down on the floor where Bruno's feet would rest. The buyer of the vacuum was in the bathroom, and she could hear the water running, but like the business in Vietnam, as well as whatever it was that had turned him to a stranger, the reason for it was yet to be talked about. Leah had stumbled around it for a week, thinking to herself, *Have patience; he'll explain.* Bruno hadn't. Of all that had happened since '69, the purchase of a vacuum cleaner seemed the most unmerited, the most unexpected, and if not those two, then certainly the most ridiculous.

She set her saucer on the couch cushion and stood up and stepped into her slippers. Padding down the hallway she came to the small alcove off their bedroom and put a hand to the doorknob and turned it, testing for resistance. There wasn't any. She had known the bathroom door would not be locked, because Bruno didn't need a lock to shut someone out. For four years, seven months, and twenty-two days, it had been this way.

Stepping away from the door, she walked down the hall and back into the kitchen and stood near the large window, glancing up at its arched top where, through the fan of wooden mullions, the orb of the sun tried to flicker. Hidden sun. Timid sun. As though it were afraid of what it might see and chose to wait until the world was up and turning before fully opening its eye. The pipes were old and loud, and the bathroom shower was set full tilt, and the kitchen faucet was vibrating. In a few minutes he would be done, and she could run hot water in the sink and set the dishes to soak. With false bravado, she slipped out of her housecoat and stood naked but for her panties, one hand up to the bruise that covered her arm from elbow to wrist, fingering it gently, while at the same time a less gentle thought formulated in her mind. How could he have had time to notice the nonexistent need for a new appliance but not an injury to his wife?

She laid the housecoat on the back of the chair and walked to the bathroom door and stood listening to the water running as she ran the course of speculation. *Does he take off the brace? Does he stand? Does he sit? Does he see this bruise but not want to talk about it? Have curiosity and concern died, too?* Her only answer was the sound of running water. A secretive sound that refused to give out clues.

Steam feathered out from under the bathroom door and rolled along the floor until it hit the baseboards and curled like tiny crested waves. She could feel them on her ankles. Stepping out of her slippers, she pushed open the door.

At first it seemed as though she were peering through her kitchen window again, such was the haze. Billowing wreaths of it cascaded over the top of the shower curtain, and filled the room. She could see the outline of her husband standing stock-still behind a pale blue plastic shower curtain. Reaching to wipe the mirror clean, she saw her face, her hazel eyes, her hair that needed brushing. She would give him two minutes, and then she was shoving the shower curtain aside and facing him.

She got to keep her two minutes, because he said, "I'll be done directly," before her hand had left the moist surface of the mirror.

"I can wait." She looked to the floor and got the answer to question number one. A towel was thrown over the brace, though a pale pinkish corner was visible. Its padding resembled the soft meaty tissue in the palm of a hand.

"Leah."

"What?" She swiped the mirror again, the squeak of flesh against moistened mirror high-pitched.

"Is there a reason you're in here?"

"I have to pee." It was lame and she knew it, but he was pretending to be lame and she knew it, so she figured they were just about even.

"Can you wait until I get out, then?"

"No," she said while steam billowed and fell. She thought Bruno might have said "Fuck," but she wasn't sure. Lifting the lid on the toilet, she pulled down her panties and sat down and peed and kicked her panties off to the side.

"Are you done?" he said.

"Just about."

A small window over the tub brought in morning light, and Leah could see Bruno's outline. His thick torso. His head, which seemed terribly straight for someone so damaged. A bottle of Breck shampoo and her Lady Gillette and English Lavender soap were in a drawstring mesh bag hanging on the cold-water tap, and the thought of Bruno being naked in front of her bath toiletries was both erotic and irritating. She wiped herself and flushed the toilet, and this time she was sure he said "Fuck."

"Bruno," she said, jerking back the shower curtain to expose his charade, and saw his strong legs runneled with water, the dark hairs flattened against his skin. Her eyes traveled up his legs to his thighs and the squareness of his rear. He was trying to turn away from her, but she could still see enough, and from her vantage point Bruno looked enough like her husband to be a man she could live with. It was only when her eyes traveled higher up the wide expanse of chest and his contorted arms and she saw a human pretzel of a man leaning perversely into the tiles, struggling for breath, his right arm twisted up behind his neck so that his elbow might cradle his head, that she said, "Shit."

"Get out."

"Listen, I . . ." she said, reaching out to him, searching for words.

"Get out."

Leah could see the chill bumps on his skin, and she leaned into the tub and felt the water and realized it was cold. She turned up the hot and tested the water with her hand until it was comfortable. Her head and neck were trapped in the stream, and her hair became dripping wet, portions of it clinging to his wet knee. Bruno stood on the ribbed rubber mat she had bought at the five-and-dime, the bar of soap near his toes. Leah stared at it. "Were you through with the soap?"

"No."

"Here, then," and she picked it up and was reaching for his hand to place it there when he shifted slightly and she saw it. He was fully erect.

"Shit," she said, wondering what had become of her vocabulary, why it had been reduced to that one word.

"Leah, I—" he managed.

She put the soap in his hand and bent to the floor and picked up his towel and laid it across the edge of the tub and walked toward the door.

"Leah, wait."

But she couldn't. She had to leave.

Leah saw the buzzards as soon as she pulled out of the yard. Black spiraling kites off in the distant gunmetal sky. She drove slowly, pulling out of the long front drive and turning left at the mailbox. Should anyone be watching, it would appear she was headed to town. Her hand was on the steering wheel and she was turning her ring against it, the knob of the diamond catching against her palm as she remembered her overtures. Like many women who pretended not to be, Leah was shy, and it took a lot out of her to reach out to Bruno time and again. She remembered those times and places and dates and all the rejections as she passed the thick neck of the woods and tall pines spread their spear-shadows across the hood of her truck. He said he couldn't, and this was the reason he turned away from her at night, but she had seen proof that he could. She drove on down the ribbed dirt road, her hand jerking against the steering wheel of the truck.

The road ran between trash trees to the north and crop pines to the south. Trees planted by Bruno's grandfather, Reinhold Till, for his grandchildren, assuming there might be some one day. Everybody needed paper, Eilene was fond of telling her. Either to write on or to use to wipe the ass. Paper was the only sure thing nowadays, and to get paper, you needed trees. Close to fifty acres had been set aside for use by the southern letter-writing, ass-wiping population, but when Leah looked at the trees these days, instead of seeing money waiting to be collected, she saw dead soldiers waiting to fall.

The south gate was just beyond, and she stopped the truck and opened it and drove through, watching with pure amusement the gate swinging shut behind her. Sonny had invented the means by which the gate swung shut, placing a pressure foot connecting to a buried cable that, when pressed by the tires, flipped a toggle to release the gate. A man in love with gears and levers and anything mechanical, he could make money selling it, if he'd but try. Of all his lame-brained inventions, the automatic gate-shutting device seemed the only one with promise.

She took a deep breath and watched the buzzards sailing on the breeze. Steering across the bumpy pasture toward the strange gully she had found and the house that was buried for the most part in the earth, she realized it was the one place she could go where she might think about things, and the largest question on her mind was how in the world she had come so far from where she used to be.

{CHAPTER 9}

Eilene closed her back door and stepped out into the yard and began to walk across the wide expanse of field that separated her house from her older son's. The bluetick hound came up from the rag-rug bed and followed at her side, and she stopped and shooed him away, and he stood wagging his tail and staring at her. "I got nothing for you," she said, waving her arm. "Now git." After a moment the dog went back to his bed, circled three times, and plopped down.

Tomato wires were stacked next to the house, and inside Eilene's garden fence the ground was weed-grown, not turned over yet. The shadow of the boat was so large that there seemed little use for dragging the tiller out of the shed. Last year's tomatoes grew no larger than golf balls, and who'd want to eat one of them? The fans that kept Sonny cool were not running and a table was set between them holding empty potato chip bags and crushed drink cans and greasy rags and buckets of paint with their lids askew. A fifty-gallon drum held a net Sonny was trying to mend. Eilene sidestepped the tongue of the boat trailer and wondered if she could buy dynamite without drawing attention to herself.

Once she was clear of the mess, she brushed a hand down her camel-colored slacks and retucked her starched pink cotton shirt. A new straw hat was tied to her head with a paisley scarf, and she had a basket on her arm loaded with hot homemade biscuits, as well as a book she was reading.

The book was a backup plan, so to speak: its presence known only to Eilene, and she'd leave it that way if Bruno would straighten up and speak to her. If not, she'd pull out the book and sit smack-dab next to him on the couch and read for a solid hour. Maybe then he'd know how it felt to be ignored.

Eilene had seen Leah pull onto the main road a little before seven o'clock, and after months of spying, she had their schedule firmly stamped in her brain. Bruno showered around seven, and since the kitchen light had not been turned on, this meant Leah hadn't bothered with breakfast, so perhaps there would not be a battle over her biscuits. Even if there was, she felt ready for a fight.

Stopping at her fig tree, she examined the low, thick branches, spreading apart the fan-shaped leaves with her hand until she found the tiny tear-shaped lumps. Unless a tornado showed up and blew apart the tree, the season would be large and luscious. The best in over a decade, judging from what she was seeing. Eilene left the tree and walked on.

Bruno's yard was mowed, but mowed like a woman with a lot to do would mow. Leah used the bushhog and made sweeps as close to the house as she dared, and there were clumps of tall renegade grass growing around the pump house and back porch steps and taller clusters of hay grass gone to seed around the T-posts where the clotheslines stretched. Eilene walked up the steps and stood rubbing the cat, and then she checked the bow underneath her neck and stepped through the door into the kitchen. Her eyes were not adjusted to the gloom, and she bumped into the back of Bruno, who was standing at the cabinets, holding a tin of baking powder in his hand.

"Mornin, Mother," he said, extending his hand.

"Mornin yourself," Eilene said, shaking his hand. It was something the two boys had learned from her, these good manners.

"I saw you coming across the yard."

"What'd you say?" she shouted, setting her basket on the kitchen table.

Bruno went to the fridge and got out the carton of buttermilk. "Mother, you heard me." He turned around and stared at her, seeing her as he had seen her as a small boy when she'd come into his room to check on homework that was usually half done.

Eilene pulled a chair away from the table and sat. Was he humming? Was she losing her mind?

Sitting at the table, she folded her hands and waited. One of the many problems with pretending to be deaf was that she gave up the chance to engage in conversations that really mattered. Like blessing him out for leaving the door shut when he'd admitted he had seen her coming across the yard. Her friends' sons took their mothers on dinner cruises in New Orleans and to visit the alligator farm in Ocean Springs and once a year to Bellingrath Gardens. Eilene couldn't even get a door opened for her. In spite of these notions, she made her face the picture of geriatric contentment.

"I brought you some buttermilk biscuits!" she yelled, pointing to her basket.

"I've tasted your biscuits. I think I'll make some of my own," he said, bending to lift the pastry bowl from under the cabinet. It had been years since he had thrown together flour and shortening, but since stepping out of the bathroom into a house that was empty, he had wondered if, like the erection he had maintained in the presence of his wife, it might be something he still knew how to do.

Her son had clearly insulted her but Eilene managed to keep the slight smile on her face.

"WHAT ARE YOU DOING, DEAR?" she yelled.

Bruno winced at the decibel level of her voice and made a decision. Walking over to a kitchen chair, he pulled it out and sat across from her. He couldn't help but notice that in spite of her age (what was it these days? sixty-five?), she had managed to keep her appearance similar to what he remembered it being when he was a small boy. She had always been neat as a pin. Always wore a hat out-of-doors. Always starched her shirts. Always slipped into loafers and a pair of girls' white socks. The only difference between the Eilene of today and the woman of twenty years back was the lacework of wrinkles next to her eyes, and the silver-gray hair, and, of course, the not uncommon demeanor of a woman forced to live with one of life's bigger disappointments. Bruno was not thinking of Sonny this time. He was thinking of himself.

"I tell you what, I'll make a deal with you. If you'll quit pretending you're deaf, we'll have a conversation. Otherwise, I'm going out to the barn and work on the tractor." He studied her, grinning slightly.

The truth showed between her blue eyes, which had remained, after all these years, incredibly bright. Slowly, thoughtfully, she untied her scarf and lifted her hat off her head and sighed. Here was the son she had never figured out. The son least like his father.

"You seem unusually cheerful today," she said, brushing her fingers through her short gray hair.

"Now, that's much better." Bruno tried to lean back against the chair, but the brace ran the risk of lodging between the slats. "You're lookin spiffy this mornin. Where you off to?"

"I'm goin to town later on. But first I thought I'd do my good deed for the day." She patted the basket and then leaned around Bruno to look in the living room at the strange tubed appliance. "Is that a vacuum cleaner?"

"Yep. It's an Electrolux. A fine machine. At least that's what the instruction manual says."

"Bruno, you've got wood floors throughout and a fine dust mop standing right over there." She pointed to the wall next to the fridge. "Why in the world did Leah buy an appliance she doesn't need?"

"I guess you'll have to ask her. Now, if you'll excuse me, I have some biscuits to make."

"I brought you some fresh hot ones."

"Like I said before, I've tasted yours, and they're not any good."

"Believe me. These are good," she said, and Bruno turned to her.

"The bad food was a game, too? Like pretending to be deaf?"

Eilene clamped her mouth shut and wished she had brought along her hair net; she felt so damned naked. If her two friends, Bea and Velma, hadn't abandoned her in light of recent stupid hobbies—ceramics and ballroom dancing—Eilene would have had a place to go, and a decent cup of coffee to drink, and two pairs of ears willing to listen to her catalog the shortcomings of her children. The two women had been pleading for months that she join their group of Santa-painting, fox-trotting senior citizens, and Eilene was beginning to regret her refusal.

She pointed in the direction of her house. "It's that darn boat," she said, her hand trembling slightly. "I thought when I bought it for him, it would be a way for him to get out of the house and make himself useful."

"How much did you pay for it, anyhow?"

"None of your business."

Bruno was silent.

Eilene brushed a biscuit crumb into her hand and put it in the basket. "I thought maybe he would set up a small fishing business. But no, he has to take something that's perfectly fine, and turn it into something that will never work."

"I think the key word is 'work.'" Bruno lifted out one of her biscuits and bit into it. "These *are* good."

"He could have taken small groups of people wanting to fish. The gulf waters are teeming with all sorts of aquatic life."

"Not to mention, it's a great place for a fat boy to drown."

"Bruno, hush." She put a hand to her chest. "It really grieves me the way you talk about him."

"Sorry."

"Your brother wants to work, he just can't."

"He does *not* want to work. He has *never* wanted to work."

"That's not true. He flew all those miles—"

"To Australia. To New South Wales, to be exact. I know. I was the one who took him to the airport and put him on a Qantas jet. If that waste of money doesn't prove my point, I don't know what will."

"It wasn't his fault. His intentions were good."

"Then whose fault was it?"

"The person who placed the advertisement in *Field & Stream*," Eilene said.

"There you go."

"There I go what?"

"Blaming the wrong person."

It had been a good ad. Well designed. A big dollar sign next to a rabbit lying on its back with its tiny feet in the air. Rabbits were eating the Australian crops and a bounty was offered. Fifty dollars a head. All you needed was a gun. She had seen the words with her own blue eyes. She guessed there were hundreds of young men who had gone over there and made the thousands of dollars they were promised. Sonny just wasn't one of them. After going into her household fund and forking over fifteen hundred for a one-way plane ticket, and buying him gear, and making sure he had the proper shots, she had made him promise (promise, by God!) that he would make the endeavor work. It was in the middle of his third week away that Eilene got the phone call begging her for money so that he might come home. The rabbits that were there ran too fast, he said. And the climate was unbearable, he whined. And that easy-money "bounty" advertised in his sportsman magazine apparently didn't exist, he complained. And to make matters worse, an itchy rash had attacked his balls. "No sir," she firmly told him. "You said it was going to work, now *make* it work. I don't care if you have to sweep out bars or clean toilets. I've not got the cash to fly you halfway across the world time after time." Slamming down the phone, it was the first time Eilene had been positive she'd taken the appropriate steps in teaching her younger son a thing or two. Learning to make do was a good lesson for anyone, even Sonny. It would give him new confidence, as well as a fresh outlook on life. It would make him pursue his own natural resources, resources she was sure were there but needed only a slight poking with a stick. A week later the government car pulled up into her yard and the man in a suit handed her a notification that her son had gone to the American embassy located next to the Parliament House in Canberra and declared himself destitute. Since he was an American citizen with next of kin living peacefully in Purvis, Mississippi, the only recourse was for those kin to fork over the money. Either that or a lien would be placed against the farm. One way or the other, Sonny was to leave New South Wales. So outraged she felt she might begin to shatter from a point deep inside (near the betrayer womb that had nurtured this child), Eilene gathered up her grandmother's silver and headed to Vicksburg, where she knew a dealer who would give her a fair price. Sonny flew home the following week, declaring the week spent in a hotel courtesy of the stand-up guys at the American embassy the best week of his life.

Eilene rubbed at her temples. This was not going as she had planned. "Where's Leah?"

Bruno got up and went to the cabinet and retrieved two cups and two saucers. Lifting the percolator, he filled his cup and then his mother's. "She's out tending the cows," he said, setting the cups of coffee on the table and reaching for one more biscuit.

"She headed out in a direction opposite the cows."

"There's feed bills to settle." Bruno sipped from his cup and then looked at her. His movements were so constrained by his brace that Eilene wanted to wince, and he seemed to know this and took great strides to act casual, the end result being a man whose every movement appeared in slow motion.

"Are you spying on us, Mother?"

"No. I'm not spying. I've just always been very observant."

Eilene reached into her basket and lifted out *Testimony of Two Men*. In her opinion, Taylor Caldwell was a genius. The flyleaf had indicated the book was about two brothers who hated each other and this was the reason she had checked it out from the library. She was quite taken with the dark and angry Dr. Jonathan Ferrier, who was so misunderstood by the residents of Hambledon, and she already hated Harold, the lazy brother who refused to work. The only wrinkle in the novel was the poor treatment Caldwell had given Robert Morgan's mother, who was being portrayed as a buffoon. If Eilene knew how to get a letter to the actual writer, and not the Doubleday publishing house in New York, she would register this complaint. Eilene opened the book to her marker and looked up at Bruno, also guilty of exhibiting poor treatment to his mother. "You could ride along with her, you know."

"She's got enough to tend to, she doesn't need one more thing."

"You see yourself as a cripple. That's your problem."

Bruno had lots of problems, but clarity of vision was not one of them. "Mother, I think you should mind your own business."

"It's sad how soon children set aside their terms of endearment."

"What are you talking about?"

"You used to call me 'Mama,' not 'Mother.' "

"I used to be seven years old. At last count, I was older than that."

Eilene sighed, wondering if the loudness of exhalation would weigh on Bruno's sympathy. The truth was, she didn't really care what the boys called her, as long as they stopped calling her. "The reason I'm over here is to remind you of the Fourth of July."

"It's just now the last of May. Why hand out the invitations so early?"

"Because last year you didn't show up, and this time I'm not allowing the excuse that you weren't properly informed. You can get Leah to fix her German potato salad and tell her I've already phoned Dora and Merle and they said they would love to attend. Dora said it's been months since Leah phoned her. You can accuse me of being a busybody, but that's just not proper behavior, coming from a daughter." She waited for Bruno to agree with her. When he didn't, she continued: "Anyhow, Dora's making one of her wonderful Jell-O salads, and Merle will act as bartender for the day. I'll barbecue the ribs and we'll spread the food out on the tables in the front yard. All I need you to do is buy the fireworks for later that night."

"What's Sonny going to do?"

"He's got his hands full, I'm afraid, just tending to the business of showing up. It's been a long time since I enjoyed watching him sweat." She smiled, a faraway look to her eyes.

"Why the drama?"

"Well, he lied to me. Again. And now he's running scared."

"He lied to the embassy officials in Canberra, and that didn't seem to scare him too much."

"This time is different. This time it's his *mother* he's lied to." She looked at Bruno, who couldn't help but smile at her.

"What'd he lie about?"

"He *claims* he has a girlfriend, and I know it's all foolishness, of course. But I've given him an ultimatum that I'll extend to the Fourth of July: under no circumstances is he to show up without her."

Bruno shook his head. God, he hated his brother. It was not as if anything Sonny did affected Bruno personally, it was just that he couldn't stand him. The lard-ass just rolled along through life, piddling with his little inventions and his grandiose plans, so sure the world thought he was a great guy, there were any number of people who would give their eyeteeth to be just like him. *The fool actually adores himself,* Bruno thought. *Unconditionally.* This unexpected moment of clarity dispelled all the other reasons he normally hid behind when explaining his constant irritation with his brother. *He likes himself and thinks he's great. And* this *is the real reason I hate him.*

"Can you imagine what type of girl would actually give him the time of day?" Eilene asked.

"No. But I'd sure buy a ticket for it," Bruno said.

"You and me both." Eilene closed her book and looked at her son. In so many ways, he was the same as before, his strong face, his blue eyes, his large hands that were beautifully shaped, his quiet nature and obvious intelligence. He was such a blessed contrast to his younger brother, who had none of those things. Bruno wore his shirts halfway buttoned, to accommodate the brace that began at his breastbone and continued upward until his head was cradled, but it did little to interfere with a resemblance drawn from Reinhold Till, also a quiet man of obvious intelligence. Eilene looked away and sighed, and it was a genuine sigh. She was unaware that her geriatric contentment had slipped and left exposed an authentic state of melancholy and that Bruno had registered it as real and, as a measure of comfort, reached out and laid his hand over hers.

{CHAPTER 10}

Leah lowered the can of diesel fuel by the length of rope, watching it settle to the ground next to the busted stock of the .30/06. She had already tossed down a rake and a blanket in case the fire got out of hand, and the matches and a carefully rolled joint were in her shirt pocket. Since she had a cremation to attend to, the various methods of burning were on her mind as she caught on to the handholds and worked her way down the side of the cliff. She had burned with a fever when she was a little girl suffering with strep throat, and burned with desire once she was older and realized Bruno was who she wanted; and as recently as this morning, she had burned with an anger that had been kept on the back burner far too long. And now she was set to sit back and watch a carcass disappear into flames. Of all the types of burning, she supposed logically, the one she was about to inflict on a dead cow was the least painful.

The pyre she had built was wilted with the heat. The pine limbs were brittle; the leaves of the sycamore, brown and curled along their edges like minature boats. There had been too many days without rain, and she raked around the cow, removing the dried brush and deadfall, not stopping until a track the width of a small car isolated the body from the rest of the trees. She looked up at the sky. One benefit of being down in a hole was that the wind didn't seem to be such an issue, at least not as much as it was high above. She had no fear of a brushfire, or of being roasted alive inside a pit, and she supposed the reason she was not afraid of either of these things was that she had recently discovered there were other things that scared her more. Admitting defeat, just one of them. Unwilling to think about it at the moment, she doused the limbs with diesel fuel, stood back, and tossed a match. A deep *whoomph* sounded, and she felt the percussion of heat-driven wind and took backward steps, her arm across her face to shield it from the flames.

Once the pyre was sufficiently lit, the smell of scorched cowhide commingled with roasting decay and assaulted her nostrils, and she backed farther away. The whole business smelled like somebody was trying to grill a truckload of rotten hamburger meat. Turning until she was headed in the direction of the sunken house she had found, she noticed for the first time the elements of homesteading scattered all around her. A rusted tub turned upside down. A broken plate. An old muddy whiskey bottle. Not that whiskey was a necessary part in homesteading. In fact, it probably did more damage to the initiative required to accomplish something meaningful than anything else. She had been drunk once or twice in her life—that field high overhead was one such locale for one such time—and look at her now. A woman down in the middle of a gully, scavenging the ground around her as though nothing else mattered. She realized there was something other than liquor that kept a body from getting anything accomplished. The stagnation produced by making too many wrong decisions was more paralyzing than a whole case of Jim Beam.

Leah bent for a stick and scooped away debris from what used to be a shovel, and a small lump of white scooted to the side. "Jesus, it's a tooth," she said. She picked it up and used her finger to roll it around in the palm of her hand. *A real person lived here,* she thought. Not that she had imagined gnomes or elves being the past residents, but she had to admit that the odd shape of the house, the way it seemed to have been stretched and sucked for the most part down into the earth, seemed the stuff of nursery rhymes or fairy tales. *Or nightmares*, her more sensible side reminded her. Leah went to the pool at the base of the falling water and sat leaning against the wall, dipping her fingers in the cool water. She rinsed the tooth and then held it up for inspection. It seemed to be a molar, and she felt along her teeth with her tongue as a way of comparison. The tooth she held in her hand was slightly bigger than any of hers, and it appeared the person took great store in dental care, for there was no sign of decay. Not a cavity to be seen. Just what appeared to be a perfectly healthy tooth, knocked out of the mouth and deposited in the earth. Perhaps as a result of the fall. She looked at the house. In spite of its almost cartoon trapezoid appearance, it had gone from being a symbol of fantasy and become a dwelling place where somebody bathed in a tub, drank whiskey out of a bottle, and apparently had the good sense to brush his teeth. She set the tooth in the water near the edge of the pool, where she could look at it should she want to.

Leah stretched out her legs and then pulled them up to her and rested her chin on her knee. She sat this way for a while, the sound of cicadas rising and then falling, rising and falling. Sunlight moving across her boots and the top of her head, and still she sat. The billowing smoke turned to a tower of black, and still she sat. It was while she was watching the rise of thick, oily smoke that she realized there was another type of burning after all, one much more painful than the others—the burning one feels from the embarrassment of being wrong.

The single child of Merle and Dora Maxwell, Leah had spent an uneventful childhood surrounded by a vast number of dolls on her bed. She had as many as her nearest neighbor, only Leah's were better because their hair was left alone. Her bicycle was better, too. Blue. Newer than her neighbor's, and it came equipped with a basket and a bell. And since her mother understood how to cut on the bias, when it came time for poodle skirts, Leah had seven of them. One for each day of the week. It was almost idyllic, this place where Leah lived. This closed-off street of Balanced Meals and Baton-twirling Lessons and Roller Skates that always had an extra key. Soft breezes blew through the wisteria plumes. Rain fell evenly and ran circumspectly down a series of concrete drainage openings. There were sidewalks, and every evening whole families took walks. With the possible exception of the holding pond meant to be a lake but which turned out to be a swamp, everything about Pinecrest West went according to the original plans of the civil engineers, one of whom was Merle Maxwell. The community was a series of ranch houses built around tiny blocks, each with its own fire hydrant and seasonal theme. During Thanksgiving on Loblolly Lane and Fraser Fir Place, fathers took turns dressing as a giant turkey, handing out candy in exchange for ears of dried corn. Christmas week, every family in every house participated, each street decorated as one of the twelve days of Christmas. Colorful contruction paper partridges filled the trees on Red Cedar Lane. Hula hoops painted gold hung from the trees on Hemlock Branch. Glittered wooden swans swam on yards laid out with mirrored boards.

Leaving home and going to the University of Mississippi woke Leah up, and she found herself moving inside the crush of young people who had no idea where they were going or what they wanted to do. Walking the narrow streets of Oxford, the Confederate soldier usually within view, she thought about Faulkner and wondered if, when drunk, which rumor had it was his perpetual state, he found the circuitous route around the city square as depressing as she did, if his drunken circle made him feel as though he faced irrevocable history again and again. If this might be the reason he said "The past isn't dead, it's not even past."

Home for the holidays, she looked around her room; the pennants and pom-poms and shelves holding dolls and the white vanity table with its matching mirror and brush set all seemed artifacts from a lost civilization, an obsolete place where children were dressed in finery before being sacrificed. It was only a matter of time before she saw her parents the same way: stone relics on which blood had been spilled, carved bulbous limestone lips overgrown with decay, timeless altars whose time was done. The fifties were gone. The sixties were here. And while Dora and Merle might have thought the sixties would extend uneventfully into eventual peace and sameness, Leah had other ideas and began to pronounce sentences on her parents based on their dinner-table testimonies. The term of their incarceration was determined by their hardheadedness and refusal to listen. She might visit them while they were in prison, or she might not. It depended on their receptiveness to rehabilitation. The sentence was pronounced first on her father because he was the one who disappointed her the most.

Her father was a walking paradox. An engineer who made his money with the TVA, who liked his Scotch and good cigars, who went on record in recognizing integration as a necessary rung on the evolutionary ladder of society but thought the ladder itself leaned into a window behind which the total downfall of humankind waited. Merle voted somewhat liberally for a central Mississippian, and he had renounced all methods of religion as self-serving and idiotic, yet he went fishing twice a year with a die-hard white supremacist who lost a bid for the Senate, and he roamed the golf course of the country club like a man in search of salvation. During her second year in college, Leah discovered the type of man her father really was: a relativist. One who no longer believed in absolute truths or absolute morality but in the burgeoning balloon of moral grayness, where ideals changed and shifted depending on whatever situations surrounded it. This in itself would be bad enough, but Merle took it one step further: he was a complacent relativist, one who lacked the convictions of his beliefs, a man who failed to recognize the irony of his words.

There was very little to say about Dora, other than she was a woman who collected piquant sayings and salad recipes with equal attentiveness. Gregarious but dim, Dora was renowned throughout Pinecrest Woods for her Lime Jell-O Coconut Salad, and her favorite saying for the month of June was "America the Beautiful. Let's Keep It That Way." She served drinks to her bridge club festooned with tiny American flags to drive home her point. The week the bridge club meeting was held, two black men were mauled beyond recognition by police dogs for refusing to get out of the whites-only line at a Greyhound bus station; a third-grader in Neshoba County required forty-seven stitches in her head because of a thrown brick; and five black churches were burned to the ground near Jackson. In the middle of the news stories, Dora called Leah at college to tell her how festive the flags looked stuck inside the tall glasses filled with Tom Collinses.

At first Leah maintained proper reticence on her visits home, sitting at the polished dining room table, aware she was shedding the skin of parental adoration in great flaky sheets that fell to her lap, but able to tolerate it because, after all, they were her parents. She tried to listen to them talk, but the words became metal somewhere between the wilted spinach salad and the pork loin and spring peas, and Leah's role of silent historian lost its appeal. She'd had her fill of magnolia-scented community teas, magnolia-themed community garden parties, magnolia-colored community action committees; she recognized with a cynical air that what really went on in Pinecrest Woods was social activity tuned to an underlying worry: How to Keep the Colored People (as Well as the Jews) Out. Unable to be quiet about it, Leah laid aside her robe of observation and opened up the briefcase of chief proscecutor. The case was presented (as usual) at the dinner table. Leah's prosecutorial plan was one that seemed innocuous in appearance: she would talk about drinking water.

"I've been to town and I've seen them and I know they're there, but to bring it up now is ridiculous," her mother said while she spooned whipped cream onto the Nova Scotia Pudding Delight. "They have the same water we do, and that water comes from the same big tank, and so why does it matter if they drink out of our water fountains? Personally, I think they probably prefer to have their own water fountains. They're a lot less crowded than ours, and if I was out walking around town it might discourage me to see a huge crowd waiting to drink water from a single fountain."

"I think you've missed the point, Mother. Nobody's talking about eliminating water fountains. There will still be the same exact number of water fountains, just made available for everyone."

"I think *you're* wrong. I think they *like* having their own water fountains."

"Have you asked them if they like their own water fountains?" Leah said, taking her knife and scraping off the whipped cream. Accepting and swallowing and actually enjoying whipped cream on her dessert seemed something the old Leah would do. "Have you asked them if they like having 'colored only' hanging overhead?"

"Well of course I haven't. Who would I ask?"

"That's my point."

"What's your point?"

"You have no one to ask. They stay over there. You stay over here."

Dora looked at her daughter, this stranger who used to wear poodle skirts. She didn't recognize her. She looked at Merle, the Great Mediator of Meaningful Discussions, for help, but his head was lowered over his pudding cup.

"Of course they stay over there and we stay over here. Where else would we stay? This is not something they thought up on their own.

Everything was fine until a few years ago. And you're wrong. I do have someone to ask. I could ask Zola."

"The maid?"

"Why not? I'm sure she has an opinion on it."

"Have you asked her how she feels about it?"

"No. But I will if it'll make you feel better." Dora took her napkin from her lap and folded it, pressing her nails to the crease, smoothing a hand over the perfectly starched lacework. "All this business is originating from some other point than the South. I know it. Merle, tell her how you feel about this."

"No," he replied.

"Okay, then I will," Dora said.

"Mother, you don't have to. I think you've explained enough."

"You're taking that tone again, and I've not explained anything at all, and I don't think it's fair. It's like the time that Jewish family was planning on moving into the neighborhood and you were home and we were talking about it and all I said, *all* I said, mind you, was how left out they would be at Christmastime. That's the *only* thing I said, and you attacked me. Attacked me, Leah, and that's not fair."

"You've explained how you feel without meaning to explain it," Leah said. "The sad thing is, you can't help how you feel."

"I've not explained my feelings at all. But I will. Not that I think you really want to listen. People don't like to change, Leah. And this is what we're talking about here. Change. Changing the way things are done makes people uncomfortable. And I tell you this: I think if you stop and ask anyone, they'll tell you they like it the way it is right now. If people from the North would leave things alone, we would be fine. Life would be fine. We've been good to these people—"

" 'These people'?" Leah said.

"You know what I mean."

"Yes. I know exactly what you mean."

"Stop baiting your mother," Merle said.

Dora eyeballed the two of them, wondering what she had missed.

"I don't think I'm baiting anyone," Leah said, watching her father, setting him up for questioning. "You were part of a progressive movement,

Dad. You were there. You saw what the Depression did to the Tennessee Valley region. You told me about it. How can you take this stand? Or not take a stand? Or do whatever you call what you're doing."

"I was paid to do a job, Leah."

"It was more than a job, and you know it."

"Wall Street ruined the country," he said. "It was up to us to help fix it."

Leah sighed.

"People were starving. Black and white alike. The issue here in Mississippi is not starvation," he said.

"I think it is. A different type of starvation. And it's not just a Mississippi issue. It's everywhere."

"I thought you wanted to know how *I* feel about it," Dora said. "I thought *I* was having a discussion with Leah." She glared at Merle, who always managed to make her feel shoved aside.

"Dora, I don't think you know what she wants to discuss," Merle said.

"Of course I don't know what she wants to discuss. I haven't heard what it is. How could I know ahead of time?"

Merle looked at his daughter and then looked over to the bar, its reliable grid holding bottles of gin and Wild Turkey. The bar was next to the living room, a sunken living room his wife was proud of, with a parquet floor he had just paid to have refinished. A television stood in the corner near the rubber tree plants and the bookcases holding *Reader's Digest* condensed books. All he had to do was walk over to the bar and pour himself a drink and he would be set.

"Do you know what's happening in Greensboro?" Leah asked.

"Myrtis Gleigmier lives in Greensboro. She says it's a beautiful city. The climate is in*cred*ible."

"But do you know what's happening there?"

"Why, I'm sure lots of things are happening there. Aren't they, Merle?"

Merle just shook his head.

"I'm not talking about a cotillion or a garden party, Mom."

"How could I know what's going on in North Carolina, since I don't live there?"

"You said you have a friend there, maybe she's mentioned it."

Dora blinked her eyes rapidly and rearranged her silver spoon. The Nova Scotia Pudding Delight was a failure. Too much walnut extract.

Next time she'd use less. "I haven't seen Myrtis in years. Last time I saw her, she was just about to become a grandmother, and not taking the news any too good, either. Her son married that German girl. Remember her son, Rudy? I think you went to school with Rudy. Well, they wanted Rudy to study agriculture at Auburn University so he could take over his father's nursery business, but no, Rudy had to go to Chicago to school, and I told her then it was a big fat mistake. Strange things happen when you go away. Myrtis didn't believe me at first, because no one in her family had ever been farther north than Batesville. But it happened, just like I said. Tell her, Merle. Tell Leah what happened."

"I don't know what you're talking about."

"You do *too* know what I'm talking about. We've already talked about this. He knows exactly what I'm talking about, he just doesn't want to agree with me in front of you."

"No. I don't know what the hell you're talking about, Dora." Merle clipped the end off his cigar.

"I'll tell you, then. When you go off in a new direction, you see all these foreign people, and you fall in love with a total stranger just because he or she looks a little different than you do and because opposites attract. This is what happened to Rudy. He met this strange foreign girl who's German—"

"Our ancestors are German, Mother," Leah said.

"Why, they are not! Our people are from Wisconsin. Anyway. Rudy met this girl and married her, and Myrtis is fit to be tied. She says the girl is hard to talk to because she can't say the letter 'V.' She says 'W' instead. 'I need to wacuum the den. I need a wodka tonic. I want to play wolleyball.'"

"Dora, hush," Merle said.

"'I wolunteer for ciwic duty, ewery chance I get.'"

"For God's sake, Dora. Leah's talking about the sit-ins," Merle said.

"Thank you, Dad."

"Don't thank me. You started this, and it's been a long day and I'm tired and I don't think you really want to discuss anything other than your disappointment in the way we think. Our values are being challenged here. Though why, I don't know."

"What's a sit-in?" Dora said.

"You really don't know why your values are being challenged?"

"Leah." He leaned on his arms to look at her. "I know things are changing. I have to question the motive at the root of it. There's a difference between social concern and social uprising. One annihilates the other, and you know it."

"What's a sit-in?" Dora said.

"Society doesn't change without resistance. What difference does the 'motive' make if, socially, the playing field is being equalized?" Leah said.

"Christ, you're talking like a Marxist," Merle said.

"I am not!"

"What *in the world is a sit-in!*" Dora shouted, banging her hands down on the silverware.

"Are you sure you want to know?" Leah asked, turning to her.

"Well, if it was so important for you to bring up, of course I want to know. What is it?"

Leah gave her the condensed version. "A sit-in is where Negroes go and sit in the drugstores, or dime stores, and ask for a cup of coffee. No one will serve them, since they're sitting at the 'whites-only' counter, but they sit there anyway. The first four sat in a Woolworth's five-and-dime in Greensboro, neatly dressed and polite, for an hour. The next day they showed up with over twenty of their friends. By the third day there were more than sixty. It's been on the news. I think it's spread to over fifty cities by now."

"Merle, did you know about this?" Dora was abstractly curious. The closest Woolworth's was in town, and she rarely went into town these days.

"Yes."

"It's not pretty, Mom. Most of them are students. They get beat up and jailed. They get doused with ammonia and pulled from their seats."

Dora sat up, suddenly enlightened. "This is proof of what I said earlier. About those water fountains. People don't like change, Leah. People like things to stay the way they are."

Leah's mouth was hanging open. Before she could even comment, her mother continued: "The Negroes know there's about to be a shortage of water fountains, and they're frightened. Where will they go to get a drink of water? What will they do?"

Merle was silent, smoking his cigar as he watched the news through the planter stand separating the dining room from the den. Chet Huntley was looking especially grim these days. Smoke rings drifted toward the bar. Dora began to clear the table. The discussion was over, the door to her mother's jail cell slammed permanently shut. Leah looked at the two of them and wondered how far she would have to go before it would be too far to ever visit them again.

It wasn't as far as she had thought. Leah began postponing her trips home, traveling instead in directions away from suburbia, taking the back roads, finding a type of realness in the long stretches of fence wire and swaybacked horses set to pasture. The crops of fan-leafed collards, their clusters of olive green the only undiluted color in an otherwise faded landscape. On the arteries of red clay, she passed banded trees marked for cutting and blackened stubbled fields charred from seasonal burning. She saw handwritten messages on fence posts meant to ward off strangers. She would come to a fork in the road and, depending on the way the sun was shining, choose one, considering either way a good one. She saw a mule tethered to a long pole and men prodding it along as it ground sugarcane for syrup. Farmers ducking their heads against the wind to light home-rolled cigarettes. A washerwoman leaning to scratch her knee, her line of wash propped in place by a wooden crutch. Trees with bottles on their limbs to capture evil spirits. Ruined barns. Dogs at rest. Dogs at fight. Dogs scratching fleas. Dogs, tits dragging the ground, flanked by their starving litters. She saw weather-beaten houses and shoeless children riding on the hips of teenagers, muddy yards, houses without power or plumbing. She saw a black family of five stationed on the porch of their house, looking off in one direction as though frozen in place. The father wore a cap and had his legs crossed at the knees. A daughter was leaning against clapboard siding. Another child had her knees pulled up under her dress. A baby leaned inside his oversize shirt. The mother stood guard at the steps. Leah wondered what they were seeing, how they were feeling. What their dreams were. Leah wondered if Dora Maxwell, upon seeing such a thing, would still think tiny American flags a fitting complement to vodka and lime juice.

Tired from driving, she pulled into a crowded lot near an auction house on the onskirts of Laurel. Dirt covered trucks everywhere. Her blue Rambler looked like a jelly bean trapped in a dust pile. She walked through the open doors and climbed up into the stands and sat, elbows on knees, while she watched the wild-eyed nervousness of a rust-colored cow. She had driven two hundred miles and gone in circles. She was twenty-one years old and going nowhere. She was tired of her college roommate. Tired of school. Tired of her parents. Tired of being Leah Maxwell, a woman who picked fights with her parents because she feared a stronger opponent. The auctioneer's voice seemed a monotone lullaby. A poor man's Shakespeare. Syllabic quickenings resonating in her stomach, as well as her ears, where slashes of vowels and consonants formed words that formed sentences that formed thoughts that formed dreams . . . Her senses shut down in the middle of the autioneer's litany and her head fell forward, her thick hair a curtain around her ears, her forehead meeting resistance and resting against the feel of warm cloth. Leah had fallen fast asleep on the back of a total stranger.

He stirred and she woke, surrounded by quiet. The benches were empty. Dust motes fell through warm light, a silent siren of serenity. The man smelled of sweat and salt and dust and leather. Across the back of his shirt, she had drooled a pattern that looked like the state of Florida.

"You awake now?" he said.

"Jesus, I'm sorry," she said, sitting up and running her hands down her jeans. He was looking straight ahead, his eyes on the sawdust floor.

"Don't be. I didn't need that cow anyhow."

"Where am I?" She ran her fingers through her hair.

"Same place you started out. I didn't dare move you."

"No, I realize that. I'm just confused."

He turned to her and she saw a serious, chiseled face, pale blue eyes, dark brown hair. She noticed a natural frown line between his eyebrows that was sure to be a problem for somebody at some future date.

"You're in Laurel, Mississippi. At the stockyard. You were sleeping so good I hated to wake you." He lifted a piece of straw from her hair.

She didn't know what to say. How does one explain falling asleep on a stranger's back? How does one explain climbing up into the bleachers of a crowded stock auction looking for peace and quiet? It can't be done. The bewilderment must have shown on her face.

"My name's Bruno Till. I live down in Purvis," he said.

"I'm Leah. Leah Maxwell," she said. And when Bruno smiled at her and took her hand to help her down from the row of hard benches, she felt like she had finally made it home.

→←

Reaching down, she pulled off her boots, then her socks, and loosened her shirt from her jeans. She lit the joint and inhaled, her head tilted back and her eyes shut. Her mother had told her there was not enough between the sheets to make the marriage work, and Leah had not been in the mood to listen. Why should she listen to a woman who spent her life reading grocery-store magazines? How could that woman know anything at all about goings-on between the sheets? And what in the hell did the business between the sheets have to do with anything at all. Maybe for the generation to which Dora belonged, sex was nothing more than a really great insurance policy to be pulled out and relied upon whenever a crash seemed imminent. If you happen to burn the roast, don't worry, we got you covered. If you can't seem to get the rudiments of Jell-O salad making off your mind, don't worry, just spread your legs and he'll soon forget how incredibly stupid you are. At least for the next seven to ten minutes. Maybe what Dora was telling Leah was that she recognized in her daughter a certain liability, or perhaps the need for a disclaimer printed on a tag around her neck. Maybe she was really saying that her daughter didn't have the manipulation skills needed to play the game, and if this was the case, then Leah chose to take it as a compliment. Then again, she was the one who had stood naked that very morning trying to force information out of her husband. The irony wasn't wasted on Leah that the thing that had set her off was the very reason she had thrown a hairbrush at her mother's head.

Leah's decision to marry a man neither of her parents had met ignited the biggest conflict within the Maxwell household of all her years living at home. The screaming between mother and daughter seemed to last for days, until the two of them were as weary as they had ever been but refused to admit it, even to themselves. Every ending to every conversation bounced back to the topic of sex, as though Dora assumed it was all young women Leah's age thought about, using the phrase alternately as a threat and a bribe. "Leah, there's not enough between the sheets, dammit!" A clearly defined threat. And moments later, "Dear, think about it. Is there really enough between the sheets? What if the perfect man is still out there waiting for you?" A half-assed bribe. In many ways it was like the time Dora promised Leah a new pair of roller skates if she would try ("Just try, for God's sake!") to learn to like broccoli. Once it finally dawned on Dora that Leah had no intention of ever learning to like broccoli, or even *pretending* to like broccoli, she was spanked and sent to her room for the night. "You're too smart a girl to fall for this," Dora finished, pulling out her next to last weapon: Leah's obvious intelligence, which no one had ever denied. The remark sent Leah through the roof.

"For your information, Mother, Bruno fucks me like a goddamn bull rider!" Leah had finally shouted, the words so crudely delivered that she thought for a moment her mother might be the victim of a sudden stroke. Dora recovered, though, her hand to her throat, her eyes refusing to meet Leah's, bouncing instead around the room.

"Well, seeing how you won't listen to me about *that*, you've at least got to consider the money we've wasted on college tuition," Dora had told her, resorting to tears, her final weapon in the heavy arsenal of defense. "Do you have any idea how much money we've thrown away? All because you've decided to settle for an ignorant country bump—"

The hairbrush whizzed by Dora's head, barely missing, as Leah ran out of the room. Her father was pushing a wheelbarrow along the overgrown azaleas that bordered the yard, moving methodically, pushing his glasses up on his nose occasionally as he bent and lifted drying weeds and clippings, stopping to count the nodules along the stems of winter roses. He was next to her bedroom window, his back to her. When he turned, he shrugged and said, "Come on over here and help your old man." Standing, she had gone to him, moving behind him, picking up the cutoff pieces of azalea bush as quickly as he sent them to the ground.

"She'll adjust," he said to her.

"You think?" Leah asked.

"Yep," he answered. "A whole lot quicker than me."

She wasn't offended by his words because they came from an entirely different country than her mother's, and when Merle took her hand and squeezed it, Leah squeezed in return. And that was all he ever said about the upcoming marriage.

A month later he walked her down the aisle and kissed her on the cheek and handed her over to a waiting Bruno, who looked terribly uncomfortable in his brand-new suit, but the distance between Leah and her father had widened, and she wondered if this was the case with most fathers and daughters, if distance was required to overshadow the embarrassment of the petty surrender men made "between the sheets." Whatever his reasons, Leah missed her father. A part of her felt that what she needed at this very moment was someone who was fully aware that the world collapsed periodically, but chose to go on living in spite of it.

{CHAPTER 11}

Willem found the girl at the Lamar County courthouse brazenly inefficient. All he had wanted was to be pointed in the direction of the deed and land-transfer section, and instead of doing that, she had handed him an application for renewing a boating permit.

"I don't own a boat," he explained for the second time. "I've never owned a boat, and wouldn't know what to do if I *did* own a boat."

"That's easy enough to fix. There's a boatin class for first-time boaters that's held once a month." The girl pushed her hideously large glasses higher on her nose. They seemed to encompass the entire surface of her face, and Willem reminded himself not to refer to her as a human fly, since that was exactly what she reminded him of. Her reddish hair was frizzed out in a perm that triangulated along her shoulders. He amended his thought: an *Egyptian* human fly.

"Miss—" he said.

"Hey, I'm married," she said, wiggling her fingers, where a minuscule diamond rested next to a gold band.

"Beg your pardon?"

"You called me 'miss.' I was explainin that I'm not a miss, I'm a miss*us*."

"My condolences to the husband, then."

She stared at him, undecided if this was an insult or an attempt at an apology.

Willem leaned back and forced his eyes to meet hers. One thing about being in the South, everyone he met seemed to have problems that completely overshadowed his nervous condition. "What I'm tryin to find is the place where deeds are recorded."

"You're not here to register your boat?"

"No, ma'am, I am not."

"Then why are you standin in front of my counter?" She leaned across the wood and pointed to a sign: VEHICLE REGISTRATION AND LICENSING.

"The reason I'm standin here is because I need directions to the deed and claim office."

"I'm sorry, I cain't help you there," she said, trying to peer over her glasses, which was virtually impossible: she would have had to stand on her head. "Try that fella over yonder." She pointed to the information desk. A place Willem had already visited. Of course, when he had visited it moments earlier, no one was there, and this was what led him to the Egyptian Fly Lady. Now he saw a man who immediately reminded him of a large tadpole, sitting on a stool, his chin resting on his chest as he slept.

"Thank you for your time," Willem said.

"Don't mention it," the girl snapped back.

Willem caught a reflection of himself as he made his way to the sleeper on the stool. He thought his pith helmet looked fitting. And the khaki pants and matching khaki shirt seemed to set him apart from the rest of the town's occupants, giving him the distance he needed to function at the height of his abililty.

"Excuse me," he told the sleeping man, who answered by lurching to his feet and retucking his shirt into his pants.

"Where can I find the deed office?" Willem asked.

"Christ, I ain't seen one of them in more than twenty years," the man said, staring at him with his mouth open.

"The deed office?"

"No. One a them hats. Where'd you get that sumbitch, anyhow?"

Willem lifted the hat from his head and set it on the counter.

"You on some kind of safari?"

"No. I'm not. I'm just looking for the deed office," he told the man.

"It's back yonder a ways," the man said, using his head as a directional pointer. He lifted Willem's hat and tapped it against the counter. "It's a hard sumbitch, ain't it?"

Willem took it from the man and turned and walked away, regretting the purchase, wishing he had never set foot inside Lulu's Antiques on School Street.

It was as simple as following ill-placed signs, and he eventually found the narrow corridor that led him down the proper flight of stairs, which took him to the basement portion of the building. The room designated for records was cool and musty-smelling and painted two shades of green: a dark olive near the floor and a pale green above black plastic border tape that Willem guessed was meant to be some sort of economical chair rail. He leaned back and looked. Even the ceiling tiles were green, and to make matters worse, a green-visored woman was sitting behind a green-tinted teller's window, sleeping on her hand. It was like being trapped inside a low-budget Emerald City where every single Munchkin was fast asleep.

Willem tapped on the glass, and without opening her eyes, the woman shoved a clipboard through a narrow slot. "Sign in," she said.

Willem signed his name and slid the clipboard back to her, wondering if she needed to read his name before pressing a button to let him in. All he saw was her head resting on her hand, and he stood, his hands in his pockets, his palms sweaty.

"Well?" she said. Her eyes were still shut.

"Excuse me?"

"Are you goin in or not?" She opened one eye and studied him.

"Yes. I was just waiting . . . I wasn't sure you saw my name."

She leaned down and studied the clipboard. "Looks like a name to me. Go on in."

It was an awkward moment, and Willem felt his resolve slipping away. Hopefully no one would be in the room and no one would come in while he was there, and if the gods were with him, no one would be around once he decided to leave. A world without people. Ahhh, what a dream.

The deed records were kept in books the size of small library tables and filed according to section, township, and range. Pulling the map out of his pocket he spread it open and walked over to a crude legend hanging on the wall. The whole county's drainage system had recently been redone, and the resulting access roads were the culprits behind his confusion. He found what he thought was the area—C 23—and walked down the corridors until he found the corresponding book. Climbing a stepstool like those used in libraries, he pulled it out and went to one of the tables. The pages seemed a large tangle of confusion, transfers and recording dates, nothing written in the same color of ink, some dates penciled in, which he found extremely risky. A person could do an amazing amount of damage with nothing more than a five-cent eraser. As he ran a finger down the listings, the first item that flagged his attention was the name Reinhold Till. He kept on scanning and finally stopped at Fremont, a lump forming in his throat. One hundred and forty-three acres. Christ, he had no idea he owned that much. Directly below Fremont, a notation had been made regarding tax default, and Willem leaned forward for a closer look, comparing the name to one listed two lines above. "Son of a bitch," he said.

He heard a woman's voice out in the vestibule and glanced around. All he could see through the frosted glass was a ghostlike form that seemed to be wearing a hat. Not wanting to be discovered, Willem quickly jotted down the coordinates and folded the paper and put it in his pocket. Hearing the door open, he realized he wouldn't have time to put the book up and decided, *What the hell, at least I know what I need to know.* Making sure his helmet was tucked under his arm, he walked across the room and stood aside to allow the woman to enter, a sentry posted from the age of chivalry, a tall old man who had the poor judgment to buy his fashion accessories from an antique shop.

The woman was elderly and petite and when she brushed past him, she said, "Good mornin," leaving in her wake the smell of fresh biscuits. "Good morning," he said, noticing her straw hat and paisley scarf and the neatness of her pink shirt. The wardrobe features he liked the best were her black loafers and white socks. With his hand on the knob, he turned and looked at her one more time. She was standing in the middle of the room, turning in a slow circle, as if waiting for a clue to pop up and show her the way.

"You need any help?" he asked.

"Sugar, the help I need nobody but Christ can give."

Willem could not believe she had called him "sugar." The presumptive familiarity these people operated with made him sick. Now that he thought of it, it had been an overly friendly waitress in Ruby's Royal Truck Stop that caused his anxiety level to break the sound barrier.

"There's a legend on the wall." He pointed to the spot next to the metal bookcase.

She looked at him and opened her mouth as though she wanted to speak, then turned away. "Sugar, I've been here before. I just wanted to enjoy the peace and quiet."

"My name's not Sugar," Willem said before thinking, placing the helmet on his head and walking out the door. Patting his pocket, he walked up the stairs, his path surer this time, and it was a good thing, since he was practically running. Downstairs, Eilene Till was standing before the same open book, laughing, her finger traveling down the same row of numbers until it settled on Reinhold Till.

{CHAPTER 12}

It took Bruno most of the early morning before he decided to call her. The small business card was damp from being held inside a sweaty palm, and he had walked the path to the telephone at least fifteen times in the last ten minutes. He looked at his watch. Ten-thirty. *All I have to do is say I have some questions about the filtering system*, he thought, putting his hand to the black receiver and then removing it, delaying the phone call for one more look in the bathroom mirror. He almost didn't recognize himself due to his heightened color. Shit, he felt like he was about to ask a girl to the prom. Picking up his toothbrush, he spread a gob of Pepsodent on it and began to brush his teeth.

When he walked back to the living room, the folly of it all rose up and slapped him in the face and he sighed. He wouldn't be able to do it. Not for a noble reason like marital integrity, either. He was just too damn scared. Turning to the wall that held his *National Geographic*s, he had just decided the article on the Mayan ruins featured in the January 1970 issue might be compelling enough to reread when the phone rang.

Moments later, he was sitting in his chair, his hands flattened on the lace armrests, his heart pounding, wondering what had motivated the girl to up and call him when he had been standing there trying to figure out a way to call *her.* Bruno looked up to the ceiling where Leah had wanted him to hang a ceiling fan. There still wasn't one there, and now he wished he had listened to her, for he was sweating like a whore in church, and while he couldn't see them to be sure, he knew that rings were beginning to form underneath his arms and across his chest.

"Shit. This is childish," he said. Marching back to the bedroom, he forgot himself and had to pivot and turn toward the guest room, where he had been sleeping for the past week. The bed was mussed, and his clothes were folded in stacks on top of her old sewing machine. A pair of pants competing with the zipper foot, his shirts thrown over the spare bobbins. If Leah had objected, and he had really expected her to, he would have come back to their bed after a couple of hours of sullen behavior, but she hadn't. In fact, he would give his eyeteeth for an objection or two. A word about anything. The dry weather. The pervasiveness of deerflies. The nuisance of dandruff. Any topic at all would do. But she was still playing the quiet game just because he had refused to answer her questions about the Electrolux and why he had bought it ("On *time*, for Christ's sake, Bruno! We're *barely* making do. The hell we gonna pay for this?"), and while he was prepared to eventually forgive her for taking over all his work on the farm and rendering him a gimp not only in body but in mind, the slap-on-the-face insult she had thrown his way by questioning his consumer skills had really pissed him off. Bruno was the first one to bed that night, making sure Leah saw him enter the guest bedroom. He lay there expecting her to open the door, no, *wishing* she would open the door and at least inquire as to his comfort, of which there was absolutely zilch. But no, Leah Maxwell Till was making it clear just how irritated she was with him and walked right past the guest room door.

It was the first time the two of them had existed inside such a large, echoing chamber of ill will. Even when he first came back from Vietnam, there had been the comfort of words between them, mainly because Bruno had been optimistic then, believing the doctors were all simpletons who didn't know what they were talking about. Only after he realized the doctors did have the inside scoop as to his recovery, and had even been overly confident about the amount of damage from the shrapnel, did he clam up. Leah had grown quiet right along with him, her acquiescence based on the fraudulent belief that as soon as Bruno adjusted, he would be back to a close proximity of what he had been before.

Proximity. Now, there's a word for you.

Bruno was within four feet of the can of baby powder sitting on the table on the far side of the room. All that was between him and the can was the guest room bed. But to reach the can, something he needed right now because he was pouring sweat, he would have to lie prostrate across the mattress and rock along like an elephant seal. Among a long list of things it had destroyed, the injury had ended his ability to crawl on his hands and knees, and while the physical therapists at the VA hospital in Jackson had told him repeatedly that unless he learned to crawl again, the muscles would *never* heal, each time he raised up on all fours, his neck reacted as though attached to a bit. He couldn't help but envision a horse with its head thrown back, strangling on its saliva.

"Shows how much *they* know," he said, his nose in the rumpled sheets, his hands fanned out and searching for the table. He finally retrieved the can and rolled onto his back and unfastened the top buckle of the brace, which gave him enough room to sprinkle the powder down inside. Rebuckling, he pushed himself to his feet.

She had said apologetically that she would have to bring her little boys with her, and Bruno found himself wandering around the house looking for something that might engage two youngsters. He supposed the set of steak knives was out of the question. Opening the back hall closet where he and Leah kept their leisure-time paraphernalia, he saw how grim the two of them must have become over the years. Hell, there wasn't even a television in the front room, and here inside this closet holding winter coats and clothes destined for Goodwill was a lonely screen leaning next to the projector and a stack of home movies; to the left of his old bowling-ball bag, a cracked wheel for holding poker chips. The fact that it held only two chips seemed sadly pathetic.

Outside in the drive, a truck door slammed, and Bruno raced as fast as his unequalized weight would allow to the kitchen, remembering in the nick of time where Leah kept the playing cards. All kids liked playing cards. Even kids who couldn't add, or didn't know the difference between a queen and a jack, liked playing cards. He couldn't think of a single kid who didn't like to shuffle and fan them open in his hands while pretending to be a tough guy. The kitchen drawer had barely left his fingers before she knocked on the door. Waiting the appropriate number of seconds, he brushed a hand over his short hair, then walked to the door and opened it, seeing the two little boys. The older one had his hands cupped around his face and his nose pressed to the screen.

How did I act before? he wondered. *Was I bored? Pissed off? A pain in the ass? All three?* However he was then, it was important that he be that same way now. Settling on slightly bored and moderately pissed off, he pushed open the screen.

"Good mornin," Alyce said, placing her hands on the heads of her sons and herding them inside. The two of them stood awkwardly next to the front door like two frightened doorstops.

"Go on. Stop bein shy. He's not gonna bite."

Bruno's hand went up to his brace. Obviously they had never seen a grown man wearing a flesh-colored plastic barrel around his neck.

The older boy took the lead and went to the couch and sat, his legs dangling off the edge. His eyes never left Bruno's brace, not even when he said "Come here, Ben" in a protective tone and patted the cushion next to him in a gesture that was too old for a child to be using. Once Ben was there, Joe slung his arm around his little brother and glared at Bruno. *What the fuck did I do to* you? Bruno wondered.

"How's it running?" Alyce asked.

She might as well have asked Bruno "How's it hanging?," and for a moment he wondered if she had. Confusion must have shown on his face, because she tilted her head and studied him. "Are you okay, Mr. Till? Is this a bad time for a courtesy call?"

"Oh," he said. "No. I'm just . . ." *out of breath from scrambling across the bed for my powder, and rummaging through the closet looking for games and racing through the kitchen searching for cards . . .* He held out the pack of playing cards. "I thought they might like to play with these."

She held the deck in her hand and looked over at her boys, who were sitting quietly. "Boys, you wanna play with these?"

Ben nodded enthusiastically. Joe shook his head and put a hand to his brother's head and made it quit nodding.

"Maybe in a little while," she told Bruno, handing the deck back to him.

He couldn't understand why, but he was embarrassed by the rejected offer. "There it is." He pointed to the vacuum cleaner. "Right where you left it."

"Don't tell me you ain't used it."

He tried to smile. "Okay, I won't."

"You haven't? Really?" Her hands were on her hips, and she was studying him with pure disbelief. Bruno turned and made his way to the chair. *His* chair this time. The frantic activity had worn him out. It was time to give in to the wave of reality that had chased him for weeks. *Here is the chair belonging to a man incapacitated. Watch now while he quits pretending it belongs to someone else.*

"What's the matter, Mr. Till?" Alyce asked, looking him over, noticing the sweat rings under his arms and the generalized put-upon attitude. She went to the couch and sat, her knees in close proximity to Bruno, who had already noticed the blue jeans and long-sleeved white button-down shirt. He had hoped for a swinging skirt and almost sheer peasant blouse, but now that he could see how tight the jeans were, he was beginning to forgive her. Her arms were between her knees and she was leaning forward.

"How about callin me Bruno?" he said.

"Okay, then. Now, tell me what's bothering you, Bruno, because something is, and don't pretend it's not. Does it work when you boys pretend?" she fired the question at her children.

A long, drawn-out chorus of "Nooo."

"There, you heard them. Now, spit it out."

The word "spit" made him think of blow jobs and how Leah used to spit into a towel. He blushed and said, "It's a lot of money, Alyce," tucking his lips next to his teeth in what he hoped was a thoughtful expression of regret, but in actuality made him look a lot like Howdy Doody.

"Jeepers. I was afraid a that."

Jeepers, he thought. *The gal actually said "jeepers."* "How come you don't sound surprised?"

"'Cause I had to go yesterday and pick up the only other one I sold."

"Who else bought one?" He was immediately jealous.

"The Colemans. Over on the highway."

Bruno thumbed through his mental resources and tried to place the Colemans and couldn't. There was a county map in the drawer, and he was tempted to go and get it and spread it open on her blue-jeaned knees and demand that Alyce point him toward the general vicinity.

"—husband died six months ago and she figured a new vacuum cleaner would be a good gift to give herself. Oh well."

She leaned back against the couch and crossed her arms behind her head and seemed to be studying the facing wall. Today her hair was free of its bandanna, and it was beautiful hair, abundant and glossy. She had it parted on the side, one portion tucked behind her ear. He saw that her ears were pierced, and the image of a needle pressing against her skin and puncturing it seemed so exotic that he almost lost his breath. While he *could* remember that Leah spit into a *towel,* he couldn't remember whether or not her ears were pierced, and this seemed to speak volumes.

"She sure seemed embarrassed that I had to come back and pick it up. She was cryin a little bit. Even baked me a pound cake."

"How come she changed her mind?"

"Same reason you're about to. Cost too much—"

He held up a hand. "I didn't say we were definite about returning it."

"Well." She huffed out a breath of air and sent her bangs flying. "It won't hurt my feelings if you do. I mean, you were nice enough to let me in—"

"Nice." Now, there's a word for you, he thought. Bruno was about to demonstrate the number one reason he was not nice when the older of her boys pointed a finger and said, "Mister, what's wrong with your head?"

"Joseph Claude Benson!" Alyce said, leaning over the younger boy and pressing her hand to the older child's knee.

Joe reacted by turning his large blue eyes in her direction. "But Mom."

"Mr. Till was injured in the war," she said, and Bruno was taken aback. *Hell, does the whole town talk about me?*

"What's a war?" Ben asked.

"It's where people fight."

"Like you and Daddy?" Ben asked around his thumb.

A pall descended on the four of them, and Bruno sat back and wondered how they were going to get out from under it. Alyce didn't blink an eye and said, "No. Not like me and Daddy. In a bigger way."

"Does people get killed?" Ben asked.

Jeepers, Alyce, how you gone introduce death to a child? Bruno wondered, lifting his eyebrows, curious as to the way she would handle this.

"Sometimes," Alyce answered. "And sometimes they just get hurt. Like Mr. Bruno." She licked her lips and looked at Bruno as she retucked her hair behind her ear, her face firing to a deep crimson. He shook his head and tried to convey to her that he was perfectly fine with the explanation.

Joe was watching, not afraid anymore but still not liking Bruno. Even if his neck was thick like Humpty Dumpty's, everything else about the man was too big to like. Too different from his daddy. He wanted all men to be the same, because if they were, his daddy wouldn't seem so different.

Ben scooted up on the edge of the couch and addressed Bruno. "Does it hurt?" He pointed to Bruno's neck.

Alyce turned to Bruno, apparently curious about the same thing. Bruno realized they were asking questions his wife had never asked. Of course, rule number one from the hospital bed was that she not talk about it until he was ready to talk about it, and maybe in the year 2050 that time would come.

"Boys, maybe Mr. Bruno don't want to talk about it," Alyce said.

"Hell. It's no big deal. I don't mind talkin about it."

Funny thing about lies, once you tell one, it snaps shut around you like an elastic cocoon and the only way to free yourself is to tell more lies until they grow so large they burst the sac. He would have crossed his legs, but that involved too much time and too many pitfalls. He had broken three matched sets of cups and saucers trying to cross his legs.

"The only time it feels bad is when I take this thing off." He tapped on the front of Thomas Type Model 802, customized for his personal needs at the factory where a hinged chest plate and straps around the back were added. His forefinger slipped into the tracheotomy slot he no longer needed, but, like most things no one needed, was there anyway. Seeing Ben open his mouth to ask more, Bruno continued: "When I got hurt, it damaged the muscles back here." He reached around and touched the back of his head. "And they're still gettin better."

"Are them muscles really gonna get well?" Ben asked, curiosity in his eyes.

Bruno looked at Alyce and thought he saw curiosity resting there as well. "One day," he lied.

Alyce brightened and unbuttoned her sleeves and began rolling them up. "See, boys, when you get a boo-boo and you cry and carry on and I promise you in a little while it won't hurt, ain't I tellin you the truth?"

A single response of "Yes, ma'am." Joe was having none of it. That one was pressed into the corner of the couch like a saggy pillow.

Bruno was hoping this might be the end of the discussion of his injury and that Alyce would sit back and talk to him a while and maybe later he could go into the kitchen and make the two of them some coffee.

Joe dashed his hopes in an unexpected way. He leaned forward at the waist and addressed his mother. "If things get better, then how come you still cry at night over Daddy?"

Everything that she had been pretending to be fell off of her, and her shoulders slumped and she lowered her head. And then she seemed to get mad over it and stood as though poked in the ass with a cattle prod and took each boy by the hand and jerked them off the couch, pulling them toward the door, not trusting herself to say good-bye. It had been a hard night and it seemed it was going to be an even harder day, and if he wanted to return the durn vacuum cleaner, he could durn well bring it to her own durn house, and as soon as she got this durn kid in the truck, see if she didn't pop him on his durn Jiminy Cricket ass.

Bruno lurched to his feet and headed after her. At the screen door he opened his mouth to say "Wait," but she was already down the steps and slinging open the door to the truck. There was a look of compassion on her face as she lifted the smaller boy to the truck seat. Then she turned to Joe, one hand on her hip, the finger of her other hand pointing to the cab of the truck. Apparently a child as astute as that one was old enough to climb up on a truck seat by himself.

[CHAPTER 13}

One of the stranger things about the Li'l Miss Roustabout Club was that you never knew what kind of character was going to walk in. Take, for example, that old geezer over there all dirtied up. Sonny, locked inside a mood of serious awareness, peered across the bar to the fella wearing the pith helmet and wondered who the hell he thought he was, showing up in the middle of the afternoon and taking over Sonny's favorite bar stool. Not that it had his name on it. Hell no. Even though he *had* thought long and hard about carving his name into the seat before he realized somebody might take notice of it and tell his mama. But seeing how his ass had been plopped down on it for the better part of a week, Sonny figured he hadn't needed a knife at all since everybody, including dim-witted Sparechange Dinkins, seemed to know it was Sonny's stool and made sure it was waiting for him every afternoon when he walked through the door. Everything had been fine until this old guy had claimed it. And he had claimed not only the stool but also Conchita's attention. How many beers was that, now? Two? Three?

"Conchita. Conchita." Sonny rolled the name around on his tongue and drank from his beer. There was a roll of LifeSavers in his front pocket for later when he decided to head for home and face his mother's interrogation. Sparechange Dinkins darted up to the bar and leaned over Sonny's hunched back and tried to shake his hand. Sonny, not in the mood for it, swatted the man away. Conchita was directly across from him, busy wiping down the bar with a filthy rag. She had charged across his spot moments earlier, and the whole surface area smelled like a pair of pissed-in underpants. *Somebody ought to tell them to wash their dishrags once in a blue moon if they want to keep from making the customers sick to their stomach.* He thought of his place and how his mama felt like the day couldn't end without scrubbing down the entire kitchen with a brew of vinegar and water, and how once the Easter-egg smell finally disappeared, everything seemed so clean and fresh. And then he stopped thinking of his mama, because thinking of his mama while sitting on a bar stool at the Li'l Miss Roustabout made his ass pucker. Sliding a beer down in front of him, Conchita leaned on her elbow and smiled, and Sonny winced. Hell, he wished she wouldn't do that. He certainly appreciated the beer, but the bucktoothed smile made him feel like he was going to puke.

"Thank you, darlin," he said, remembering his manners. "Who's that old feller over yonder?"

"Nobody for you to worry about." She placed a warm hand over Sonny's and stroked the top with her middle finger. He rotated his arm and looked at his wristwatch. Four-thirty. Joe was thirty minutes late.

"What size shoes you wear?" Sonny asked, patting his pockets, wondering if he had enough dollar bills for later on, when the dancing started. He had lifted the huge pickle jar full of pennies from his mother's closet and rolled them in his bedroom and come up with twenty-seven bucks. He sucked on a toothpick. "You look like you wear about a size six."

"How come you keep askin me about my shoes?"

" 'Cause you ain't give me a answer yet. As soon as you tell me, I'll quit askin." Sonny flashed his best smile and reached out to rub her arm. Contact was allowed before five P.M. Once the halter top came off, no one, not even a brand-new boyfriend, was allowed to handle the merchandise.

"I wear a size seven." She really wore an eight. But an eight sounded *so* much larger than the six he thought she was, and while it was one thing to have large tits, it was another to have big feet.

"You gonna buy me some shoes, Sonny?"

"I'm doin one better than that. I'm *makin* 'em for you."

She yawned. Fuck, she'd heard it all now.

Sonny heard Joe's *ahoogah* horn blasting from a spot down the road. Lord, that fucker had himself a car! Looked great. Sounded great. Was great. The old geezer wearing the safari hat climbed off his stool, his beer clutched in his hand as though it were a homing device leading him to a corner booth. There was dirt all over the back of his shirt and the rear of his pants. Sonny watched him slide into the seat that faced the wall, the tiny red lamps sending out a glow that made it look like his face was peeled from the nose down. While Sonny watched, the man leaned under the table and did the thing that Sonny had always wished he would do: he unplugged the cord to the tiny light.

"What're you and Joe up to?" Conchita asked, her hand over her mouth as she smothered another yawn. The hours at the club were crap, but at least she wasn't ripping sheets off the bed and cleaning smelly toilets like her mama.

"Nothin. How come you think we're up to something?"

"Cool it, big boy. I was just askin."

He reached out to her, but she slipped away and, with a glance over her shoulder, took her little notepad over to where the old geezer was sitting in the dark.

"Be like that, then," Sonny said.

They could be a pack of vampires, the way they all flinched when the door opened. Sonny knew it was Joe, even though his back was to him, from the power of his cologne.

"Without a doubt," Joe said as he pulled his stool close and slapped Sonny on the back.

"Without a doubt what?"

"Without a doubt, you look a man ready to make some money."

"Keep your voice down," Sonny said, glancing around. Conchita was still talking to the old guy. He wished she would get over here and talk to him before she climbed up on the stage and pulled off her shirt.

"I put a little map in your heap out front," Joe said.

"It ain't a heap. It's a car. A good one. And who told you you could go in my Pontiac?"

"You know what Pontiac stands for?"

Sonny gave him his best bored look and sipped his beer. "I expect you'll tell me."

"Sure will. Poor Old Nigger Thinks It's a Cadillac. Get it?"

Sonny swatted at Sparechange Dinkins, who was reaching for the bowl of peanuts.

"Hey, that's a joke," Joe said.

"It ain't funny."

"Don't get pissy on me. Personally, I like Pontiacs."

"You still didn't have no right to go in my car."

"I just laid it on the seat. It ain't harming a soul. Shows where the storm drains are at. Besides, it's your mother's car. It ain't yours."

"And if I forget to pick it up and she sees it?"

"That's your problem, big boy." Joe tapped on the bar with his knuckles, and Conchita meandered to the counter, and Sonny stared at the two of them, the overuse of the term "big boy" not lost on him. Joe had sworn he'd never touched the girl, and now Sonny was beginning to wonder.

Joe said, "Give me a beer, darlin."

"Hey, asshole, Sonny's the only one who gets to call me darlin."

"Well I'll be go to hell. Look at you two lovebirds." Joe leaned back on his stool and studied the two of them. When she returned, she had two beers, and Sonny was so proud of her display of affection (the free beer!), he blushed, thanking God for little red lamps that made all the faces red.

"I bet that old guy over there ain't from around here," Conchita told them, nodding at the dark corner.

Joe leaned toward her. "You know what? I'm needing to talk to my buddy here. You think you could manage to give us a few moments of privacy?"

"Watch your mouth, Joe," Sonny said.

"Save your breath, Sonny. I know when I'm not wanted." Conchita flounced away, heading to the stool across the way, where she crossed her legs and lit a cigarette and smoked as she sipped hot coffee.

"Why in the hell do you have to be that way?" Sonny leaned back and looked at Joe, who had pulled out his pocketknife and begun to carve his initials in the top of the bar: J.C.B. +

Joe shrugged and said, "I'm guessing twenty thou, easy." He began to carve an extra-large heart in the wood, and Sonny waited for him to put the wife's initials underneath his, but he didn't. Instead he bent down and blew the tiny fragments of wood to the floor and then pocketed his knife. "Without a doubt," he said again.

"Without a doubt what?" Sonny was repeating himself but couldn't seem to help it.

"Without a doubt, old man Russo ought not to have turned down my kind offer to set up a security system."

"Still—"

"Listen. You'll not be anywhere near the spot. The place I need you is marked on that little map in your car. Once you make sure the coast is clear, your debt is wiped clean." Joe ran a finger across the bar in demonstration.

"What makes you think you can get away with this?"

" 'Cause my name's Joe Benson, and I been gettin away with shit all my life."

"Where you goin once you're done?" Sonny bent over his glass and slurped his beer.

"Me*hee*co. The land of brown-eyed gals and fifty-cent margaritas."

"I only got one question for you." Sonny swiveled on his stool and waited until he had Joe's full attention. "A couple of weeks ago, you said you were doing this to pay off the wife's hospital bills."

"I said I needed the money from *you* to pay off the bills. This is an entirely different venture." He flashed a smile at Sonny.

"It still seems weird to me that a man who had to work so hard to marry a woman would up and run away."

Joe peered up at the Jax beer sign that was glowing yellow and blue, and then he reached for a napkin and rubbed across his artwork on the bar, tapping a finger at the open space below his initials. "Spoken like a man who's never been married."

"What day?" Sonny asked, feeling a knot of apprehension tighten inside his stomach.

"July the third. Late in the evening. That way I'll be in and out and won't nobody know it till the fifth. I'll celebrate Independence Day in style. Down on some white-sand beach with two bimbos stretched out naked by my side. Each with tits the size of watermelons."

Sonny sat huddled over his drink, rubbing his head. There were so many blasted things to deal with. Joe. Making sure he had use of the car. Talking Conchita into keeping her mouth shut about being a stripper when he introduced her to his mother.

"She's a durn theater dancer from Hattiesburg!" was the lie Sonny had shouted to his mother. "What in the hell is a *theater* dancer?" she demanded. "Are they different from other kinds of dancers? Do they only dance in theaters?" "You'll have to ask her, Ma," he stammered. "Oh, I intend to," his mother said in a tone of voice that made his heart flutter. "You better believe I intend to." She had been peeling tomatoes and spacing them evenly on a platter in spite of the fact that Sonny had reminded her a thousand times that he preferred to eat his tomatoes with the skin left *on.* "Oh, Sonny, this just don't sound right!" she yelled, waving the knife around. "Dancers are fly-by-night and terribly unreliable." "Now, Mama," he pleaded, holding out his hands. "Where exactly is this theater where she dances?" she wanted to know. Shit, he felt like he had been hit with a board. He wished someone offered a mail-order course in lying so he could learn to do it better. "She's a traveling dancer," he finally managed. "Appears with a bona fide troupe from here to Jackson." "Oh. I *see,*" Eilene said, her head lowered over her platter. "A *traveling* dancer." She pushed her glasses farther up her nose and came and stood next to him, her eyes a mere inch from his face. "This girl's a traveling dancer." At this point Sonny had shrugged. "Similar to the traveling lodge, I guess," Eilene said.

"Without a doubt, you're a brass-plated fool," Sonny told Joe, gritting his teeth.

"Without a doubt, you're wrong once again," Joe said as the jukebox kicked on, jarring the glasses on the bar. Both men turned to watch Conchita step up onto the stage, wearing a garter belt and stockings and nothing else. As she spun around the pole, Sonny noticed with something akin to pity that the girl had a run up the backside of her fishnet hose.

Willem had seen the Li'l Miss Roustabout around one-thirty that afternoon as he drove away from town on the Purvis–Columbia Road, headed for the section of land described as NE 479. A wood-frame First Church of the Redeemer was directly across the road from the bar, ramshackle and in dire need of paint, with a red dirt parking lot and an overgrown wooden sign and windows that were out of square. The Roustabout was equally sad-looking and proved Willem's theory that while the majority of the county was busy recruiting for Jesus, or getting drunk in avoidance, all efforts seemed to take a fierce toll on the spaces these participants occupied. Approaching the club again around four o'clock while on his way back to the Rocky Creek Inn, Willem swung his truck into the parking lot, aware that there were only two cars there at the time, unlike the church parking lot, where a hay truck was parked and young men in white shirts and black pants were unloading speakers and electric pianos and beginning work on a patched army-issue tent of the type front-line medics used.

The Roustabout, brick and square, had the feel of a place that had never seen better days. Its glass front had been painted black, and the door was split from the bottom to the doorknob and repaired with a sheet of plywood that had also been split, as if something inside was determined to get out and had kicked at the door repeatedly. Across the road, a religious enthusiast did a roll down the horrible-sounding electric piano, and in an act of self-defense, Willem pushed open the cracked door and made his way to the first stool he found, pleased to see there was no one around. Just an overweight guy who had come out of the rest room in the back and stood watching Willem before settling reluctantly across the bar. Willem wondered momentarily what he had done to merit such scrutiny. Holding up a finger to the girl tending bar, he ordered a draft and then remembered his hat was still on his head. Lifting it off, he set it by him on the bar and rested his elbow on it. His hand was scraped raw and he had a sore knee, but he had found an old logging road that approached the land by the west and driven down as far as the road allowed, and then he had walked until he saw the top of the toppling pine, not really seeing it at first. Someone was burning something, and for the first half hour, all he had seen was a tower of black smoke. It was only after the wind began to pick up that the point of the tree appeared.

The beer made him feel drained and emotional and overly sentimental, and Willem turned his hands over, noticing how knobbed and old they were, and then he heard a strange-sounding car horn that made him forget all about his hands. *I've heard that horn before,* he thought, looking at his reflection in the mirror behind the bar. *But where?* It took a minute for it to dawn on him, but once he remembered the lime-green pimpmobile and who was likely to be driving it and how he was staying at that person's motel, he picked up his drink and made his way to the most isolated spot in the room. Once there, he was bothered by the red light set next to an overspilling ashtray, and reached under the table and jerked the cord from the wall. Not bothering to look around and see if anyone might object. For the first time in his life, not worried about offending anyone at all.

On the wall in front of him was a pay phone with a black metal case hanging off the bottom where a phone book should go, only there wasn't one, just a square of metal that rattled against the paneling every time one of the locals entered or exited the rest room. The room was L-shaped, with a row of six booths to the side, a wider section where seven or eight tables were grouped close to a stage, and, in the center of the place, the bar. Willem was tucked away at a spot where visibility was at its worst, which suited him just fine. No one felt inclined to bother him, except the girl with the smelly rag in her hand who brought him his second and third beers and the poor wretch waltzing around the place who was clearly not right in the head. The door to the rest room swung open, and that one came stumbling out with his belt undone and one side of his shirt tucked in while the other side flapped against his pants. The look on his face was one of bewilderment and fear, as though he had gone in and emptied his bladder and returned to find himself in some other place at some other time. Willem hoped he would settle down and walk on by and bother those two sitting at the bar, but this wasn't to be the case. Thin beyond belief, the man seemed an overgrown child, with eyes as dim and black as those belonging to some lower primate. He leaned his head down to study Willem's face. Willem turned himself in the booth until his back was leaning against the wall while he watched. *I've come a ways,* he thought. He realized this person would have sent him scampering for the door weeks earlier.

"Whatcha need?" he found himself asking, somewhat amazed.

"Sparechange Dinkins, here," said this high-pitched cricket voice while the monkey eyes blinked and blinked. "Pleased to make your acquaintance, I'm sure." The fellow extended his hand. Willem was not fond of shaking hands with strangers but made himself do it. The handshake was vigorous and rhythmic, as though the man had calculated exactly how many times his hand would need to pump up and down before finishing the job.

"Likewise," Willem said.

"Without a doubt," Sparechange said as he waltzed away in search of others to greet, and since the only other two inside the place were the owner of the green car and his companion, Sparechange hit the proverbial wall. Alyce's husband stood and grabbed the man by the front of his shirt and shoved him hard. "Get the fuck outta my face!"

The push sent the fool into a spin from which he collided with the woman with the overbite, his hands up in a defensive measure that landed square on the woman's tits. Sparechange got slapped for it, the sound echoing in a way that defied acoustics.

Alyce seems like such a sweet young girl. How in the world does she put up with such an asshole? Willem wondered as he looked at the telephone numbers written on the wall in front of him. They traveled in an ever widening circle until they merged with the door frame. Some numbers written in ink, but most scrawled with a pencil. Willem recalled the deed book at the county courthouse and how much of the documentation had been penciled in and wondered if the culprit might be a regular.

"Without a doubt," a peeping voice said, and Willem watched in alarm as Sparechange slid into the booth opposite. "Dawg. I felt a tit. A real live one."

Willem wondered how many dead ones the man had felt, since his comment implied he knew the difference. "Listen," Willem said, holding up a hand.

"No-no-no-no. Wait, now. Just wait." Sparechange bent to sniff the table. "Shit, this table stinks." He peered up at Willem through greasy hair that fell into his eyes.

"You might wanna try over there. I bet that table don't," Willem said pointing to the one to his left.

"Hell. This one ain't too bad. I guess you get used to it after a while." Sparechange lounged against the padded booth as though he intended to take a nap.

"Look, fella—"

"Just hear me out. Just hear me out." Tapping his fingernail on the table, he said, "Hang on for one second and then I'll leave." He looked over his shoulder and then back at Willem. His hands were wadded together as though he might be constructing a prayer. He made a steeple of his two forefingers. "Are them guys still watchin me?" he whispered out the side of his mouth.

"What guys?" Willem asked with a sigh.

"Them two over yonder."

Willem scanned the room. The only people he could see were the two at the bar, and they didn't seem to be paying attention to anyone or anything. "I think you're safe for the moment." He paused, then said, "Buddy, you need a ride home?"

"No-no-no-no! You don't understand. Wait now. Just wait a minute." He sucked in a breath and mouth-farted.

"Hey—"

"Sorry. Hang on a minute." And then he began to whisper. "I need to stay here." Sparechange again tapped on the table with his ragged fingernail. *Tap tap tap tap tap*. "Here's where I need to stay. Here. Right here. Cain't go home yet. Nosiree."

Willem leaned back in his booth and folded his arms over his chest. It seemed he might be watching a caricature of himself on one of his worst days. That time on the train to Chicago came to mind. He reached for his Pabst and lifted it by the neck and looked to the bar. His beer was gone, as well as the nice buzz, but something else had taken its place that defied naming. Fatigue? No, that wasn't entirely right.

Sparechange rested his head on the table and covered it with his left arm and feigned a snore.

Jesus God, Willem thought, shaking his head. *At least I never did* that.

The snoring stopped, and Sparechange whispered against the table. "Hey mister, can you hear me?" His voice was muffled.

"Yeah, I can hear you."

"You sure?"

"I just answered you, didn't I?" Willem said.

"Okay. Listen up, 'cause here's the thing. That one over there. That skinny man sitting next to the big guy is a common miscreant."

Willem looked over at Alyce's husband. "A miscreant?"

"You know. A thief. A ne'er-do-well."

"A ne'er-do-well."

"Without a doubt," Sparechange said.

Willem looked for the girl who had brought him his beer. *Empty,* he thought. *This is how I'm feeling: amazingly empty.* He wiped a hand across his forehead and then held it out. It wasn't shaking.

"He's gone break in a place. There's a map in the car."

"You don't say."

"That's right. Inside the Pontiac. The Poor-Old-Nigger-Thinks-It's-a-Cadillac car. That's what he's tellin Big Boy over there."

The door opened and closed, then opened again, the room beginning to fill as the hour approached five. Willem noticed there were bruises on the fella's arms and had no problem guessing where they came from."I drive a GMC myself," Willem said, for no other reason than he wanted to talk about it. The truck, as well as his life, suddenly seemed remarkably stable.

"You do?" Sparechange raised his head and stared at him.

"A nineteen sixty-eight." Willem began to pick at the label on his empty beer bottle. "Custom job. Olive green. Used to be my company's truck. And since I owned the company, I guess that made it mine."

"They been talkin about it for weeks." Sparechange picked his head up by the hair and slammed it down on the bar in a type of antic the police might use, and Willem realized the man had no desire to talk about his truck.

"Buddy, you're gone get hurt if you don't quit this."

Sparechange shook his head and covered his face with his arm, muffling his words even more. "They think I'm so stupid I can't hear. They think just 'cause I got struck by lightning, I'm a fool."

"You got struck by lightning?" Willem asked.

"Yep. Out by the railroad tracks. A nigger found me and drug me to the hospital and they brung me back."

"Brung you back?"

"Brung me back from the dead." Sparechange raised his head and looked at him in amazement. "Aint you heard about this?"

"No."

The man tilted his head, his dark eyes suspicious. "I was dead as a doorknob till they pounded on my chest and blew in my mouth."

Willem finished peeling the label off and looked at the guy, who seemed to be holding on to his last thread of reality. He said, "I seen a cow struck by lightning once upon a time out in a Louisiana field."

"Hellfire, did you really?"

"Yep. Threw that cow ten feet in the air."

"Holy shit."

"Never will forget the sight of it." Though he had done just that. For fifty or some-odd years, he had forgotten it, beginning to understand now, at this twilight phase of his life, the reason he was afraid of storms.

"Did a nigger carry it to the hospital?"

"Nope."

"Did you?"

"The cow wasn't as lucky as you. It was dead before it hit the ground."

"Man oh man. Whose cow was it?"

"Don't have any way of knowin. A friend I was with told me he believed God thought it was His."

"'Cause He struck it with lightning?"

Willem nodded.

There was a slight pause and then, "That's about the stupidest thing I ever heard." Sparechange began to pat at his pockets.

"I don't smoke," Willem said, trying to save him the trouble of asking.

"Hell, I don't, either. What I'm looking for is a piece of paper to write on."

"I'm fresh out."

"Okay, then, listen up. We got no choice but to do this the hard way." Sparechange brushed his hair out of his face. He tapped his fingernail on the table. "You know anythin about concrete?"

"A little."

"You ever rolled around in it right after it's been poured?"

"Can't say that I have."

"You ain't? Well, I sure have. More 'n once. So you tell them when they come askin that concrete burns like hell and it don't *never* cure." He blinked. "You think you can remember that?"

Willem sighed. "Sure. Why not."

"Good." Sparechange glanced around. "Conchita's gone start dancin any minute now," he said, looking at his hands. "It'd almost be worth gettin slapped just to touch them boobs again." And with that, he was up and waltzing around the room, disappearing finally behind a group of truck drivers leaning against the bar.

{CHAPTER 14}

That evening as she drove toward home, Leah rolled down the window of the truck so that she might feel the air brushing against her arm. The weather had turned cool, and the late afternoon light seemed to belong to the family of fall instead of late spring. The news on the weather radio she kept in the bedroom indicated a high-pressure system was sitting over lower Mississippi, promising blue skies and cooler temperatures and a break in the humidity that seemed perpetual. Leah unbuttoned her overshirt and fanned it with her hand. The cremation had not gone as planned. The pyre had burned for a while and then petered out, and no matter how many matches she struck and how much kerosene she poured, there wasn't enough combustible material to get it going again. She wished someone had told her that a half-burned cow was worse than a rotting one. The smell was egregious. If not for the buried house, she might never go back again and just leave the bones to be rocked by the elements.

She turned left on Old Clement Road and drove a ways and slowed down as she approached a woman standing and then bending along the weedy shoulder. Leah pulled up and stopped the truck, the engine ticking, the needle in the water-temperature gauge climbing a bit toward the red.

"What a wonderful turn of luck," Eilene said, opening the door and climbing in, setting her bucket between them in the seat. "It's been a lonely day, and now you come along."

Leah glanced at her as she eased the truck back onto the blacktop. Eilene had never bothered to use her shouting voice with her, and Leah had never mentioned it. Now that she thought about it, the two of them had always had a somewhat honest relationship. Tense but honest.

"Blueberries?" Leah asked.

"No. Dewberries. Not enough to even fool with. We had that spell of hot weather last month, and I thought there might be some. I was wrong." Eilene hiked up her leg on the seat and said, "You got an extra cigarette?"

"Right there." Leah pointed to the dash where, amid the clutter, a pack of Pall Malls was shoved. Eilene reached for it and shook out two cigarettes and lit them both, handing one to Leah.

"Thanks."

They rode that way for a while, neither seeming to mind the silence.

"I talked to your mother yesterday," Eilene said, pulling open the ashtray and lifting a bent harmonica from the bed of butts. She looked at it, turning it this way and that.

"I don't know whose that is," Leah said, glancing at it.

"Bruno played one years ago. When he was a little boy."

"Then I guess it's his," Leah said, pissed off for a reason she couldn't understand. "What's new with Mom?"

Eilene settled back in the seat. "She's making one of her special Fourth of July Jell-O salads, and your dad's agreed to tend bar. Not that we have a bar. But you get the picture. Dora says she got some new cocktails she wants to try on us."

"Figures."

Eilene looked at Leah, saw the smudge under her eyes and the cracked lips and the hollow cheeks. "This outdoor work's ruining your skin," she said.

"Can't be helped. I'm late now for the evening feeding. Soon as I drop you off, I've got to head out to the fields again."

"I thought you just came from the field."

Leah picked up the corner of her shirt and wiped at her face. "I did.

There's a dead cow in the back plat, and I was disposing of it. Or trying to. Didn't have much luck."

Eilene studied Leah, all her stubbornness, her weariness, the brittleness of her disposition. "Good Lord, Leah. You could leave it alone and let nature take care of it."

"Nature's not been too reliable lately."

Eilene shrugged. She had to agree.

"I just hated to imagine the cow left there. I have to admit, I'm about ready to rethink my position now."

"What's dead is dead," Eilene said.

Leah stared at the native pastureland out the windshield.

"I was talking about the cow," Eilene explained.

"Were you?"

"Of course I was."

"Funny, it felt like something else for a minute there."

"Nope. You'll not hear it from me."

"Hear what?"

"Whatever you thought you were hearing."

Leah shook her head, too worn out to read between the lines.

They were approaching the long drive that led to Sonny and Eilene's, and Eilene said, "You can let me off here."

Leah ignored her and turned in to the drive. No way she was going to go through the guilt of making the woman walk if she didn't have to.

"I said I would walk."

Leah didn't respond.

Once they were at the side parking area next to the scuppernong trellis and the concrete birdbaths, Leah looked across the expanse of yard and saw an unfamiliar truck up on Bruno's portable ramps in her driveway. The ramps were red and had been in the barn for close to two years, hanging high up on the wall at a space it would take a ladder to reach. The truck's hood was raised.

Before Leah could open her mouth, Eilene said, "I declare. Twice in one week," and opened the door and eased down to the ground, her bucket on her arm. Without a look at Leah, or a thank-you or anything, she opened the side door and disappeared into the house.

Leah made a U-turn and headed back down Eilene's drive. Two little boys were playing chase in her front yard, and a young woman who seemed more teen than woman was sitting on the steps holding a blue-green can in her hand. Stopping at the mailbox, Leah opened the door and lifted out the mail and then pulled in the drive, swinging around the jacked-up truck. Making a wide circle, she maneuvered until the truck was in front of the hay wagon, which had been loaded the night before. Once it was hooked up and ready to go, Leah walked into the house and put the mail in its wooden box and went to the sink and washed her hands. The front door was open, and Leah saw the woman's back through the screen door, and how she was sitting as still as a stone, and the can of Fresca on the porch beside her. Going to the icebox, Leah opened it and saw that all the Frescas were gone. All that was left was a single pink can of Tab. "Thanks a lot," she said, reaching for it. Lifting the lid off the tea canister, she reached inside and pulled out her plastic bag of pot and her Zigzags and stepped out onto the porch, where she watched the cat for a moment. Its rear leg was hiked over its head as it preened itself next to her potted geraniums.

Popping the can, she took a swallow of the soda and then wiped her mouth on her sleeve and climbed back into the truck and steered across the field, driving along the uneven fence line, the truck bouncing and throwing debris on the floor. *How many times has he watched me throw hay bales in the back of the truck without an offer to help? How many times has he watched me pull the cord on a hand mower that refused to crank? How many dinners were there that were cold even though the food was hot?* Leah knew his habits and restraints, the limits to him, and climbing up a ladder and lifting down repair ramps certainly seemed one of them. But those were Bruno's legs sticking out from under the girl's truck, and she couldn't think of a single explanation he might have that would make his behavior seem fair.

→←

"Shit. I shoulda done this months ago," Leah said, slinging clothes into her suitcase. She had packed only twice in recent years. Once when she was leaving the home of her parents to marry Bruno, the other time when she was on her way to the VA hospital in Jackson.

Bruno watched her in the waning light of the living room as he stood next to the front door, trying to decide whether to shut it or leave it open. He could feel the late afternoon breeze picking up, and it felt nice as it swept into the house, ruffling pages of magazines set on the coffee table. And the light was late afternoon light, golden and rich, also good. But the evening sun was pinpointing Alyce's empty Fresca can as the wind blew it across the porch, and this was bad. Bruno looked at his hands, still covered with grease.

Leah had just come from the shower and was standing in the middle of the kitchen. Her hair was loose and thick, with wet tendrils clinging to her neck, and she was naked underneath a white undershirt that belonged to him. He had forgotten how pretty her legs were, and her lean, angular shoulders.

"Why didn't you just tell me?" she said. "Why'd you have to let me go on hoping for all these months? Shit. I feel like a fool." She went to the back door and opened it and walked out to where the washer was, her form appearing and then disappearing across the kitchen window, the cat scurrying across the yard in alarm. *I'd run, too, if I could,* Bruno thought, more disturbed by the fact that his wife was out-of-doors practically naked than by the threat of her leaving. *Shit, she's walking to the clothesline. Please, God. Let Mother be taking a nap.* When Leah came back in, she had her jeans in her arms, the legs stiff like a run-over corpse. She threw them into the suitcase and stomped past him and down the dark hall into the bedroom. Shirts were in her arms when she came back. Not her work shirts, either. Her dressy shirts. The kind you wear when you're trying to get a job in an office or meeting friends for drinks after work.

"What is it, exactly, that I was supposed to tell you?" he said quietly.

"That you don't want me. That you've not wanted me for a long time. That you've probably *never* wanted me."

She stomped back into the kitchen, and Bruno said, "Leah, you're overreacting."

"Don't you dare," she hissed as she threw her plastic zipper bag holding pink sponge rollers next to her clean bra and blue box of tampons.

"What?"

"Don't you dare accuse me of overreacting."

"Okay, I won't. But tell me this. What'd I do that was so bad?" He held out his greasy hands and quickly lowered them by his side. They might as well have had blood on them.

"Not a damn thing, and that's the point."

Leaning against his bookcase, he watched her. The suitcase was open on the kitchen table, and he noticed for the first time that it was the big suitcase, and he found this troubling.

"Listen. I called her to come pick that up," he lied, pointing to the vacuum cleaner.

"Then how come it's still here?"

The lie had not been completely worked out yet, so he ignored the obvious flaw in it and said, "She was all set to leave, and her truck wouldn't start, and her boys were carrying on like kids do, driving me crazy. Why the hell you think I'm covered in grease? I was tryin to fix her truck so she'd leave, goddammit!"

Leah turned to him, frowning. "Don't you dare insult me."

"The hell does that mean?"

"It means don't stand there and pretend."

"Pretend what?"

"That I'm stupid. That you think *she's* the reason I'm leaving. What? Some podunk country girl wearing tight jeans? Shit. You're even dumber than I thought."

"You never thought I was dumb, and you know it." He looked over at his chair but decided he didn't want to sit down. Leah was leaning against the kitchen table, and he could see it below the hem of his T-shirt, soft brown and curling, and he wondered how she could stand there and be so unaware of it when it seemed to him to be the only thing in the world worth looking at. He looked away and said, "I'm sure you thought I was a lot of things. But dumb wasn't one of them."

Leah knew he was telling the truth and looked past him to the bookcase. "You certainly sound confident for a man who sits and rereads old magazines all day long."

"I don't think comparing IQ scores would do anybody any good," he said, folding his arms. "Not at this point. Maybe back when we first met, it might have sent you runnin back to one of those college boys. But you seemed sick of college boys, as I recall. College boys couldn't fuck worth a shit was what you told me out in the back field."

"Shut up!"

"No. *You* shut up."

She put her fingers to her temples and rubbed. "You're twisting the conversation around to something that has no point. You're so fucking good at that, you know. Fucking good at sidestepping the real issue. Fucking good at making me feel fucking stupid."

He lifted his eyebrows. It was their first real fight in all their years of marriage, and it was like waking up in a strange country where the language was incomprehensible. "I think you don't need any help from me to do that. You're the one acting like a crazy bitch who only knows one word."

"You fucking *ass*hole!" she screamed.

Bruno watched her. He thought she might be about to cry, and he didn't want that. He had seen her cry only once and didn't think he could bear seeing it again. "I can't believe you just called me a fucking asshole."

"Oh, excuse me. What I should have said is that you're a *non*-fucking asshole."

"Jesus," he whispered, feeling like he'd just been kneed in the nuts. "Is that what this is all about? You wanna fuck? Come here and we'll fuck." He used his middle finger to point to her crotch and the blood was up in his face and he was so mad he felt the manic desire to pull the bookcase down on top of himself. Just to punish her.

"Go to hell," she said.

"I'm already there." He meant the fight with Leah was hell, nothing more, but she took it the wrong way and said, "Oh *please,*" as she pointed to his neck. "You wear that thing like a badge of honor. You *like* that thing. Don't stand there and tell me you don't. It's your new best friend. If you didn't have it, you might have to talk to me or pay attention to me or . . ."

"Or what?"

"I don't know what. Something besides sitting in a chair all day long and making phone calls to teenagers who had the poor luck to get knocked up not once but twice."

"You don't know anything about her."

"Oh? And you do?"

"Not really. But this isn't even about her."

"Then tell me what it's about," Leah said, hands on her hips, wondering if he knew.

He looked out the window. He knew, but he wasn't about to say.

"See? You don't even know."

"I know."

"Then what?"

"Like I said before, it's about you being a crazy bitch." He walked across the living room and into the kitchen, and Leah saw the look on his face and stepped back until her rear was leaning against the table.

"Don't worry. I'm not going to touch you."

"Like *that's* a big surprise."

"What did you say?" He turned to look at her with the dishwashing liquid in his hands. A yellow bottle of Joy, of all things. She was standing next to the table with both hands holding to its edge as though she might be hanging on for life, and he could see the bruise on her arm and how it was healing up all yellowish and green, and he looked away from it. She had gotten hurt working in the field, and it seemed one more way that he had failed her. "Look me in the face and say it again. I dare you."

"I said, 'Like *that's* a *big surpise*.' You haven't touched me in three years. Why start now?"

He turned away from her and began to wash his hands and arms, the yellow liquid turning green and then gray and then black. "You're right. Why start now."

"I guess you spend your shower time thinking about Miss Tight Jeans and beating off."

"Not anymore." Blood was pounding in his face, and he felt as though the brace was too tight and he might be about to choke.

"The hell does *that* mean?"

"It means, Leah, that walking in on me this morning is just one more way that you've fucked up my life."

Leah flew across the room at him, fists raised, and pounded on his brace with both hands. It was so unfair. So goddamn unfair. Hitting the brace wasn't doing anything but hurting her, and he was too tall to slap, so she pushed him as hard as she could and he lost his balance and fell sideways into the refrigerator. A large soap and oil handprint smeared across the freezer compartment, and he cut his head on the metal handle, and a thin stream of blood ran from his scalp and pooled inside his ear. She looked at his face and thought, *Oh shit, I've done it now.*

All he wanted to do was grab her and shake some sense into her, but grabbing her wasn't easy because of his slick hands, and every place he touched slipped away from him, and her shirt became black when she spun away and ran down the hall, a black handprint between her shoulder blades like a hole. He heard the click of the lock, but it was already too late, he already knew what he was going to do.

Kicking the bedroom door in was easier than he thought, and catching her left foot by the ankle and pulling her across the bed was even easier than that. Catching her other foot was harder. Leah kicked at his face, and her heel slipped off his bloody forehead and slammed into his nose. She kicked at him again, and he heard the crack of bone where her toe met the brace. He blocked her third kick with his arm and fell across her.

"Get *off* me!"

"Not a chance," he said to the side of her neck, pulling her shirt over one arm and pinning that arm to the bed. He did the same with the other arm until her hands were held together in one of his hands and she was naked, and then he began to undo his belt and work his pants down his legs.

"Get the fuck *away* from me. I hate you!"

"Then this won't matter," he said. He could smell the pot on her breath, and he thought of the back field where he had fucked her and how sweet it had been, and then he was smelling the grease from the truck and seeing dark smears across Leah's naked body and the bed linens and the side of her head where his hand was wadded in her hair. Both windows were raised to let in the breeze, and voices were carrying across the field. His mother's and then Sonny's. Something about his mother needing something fixed, and Sonny saying, I cain't get nothin done for havin to take care a you, and some rebuttal from his mother that Bruno couldn't hear.

Leah bucked against him and he fell to the side and then he rolled over on top of her and it had been so long since skin had met skin that the feel of it froze them both in place. And then she cussed him again and tried to pull his hair, but he said "Leah, be still now," and put his open mouth on hers and left it there, fixed in place until she opened hers and they began to breathe each other's air. The curtains stirred and he could see twilight stars and a slash of a moon and then he didn't see anything at all. Just Leah, who was still crying, only a different type of crying now, and her arms were around him, low so that she might feel the skin of his back, and then she was clawing at his ass and her knees were up around his waist and her head was thrown back and he began to push into her, slow at first and then fast as he could, as though speed would take them both back to a sweeter time. That time before.

He left her while she was asleep, the sheet pulled over her. Her face was to the window and her breathing was calm and evenly cadenced, like a child's. His duffel bag was in the back room, and he went there and shoved the clothes he had gathered into it and looked around the dark house for anything else he might have missed and then he went and stood at the bedroom door and looked at her. Her hair was spread out over the pillows and the bed was streaked all over in black and brownish red. Like someone had tried to clean a carburetor and cut his hand doing so. And then he shook his head and thought, *No, the bed looks like some terrible act happened there.* And he supposed it had, since what he had done to her began as an assault before turning into something else. He dabbed at the cut on his forehead and looked at the handkerchief and was relieved to see that it was still white. Spent and tired, he walked down the hall and out the back door. Once they were done and Leah had pulled the sheet up to her and rolled away from him and fallen into sleep, he had lain there with his arm over his face for close to three hours, weighing things, realizing finally that he had no choice but to leave.

And so it's midnight and Bruno walks across the porch and then the yard and the night is cool and clean-feeling and the sky's crowded with stars that seem bright but hard. He pulls open the doors to the barn and goes inside and checks the cables on the tractor and takes the diesel can off the shelf and tops off the tank for her. After the barn doors are shut he walks to the small lean-to where Leah keeps the Rambler parked and fishes the keys out of his pocket and stands looking at them, wondering which one is the right one, it has been that long. The car smells of mice and mildew and a thin sheet of dust covers everything, but it cranks on the first try and Bruno pulls out of his driveway during this middle hour of night, driving slowly until he passes the far gates that lead to the main road. Once there, he speeds up and drives steadily east through the stillness until he sees it blinking on and off and on and off, a blur at first and then a word that spells out more than it can possibly know. Pulling into the small lot where her truck is parked underneath the blue vacancy sign, he sees another truck down near the end of the building and parks next to it, in front of room number four, and turns off the engine.

[CHAPTER 15}

How come that man's here," Joe asked, and Alyce turned from the hot skillet where she was scrambling eggs and said, " 'Cause he needs a place to stay, and that's what this place is, a place for people to stay."

"How come he got beat up," Joe wanted to know, and Alyce turned again from the skillet and said, "I don't know that he got beat up. I don't really know what happened to him. Now, go get your brother, and both you boys wash your hands."

"But it's just now mornin and I ain't dirty."

"I know it's mornin, but you were playin with that stray cat."

"The cat ain't dirty. The cat's always clean, 'cause it licks itself all over."

"It licks its bottom, too. Think about that."

Joe sat and thought about it a moment and then left the kitchen and headed toward the back of the house, where his brother was sitting on the floor watching *Captain Kangaroo.*

"Mama says come eat."

"Buh tha rabbah bou tha geh it."

"The rabbit always gets the carrots. Take your thumb out of your mouth and come on."

Ben removed his thumb and wiped it on his pajamas and followed his brother to the kitchen.

"Right there," Alyce said, pointing to the kitchen sink. She had put the red stool in front of it and the water was already running. "Both of you. Wash your hands."

They did as they were told and then sat at the table waiting for her. Two little boys still heavy-eyed from sleep. She set the steaming plates in front of them and they ate silently and with abandon, shoveling eggs onto their forks, tearing toast into pieces and cramming it into their mouths, slurping their milk.

"Mama?"

"What, Joe?"

"Ain't today a holiday?"

"Yep. Memorial Day."

"What's it a holiday of?"

"It's when we remember people who died servin their country."

"Oh." Joe drank his milk and then wiped his face with the back of his hand. "We don't know none of them, do we?"

"Not right off hand."

"Then can we go to the woods and look for worms?"

Ben looked at his brother and then his mother and nodded enthusiastically.

"I got the motel to run. You know that."

"Where's Daddy at?"

Alyce looked at him and was tired of pretending and said, "I don't know, Joe. Maybe he's workin."

Joe crimped his mouth up and appeared to be thinking about it. "Can I look for worms out in the yard, then?"

Alyce looked at them. It really didn't take much to please them, and it hurt her heart because they never asked for anything. Not bikes. Or balls. Not a slingshot or a pair of skates. She leaned on her arms and smiled at them. "I tell you what we'll do. You two can go out in the front yard and try to find you some worms, and then we'll come back inside and make kites out of old newspapers. How does that sound?"

They were both nodding and grinning.

"Mah kah wah—"

"Take it out, Ben," Alyce said.

He removed his thumb from his mouth and said, "My kite will be better than his." He grinned at his brother.

"Will not," Joe said.

"Will, too. 'Cause it'll have a bear on it," Ben said.

"There ain't no bears around here," Joe said.

"I'll cut one out of a colorin book, and there will too be a bear."

"Well, I will, too. Only mine'll be a lion, and lions are better than bears."

The bell over the front door jingled, and Alyce put a hand to her hair and flipped it behind her ear in one fluid movement. She was irritated with her heart and the way it was behaving. Stable and rocking along for these seven years, it had suddenly developed a gallop. She was even more irritated to see that it was Dolores Corrales standing in the office and not Bruno Till.

"We're back here," she called, and the woman joined them, her arms full of white towels and white sheets so that her face was all but hidden. She was square as a packing crate and wearing her white domestic's dress and white orthopedic shoes and white hosiery rolled to a point below her knees. Alyce was reminded briefly of a Maytag washer walking about on feet.

"Here. Let me get those," she said, taking the woman's burden and putting it on the low bakery table on the far side of the kitchen.

"*Buenos días, conchitos.*"

"Good mornin, Dolores," both boys chorused as they finished their milk.

"An where ees Meester Joe?" Dolores asked, her hands on her hips as she looked around the room with broad exaggeration.

She asked the question every morning she worked, and every morning the answer was the same. Alyce said, "Not here."

"*¿Qué le pasa a este hombre?*"

"Please speak English."

"What's the matter with thees man?"

Alyce looked at her and shrugged.

"*Madre de Dios.* Men!" She threw her hands up in the air. She ruffled the boys' hair with a great brown meaty hand.

"We got a family from Texas comin in around two. A husband and wife and their two kids. Their granny over in Hattiesburg died, and I need rooms two and three made up."

"*Sí.*"

"And Willem Fremont down in room six needs his room done."

"*Él no me deja pasar para cambiar la sábana.*"

"Dolores, please." Alyce lifted the plates off the table and put them in the sink and ran the hot water and squirted liquid soap.

"She said he won't let her change the bed," Joe said, looking at Dolores, who nodded.

"Is that really what you said?" Alyce wanted to know. She stood looking at her older child. Her hands were on her hips.

"*Sí.* Thees boy knows."

Dolores held up a finger indicating *watch this,* and then she looked at Joe and spoke slowly. "*Estaba escondiéndose en el baño cuando toqué a la puerta.*"

Joe squinted as he listened and then nodded. "Did you say he was hidin in the bathroom when you knocked on the door?"

"*Sí. Sí.*" Dolores nodded excitedly and rubbed at the boy's ear, and he pulled away from her touch. "Thees little ones, they learn early." She looked to Alyce, who was standing with her mouth open. "They *know* theengs," Dolores said again and peered at Alyce and a different meaning was in her eyes this time and Alyce looked away and out the kitchen window at her small square garden and the tomato sticks in the ground.

"Can you have them done by two?"

Dolores nodded.

"And there's one more here besides Mr. Fremont. But he's not to be disturbed."

Joe looked at Dolores and said, "He's down in room four and he got beat up."

"Joe, what did I tell you?"

"Well. He *might* a got beat up."

"We don't know about it. And even if we did, we ought not to talk about it."

"Leesin to your mother. She knows theengs, too."

The doorbell jingled again, and again Alyce flipped her hair behind her ear and stood up and headed for the small office, overly aware that instead of a loose T-shirt and her worn-out jeans, she had on her newest jeans and a shirt. She checked her breath in a cupped hand and then blushed because she knew herself, and she was ashamed of what she knew. Relief and dismay, this was what she was feeling when she saw who it was. Relief it wasn't him and dismay it wasn't him, for the person standing in front of her desk was the old one. Willem.

"Good mornin, Mr. Fremont," she said, trying not to look disappointed.

He swept his safari hat off his head and smiled at her. "Good mornin, Alyce." The girl looked fresh and made up with shiny hair and pale pink gloss on her lips.

"What can I do for you?"

"I was wonderin if you could tell me where a hardware store might be?"

"We got 'em all over, but that ain't gonna help you today."

He frowned at her, puzzled.

"Memorial Day," she said. "A holiday."

"Oh."

"What is it you're wantin to buy?"

"A small bush ax."

"A bush ax?"

He fumbled for a reason and decided on an outright lie. "I like to bird-watch and thought I'd go out into the woods and see what I can find."

"You bird-watch?"

"I love birds. White-eyed Vireos. Cerulean Warblers. All of them. I've yet to see a Painted Bunting, but it's May, and they're migrating up from South America. Today just might be my lucky day." He grinned at her and she smiled back. "I thought a bush ax would give me an edge should I see a snake or something."

"There's a shed around back where the lawn mower is." She sat down at her desk and pulled open the drawer and stirred through its holdings. "Here's the key to the padlock. Help yourself."

"You sure you don't mind."

She waved away the suggestion as though it were a gnat. "I ain't sure there's one there. But if there is, just return it when you're done."

Willem could hear the Hispanic cleaning woman talking to the boys, and he grew nervous at the thought of her. "My room's fine, by the way. No need for it to be cleaned."

Alyce held up a hand. "Now, Mr. Fremont, we need to get in there and get you some fresh towels and clean sheets. You paid a cleaning fee, and it's part of my job to make sure you get your money's worth. What kind of businesswoman would I be if I didn't take care a you?"

To carry it any further would make him look like a fool. Besides, he would be gone before she made it all the way down to six. The woman had already walked in on him twice: once while he was in the middle of shaving and the other time while he was mid-shit on the toilet. "Whatever you say." He pocketed the key as he turned to the door.

"Good luck findin it."

"Beg your pardon?" He turned back to her.

"One of them painted-button things."

"Oh, that. Thank you. I'll do my best."

As soon as he left, Alyce swiveled out of the desk chair and headed back to the kitchen and on into her bedroom, unbuttoning her shirt and jerking it off her shoulders and tossing it on the bed. *I ain't gonna do this,* she told herself. *It ain't right, and I ain't gonna do it.* She pulled yesterday's T-shirt over her head and unzipped her new jeans and stepped out of them and pulled on yesterday's jeans that were smudged and dirty from garden work and then she gathered her hair back in a severe ponytail and fastened it with a barrette. Her final penance was ripping a Kleenex from a box and rubbing the lipstick from her lips.

→←

Willem drove down to the end of the old logging road and put the truck in park and got out and checked his pocket for his knife. There was a heavy chain blocking his access, and while the lock was a sturdy one, he had discovered the day before that the hook was loose in the post and easy to work free. Lock and all came away in his hand, and he dragged it to the other side and then drove on through, stopping one more time to pull the chain back across the road and refasten it to the post. He had a feeling no one checked on these back roads, but he was a man well acquainted with bad timing, and should someone decide to check rural road number 487, he was sure they would pick this day to do it.

The woods were mostly pines, close-set and thick, with dead branches waist-high in some places. Intricate spiderwebs stretched from tree to tree, and dew was still in some of them and the dew looked like diamonds. The path Willem walked was sand and formed by rain runoff and wound its way down a grade until it narrowed and finally disappeared. Willem passed the hole he had stumbled into the afternoon before and took Alyce's bush ax and used it as a cane, poking it ahead of him as he periodically checked his compass. It was pure guesswork, for the most part, but a feeling of being there before was with him, and an hour into his walk, he was struck by the notion that the land he was walking on was his and he had walked this way before. He came to an old river oak where old wire fencing was girdled tight at shoulder height, grown over and crusted, and he stood before it and pressed his knife into its seam and measured it with his finger. An inch. He wondered how many years that meant, and then he walked on, sure that no matter the years, the fence was his. Now walking hesitantly, he heard the sound of falling water and shut his eyes, for the direction was off. He had expected it to be north, but it was east, and he knew that he was approaching from a direction opposed to memory. Taking the ax, he measured forward a foot at a time, and when it slid off into nothing and slipped from his hands, he was prepared for it and caught hold of a tree and looked.

It was like coming across a lake full of trees. The crowns were thick and violently green and level with his waist, and he might have walked off into the top of insubstantial limbs and fallen to his death if he had not been aware. But he was ready for it and eased himself to the ground and sniffed deep and smelled the odor from the day before: rancid meat that had been burned. Across the way was the artesian well. It was yet to be seen, but he could hear it plain enough. *Now to get down there,* he thought, standing and beginning to walk around the perimeter, considering the possibilities. All seemed grim and likely to kill him one way or the other, but he finally found a narrow ridge where the earth had buckled and set trees to growing crossways, their limbs a type of natural scaffolding, and he eased his way down through the middle of them, feeling like a prisoner going in instead of one trying to escape.

The first thing he did was find Alyce's bush ax. Once it had been retrieved, he turned and walked through the trees toward the house, not seeing it at first, for the foliage was wild and thick, and honeysuckle and scuppernong vines had grown over it completely so that it looked more like an arbor than a house. It was only when he saw the door and the old doorknob that he realized what it was. Leaning the ax against what used to be a wall, he hunkered down and knee-walked through the opening and found that the lean inside was such that he couldn't stand upright, so he sat on the ruined floor and studied the ruined walls and looked at the scattering of fallen stones from off the ruined fireplace. He wondered if there was anything within eyeshot that was not somehow busted and thought there probably wasn't.

"I haven't got there yet. But I'm not far off," he said out loud, and then he pushed to his feet and squatted toward the opening and pulled back the thick wall of green and was about to step out into the light when he saw a flash of blue walking through the trees and then the plaid of a work shirt commingling with the variegated colors of the leaves and finally a dark-haired woman stepped out into the light and headed directly for him, walking with purpose, as though she'd been there for fifty-two years waiting for him.

{CHAPTER 16}

Dora Maxwell knew in her heart of hearts that she was perceived as being one-dimensional, and it bothered her. And while she tried to convince herself on this perfect Memorial Day, with its perfect low-humidity weather so rare for Mississippi, that perhaps her hormones weren't firing as perfectly as they should and this was the reason she was feeling a little on the blue side, her heart of hearts reminded her that she had felt this way on countless other perfect days, even *before* menopause. Way back in high school, even, when out of nowhere her mood would shift ever so slightly (never when she was alone, she reminded herself, which seemed proof positive that *she* was okay), but always when she was with her group of friends, all popular girls organizationally motivated who dragged Dora along as they joined clubs she had no use for but joined nevertheless. A filament of fatigue would rest on her shoulders as they fastened their pins to their collars and signed their names in the ledger book and then huddled together like feminine-garbed football players deciding among themselves who would be the club's president and vice president. The same two girls were chosen each and every time. Denise Schuler and Mavis Clayburne. For all six clubs to which Dora belonged, these two girls sat at the helm. Once the huddle was disengaged and it was time to hand out the scraps, they would look over at Dora and assign her the position of recording secretary. Who wants to be a recording secretary? Nobody, that's who. Especially not Dora, who wanted to be the president or the vice president, or at least considered for either. But no, let's make Dora the secretary instead, and if that slot's already taken by the unattractive girl headed to Millsaps for a degree in library science—a girl who approached the club with a sincere heart, unlike Dora, who was for all intents and purposes, dragged into it—then let's make Dora the event planner, which clearly indicated one thing: she was perceived by her peers as one-dimensional and capable only of mundane responsibilities. Like decorating the gymnasium with balloons. Or wrapping two hundred paper stars in aluminum foil and tying them to a basketball goal for the "Shoot for the Stars" Sadie Hawkins dance.

That was then and this was now, and Dora realized she was long gone from those high school days; that she was fifty-four years old, for God's sake, and had a suburban house that, yes, needed new shingles and yearly treatment against mole crickets but was absolutely mortgage-free; that she had a daughter who had *almost* finished college, which was a helluva lot more than some of those club presidents could say about *their* kids, one of whom ended up panhandling on the streets of San Francisco, where she changed her name from Sally Lyon to Saffron CoolFire; that she had a husband who had never, at least to her knowledge, seriously considered leaving her for another, younger woman, who was now in his fifth year of retirement and had settled into the routine yard work and golf and occasional fishing and quit bothering her so much; that she had loads and loads of accomplishments she could put in her basket of happiness and tote around, and on most days, she was able to do this. But here on this perfect Memorial Day in the year 1974, Dora's *now* felt as uncomfortable as her *then*. Ever the club recording secretary, she listed the possible reasons for her melancholy and came up with only one viable answer: even her own daughter thought she was one-dimensional.

Oh, Leah didn't come right out and say it, but Dora didn't need her to open up her mouth and verbalize her feelings. Leah's belief and its accompanying irritation vibrated off her body like tones off a struck tuning fork. Tones the whole Meridian community could pick up and store away for future reference. Tones that might hold sway when deciding who should be nominated for club president of SLAG, the Southern Ladies' Awareness Group. Tones suggesting to one and all that Dora Maxwell and her one-dimensional self was better suited for the lowly position of recording secretary.

Dora realized, of course, that the entire Meridian community couldn't possibly witness Leah's seismic rumblings, but Meridian as a whole didn't really matter, since Leah's habit was to express herself within earshot of some of Dora's closest friends, which, in Dora's opinion, was far worse. Take, for example, the time Dora invited Leah to join her at the SLAG annual luncheon, held that year at the really elegant Magnolia Club on Brisbane Lake.

True, Dora was showing off a bit, but even that felt justified and long overdue. There were so many things to be thankful for, really. And was it so bad that she wanted Leah next to her at a table where Denise Schuler Lyon and Mavis Clayburne Stroh would both be seated? Did it make Dora a horrible person because she wanted those two women to sit up and take notice of what a wonderful job she had done raising her daughter? After all, Leah Maxwell was still Leah Maxwell, unlike Denise's daughter, who was now Saffron CoolFire and singing on street corners in San Francisco and going home at night to a commune that specialized in growing rutabagas. Not only that, but Leah Maxwell was still living in Mississippi, which was a lot more than Mavis Stroh could say about her son, whose last known address was some goat farm in northern France, where he was trying desperately to "find" himself. Was it so wrong to try to point out to her friends that while she had never been chosen as president or vice president of any of the clubs, Dora had managed to raise a daughter who would never dare to be a disappointment? Dora didn't think so. So, yes, she was showing off a bit, but as SLAG's recording secretary, she had worked her fingers to the bone decorating and arranging floral deliveries and making sure the caterer got the orders right, and she felt a bit of showing off was not out of line. Leah didn't have to know that the ticket was free, did she? Or that Dora had made a point of rearranging the place cards and slipping hers and Leah's names off table fifteen and putting them at table one, considered the best table in the room. And what did Leah do as far as showing her gratitude? She dared to talk, that's what she did. Oh, and she was so sly about it, too. It wasn't your everyday *I'm trying to be courteous* talk. It was talk that involved thought. Talk that *meant* something. Maybe not to everyone sitting around the table, but at least to Dora.

Five minutes into the first course, Leah had casually tucked her hair behind her ear (a warning sign that Dora recognized instantly) and turned to Mavis Stroh and inquired about her husband's pro bono work at the firm. Of course, there wasn't any pro bono work at his firm. Clyde Stroh, Sr., was a corporate lawyer representing the big oil companies in Louisiana, and Leah, who had played softball with Clyde Jr. and gone to the movies with Clyde Jr. and eaten dinner at Clyde Jr.'s house more than a dozen times, probably even kissed the pimply little oinker, knew damn well the type of firm that bore the name of Clyde Stroh, Sr. Who the hell out in an oil field needs pro bono work? Leah raised her eyebrows and smiled in the face of Mavis's discomfiture and innocently carved at her glazed carrots.

"But Clyde and Mavis *just* got back from a *wonderful* week at the Wolf Bay Lodge up in North Carolina," Dora had stammered, embarrassed for her friend, trying to be a good recording secretary and throw the SLAG vice president a bone. "Tell Leah about it, Mavis. How wonderful and quaint it was. About that albino squirrel you saw."

"Oh, Leah's a college girl now. I'm sure she's not interested," Mavis said, her face flushed.

"No, Mrs. Stroh, you're wrong. I'd *love* to hear all about your squirrel," Leah had said with a straight face, putting down her fork. Like Dora was so one-dimensional she couldn't recognize a double entendre when she heard one.

"We saw the squirrel on our last day there. Actually, I was the only one who saw it. Clyde missed the boat because of his bad back. You see, we were supposed to be a part of the Wolf Bay nature cruise. They go up and down the river and stop at little catwalks and let you get out your binoculars and look at the birds and the turtles and maybe an alligator or two. But you know Clyde and his back—"

"*Oh, Leah*. He has *such* a bad back," Dora interrupted. "Really, really painful. It breaks your heart to see the man try to climb out of the car." Dora had reached out to Leah and placed her hand on her arm. Leah pulled away, and Dora was sure the entire table noticed.

Mavis continued, "Anyway, Clyde's back was bothering him especially bad that day, and he's never been able to quit those filthy cigars. Not that smoking has anything in the world to do with back pain. But I told him he abso*lutely* couldn't smoke in our room, because I was not about to go to dinner that night wearing a dress that smelled like a Cuban Monticello, and he said, Okay dear. How's about I go play gin at the clubhouse, so—"

"*Oh, Leah*," Dora gushed. "You should just sit back and *watch* that man play cards—"

"Mom, let her finish," Leah said. "I'm dying to hear about her squirrel."

Dora sniffed and looked around for the coffee cart, sure now that she would never be president or vice president of anything.

"I thought about going by myself, since the cruise was part of the Wolf Bay Lodge package and we'd made our reservations a year in advance, and it seemed like *such* a waste to miss out on the major feature of the resort." Mavis began circling the air next to her right ear with her finger. "But I've always had this really annoying inner-ear problem and was worried I might fall off the boat or something. And how embarrassing would that be? Besides, the grounds are *so* lovely there. Everywhere you look, all you see is outdoors. There's all this Kentucky bluegrass that really *does* look blue. It's in*credibly* beautiful. And lovely old magnolia trees growing close to the water. Anyway, I was sitting in the gazebo and I had just rung the bell for a drink. It's really a quaint place, Dora," Mavis said, turning to Dora, who brightened immediately upon being included in the albino squirrel story. "You really *must* see if Merle won't take you and Leah there one day."

"*Oh, Leah*, wouldn't you just love that?" Dora asked, even though she knew Leah would lock herself in the bedroom at the mere suggestion of the trip's becoming an actuality. Not only that, but Merle would never *ever* be seen at a place where folks had to dress for dinner.

"Sure, Mom. Sounds great."

"Anyway. Where was I?"

"You had just rung a bell. You were about to see your squirrel," Leah said, buttering her bread.

"Yes. I had just rung the bell for a drink. The gazebo's really rustic, Leah. I've never seen such craftsmanship. And while you wouldn't think a thing that looked so 'woodsy' would have this, there was a little control panel that was connected with the main house, and all I had to do was press a button and a Negra would come running. Just my finger on a button. Isn't that something?"

Dora dropped her spoon against her saucer and chipped the plate and quickly covered the damage with her napkin. "Leah, dear. Do you need more coffee? I was thinking about ordering some."

"No, Mom. I'm fine." She turned to Mavis. "So you just pressed a button and ordered a drink?"

"How about some tea? Would you like a cup of hot tea?" Dora asked.

"Mom. I don't need a thing." She turned back to Mavis. "So you pressed this button?"

"Oh, mercy yes. Quick as you can say Davy Crocket, a Negra would come runnin with a little order pad in his hand." She paused. "No. I take that back. They did *not* have order pads. Maybe in the main dining hall, they had order pads. But not for running back and forth to the gazebo. They *remembered* the order. They're so different from our Negras down here. So smart." She looked around for the servers, who were all black. "And so well mannered."

"Leah, would you like another piece of bread?" Dora asked, knowing that an all but invisible line of sweat was popping up on her forehead.

"No, Mom. I'm just fine."

"I have never in my life seen anything like it. Just press a button and one comes running."

"If you pressed the button twice, would two come running?" Leah asked, and Dora, never one to stare at a car wreck, shut her eyes and held on to her coffee cup for support.

Mavis appeared to be thinking about it. "You know, I have no idea. I only pressed it that one time. We left early the next day."

"So, when exactly did you see the squirrel?"

Dora opened one eye and peered in her daughter's direction and wondered what was wrong with her. Here was the perfect opportunity to pull out her big "Let's Defend the Negroes" gun, and she was sitting sweetly in her chair, buttering her bread, smiling as Mavis Stroh went on and on about a dumb albino squirrel that climbed up on a gazebo bench with her and stuck its nasty little albino paw in Mavis's Magnolia Mudslide and licked the Kahlúa off its nasty little pink toenails.

And then the realization dropped on her head like a brick. Leah, observant student of humanity, had realized that Mavis Stroh was much more than a one-dimensional person, and this was the reason she excused her behavior, which was obviously in bad taste even to Dora. Her daughter had found Mavis Stroh to be complex (which equaled smart and at least three-dimensional in Dora's book), and this was the reason Leah smiled so sweetly and innocently and pretended to enjoy a story that even Dora realized was incredibly banal. The day was spoiled from that point. Not even the advent of Baked Alaska topped with individual sparklers cheered her. And for the first time in a great while, Dora was the one who refused to speak the entire way back to Meridian. Even as Leah repeatedly asked her what was wrong, Dora just shook her head and kept her eyes on the road while tears gathered against her mascara and threatened to ruin the new linen suit she had sweated and exercised for three months just to fit into.

That was only one time in particular that Leah had set her mother apart as unworthy of her camaraderie or good humor or plain old graciousness. Only one time that she had sent out a patronizing tone that indicated to Dora's friends just how low on the esteem totem pole Dora was placed. There were hundreds of others. Dora was just too tired and too blue, on this perfect Memorial Day, to dwell on them.

She had heard the phone ringing while she was in the shower. The bedroom phone with its old-timey bell that Merle had wired to speakers throughout every single room of the house so that neither of them would ever have to miss a call, not even when they were out in the yard. A system that irritated the neighbors, Dora was sure, just about as much as it irritated her. What could possibly be more annoying than hearing somebody else's phone ringing off the hook while trying to enjoy *What's My Line?* or *The Sonny and Cher Show*? She adjusted her shower cap and then the hot-water faucet and stood underneath the warm stream and opened her mouth and gargled. *I take showers in the dark. That doesn't sound too one-dimensional to me,* she thought. *In fact, that sounds like a woman who knows how to appreciate subtlety. Who loves the way natural light looks as it filters through the azaleas and into the cloistered bathroom. Who loves those lovely ghost shadows of the telephone pole and the greening tree. Who loves the way everything—toilet, sink, even the plastic waste can—looks almost not there from behind the shower curtain.* She reached for the soap and began to shave her legs. In the dark. Savoring the feeling of being cocooned.

There was nothing that ruined a moment more than when Merle chose to clomp his way into the bathroom and flip on the light, obviously assuming his wife was so one-dimensional she didn't have the good sense God gave a goat.

Dora dropped her metal razor when the light blazed on over the tub. "For God's sake, Merle. You scared the life out of me."

"Didn't you hear the phone?"

"Of course I heard the phone. The whole neighborhood heard the phone. But what was I supposed to do, jump out of the shower and answer it when I knew perfectly well that you were sitting in your La-Z-Boy in the living room?"

"Well, I did answer it, and it was Leah," Merle said, walking over to the toilet and lowering the lid and sitting on it. His presence was an unwelcome intrusion to Dora, who wanted the bathroom and its illusive cocoonism all to herself.

"Would you please turn off the light?"

"The light? What in the Sam Hill do you want the light off for? This is a bathroom, for God's sake."

"Of *course* it's a bathroom. I never said it wasn't a bathroom."

"Then how come you want the light off?"

"Oh, never mind," Dora said. "What'd Leah want?"

"That's the strange thing. She never said. She just said she needed to talk."

"Well, what did you talk about?"

"Nothin. That's what's so odd. I kept asking her about Bruno and his family and the farm, even the weather, and all I got were one-syllable answers. It was like she was sixteen again and sitting around the supper table pouting because we wouldn't let her go to the drive-in with that Stroh boy."

Dora leaned out from behind the shower curtain and saw him rubbing his head. It was a habit of his, the way he rubbed his head when he was worried.

"Did you tell her how excited we are about coming down on the Fourth of July?"

"No."

"Did you remind her to put green olives and not black ones in the potato salad?"

"No, I did not. Hell, Dora, I just told you how quiet she was."

"Just because she was quiet doesn't mean you had to be. There are lots of things a father could talk to a daughter about."

"Well, excuse me for not remembering any of them."

She peered out and saw he was still rubbing his head. "Maybe it was me she needed. Maybe it's one of those female things. Like heavy periods. Or a bad yeast infection."

"I don't even want to hear about it, Dora."

"Why not?" She jerked open the shower curtain. "It could've been something like that. Did you tell her I was in the shower? Did you tell her I would call her back?"

Merle was silent.

"She didn't even *ask* to speak to me, did she?" Dora said, her shower cap riding down onto her eyebrows.

"I answered the phone. That's probably why."

"Did you even think to ask her if she *wanted* to talk to me?"

"No. I'm sorry. I guess I should have."

So it's still the way it's always been, Dora thought. The now between father and daughter was just like the then. A closed club where the two of them could alternate as president and vice president according to their moods while shoveling leftover chores, like meal preparation and trips to the cleaner and making sure all the household ashtrays were emptied out, to recording secretary Dora. The only peculiar aspect to it was how it still managed to surprise her.

"Merle, I'll be out in ten minutes. Now, please give me some privacy and turn off the light on your way out." She pulled the shower curtain to the wall and sealed herself in.

Merle sat on the toilet watching the curtain, worry threatening to bring down the stoic face that had weathered any number of household upheavals. The worry was not for Dora, who wanted to shower in the dark and engage in the dangerous activity of shaving her legs like a blind woman, but for his daughter, who was nowhere near.

{CHAPTER 17}

Eilene sat across from Sonny reading *Testimony of Two Men* and wondered why in the world she had ever wanted children. And then she reminded herself that she had never really wanted children, they had just appeared and she had accepted them. She looked at the back of the book, where a picture of Taylor Caldwell filled the space, and noticed her simple strand of pearls and simple black dress and the simple hairstyle that was simply coiffed. There were rings on her fingers that didn't look like wedding rings and a watch on her arm that definitely didn't look like a Timex. An overall picture of an elegant New Yorker, with arms that were a little loose near the elbows, but who could fault the woman for not doing her proper exercises when she had all those books to write. An overall picture of a woman who was childless, Eilene would bet. How else did she manage to keep that simple demeanor and unharried look. Eilene went back to her reading, finished the last paragraph, licked her finger, and turned a page.

"How was your date?" she yelled, folding down the corner of the page and turning to her son so that they might have their morning chat and get it over with. She was on page 482 and Jonathan Ferrier and his lovely

Jenny, having a heart-to-heart inside a small grotto, had just been interupted by Harold, the lazy worthless brother. There was going to be a fight between those two, and Eilene could hardly wait to get to it.

Sonny was working on his second bowl of oatmeal, pouring on honey and sprinkling it with cinnamon and leaning over to spoon it into his mouth with optimum speed. His coffee cup was empty, as was the coffeepot on the stove, but Eilene was done making coffee for the day. Four cups were enough for anyone.

"It was okay!" He prided himself on remembering to speak loudly.

"Just okay?"

He looked at her and put down his spoon, as though putting down an eating utensil would eliminate an unnecessary distraction and help him keep his wits about him.

"You were out awfully late," she said.

"Ten o'clock ain't late. Not for a grown man. And I moved them paint buckets like you asked me to. And by the end of the day, I'll have them sawhorses moved and you can till up the ground for your tomatoes."

Eilene smiled at him, noticing he had taken to shaving every day instead of once a week. She supposed this was a sign he was serious about the girl. If there was one. And if there wasn't, he was doing a great job of pretending one really existed.

Eilene opened her mouth and yelled, "I wish you would ask her where she's gonna be dancin next. I'd love to go and watch," and then she smiled at him and tilted her head in order to study his reaction.

Sonny picked up his coffee cup and put it to his mouth before realizing it was empty. He set it beside his empty bowl. "It ain't your kind of dancin." His face flamed red all the way to his ears.

"What's that supposed to mean?"

"It's ballet and tap. Fancy-schmancy kind of dancin. It ain't country clog-dancin."

"Why, Sonny, ballet's wonderful. I love ballet. Where in the world did you get the idea I liked to clog?" Eilene lifted his bowl and carried it to the sink and then looked at the coffeepot. One more cup might keep him talking. "I saw *Romeo and Juliet* when I was a girl up in Atlanta, way before I met your father. Oh, I just love the ballet." She turned to him because he was tiptoeing out of her kitchen. "Where in the world are you going?" she yelled.

"I need my durn battery charger back." He pointed next door. "He's had it for over a week. How long does it take one man to charge a battery on a tractor, anyhow."

Eilene clapped her hands. "I know what I'll do. You go on over to Bruno's, and while you're gone, I'll check the newspaper and see if there's a ballet anywhere near, and the two of us can surprise her by showing up for it."

Sonny's face drained, and he put his hands to his pockets and glanced down to his shoes, and his generalized tortured expression was such that it pained Eilene, who had breast-fed this great big boy for almost three years (not because she wanted to but because he would pull at her shirt until she let him). She felt a rush of pity, and the sensation was similar to the way her breasts felt when her milk used to let down. "Go on, Sonny," she said quietly. "I've got the kitchen to clean. It was just a suggestion. A foolish one at that."

His look of relief hurt her even more and she turned to the sink and attacked it, filling one side with hot water and soap and the other with hot water and vinegar, dumping the dishes in the soap and watching clots of oatmeal float to the surface.

"There might be a ballet somewhere. I guess it won't hurt to look," he finally said, and Eilene was so startled she almost began to believe there really *was* a girlfriend. "I got to get my charger back," he said, walking out the door and down the steps, his large shape visible to Eilene, who waved her hand toward him and yelled out the kitchen window, "I'll be good and wait until the Fourth!" Sonny didn't acknowledge that he heard her, just kept walking across the yard, so lost in thought he failed to stop and admire his boat and its third coat of paint and its brand-new wooden trawl boards that hung from the steel booms like great flattened birds.

Eilene was finishing her chapter, disappointed there had not yet been a showdown between the tragic Ferrier brothers, when the phone rang. She sat back in the chair and stared at the wall where it was mounted next to Sonny's automated fan switches, the sound so uncommon to her morning routine that it took her a moment to realize what exactly the loud ringing was.

She was still talking when Sonny came and banged on the kitchen window and shouted at her, "You ain't gone believe this one!" while Eilene made shooing motions with her hand.

"No. You don't have to worry. Tell Merle I don't need any help with the tables. I've got these big boys, you know." A pause. "Oh, he can do it. He's always been able to lift stuff for me. Uh-huh. I just ask him is what I do, and he does it. I never hear a peep out of him. That's true. But a neck injury's bad on anyone. Old or young." Outside in the heat, Sonny was hopping from one foot to the next.

"No. You don't have to worry about the cost. We trade off with the slaughterhouse. It's our beef we'll be eating, and I wouldn't have it any other way. I know what our cows eat." A pause while she watched Sonny, who almost didn't seem like Sonny, he was so agitated. Eilene put her hand over the mouthpiece and looked at the kitchen window and hissed, "What in the world's the matter with you? This is long-distance. It's Flitter Brain."

Sonny pointed next door. "Ask Dora if Leah's up in Meridian."

"Why would I want to ask her that?" Eilene's hand was still over the mouthpiece of the old black phone.

"Just ask her and see."

Dora was rambling on and on about Singapore Slings, a drink made with vodka and cranberry juice and grenadine all blended together and topped with paper umbrellas. A drink that sounded absolutely ghastly. Eilene tried to imagine Sonny or Bruno holding one in their great big country hands and couldn't. It would be like putting party shoes on a pig. "Sounds complicated. You need to remember, I don't have one of them blender things." She held up a finger to Sonny, who was about to shout again. "Have you talked to Leah? Maybe she has one."

"Ain't you gonna ask her?" Sonny yelled through the window.

She covered the mouthpiece again. "Cain't you see I just did?" she hissed at Sonny. "Cain't you listen and pay attention for once in your life? Don't you know when somebody's tryin to be subtle?" He stood looking at her, and his mouth opened and closed as he tried to remember if he had heard the words, but couldn't recollect.

"No. Sonny was just telling me he found a tool he thought he'd lost." A pause. "Sonny, Dora says hello." He just stood in the sunlight shaking his head, bewildered by the game, puzzled over the conversation he had missed and the words he had not spoken. "He says hello to you, too. Now. About that blender thing. I'll save you a phone call, then. I mean, goodness, I live right next door. It's easy enough to walk over there and ask her my own self."

Eilene nodded. "Dear, we're game for it if you are." She rolled her eyes. "Okay, dear. Yes. I'll tell her how excited you are, and yes, I'll be sure and remind her about the green olives. Now, give Merle a hug and we'll see you soon."

She put the phone in its cradle. "Lord have mercy, that woman can talk on and on about the most nonsensical things. Now, what in the world are you talking about?"

"They ain't there. And the house is locked." Sonny held up the battery charger in one hand as proof of where he'd been, as though Eilene were suffering from short-term memory loss and needed a reminder of the reason he had gone in the first place. "I got this out of the barn, and I looked over and seen the Rambler was gone from out of the lean-to. Truck ain't there, either, and I went and tested the back door and it's locked. I didn't even see that cat nowhere. It's like they've up and moved."

"Stop being ridiculous."

"I ain't being ridiculous. There ain't nobody there."

"You'd like that, wouldn't you?" Eilene shouted, untying her apron and putting it over the back of her chair and walking to the door, lifting Bruno's spare key from the fishhook. It had been hanging there for almost seven years and Eilene had never used it, but then again, as far as her memory stretched, Bruno had never locked the door.

"Why'd you want to go and say something so hateful?" he asked her.

Because I know you, she thought as she stepped down the porch steps and into the yard. The day was hot, and she was halfway to Bruno's before she realized she had left her straw hat in her bedroom. She turned to go and retrieve it and bumped into Sonny, who was following a few steps behind her. "Get on back to the yard," she said, shooing at him like one would shoo a cow.

"You don't know what you might be walking into."

"Whatever it is, I don't need you with me."

He stood staring at her, his eyes going from her face to Bruno's house and back again.

"Go move them sawhorses like you promised you would. And drag that tiller out of the barn for me. I'm already late for setting the plants, and I don't plan on waiting one more day for it. Besides, I'm sure nothin's wrong. Maybe they went to town."

"In two vehicles? Are you crazy? That Rambler ain't been took out of the lean-to for over a year."

Eilene turned to him and pointed toward the spot where her tomatoes needed to be, and Sonny sauntered away, his hands in the pockets of his overalls.

Something was beginning to bother him. Something important had just happened, and he had recognized it as important when it happened, but now it was fading to nothingness, shifting clean away from him. By the time he got to the two sawhorses, loaded with paintbrushes that were stiff with dried paint and empty potato-chip bags and empty soft-drink bottles, he had totally forgotten that for a few minutes there he had used his regular speaking voice when addressing his mother, and even though her back was turned to him, she had understood every single word he had said.

Eilene knocked on the back door and peered through the glass between the ruffles of the curtains and saw a great black smear across the top of their refrigerator. She leaned closer to the glass and studied its shape. It looked like a man's hand, and she remembered the grandchild of one of her friends and how he smeared paint on paper with his fingers. It looked like that. She tested the doorknob and called out, "Leah?" The house was dark and there was no response and when she looked to the left, she saw a large suitcase opened up on the kitchen table, overspilling with clothes. All of them Leah's.

Walking around to the front of the house, she saw empty Fresca cans and a pack of playing cards on the front porch, next to the concrete planters holding ivy. She pulled open the screen door and tested the doorknob. Locked. "Bruno!" she called out once and then once more, and then with a shaking hand, she inserted the key into the lock and pushed open the door and stepped inside the living room.

The room seemed the same as it had always been. Magazines on the coffee table. Cushions arranged on the couch. The bookcase holding old *National Geographics* and farming periodicals, and bookends made out of horseshoes, and the framed picture of Dora and Merle Maxwell, Dora holding in her hand a drink decorated with a tiny American flag. Bruno's chair was in the corner next to the standing lamp, its shade peering over the top like a curious stranger. The vacuum cleaner was still in the center of the room. She walked into the kitchen and saw a coffee cup and a piece of uneaten toast on the counter, and she went over to the cup and saw that it was half full. She felt the side; it was still warm. She lifted the toast and saw a pale yellow center to it where a pat of butter had melted. There had not been a bite taken out of it, but the edges were picked off in one corner as though someone had played with the toast before refusing it. "I don't like plain toast, either," Eilene said, siding with her son and assuming the toast was his because she had never seen Leah eat much of anything. Black smears that matched the one on the refrigerator were on the white enamel sink and the stainless-steel faucets, and Eilene bent and sniffed. Grease. Car grease.

A chair was shoved to the side, and whoever was packing the suitcase was doing a sorry job of it. Stuff looked thrown in. Pink spongy hair rollers and tennis shoes. Dressy shirts and stiff jeans. Turning on the light in the kitchen made her feel better, and she left it on and headed down the dark hallway, flipping on the light switch as she went, illuminating the hall with its photos hanging on the wall. Pushing open the door to the bathroom, she saw the shower curtain pulled back and water dripping off the showerhead and a red enema bag with its white tube and nozzle hanging over the side of the tub. Leah's robe was thrown on the floor, and spots of blood were spattered all over the sink in drops the size of pennies and quarters and nickels, and a great deal of blood was on a washcloth wadded up next to the toothbrushes. "Good Lord," she said, backing out of the room and pulling the door to, her heartbeat accelerating to a level it was unaccustomed to.

The guest room was across the hall, and she pushed open the door and saw that someone had been sleeping there. Bruno, she assumed, since those were his clothes piled on top of the sewing machine. She lifted one corner of the soft quilt on the bed and saw how he hadn't pulled up the sheet but left it down near the foot and pulled the cover up over it, half making the bed the same way he had as a young boy. The window shade was rolled up, and light filled the small room, and the light seemed stark and cruel, like the light in an old country schoolroom in summertime, or a wooden church house in the middle of the week. The ceiling fan over the bed was running, and Bruno's talcum power was on the small round table against the wall, and since Bruno never went anywhere without it, she assumed he was the one out in the fields and that Leah had left in the old Rambler, minus her suitcase, which meant she had left in a hurry.

"Oh, dear," she said, a picture of their life forming in her head, and the picture was so sad and so loaded with details previously overlooked that she stood with a hand on her chest, afraid to go to the other bedroom for fear of some worse aspect of it waiting for her. But she did, stopping once to open the closet door at the end of the hall, seeing the space where the suitcase had been and Bruno's old suits and the projector screen and projector and the square boxes holding home movies and one or two board games and Leah's wedding dress sealed up in a white bag with a zipper running all the way from top to bottom, like a body bag.

Finally Eilene stood before their bedroom door and waited, tapping once and saying, "Leah?" and hearing nothing and then saying, "Bruno?" and being met by silence, hearing only the ticking of the kitchen clock, its sound carrying even that far. She pushed open the door and studied the room. She had never been slapped in her life, but she supposed if she had, it would have felt similar to what she felt as she looked at the room. The surface of the bed was smeared with God knows what, and pillows were shoved against the iron bed frame, and the pillows were covered with it, too, and something else that was brown like rust or old blood. Someone had begun to remove the sheets and then stopped, and one corner of the mattress showed. The coverlet seemed ruined, and when Eilene lifted it, she saw a bootprint, as if Bruno had stepped on it while it lay on the floor, where drops of blood formed a trail out the door. She leaned out and saw the trail led to the bathroom, and she looked again and put her hand to the door frame. She had never seen such a mess in her life, and as she looked across the room and through the windows, it seemed perverse to her that a breeze was blowing through the homemade curtains and that music was coming out of Sonny's radio and way over there inside the kitchen of her house, dishes were soaking in her sink.

Closing the door behind her, she stood in the hall and wondered what to do. It was the morning hour, the time to tend the cows, and the truck was gone and wouldn't be due back until around eleven o'clock. Walking toward the kitchen, she turned off the light and checked to make sure everything was as she had found it, and then she went to the front door and out onto the porch, taking care to lock the door behind her. If Leah had been in Meridian, Dora would have mentioned it. A woman as simpleminded as that wouldn't think to hold back information or play games about it. So, no. Leah wasn't there, which meant she was somewhere close by. Eilene looked at the front yard, at its mausoleum stillness, and wondered where Bruno could be. As she walked around the side of the house, she saw the open doors to the barn and the fresh tire tracks, indicating a truck had backed up and then pulled out toward the field. Rain had fallen during the night, so the tracks were fresh morning tracks. Someone was tending the cows. And someone inside the early morning hours had made coffee and drunk a little of it before leaving, and should a stranger be the one responsible for the chaos inside the bedroom, Eilene didn't figure he would've taken the time to put a pat of butter on a piece of toasted bread. Feeling a little bit better, Eilene decided to wait until noon before she did anything. She wasn't sure what she would do even then, but if Leah or Bruno wasn't back, some action on her part would be required, and she would cross that bridge when she came to it. Eilene watched as Sonny squatted to sand a portion of his boat and noticed how fat and white his arms were. Her simple son who had no desire to be anything other than simple. Suddenly he seemed less a burden than he had thirty minutes earlier.

→←

Willem could see her from where he sat leaning against a wall. The woman hadn't been heading in his direction after all, for at the last moment, she had veered off toward the artesian pool and, once there, had pulled off her boots and set them beside her and taken off her socks and stuck them down inside the boots. She had a piece of paper in her shirt pocket, and she pulled it out and removed the pencil that was stuck behind her ear and began to write. Willem reached for an old shovel and propped it against the wall of greening vines and watched her, and then he leaned back against a wall and put a hand to his chest and rubbed in circular motions, for the thing was happening again. He had no idea what it was or what caused it, but it was there regardless, compressing his heart until he felt like it would surely explode. He put a finger to his pulse and tried to count, but once he reached 180, he removed his finger and leaned against the wall, the sound of rushing blood resonating against his eardrums. It seemed logical in one sense that it would be happening here. It all began here. Years ago, while he slept in that rope bed over there and the ground shifted and the house fell. So yes, he supposed it was only fitting that here was where he would suffer the most. All those other times it had happened, the logic had been missing. What reason did he have to fear a supermarket or his office building? Or the National Bank? Or a shoe store?

He looked to the canted ceiling and became afraid of it. What if it had been waiting all this time to finish the job? Maybe because it hadn't killed him the first time, it was anxious to get done with a task that was long overdue. Willem stared at the crown beam for so long that it became hallucinatory and overtly menacing and seemed to be sliding down closer to him, and he slouched down away from it and rubbed his heart and saw the ring of dots around his vision and how they were breaking apart and patches of nothingness were taking their place. He would faint soon. Or he would scream. Either one could happen, because both of those things had happened before. He just didn't know what to do about it. His head felt heavy as an anvil, and he peered to the side and noticed his surroundings and how everything seemed to be moving with his pulse, and he began to think he was being ferried across the floor by the beating of his heart. A thought similar to the one he had had way back in Texas when he imagined the whole room could see him vibrating against a red Naugahyde booth. Taking a deep breath, he reached out a hand and drew a line in the dust with his finger and set the heel of his boot on it and watched. It seemed he was staying put. It seemed everything he was feeling was an exaggeration, some type of joke his brain liked to play on him. He felt his pulse again and stopped counting at two hundred. He watched the line in the dust for a long while, until all the dots were done being connected and there was more gray in his vision than walls and fireplace and dirt, and right at the moment he felt his body giving way to a faint, he heard the splash of water and looked out toward the pool and saw the woman bending over it, bathing herself. Her shirt was off, and she was rubbing water on a bruised arm and shoulder, and her underwear was white against her chest, and the sight of her brassiere embarrassed Willem, who was old enough to have seen his share but looked away from it regardless. He looked at her pants instead, and how she was up on her knees as though kneeling in prayer. She finally put her shirt back on and pushed her way against the cliff wall and leaned back her head and took a cigarette from her shirt pocket and lit it, cupping her hand around the match. Just watching her helped slow his heart, and he felt the large thing begin to move away from him, and the noise of rushing blood begin to soften until he could hear the birds sing again as they floated down from the tops of the trees.

He thought perhaps if he moved closer to the wall of vines, he would feel a little more free and less like being inside a grave, so he scooted over to the doorway and it helped a little, and the last of the gray dots went away, and he watched the blue pieces of sky through the honeysuckle leaves and thought how like being underwater it all seemed. Up there was the sky, and should he rest on his back, it would seem like he was in an underwater cave, submerged completely but somehow able to breathe, weightless and calm, his movements not his own but orchestrated by the currents, all of them gentle. Not a bad way to die. He was thinking about all this and missed seeing the woman stand and leave the area. All he knew was that one minute he was pretending he was a fish, and the next minute he was back in the here and now and looking toward the pool, and she was gone. He glanced through the trees, but there was no sign of her. It was as though she had never been, and he began to question his sanity and wonder if he had finally crossed over to a verifiable mental illness. One where music came out of lamps and colors took form and walked across the room. One that might be treated with medicine, and wouldn't that be a sweet relief? Crawling out into the light, he blinked and tried to reintroduce his back to its standing position. His legs were asleep, and as he walked toward the water, it seemed small knives were stabbing him all over his calves.

No. Whatever was wrong with him was still wrong, because she had not been an illusion or some type of enchantment offering him temporary relief. She was real, all right. A Coke bottle was floating in the pool, and the letter she had been writing was rolled into the mouth of it as proof she had been there, just a portion of white sticking out over the green.

He squatted and reached for it, the bottle floating away from his touch before meeting its own wave and floating back to him. When he unrolled it and read, he was struck by the same feeling he'd had when he saw her in her underwear. The writing was just so female, so neat and foreign to him. Something he had no business looking at.

"Silence" was the title given it, and next to the title the name of Thomas Hood had been written, and a question mark was next to his name, and underneath the name, these words:

There is a silence where hath been no sound,
There is a silence where no sound may be,
In the cold grave—under the deep, deep sea,
Or in wide desert where no life is found,
Which hath been mute and still must sleep profound;
No voice is hushed—no life treads silently,
But clouds and cloudy shadows wander free . . .

That was the end of it, but below the last line she had made a notation: "My apologies to you, Mr. Hood, for not remembering the rest of it. Please believe me when I tell you how lovely I thought it was . . . Yours, Leah.

Willem sat back on his heels and thought about it and tried to figure out what it all meant and why she had written such strange words and how those words had mirrored what he had been feeling while he studied the sky through the overhanging vines. And finally he rolled the note back up and slid it into the bottle and set it adrift across the pool, where it bobbed once or twice and then canted to the side and was still. The sun flashed against a white stone near the lip of the pool, and he stuck his hand in the water and pulled out a tooth, and it was like touching a part of his body that logic said would be forever lost. A torn-off arm or a set of missing toes suddenly recovered after fifty-two years. He ran his tongue around his mouth and felt where the teeth had compensated for their missing brother and leaned together to fill in the gap. It was his tooth and someone had found it, or rain had washed it into the pool. He placed it back where he had found it and stood up, his back cracking from age. The smell of her cigarette was still in the air, so she was real, all right, and while he walked back across the weedy plat, he could hear the whine of an old engine and the sound of shifting gears, and he stopped in his tracks and listened to it the way one might listen to a song or a hymn, until it had faded completely and all he could hear was the sound of the birds, and then he walked on.

{CHAPTER 18}

Bruno had made his own bed, literally, and was lying on it. *Mother would be pleased,* he thought as he smoked and watched his exhalations hang suspended inside the small airless room. After a moment the smoke would begin to fall across his duffel bag and his shirt and shoes and the old console television in the corner. He watched until all had settled, and then he exhaled again and new patterns appeared. It was almost hypnotic, the designs he was seeing. A baseball glove in the corner. A gun near the top of his shoes. Aware of his overindulgence and more than a little embarrassed by it, he rolled to his side and ground out his cigarette and pushed himself up until he was sitting by the side of the bed staring at the rubber-backed curtains that were pulled against the light. He could hear them out in the parking lot, where they'd been since six o'clock in the morning. Those two kids of hers who apparently fell asleep talking and rose doing the same. Once around mid-morning he had heard Alyce say, "I'm not gonna tell you again to leave that cat alone." There were several things she didn't intend to tell them again. She didn't intend to tell them about the cat again. Or playing too near the road. Or to quit knocking on the motel doors where guests were trying to sleep.

Perhaps "guests" was the wrong word, since that word by its very definition seemed to imply a crowd. There were only two people staying at the place, as far as Bruno could tell. The old one down in room six, and himself, and for only two people, there had been a flurry of activity. Around six A.M. Bruno heard a motel room door open and then the noise of a truck engine kicking over and then the noise of a truck leaving. Shortly thereafter, another car pulled up and another car door opened and then shut and a conversation was held in Spanish. The Hispanic cleaning woman saying farewell to her ride, Bruno guessed. After that he heard Alyce's voice and leaned into the curtains and saw her standing and talking to someone next to the old Coke box. He couldn't see who she was talking to, since that person was in a shadow, but he saw Alyce and how dressed up she was, with wavy hair and a neat shirt tucked into her jeans. She began pointing here and there across the property and pulled out a notepad and wrote on it before sticking it in her rear pocket. Presently the two of them went into the storage room, where their voices carried through the walls and sounded like mutterings from the bottom of an open pit mine. They came out dragging a large cardboard box of Peabody's Quick Clean, and Alyce sliced through the top with a box cutter and pulled open the flaps and lifted out gallon cans and set them on the concrete. Bruno ducked away from the window and went to his bed again. Voices rose and fell. Female voices and the voices of children bickering. And then he heard the sound of the old man's truck returning and the noise of shoes crunching across the parking lot. A tall shadow ranged across the front of Bruno's window, and after a short period of time, the shadow was back again, carrying something the size and shape of a garden hoe. Bruno shook his head and said, "Shit, what is this, a damn class reunion?" All the activity seemed harried and frenetic, not because it was either of those things, but because Bruno was listening from behind the thick rubber curtains, where all he saw were low-definition shapes and blurred movements, which added an unmerited mysterious element to the day-to-day running of the motel.

"What in the world am I doing?" he asked himself, running a hand over his cheeks. He needed to shave, but he had forgotten his razor, which he guessed was a good thing, since having access to a razor would mean looking at his reflection. He looked like he'd been run over by a truck and didn't care to be reminded of it. Touching his nose, he guessed it was broken for sure, but at least he could open his left eye now. That last tour in Vietnam, he had spent hours worrying about whether or not Leah was able to take care of herself. Wasted hours spent on a wasted worry, he now realized.

He looked at his duffel bag. Underwear was something else he had forgotten. Wondering exactly what he had managed to pack, he went to it and spread it open, fanning at the air with his hand, for the smoke was thick. Two pairs of pants. Two shirts. A can of shaving cream. Aftershave he didn't need because he didn't have a razor. Socks, thank God. A carton of cigarettes that would last little more than two days at the rate he was going. He looked over at the ashtray and where it spilled onto the old scarred table with its giant green pear-shaped lamp.

The entire room was done in cast-off furniture, and Bruno felt as though he were standing in the prop room of a play featuring Alyce Benson's life. There was the old wooden console TV in the corner, its rabbit-ear antennae doctored up with aluminum foil; he guessed at some point in their marriage, the couple had purchased a newer set. The ugly green lamp with its towering beige shade meant Alyce had bought herself a newer one, maybe one of those modern swag lamps for her living room, and banished the huge green one to room four of the Rocky Creek Inn, where it dominated a table that was much too small for it. The chenille bedspread, torn along its hem, was another clue to her life. The small Formica table cracked across its top, yet another. It was almost too pitiful to endure, and Bruno went to the door and opened it and stood there looking out over the area where the two boys were trudging across the lot. One was carrying a piece of metal, and the other one was carrying a piece of pale carved wood, and they were fighting over who would carry what, and the older one seemed to be winning. Bruno lifted the chair out of the room and put it on the concrete pathway and watched them, leaving the door of his room open to air out.

He had always hated die-hard smokers, old and young alike, people earmarked by yellowing fingernails and pinched lips who did nothing but smoke, and now it seemed he had become one. He moved his head and tried to get some air to his skin, for the sun was hot and he was directly in it and the metal portions of his brace were heating up like an oven. "I guess I could fry an egg on my neck, should I want one," he said, and as soon as he was done speaking, a woman stuck her small square head out of the room next to him and stared at him through her tiny close-set eyes. He thought immediately of a turtle, a thought that was soon validated, for just as quickly as her head had been stuck out, she pulled it back inside. He could hear the sounds of metal knocking against metal, and he wondered what they were. He found out a few minutes later when the woman pulled a huge metal cleaning cart out of the room and positioned it on the sidewalk.

"Cleen sheeets?" she said, and he looked at her and wondered if he had ever seen such an unpleasant-looking woman and didn't think he had. She was wearing a white dress that wouldn't button properly, and oval vistas of skin shown around each button, and her white hose were rolled down to the tops of her white shoes. There was hair growing on her legs, and he looked away from it.

She pointed at his room and lifted a folded white sheet and said again, "Sheeets?"

He was leaving shortly, so he supposed the next guest, should there be one, would prefer clean sheets instead of smoky ones; besides, he had bled during the night on his pillowcase, so he nodded, and she pulled her cart and came and stood next to him, and he wondered what in the hell she wanted now until he realized that he was sitting in a chair that was blocking her way. He stood up and lifted the chair and walked with it out to the parking lot to let her pass. He was standing this way when Alyce came out of the office and stood with her hands on her hips and looked back and forth across the lot.

"You seen the boys?" she asked him.

"Down thataway." He looked toward the road.

She walked across the parking lot in her tennis shoes and parted the spindly limbs of the small sweetleaf, and Bruno heard her say, "What did I tell you boys?"

"But Mom."

"There's log trucks that pass all day long. Now, get up out of there right this minute."

"Yes, ma'am," one of them said.

"There's a spot underneath the oak, and if that ain't good enough for you, you can go inside and lay on your bed and read a book. I'm not telling you again."

Bruno shook his head. One more thing she wasn't going to tell them again. He saw their blond hair, slicked down by sweat, as they moved toward her, and they were so low in the ditch it seemed two heads were rolling across the grass. The two of them came to the place where the handholds were and climbed out of the ditch and stood before her, the tools, or whatever it was they had carried with them, still in their hands.

"If I catch you out there again, I'll turn you over my knee."

She was standing underneath the shade of the tree, and the breeze was blowing her T-shirt away from her. Bruno noticed she had changed out of the neat shirt and dark jeans to faded, comfortable articles of clothing, and her wavy hair was pulled back and fastened behind her head.

Ben said, "I told you Mama would get us," and Joe said, "You wanted to, too, so hush."

The cleaning woman was inside his room ripping sheets off the bed and banging the ashtray against a bigger trash can that was metal, and when Bruno glanced at her, she demonstrated her displeasure with his smoking habit by coughing into her hand and fanning at the haze. *Hell, what does she think an ashtray means?* he wondered. *If she wants folks not to smoke, she ought to go and leave off them little glass saucers.* He shrugged at her, which apparently struck a nerve, for she pointed at him and yelled, "*¡Vete a la chingada, señor!*"

"Dolores, speak English to our guests. I'm not gonna tell you again."

"Aughh!" the woman said with a snarl, waving her hand at the two of them.

Alyce said, "I'm sorry about that. I told her not to disturb you. She don't take well to receiving orders."

"Is she always so sweet?" Bruno said.

"Oh, today she's in a good mood 'cause her daughter's got herself a new boyfriend."

"You're kidding me. This is how she acts when she's happy?"

They both watched her scrub at the small sink like there was no tomorrow, scattering powdered Ajax in the air.

"You shoulda seen her the week she found out where her daughter *really* worked."

Bruno shook his head. He knew too much already and didn't want to know anything more.

Alyce cleared her throat, and he looked at her. There was a blush of apprehension to her posture, a certain tension in her hips and a slight stress to her arms, which were folded across her stomach. He thought maybe she thought he was offended by the woman cleaning his room.

"She asked me if I wanted clean sheets, and I said okay," Bruno said.

Jesus, he was sweating, and Alyce was sweating, too, in spite of the breeze that was finally beginning to blow. Bruno was very aware that he was standing in the parking lot holding a piece of furniture in his hands, and this was what was bothering him the most, he didn't know how to get rid of the stupid chair.

Alyce said, "It seems it's broke."

"What's broke?"

"Your nose."

"I guess it is at that."

"Are you goin to a doctor about it?"

"I've had a broke nose before. It'll heal, I reckon."

"Okay, then," she said, and the two of them stood there, timid with each other for reasons neither fully understood but they were aware of nonetheless. Bruno thought about the concept of conversation, how hard it was to say what one really wanted to say, how even if he knew what the words might be, he'd still be prone not to say them. The tension of bridled thoughts and unanswered questions was almost unbearable.

"We got a family comin in around two. From over in Texas. Their granny died."

"So you need the room?"

"No. I was just tellin you there'll be others coming."

"That don't seem so odd, seein how this is a motel," he said.

"It's a little odd, seein how there's never nobody here," she said. "Mr. Fremont's been here over a week, and he don't seem to be wantin to leave anytime soon. Not that I want him to." She shook her head as though a fly were buzzing her, and held out her hands. "Jeepers. I'm standin here like I got nothin else better to do." She looked at him and then looked away. "I just wanted to see if you needed anything, or if there was anything I could do for you."

"Can I use the office phone?"

"Sure. There's my desk phone, and a pay phone on the wall if you want to make any long-distance calls."

"It'll be a local one."

"Okay, then."

Irritation seemed to wash over her, and she frowned and turned from him.

"Alyce?" Bruno said.

She turned to him and waited, her hands down by her sides, a look of mystification on her face.

"This ain't your fault. You've done nothing wrong."

She waited for a moment, and when she spoke, she refused to look at his face, choosing the plants in the old terra-cotta planters instead. "It sure feels like I have." And then she walked over to her two boys, who were squatted in the dirt, digging at something underneath the shells.

After stalling as long as possible, Bruno walked toward the small office, fully intending to call home and make amends. The olive-green truck pulled up, and the old man got out and made his way up the sidewalk with his head down, holding the key with its red tag in his hand as though all his energy were located there. If Bruno had not stepped aside, the man would have run into him; as it was, Bruno ended up doing an embarrassing foot dance in avoidance and watched as the man veered to the right and caught hold of the Coke box and fed it some coins and then lifted out a drink and all but drained it in one swallow. The old man caught Bruno's eye as he walked on toward the office, and he was left with the uncomfortable sensation that he was being stared at. Once inside the office, he forgot about the man, noticing the phone across the room that seemed as inviting as a guillotine.

Ben was sitting in a corner coloring. His short legs hung over the sides of the small red wagon as he worked with quiet determination, a jumbo green crayon in his hand. It was a picture book of Mickey Mouse and Pluto the dog, and everything on the page was the color of field grass in spring, even the eyes of the dog and the ears on the mouse. The child hadn't even raised his head when Bruno came into the room, he was that intent on coloring.

He went to the the pay phone and fished coins out of his pocket and stood staring down at them, wondering if the phone would give change for his quarters. She had said he could use the desk phone, since the call was local, but that seemed repugnant to him. Like using Alyce's personal toothbrush before kissing Leah good night, or some type of foolishness like that.

The women were in the back room, talking about paint colors and how much it would take to paint the cinder bricks. Alyce said we got to figure them bricks will soak up a goodly bunch of it, and the Hispanic woman said *sí* and went into her broken English about the daughter's boyfriend being good with paint. Alyce said, I ain't got a lotta money to pay him. You better make that clear, and again the woman said *sí*.

He lifted the receiver and dialed the number and heard it ringing and ringing and ringing, and though he was miles away, he saw the phone where it sat on its table in the living room and was struck by a curious type of cognizance, an awareness, that Leah was standing beside it, staring down at it and refusing to give in. The thought infuriated him, and he slammed the receiver down in its metal cradle, and the boy looked up from his coloring book. Bruno tried to smile at him, but the child frowned and fear crossed his face. "Wrong number," Bruno said for no other reason than an attempt to reassure the child. The boy gathered his book to his chest and climbed out of the wagon and trotted past him and through to the back, where Bruno watched Alyce open her arms to him and kiss him on the face.

A car horn honked, and Bruno looked out the window and saw that a dusty black station wagon had pulled up. All the doors opened, and family members climbed out with their drink bottles and bags of crackers and loose pillows and other items of travel. Bruno noted they were all obese and unkempt; the father had slicked-over hair that curled in the back, and he was wearing a shirt that was too small for him; the mother looked just as bad as she pulled at the bottom of her shirt in an effort to hide her large stomach.

Alyce had said there would be travelers from Texas, and before he ended up hog-tied and playing the part of motel doorman, Bruno walked out of the office toward his car. Cranking the Rambler and backing across the lot, Bruno saw members of the family piled up inside the small office. The teenage children sitting in a sullen slump on the small chairs, the mother patting at her face with a Kleenex. The father was out near the car, removing luggage from the back of it and stacking suitcases on the concrete walkway in front of rooms two and three. Swinging the car onto the main road, Bruno shifted gears and happened to look back toward the building and saw the old man standing in the weeds alongside the back of the motel, peering around the front of it as though hiding from the law. Bruno wondered if he had ever seen such a crazy circus in his life and, after moments of consideration, realized he hadn't.

He drove around the town square and saw the foldaway bleachers set up next to Main Street and children and their parents sitting on them, some holding red balloons and some holding small American flags. Band members from the local school were wandering around in their hot red coats with their hats pushed back on their heads, drinking sodas and yelling at one another. Bruno saw a tuba disappearing down an alleyway and a lone trombone lying on a park bench while old uniform-clad veterans milled around the one or two jeeps on loan from Camp Shelby, south of Hattiesburg. The parade would be at three, and Bruno wanted no part of any memorial celebration related to any war. He drove down LeClede Avenue to where it intersected with School Street and drove on past the empty five-and-dime and hardware stores and the empty barbershop and the closed bank with its flag hanging motionless off the pole. He drove two more blocks and found the place he wanted, Smokey's Bar and Grill, and parked the car and went inside. The interior was cool and dim and slightly green-hued because of sheet tinting on the large window. Just what he needed. The only drawback was the jukebox in the corner, playing some of the new music that all the teenagers seemed to love, but even that was not too bad, since the volume was low enough to be tolerated. Bruno sat at the burnished bar and ordered up a beer.

"Bruno Till, as I live and breathe."

Bruno recognized the red hair and freckles as belonging to Tom Waite and said hello to him. The two had gone through all their school years together, and Bruno had always liked him well enough. Of all the people he'd had to face after his injury, Tom was the only one who continued to treat him the way he had always treated him, and it was a kindness Bruno would never forget.

"What the hell kind a wreck happened to your face?" Tom asked, peering at his ruined nose and blackened eyes. He didn't bother looking at the brace. The whole town knew about the brace.

"Livestock accident."

"A horse kick you?"

"No. Cow. I was workin with the dehorner, and she decided she wanted to keep that little malformed horn. Head-butted me," Bruno said, and then glanced around. "This your place now?" he asked, and the man leaned over the bar and worked a toothpick back and forth across his lips without once putting a finger to it.

"Been mine for three years now."

"I guess I don't get out much."

"Seems like." Tom slapped him on the shoulder, and Bruno nodded and grinned and glanced around. He saw a couple sitting back in the darkened corner, but that was it. A slow day by anyone's standard. "Business always this good?" Bruno asked.

"Hell. You ought to seen it this mornin. Folks has left now for the parade. Come five o'clock, you ain't got enough money to buy yourself a seat."

"You got anything to eat?"

"Whatcha need?"

"How about a barbecue sandwich?"

Tom nodded and yelled over his shoulder, and a young pimply boy in a white soda hat popped up behind a window near a hanging metal wheel. "Fix us up two them big boys," Tom said to him, and the boy wrote it out on a little pad and attached it to one of the metal clips and spun it around as though it were a top, then disappeared to work on the sandwiches. "He's new here. You have to excuse him. Thinks the Hobart meat slicer is a damn toy. Thinks the industrial Raetone fridge is one, too. Not to mention that there order wheel."

"I guess it's his first job," Bruno said.

"Sure is."

"I remember my first job."

"Oh yeah?"

"Workin my ass off for my old man and not making diddly-squat. If Mama hadn't pitied me, I never would a had money for a football game."

"Hell. Those were the days, Bruno." Tom leaned on his hand. "You had him, though."

"Had who?"

"Your old man."

"Yeah, I sure did at that."

"That's more than some of these doofuses has." He leaned his head toward the boy in the back, who was using a large knife to hack at the smoked pork.

"How's your folks gettin along?" Bruno asked.

"Oh, him and Mama's well enough. Still runnin that grocery store on Hardy Street over in Hattiesburg. Lovin ever minute of it, too. Even though a brand new Piggly Wiggly done moved in across the street. I'll wager the parents'll be out of business in less than a year."

"Shit, the whole world's goin to crap," Bruno said, drinking the last of the beer. He tapped the side of the glass. "Am I good for a tab?" he asked.

"Better than my brother, who's turned to a bum, by the way. Here, hang on." Tom drew it up and handed it to Bruno, who drank half in one swallow, as though he'd never had a beer in his life. He had no idea why he was so thirsty all of a sudden.

Tom said, "Speakin of brothers, how's yours?"

"Speakin of bums, you mean."

"Hey, I'm the owner of this place. I cain't afford to be rude."

"Sonny's the same. Got big plans for his shrimping business."

"Where the hell's he gonna find shrimp in Purvis, Mississippi?"

"He ain't thought that far yet. Tom, you ought to see the mess he's made of Mama's backyard."

A bell *ding-ding-ding-ding*ed, and Tom turned abruptly and shouted, "Christ Almighty, boy. I'm standin right here in front of you. Cain't you just say the order's up?"

The boy said, "But you got a bell here," and pointed to it as proof.

"So?"

"So, I thought I'd use it is all."

"Well, now that you've banged the living stew out of it, you think you got it outta your system for a while?"

"Yes, sir," the boy said in a muted voice as he ducked his head.

"I tell you what, Bruno. You think about who's gone be runnin the world in another twenty or so years, and it makes you want to pull out the Colt and put a bullet in your brain."

Bruno agreed but kept quiet about it. An olive-green truck drove by, traveling slower than a truck had a right to, and Bruno saw who was driving it and thought to himself, *I'll be go to hell.* The unwelcome sight brought to mind one of his main reasons for hating small towns. He bit into his sandwich and wiped at his chin with his napkin, nodding his head toward Tom, who was waiting and watching for his reaction. "Hell, this is good."

"My granddaddy's sauce recipe."

"You ought to bottle it and make yourself some money."

"Hell, Bruno. That might involve work," but Tom grinned at him and leaned on the bar. "By the way, he was in here last week," he said.

"Who was?"

"That brother of yours. Had himself a girl on his arm. Sat right over there by the jukebox and played the same song about fifty million times and didn't spend but five dollars the whole evening."

"Sonny was in here?"

"Sure was."

"What song'd he play?"

"I don't know. Some Elvis song."

"I can't believe he had a girl with him."

"I ain't lyin to you."

"I ain't accusin you of it. I just can't picture it, though."

The male half of the couple in the back stood up and made his way to the jukebox and put in his coins and punched some buttons, and a man in a wailing voice sang, "What's goin on? What's goin on?"

"I hate today's music," Tom said. "Nothin but noise. I went and turned down the volume on the thing, and it keeps the couples huddled over there in the corner, straining their ears to listen."

Bruno was silent as he went about the business of finishing his sandwich. He thought perhaps he might find that song again and press the proper buttons so that it would be playing when he made the dreaded phone call to Leah. A person walked across the front of the grill, past the wide window with its blue neon beer light up in the corner, and the bell over the door jingled and the old man came inside and stood there, his hat in his hands, looking around.

"Afternoon, Willem," Tom said, and the man moved with a start and shambled over to the bar and sat, putting the hat down beside him. Bruno saw that his old hands were shaking, and so did Tom, who reached over to him and shook one of them, steadying it with his other hand the way people do when they turn considerate of each other. "I thought the parade had run you out of town," Tom said, already drawing the beer and sliding it toward him. Apparently that one had a tab, too, for there was no exchange of monies.

"A good afternoon to you, Mr. Waite. I clean forgot it was Memorial Day," Willem said, bending to his beer and sucking the foam off the top and refusing to use his hands, which were still shaking. It was the damnedest thing Bruno had ever seen.

"I guess you want one of them big boys."

"If it's as good as yesterday's."

"It will be." Tom turned to the window and put his hand over the bell and motioned for the boy, who came still holding the large industrial knife in his hand. "One more big boy," he said. "And throw some of them french fries in the deep fryer."

"But I ain't learned it yet," the boy said.

"Learned what?"

"That fryer thing."

"Hell, do you know how to dump a bag and press that red button over there?" Tom pointed to the stainless-steel well with its large red and green button and its wire baskets hoisted up on a hook.

"Yessir."

"Just dump them in and press the button and when they're done a buzzer goes off. Easy as pie. You don't even have to watch over them. It's called modern ingenuity."

The boy's face was a study of consternation. He went to the freezer and took out the clear bag holding iced portions of potatoes. Tearing at one corner with his teeth, he stood with his rear end back as far as he was able to get it and leaned forward and shook the fries into the wire baskets that slid by their own weight down into the hot grease. It sounded like firecrackers were going off inside the grill.

"Tom, how long's that kid been workin here?" Bruno wanted to know.

"He's my sister's kid. It ain't but his second day."

"I hope he's smart in school, 'cause I don't see him making great strides in the food industry."

"Honest to God, I have to agree with you." Tom turned to the old man, who was sitting quietly, drinking his beer. "Willem, you met my buddy Bruno Till?" Tom asked, and Bruno blushed. Hell, they had just done a little foot dance out near a Coke box not thirty minutes earlier, so of course they had met. But to acknowledge it would let loose the information that Bruno had worn out his welcome at home and was living instead in some fleabag motel, and this was not news he wanted spread.

"He was on the losing end of a fight with a cow," Tom offered as explanation for Bruno's face. "Willem's from out west—"

The man stood to his feet and stretched out his hand. "Willem Fremont. And no, I don't believe we've met." Bruno, who knew it was a lie, appreciated it regardless and took the man's hand and shook it, finding the man's grip strong for someone who appeared so ancient. There was a haunted, pained look to his eyes. A look of constant alarm.

"You been in town long?" Bruno asked quietly.

"About two weeks."

"You on business here?"

"Sort of. More of a retirement trip."

"Willem here's stayin down at Alyce's place," Tom offered.

"Alyce?" Bruno said, wondering how far to play his hand.

"Alyce Benson. Joe Benson's wife."

"Oh," Bruno said, done with playacting. It was too hard to do, and tapped into a nerve he supposed was hardwired to his conscience. He felt guilty for pretending and, like most country men, was too unfamiliar with its precepts to carry it out much further.

"The Rocky Creek Inn," Willem said. "A nice enough place."

"So I've heard," Bruno said, telling himself that this was positively the last time he was going to hedge on the truth.

Tom was looking at the two of them as though he were a damn matchmaker, twirling his toothpick across his lips and grinning. It was a role he had brokered as far back as high school. Always making sure no one was left out. Being kindhearted enough to include kids nobody else wanted around. Bruno looked to the menu wall and wondered if Tom had pitied him back then, if this might be the reason he spent so much time in the back of Bruno's pickup truck raising hell all over the county. *Well, at least no one has mentioned the neck brace or the business in Vietnam,* Bruno thought, thankful for God's small mercies.

"Bruno here took a nasty turn in Vietnam," Tom said, and Bruno hunkered down over his beer.

"You don't say," the old man said.

"He's a hometown hero. Got wrote up in the *Stars and Stripes*," Tom said, smiling, unaware of Bruno's discomfort. The old man seemed aware of it, though, and looked away from him toward the small television set hanging in one corner over the bar. "I never had the privilege of serving," Willem said, and his eyes seemed somewhere far away from Purvis. "But I certainly admire those who did."

"How about another beer?" Bruno said, tapping his fingers on the bar.

"What do you think of that?" Tom said.

"What?"

"That there television mounted on the wall."

"Damn, Tom. Almost looks like a real bar now."

Picking up a remote control, Tom pointed it toward the set, and the screen showed a parade and male and female commentators holding microphones decorated with ribbons. "I thought customers might like to keep up with current events."

The parade was in New York City, and there were bagpipes and flag corps. Tom pressed another button, and Walter Cronkite was talking over some old footage of soldiers, harassed by protestors throwing eggs and rubbish, as they walked down a boarding ladder shoved up to a jet. Cabbage and potatoes were scattered across the tarmac. One of the soldiers had his arm up, shielding his face.

"Hell, I guess you seen enough of that," Tom said. He flicked off the television.

"Yep. I seen enough of that," Bruno said, pushing away from the bar.

"Tom. That was a helluva sandwich." He opened his wallet and slid out some bills and put them on the counter.

"You still want to keep a tab goin?" Tom asked.

"Let me call home and see what the wife's got planned," Bruno said, motioning to the phone and walking toward it, noticing that the female half of the couple was studying his neck brace. She looked away when he caught her eye.

"Your stool's here whenever," Tom said, spitting the toothpick into an ashtray and turning to Willem Fremont, who was still staring at the television set hanging in the corner, a look of intense thought on his face.

{CHAPTER 19}

He said he was not calling to upset her but to tell her he was sorry for behaving unseemly, and not only that, he thought she had a right to know where he was and that he was okay.

"Why'd you leave? That's all I want to know."

He was silent, and Leah stood waiting to hear his reason, already having mentally listed the possibilities and rejected them one by one. Fresh sheets were in her arms, and she was working on setting the place back in order. He said something about needing time to cool off and think and that he didn't want to do anything else to hurt her.

She heard only part of it and said, "*You* need time to cool off?"

He said yes, he needed time to cool off and think.

"About what?"

He was silent.

"Oh, I see. *You* need time to cool off because it made you so damn mad to rape me."

He said that he hadn't raped her and she damn well knew it.

"Oh yeah? It looks like somebody castrated a cow in our bedroom."

He said that she was a country girl and ought to know by now that cows were the ones with teats and bulls were the ones with balls and you milked one and castrated the other.

"So now you're making fun of me."

He said he wasn't making fun of her. That he understood her meaning and took it for what it was. Just one more of her mixed-up metaphors.

"I'm not talking about a metaphor here, Bruno. I'm talking about the two of us."

He said she was too mixing her metaphors, because she had just compared what happened between the two of them to a castration, and if this was the case, he was the bull who got mutilated, so on the other hand, he guessed her metaphor was right on, since she had been hacking at his balls from the day they met—

"Jesus. Is that what you really think?"

He paused and then said no, that was not what he really thought, but he was tired of fighting with her.

"That's funny, because I'm tired of the silence. There's been nothing but silence until yesterday, when I decided to open my mouth and demand some answers, and then what'd you do? You did that horrible thing to me—"

He said that by the time they were in the middle of it, those didn't sound like cries of regret he was hearing.

"Well, if they were cries of pleasure, you sure seem prone to run from them. You're the one who left, after all. I'm the one standing in the damn living room."

He said this was what he meant about making him feel off balance and that she had a way of turning what he had hoped would be a pleasant conversation into something he couldn't beat his way through with a sledgehammer.

"I wasn't aware that you were looking for pleasantries."

He said it wasn't pleasantries he was looking for.

"Well, what *are* you looking for? A pat on the back from me?"

He said no, he wasn't looking for that, that all he wanted to do was call and see if she was okay.

"No, that's not what you said. You said that at the end. But what you said *before* that was that you needed time to think and cool off, and it just seems to me if *anybody* needed time to cool off, it would be me. I don't guess you care about that, though."

She walked over to the table and threw down the bed linens and pulled out a chair and sat and reached for her cigarettes and lit one as she stared out her large kitchen window.

He said he had always cared about her and she damn well knew it.

"That's why I've got this great big bruise on my arm. Because you care so much about me."

He said he didn't put the bruise there, that the bruise was already there and she knew this, too.

"Well, you're right about that. How many days did it take you to notice it? Just for curiosity's sake."

He said he noticed it that first day and he was sorry about it, sorry she had to go and get hurt doing something he should have been doing all along, and because she was so quiet after his words, he said, "Leah, did you hear me? Are you still there?"

"I'm here, Bruno. Right here in the kitchen."

He said she never answered his original question about whether or not she was okay.

"Oh, I'm great. Never been better. It's not every day of the year I get attacked by a grown man in the bedroom of my farmhouse."

He wanted to know if she could stop being sarcastic for once in her life.

"I would gladly stop being sarcastic, if that's what I was being, but I'm not."

He said it sounded like sarcasm to him, because all he had wanted to do was check and see if she was okay and let her know that he was okay, too, because he thought maybe she'd be a little worried about him, but now he could see he was mistaken.

"The only thing you're mistaken about is me going on with work that I'm not going to do anymore. I'm through with the cows. Sick of the cows. There's no way in hell I'm liftin another bale of hay."

He said she wouldn't have to tend them anymore, that he would work it out somehow.

"Oh, I bet you will."

He said never mind what he would and wouldn't do, that all he wanted to know was if she was okay.

"I already told you I'm fine. I'm fine as wine. I just washed our fucking bloody sheets, and I'm about to hang them on the fucking line. And as soon as I finish that, I'm going to scrub the fucking mess *you* made of the kitchen and take the clothes out of the fucking suitcase and put them back into the fucking bureau drawers—"

He interrupted her by saying he was not beyond the use of sarcasm and this being the case he was pleased to see she still enjoyed the use of her favorite four-letter word.

She said, "Fuck you, Bruno," and slammed down the phone, and then she leaned her head against the back of the chair and stared out the wide window onto the open pastureland and the feathery tops of the trees, all sad fellows, it seemed.

She had not wanted it to, but her heart had jumped erratically when she heard his voice, and for a moment there she had thought the two of them would recover, but something was running wild through her and she didn't know how to stop it now, how to make it behave. And so she sat there enveloped in sadness, realizing that of all the words she had wanted to say and hear, she had not heard or said any of them.

{CHAPTER 20}

Willem liked Tom Waite well enough, but the man seemed unacquainted with the simplistic concept of solitude, of how a certain individual might want nothing more than to just sit and stare at a blank television hanging high up in a corner while he ate, of how the times had outgrown them all, and while certain people would benefit by one, there was no acceptance now for a bell worn around the neck warning passersby of illnesses. Leprosy and tuberculosis. Diseases of the sex: gonorrhea and syphilis. Worse diseases for which there were no names. Tom Waite could make a helluva sandwich, and Willem was working on his second one as proof of the man's sandwich-making expertise, but his face was blandly configured and his eyes were laced with good humor, and as a result, he wore the face of a man unacquainted with sorrow of any sort. Now, the one on the phone, Bruno Till, with that medieval-looking contraption around his neck, seemed more of a kinsman, easier to take. That one seemed to follow the religion of privacy and understood its creed, how painful but necessary it was. Willem turned his head and looked at him, saw how he was still talking on the phone and wondered where he had heard that name before, wondering if it was spelled the same as it sounded. Shutting his eyes, he fashioned a line in his imagination and placed the word there—Till—granting it a slight loop on the left side of the crosspiece, bestowing an even more ornate loop to the base of the letter's stem. In his mind, he saw the name as *Till* and remembered where he had seen it: the basement of the courthouse, on a page in a ledger, next to the crossed-out name of his father . . .

Willem tried to stop thinking about the implication and what action it might require (*Oh, excuse me, Mr. Till, but would you kindly give my land back to me? You see, way back when I was still wet behind the ears, I ran off from it, skedaddled clean to Colorado and failed to pay the taxes on it, but I'm all better now. No longer an idiot. And I'd like it back, please*) by staring at his sandwich, at the greasy red stain soaking into the king-size bun and down onto the thick crockery plate. He patted the top of the sandwich as though it were the head of a child and blinked several times, calculating distances between various objects as he scanned the room. Cash register in opposition to tin napkin holders. Utensils standing upright in wire baskets as they related to the rolling lights of the Wurlitzer jukebox shining on the tabletops with psychedelic patterns so like a beating oily heart. Willem had never had an attack twice in one day, but the peculiar humming had begun, so he guessed he was entering new territory where anything bad was imminently possible. He glanced out the window at the harmless sight of pedestrians strolling along, balloons in their hands. One little boy stumbled on a sidewalk crack and released his balloon accidentally and stood jumping for it and getting nowhere. Looking both ways, he ran across the street to a light pole in the direct path of his floating balloon and tried to scale it by wrapping his arms around it. He gained a mere foot and a half before sliding down, and Willem watched the boy's tennis shoes peel against the metal pole, and it looked like skin sliding down a bone. The image was a familiar one, and the humming grew louder behind Willem's ears.

There was a sheet of dark green rollout tinting across the front window, and because of it, everything took on a certain distortion that seemed to grow more severe as the humming grew louder. "Don't you hear the noise?" he asked Tom, who failed to hear him since he was leaning against the backside of the bar wiping a glass with a towel and talking to the boy. Willem heard snippets of their conversation. Tom saying something with the word "that" in it. How about emptying *that*. Or refilling *that*. A vague "that" sentence took on an unparalled importance in

Willem's mind, an importance the caliber of, say for comparison's sake, disarming a nuclear bomb in the middle of a stadium packed with innocent schoolchildren. If Willem could not determine what "that" Tom was talking about, the world would blow up and he would be the one they would blame. Make sure *that* icemaker's cycling regular. Was this the right "that"? Willem shook his head. *No. No. Make that "that" go away. Tell this wrong type of "that" you do not want to play.*

Jesus God help me, he prayed, leaning on his hand. He absolutely did not want to start rhyming his words. It had happened once before out in Colorado, while he was standing in line to see *McKenna's Gold*. By the time he reached the ticket window, he was shouting out stanzas that got him escorted off the premises and barred for life. He looked out the window at the surreal green-tinted street and buildings that were all leaning like cartoon images.

"Too green to go out / and too hot to play ball / so I'll sit on my stool / and try hard not to fall."

The boy in the white hat glanced at him and stopped talking to Tom.

Rhyming words was as bad as a bomb going off in a packed stadium. Every idiot on the street understood a bomb, but an old man spouting Dr. Seuss? He'd never live it down. Willem shut his eyes and tried to spell "that," because sometimes spelling a word over and over again worked like a magnet and drew in the subject and the verb and stirred them around a bit until a phrase spun out that made sense. Of course, he had spelled out the name "Till," and look where that had gotten him: stuck on a stool trying hard to spell *another* word to offset the fear that spelling the first word had stirred up. Willem strained to hear what Tom Waite and the boy were saying to each other, but it was like trying to distinguish the noise of a ticking wristwatch in the middle of a beehive. It couldn't be done.

Willem bent down and examined his barbecue sandwich and began to count the sesame seeds on top of it. He guessed there were more than a hundred. *What triggered this?* he wondered. *Spending a cramped hour inside a collapsing house? Seeing the car pull in and recognizing the family from Texas?*

Willem began to mumble to himself, and he bent lower to the bun: "Was it this/was it that?/Can you honestly say./Tell the Cat in the Hat I do not want to play."

Tom Waite stopped wiping the glass and was staring at him. "You need some more fries, Willem?"

Willem stared back for a long while and then began to shake his head, and Tom frowned and looked over to the wall where Bruno was standing with his back to them.

The humming was louder now, and since Willem had failed the required "that" test, he was now going to have to suffer the consequences, and he braced himself as the noise climbed up the back of his neck and traveled across his skull, where his hair reacted to it by standing on end.

Now, Tom Waite thought Willem was doing nothing more than smoothing down his wavy white hair, which was some of the thickest hair he had ever seen in his life, but when the man began to flail at his head, slapping it with the hand that still held the barbecue sandwich, sending globs of it to the back of his neck and down to the floor, where sheared pieces of pork dirtied the stool legs and brass foot rail, Tom said, "Whoa, now. Easy does it, fella," and reached for one of Willem's hands and tried to pull it away from his head, where it was pounding at his skull, smearing barbecue sauce against his temple.

It was the worse one yet. This one truly seemed to be the bullet with his name written on it, and since it was custom-designed, Willem thought he would say his name out loud to make sure the bullet found him and didn't stray over to the wide-eyed couple he was sure was staring at him. "Willem . . . Willem . . . willemwillemwillem!"

"What in the world?" Tom was saying.

"Willem Fremont. Willem Fremont. Willem. Willem. Willem. Willem."

"Okay, Willem. Sure now. We know it's you. Come on, now, and calm down."

Willem saw Tom's face, but it was from inside another world, a world he could see but not touch. There it was, a hand reaching out to his shoulder. Willem jerked away and pushed against the bar and backstepped to the center of the room where he could see it all. Bruno on the phone. The boy in the white hat standing next to the metal wheel holding order slips. Tom working his way down to the gate of the bar, his eyes full of genuine concern. The couple who, moments earlier, had been in a near snooze next to the jukebox were on their feet, and the sallow-faced girl was jerking at her purse and its long black handle that was tangled underneath the legs of the chair.

"Just hold on a minute," Tom said to them, holding out a hand.

"We're outta here, man," the boy said, pulling bills out of his wallet and throwing them on the table. "Come on, Sabrina. Come on, now, don't look at him."

"But my purse."

"Screw your cheap purse," he said as he jerked it free, sending the chair clattering across the room. "Now come on." The boy pulled the girl by the arm toward the front door, and once they were there, it was like trying to get two horses into the same cramped stall, the way they hung up inside the door frame, hips locked together in a frantic dance of escape.

Willem had seen it before. Or something very much like it. Only then it had been an entire family trying to enter Ruby's Regal Truck Stop out in Sherman, Texas, and now that very same family was waiting for him back at the motel. *Waiting for what?* he wondered, for other than walking out of a town he'd grown sick of and making a foolish attempt to reconcile the trauma that had ruined his life, he had done nothing wrong. The question was a mere flickering of rationale, a tiny light of reasonableness that was about to be snuffed out, since the side of his mind that was able to understand logical assumptions was shutting its door, and he saw his sane self standing inside it, staring at him with detached sadness while the humming spread across the front of his face and to his neck and on down lower to the center of his chest. Ear noise glided from a buzz to a roar and the roar had a weight to it this time, a weight like a cast-iron tub, and without being aware that he was doing so, he began to beat on his chest with his fists in an effort to get it off of him and make it stop.

The last he saw of any of them was Bruno Till, who had hung up the phone and was moving across the room toward him. Willem held out his arms to him as he dropped to his knees and saw the man's shirt and brown belt and then his knees and finally his shoes.

"Hold it. Hold it, now," Bruno said, hurrying across the shiny linoleum and reaching a hand out to lend support. But Willem had been holding it for fifty-two years and couldn't hold it any longer and fell face forward into his soggy hamburger bun, the smell of barbecue sauce his last awareness before the room turned blue-black and the roaring in his ears turned to a scream he recognized as his own, a scream that finally won the war.

→←

"Christalmighty, what do you make of it?"

He could hear them far far away, but he couldn't see them yet, for all was still gray. Huddled forms were out there somewhere talking about him, the voices sounding as though they were coming from some sort of tunnel. Willem's eyes fluttered open, and he saw a portion of the ceiling fan turning slowly, and the vision was tragic, like bent propellers of an airplane falling from the sky.

"I think maybe it's his heart," Tom said. Willem felt someone undoing the top button of his shirt, next to his Adam's apple, and tried to stop them, but his hands were powerless to do so. He always wore his buttons done all the way up. It was a lost art. It was the only way to properly wear a shirt.

"Maybe," Bruno said, lifting Willem's head and placing a towel under it. "Could be something else. I've never seen anything like it. What's in that sauce, anyhow?"

"You think it's the sauce?"

"Maybe an allergy to it. Or something."

"Our family's been eatin this sauce for fifty years."

"I was just asking what was in it."

"Nothin that would harm a soul. I thought he was choking on something," Tom said.

"Did you check to see?"

"No. 'Cause he's breathing. You cain't get choked and breathe at the same time, can you? You think I ought to check in his mouth?"

"No. Just give him a minute. Get the boy to wet a rag, will ya?"

Tom looked up and said, "Billy. Wet one of them rags for us."

Willem could see them now. The underplanes of their faces, their chins, which were out of focus and optically distorted to shapes that were terribly large. He leaned on his elbow and tried to lift himself up.

"No. You just hang on." Bruno pressed him back down to the floor, leaving a hand on his shoulder, and it felt warm and strong. "Do you know where you're at?"

Willem nodded and said, "Ruby's Regal."

"Ruby Sweegal? Is that the name of a buddy of yours?" Tom wanted to know.

Willem thought about it but couldn't understand what they meant. Hadn't they just seen him standing on the table and screaming? And then he thought, *No, that was a different time than this,* but he was still confused. "This is not Texas, is it?"

Tom said, "This is Smokey's Bar and Grill. You're in Purvis, Mississippi."

Willem put his hand to his chest and felt the wet smear of barbecue sauce on his shirt. He tried to evaluate his predicament, assess the damage, filled suddenly with an unaccountable sadness and fatigue at the thought of explanations and apologies and the looks on their faces that would tell him all the explanations and apologies in the world weren't worth a dime. He couldn't do it anymore.

"You havin chest pains?"

Willem considered this and held up his thumb and forefinger, spread just a little.

"He's sayin just a little," Tom said.

"I can see that," Bruno said.

Tom said, "We got to get him to the hospital."

Willem rolled his head from side to side and said, "No."

"There's no question about it." Tom looked toward the pay phone.

"This is not a heart attack," Willem whispered. "It's . . ." And then he was silent. How in the world could he make them understand something he didn't understand himself? "It's not my heart."

"Has this happened before?" Bruno asked.

Willem looked at him and nodded. "I got medicine back where I'm staying," he told them in a weak voice.

"Buddy, you cain't drive," Tom said.

Bruno sat back on his heels and stared down at him.

"He cain't drive, can he?" Tom said.

"Probably not," Bruno said, thinking hard about it.

Willem tried to raise himself up and fell back down again. The spell had been the worst one yet. Other spells lasted around twenty minutes and left him drained and weak for hours. All he could imagine at that moment was the small motel room, where he could crawl under the bedcover and sleep.

"I'll drive him," Bruno said. "I know where he's staying."

"How do you know that?" Tom asked.

"Didn't you tell me he was stayin at Alyce Benson's place?"

"Well, yeah, I did at that."

"Okay then."

"Mr. Fremont. Is it okay with you if Bruno here drives you back to the motel?"

Willem looked at Bruno and nodded.

"If I were you, I'd swing by the hospital," Tom said.

"We'll see," Bruno said.

"You need to listen to me about this, Bruno."

Bruno put his arm under Willem's shoulders and raised him to a sitting position, remembering the inside of the small Rambler and how cluttered and dirty it was, how bad it smelled. Men were supposed to take care of their vehicles, and it was one more piece of evidence that he was failing at the job of being a man. "I'll drive him back in his truck. Can I leave the Rambler here until later?"

"Of course you can. Still. It looks like a heart attack to me."

"Could be, but I want to take a look at his pills and see what they are."

"I'll be fine," Willem said.

They both looked down at him.

"Of course you will," Bruno said even though he didn't believe it. "Now, come on. Let's ease up and see if you feel dizzy."

The boy came bringing a drippy rag and handed it to Tom, who held it in his hand while water ran down his arm, soaking his sleeve before runneling over the tile floor. "Billy, I swear. Don't you know how to wring out nothing? Is this what you thought I meant by a wet rag?"

"It's wet, ain't it?"

Tom sighed. "It is at that."

Bruno helped Willem into the passenger side of the truck, making sure his feet were inside the truck good and taking care to secure the door. Backing out of the lot, he saw his Rambler and figured it would be safe enough, even if it turned out to be the morrow before he made it back into town. Whatever was in there that was worth stealing, the thief was welcome to it. He supposed in some dark market somewhere, there just might be a demand for mouse shit and dust.

"I apologize to you, Mr. Till, for this inconvenience," Willem said, leaning his head against the truck window.

"It's no bother."

"It feels like one," Willem said, wondering how long before the man's curiosity got the best of him and he began his line of questioning. The truck had a natural rhythm to it, the rocking motion of two tons carefully balanced on shocks. Movement was a narcotic to Willem; it soothed him and brought on the first tentative strokes of relaxation, but relaxation worried him, and he sat up straight in his seat and put his hand to the door. He was at his best when he was alert, and if ever there was the need to be at his best, it seemed to be now, in order to offset the obvious: a man so incapacitated by a nervous spell that he had to be ferried back to a motel room. He glanced down and saw how ruined his shirt was, how his flagellation by means of a big-boy pork sandwich made him appear to have been shot in the neck. "I'm not at my best these days."

"Don't worry about it," Bruno said, driving past the empty parade stands, the wind off the truck scattering paper cups and other debris.

"I'll miss those big-boy sandwiches," Willem said. "I've never tasted such good barbecue."

"My mother says the best thing to do sometimes is get right back on the horse that's thrown you."

"Your mother is a horsewoman?"

Bruno chuckled. "She digs her spurs into one occasionally. The horse's name is Sonny, and it's about as stupid a horse as they make."

"I don't know much about horses," Willem said.

It was only a matter of minutes before they were out in the country and pastureland was rolling past. Willem saw old oak trees standing solid and strong in the center of some of the fields, with cows milling about beneath them.

"Tom says you're from out west. How'd you end up in Purvis?" Bruno asked him.

Willem had expected the question. "I used to live here. A long time ago."

"Where about?"

"Way out in the country. We farmed for a while."

"Farmin can be a heartbreaker."

"That it can."

They were silent for a couple of miles, then Bruno asked, "You feelin any better?"

"Some." Willem rolled the window down a bit. "I would wish for cancer rather than this. With cancer, one would know what to expect."

"Are you sure it's not your heart?"

"They've tested me and poked at me and drawn my blood. At least a dozen doctors over the course of the years. Nobody seems to have a clue."

"There aren't any pills, are there?"

"The last doctor gave me some Valium. So yes, I've got some pills."

"Do they help?"

"Make me tired is all. And I'm already tired enough." Willem withdrew his handkerchief and began to wipe at his shirt, noticing his unstable hand movements.

Bruno glanced at him and then out the windshield, where the black highway stretched and leaned and climbed over small hills that all looked the same. "How'd you end up out west?"

"I . . . ah." He paused and thought about it. "I wasn't a very good farmer. I had a turn of bad luck and lost the land and left. Headed west and found myself in Colorado."

"That's a far spell from Purvis."

"In more ways than one." Willem sighed. "I wasn't but a kid when I ended up there, and it took me most of a week to earn my first dollar. Almost starved to death."

"Is there much farming out there?"

"No. I gave up farming. Went to work in a small woodshop. For a man who was a helluva craftsman. I built cabinets first, and later, furniture. Once I got through that first month, there were no more worries about starving. My first night out there was a bitch, though." Willem was remembering the train ride and how exhausted he had been and how he had fallen asleep on the wide wooden steps of the train depot until he was ordered off the premises by the night watchman.

Bruno drove past a series of run-down shacks and turned to Willem. "I can't help but wonder why you'd want to come back to this place. Most people wanna leave."

"I just wanted to see it again," Willem said. He was tired. Tired of everything. "Are there many Tills around here?" He watched as Bruno tried to shake his head. The brace impeded movement; but for his eyes, the negative response might have been missed. "There's just us. Me and my brother. And my mother." After a slight pause he said, "And there's my wife."

Then why are you staying at the Rocky Creek Inn? Willem wanted to ask. Instead he said, "You lived in Purvis long?"

"All my life. On the same land. I suppose I'll live there until I die."

The answer was unsatisfactory, in Willem's opinion. "I seem to remember running across a Till when I lived here before," Willem said, warning himself to be careful; a pot was being stirred, and the ingredients were untried. Likely to become caustic or, at the very least, boil over. "Reinhold, I think his name was."

"My grandfather," Bruno said. "Had great plans for his sons."

I remember, Willem thought, the memory so dusty in appearance, it would require a heavy cleaning to see the details. But what he could recall was a man cursed with the rude habit of riding up on horseback whenever Willem least expected and making inquiries about the Fremont land. A man whose comportment indicated that whatever gains Willem had made in learning to farm would amount to nothing. A man who never accepted no for an answer.

"My father was one of those sons," Bruno said, his voice steady. "He never took to it. Wanted to be a schoolteacher. Reinhold wouldn't hear of it."

The longer he spoke, the more clearly the old life appeared, sepia-toned and glazed with yellow light, the smell of the turned-over fields, the setting of foundation posts for the small house out in back of the field, the texture of the mattress beneath his back.

"Grandpa was a tyrant. Ask anybody. I'm sure they'll not hold back their opinion."

Willem had no intention of asking anyone anything. Instead he began to wonder why a man who had land and a house, not to mention a wife, was sojourning at the motel room. And then he thought of Alyce and supposed this was the reason. So *that* was the way it was. Surprised by the level of moral disapproval he felt, Willem concentrated on the glove compartment, opening it and shutting it four or five times in quick succession, not caring in the least that Bruno was watching him. The round knob felt so comforting to his forefinger, and compliant. All he had to do was press it and something happened, something immediate: the door popped open. He slammed it shut and put his finger to the knob again. Drawing comfort from the dependable rectangular door with its two round indentations for coffee cups, the inky blackness where his spare keys were stored, as well as the passbook to his bank account. When he shut his eyes and put his hand inside the compartment, he pretended he was in the dark, forced to guess at the contents, finding a ballpoint pen and what felt like fingernail clippers, and was that a comb? Satisfied, he slammed it shut again but found that his finger seemed drawn like a magnet to the chrome button. The glove-compartment door flew open again.

An uncomfortable silence ensued, and after enduring it as long as he could, Bruno cleared his throat and said, "I've known Tom Waite all my life. He'll take great offense if you rob him of the chance to sell you some more of his barbecue." *Jesus. How many times is he going to open and shut the thing?* he wondered.

Willem slammed the glove compartment and folded his arms and tucked his hands in his armpits. "I hate to offend the man, but I can't go back there," he said, forcing his eyes to the passing fields and finally leaning back in his seat.

Bruno said, "When I first come back from rehab in Jackson, Tom was the only one who still knew how to have a regular conversation with me."

"That's because you're his friend. It's different for strangers."

"I don't think Tom's ever met any strangers."

"I still can't go back."

They both saw the motel sign in the distance, the blue vacancy sign lit up with an added feature: the small red "no" was illuminated in front of the "vacancy," and Bruno wondered if that small two-letter word had ever been lit up before. As they both watched, it blinked and held and blinked and held. Bruno rolled down the window and stuck out his arm in a turn signal and steered across the lot and down to the very end, where privet and wild sassafras grew.

The black station wagon was no longer parked in front of rooms two and three, but a late-model lime-green Chevrolet had taken its place. Alyce was out in the yard talking to a man leaning against it, a man slightly built and as blond-headed as those two boys of hers. Once the truck was parked, Bruno went to the other side and opened the door and helped Willem out.

Willem fished for the keys, and together they walked to the room door and stood there. "I'll be fine," he told Bruno.

"Could be Tom is right. Maybe you ought to see somebody. I'd hate for that Mexican hellbitch to find you dead in there. Knowing her, she'd leave you where you lay and never say a word about it."

Willem extended his hand, not caring to talk about it. Enough had been said, in his opinion. "Thank you for your trouble."

He went in and shut the door, and Bruno walked on down to his room, reaching for his keys and ignoring the couple, who seemed intent on watching him. He had no wish to see Alyce's face nor anything that might be written on it.

⇢⇠

"What the hell we runnin here? A convalescent home?" Joe Benson was watching the two of them as they made their way to their rooms.

"We're runnin a motel," she said, noting her husband's coloring and the flushed look to his face that indicated drunkenness. The thing about Joe was that he never acted drunk. There was no way of knowing the level of it other than the slight mottling of his skin.

"Who beat up the cripple guy?" he asked, looking at his wife.

"I ain't got a clue."

"Hell, who in the world would beat up a cripple? I ain't never even done that."

Alyce said, "He's not a cripple."

"I don't expect he's wearing that stock around his neck for the fun of it."

"He was wounded in Vietnam. You need to keep your voice down."

"And who's old Granpappy there?"

"Mr. Fremont. Listen, Joe, if you'd stick around long enough, you might find out what's going on. I ain't got the time for this. I got stuff to do."

He reached out and put his arm around her waist. "I know one thing in particular you gotta do." He tried to kiss her, and she pulled away.

"Don't."

"What do you mean, don't? I'm your husband. Cain't I hug my wife?"

"You don't act like my husband except when it suits you. I still smell her."

"Who?"

"Whoever sat on your face. You make me sick."

She had said it before, but the look on her face told him she really meant it this time.

"I ain't done nothing."

"Jeepers, Joe. I wonder why I don't believe you."

"Because you're a class-A bitch, maybe?"

She whirled to face him, and he caught her arm and pulled her next to him and stood grinning at her.

"Daddy?" Ben had come unnoticed out of the office and was standing next to them holding the kite he had helped make. The tips of his fingers were smudged from holding tight to words he couldn't read and wouldn't understand even if they were read to him. Without taking his eyes off Alyce, Joe said, "What is it, son?"

"Ain't we gonna fly our kites?"

"You bet your bottom dollar we are. Didn't Daddy tell you he'd take you out and do that?"

"Yessir. But are we?"

"Don't Daddy always do what he says he's gonna do?"

Ben looked from one to the other and saw how they were dancing strange. How his mama's arm was locked inside his daddy's hand. He said nothing, but a look of great perplexity was on his face as he stood there quietly studying them.

"Now, that's a damn shame, Alyce," Joe said in a quiet voice through his clenched teeth.

"What is?"

"How you've turned these little boys against me."

"You've done that yourself," she said, jerking her arm free and going to her son and putting a hand to his head. The little boy lifted his kite to her and smiled, and his face was trouble-free now that she stood next to him. Tears came to her eyes at the purity of his movements, at his undiluted expectation.

Her husband said, "Ben, you run get your brother and we'll head out to do our kite flying."

Ben trotted off, raising his kite and watching the rag tail trail after it.

"Where you takin them?" Alyce asked, more alarmed than she was revealing. It was a trick, like knowing when he was drunk, this ability to hide how afraid she was of him. "I told them earlier I'd take them out to the fairgrounds."

"That's seven miles away. I ain't got the gas for it."

"But I told them," she said.

"Well, I told them I'd take them somewhere special, and I will."

"Where?"

"Where there's lots of wind." Joe grinned at her.

"Joe."

"What?"

"If you hurt them boys . . ." And then she fell quiet. She couldn't work her way past seeing them harmed in some way, and should the unspeakable happen, whatever words were called for were unknowable.

"Alyce, you really know how to hurt a guy." He put his hand on his chest, and his face was filled with mock remorse and something else that translated to plain old meanness.

"If you hurt my boys," she said again.

"They're *my* boys, too. Seems like it might pay you to remember that from time to time," he said.

Joe came whooping out of the office alongside Ben, and the two of them raced over to their father's car, kites in their hands.

"Look at that," Joe said. "If those two boys don't love their daddy, I don't know beans from rocks." He patted her on her cheek a little too harshly to be endearing and walked to the car, whistling as he went.

Joe rolled down the back window and leaned out toward his mother. "Mama, we'll fly them real high, I bet."

She nodded and tried to smile at him.

Ben scrambled over his brother and said, "I'll fly mine higher," and Joe said, "Will not," and Ben said, "Will, too."

Alyce went to them and leaned in through the car window and ruffled their hair and kissed them each on the cheek. She said, "You boys mind your daddy, now."

"We will," they said in unison, and then Ben draped his arms around his daddy's neck and squeezed. Joe Benson said, "Where'd you learn that stranglehold, boy?" and laughed as he pulled his son's arm away.

"I learned it from Mama," Ben said, and Joe Benson looked at Alyce and said, "I bet you did at that," right before cranking the car and scratching out in a throw of loose gravel and rocks. Alyce watched them until they disappeared over the small hill, the homemade kite tails dangling out the car window and catching in the breeze.

{CHAPTER 21}

Sonny Till had been one of the laziest students ever known to participate in the Purvis educational system, and coming on the heels of his older brother, who had managed to excel in sports and academics alike with very little studying, or so it seemed to Eilene, the label was a hard one for his mother to take. It stuck to her younger son's hide like the skin of a blueberry, and removing it was all but impossible without destroying what little good there might be inside.

Eilene was not caught completely off guard by Sonny's failures. She couldn't honestly say that she didn't know, for the warning signs were there. Scribbled notations at the bottom of some of his weekly spelling tests and math quizzes. And there had been the report cards, of course, but the school system had been overrun by a battalion of fresh-from-the-trenches elementary- and secondary-education professionals who thought Purvis students would benefit more without the standard grading system. The alphabet sextuplet had been banished because of something the professionals referred to as "classification-related expectations and societal trauma," and Sonny was still laboring under the reward system of "S" for satisfactory, "U" for unsatisfactory, and "I" for incomplete. *Who can make heads or tails of such nonsense? What does an "I" mean in this day and age?*

Eilene had wondered. There were so many stages of incompleteness. There was the incompleteness that was terribly incomplete, as in having never even been started, and then there was the incompleteness that was more complete than incomplete, as in the frantic student who tries his best to get something finished before the bell rings, but doesn't make it.

When the letters began arriving near the end of Sonny's seventh-grade year, Eilene had read them carefully and allowed herself the luxury of self-deception. In those early years, she was still seeing the glass as half full and in light of this optimism, took the words "testing required" as a sign that Sonny was hiding his brilliance under a bushel basket of casualness. Driving him over to the Forrest County mental-health facilities had been an exasperating, time-consuming chore, but she had done it, and once the tests were completed, she stood a vigilant watch over the mailbox for the official letter confirming her belief that her younger son was exceptional. There were no letters throughout the summer, and she resolved not to let her disappointment show. Children *knew* things, after all. Unspoken opinions had a way of surfacing when one least expected them or even knew that an opinion was being squeezed out during a moment of weakness. And she, for one, was not about to weigh the boy down with a disappointing set of her shoulders. When the first of the letters arrived during the Christmas break of his eighth-grade year, some nerve in her stomach was tweaked. Some mother nerve that reminded her adults *knew* things, too. And since the half-full glass was at risk of draining right before her eyes, she stuck the letters behind the wire basket holding her homemade bread and refused to read them. A month later she got the phone call from the principal and pulled out all six of the letters and read them from start to finish. Sonny was fast approaching the time he would begin life as a Purvis High School student, and Eilene couldn't wait for that to happen. At last he would be able to ride the county school bus, and she could pass on rising with the proverbial rooster to haul him back and forth to school and be able to get to her gardening bright and early. She read the letters quietly and with growing alarm, taking off her glasses and wiping them clean and going back and seeing the same words, "will be held back" and "incompleted work" and "failure to apply," appear before her eyes. This couldn't be. There had to be some mistake. Sonny had been tested, for God's sake. Hadn't they said he was just fine? Well, no, they hadn't actually said that, but there had been no follow-up or reassignment, so she had assumed that Sonny was maybe not exceptional but at least okay. She was his mother. She loved him anyway. But this? This vile threat? She shook the most condemning letter in the air as though it were a dirty sock.

Seeking actual evidence, she had marched straight up to the school and demanded a conference with the paid professionals who had made the terrible mistake of overlooking the potential in her obviously gifted child. All the teachers had been summoned. She wasn't about to waste her time on one or two of them. No, she was taking her good time off from canning tomatoes, and she wanted all of them there, by God, and so they came, along with the principal, Ron Wheeler, a portly man wearing a baseball cap and a shiny red athletic jacket zipped halfway up. Next to him was the guidance counselor, wearing a pocket protector loaded with pens, a slight man who looked as though he had been kicked around all his life and expected more of the same and wouldn't put up a fight even when he saw it coming. Wheeler made a point of positioning the counselor across from Eilene, who was so angry her jaws were cramping and she couldn't keep her foot from tapping against the chair leg.

They all sat around a table in the small conference room off the library, a room that smelled of mimeograph ink and cigarette smoke and burned coffee and some other chemical smell, like cleaning solvent, or maybe it was just plain old chalk.

Sonny was there, too. A greatly outsize eighth-grader who was yet to find a desk that felt comfortable. They all watched silently as he wandered around the room and tested out four chairs before he settled grudgingly on the one next to his mother, his face placid and unconcerned, relieved he had passed the inkblot test with flying colors. It was an easy enough test, really, as every single blot on the pieces of white cardboard looked like a variation of a small speckled pup. Pup being run over by a truck. Pup being splattered by a baseball bat. Pup left alone to lie on its back with its paws up in the air. Pup being pelted on the head with overripe apples. Pup with its leg hiked as it peed against a tree. The man who had given him the test had asked Sonny a couple of times if he saw anything more than a speckled pup, and when he had answered solemnly, "No, sir, I sure don't," the man had said, "Very well, then," and put the cards back in his black briefcase and sent Sonny out to his mother, who was waiting in the next room on the edge of her chair with her straw hat on her lap. And now Sonny was sitting in a cramped chair ready to watch his mother's face when they told her how smart he was. He had a feeling they were about to move him on up to a higher grade. Maybe turn him overnight into a sophomore. There was also the possibility of a little silver achievement pin shaped like a feather. Only a few students got them at the end of every year, and most of the recipients wore them fastened to their collars, but once he received his, he planned on handing it immediately over to his mother, since she was the one who had pushed him with his studies and stayed up nights listening to him spell his words.

Ten minutes into the session, he realized he wasn't going to receive a durn thing other than a tongue-lashing from his mama, and he watched with growing alarm while her face fell as she listened to the teachers' unflinching recital of past evidence of lackluster effort. There were test scores for her to see: the before-mentioned inkblot-speckled-pup test, as well as another test loaded with silly questions like which do you like the best: flowers or butterflies? Sonny had no place in his heart for either of the choices and had told them so. There was even the result of the hearing test, which he hadn't needed at all because, like he had told the lady, if a boy could hear the question being asked, didn't that prove he could hear just fine? There were also some observations by the guidance counselor for Eilene to consider and some questions about the family dynamics for her to answer. The only bright spot in the whole session came from the shop teacher, who said he had never seen anybody who could dismantle a busted toaster as fast as Sonny Till, and Eilene had said should there be a bounty of busted toasters around that needed repairing, she supposed Sonny would find himself duly employed and not standing in some breadline.

Nobody seemed to have anything worthwhile to say after that.

"Thank you all for your time," she had said in closing, shaking each teacher's hand, turning away from Sonny, and walking out the door, leaving him trapped inside a folding desk chair. They didn't even discuss it on the way home. Eilene just reached over once and patted his leg, and Sonny looked out the side window of the car and wondered what in the world he had done that was so wrong. Once supper was done, he stood waiting by the refrigerator, pencil in hand, ready for her to tell him to get to his books, but she didn't. "Ain't you got nothing to say to me?" he asked her. "Just do your best, Sonny. That's all anyone can ask." And she turned and mixed up her vinegar solution and took to scrubbing the countertops and the surface of the stove, even the kitchen table, until the whole room smelled like the inside of an Easter egg factory.

Sonny found it baffling, the way they had been all over him one day and left him alone the next. Even the most hard-core of his teachers was willing to issue him a hall pass whenever he asked for one, and Sonny spent the remainder of his years in school leaning against the lockers, watching the smooth-talking varsity players hook their thick fingers into the waistbands of their cheerleader girlfriends' flouncy skirts. He loved the squeal the girls made when they were pulled into the arms of the fellas, and he would stand there covertly spying on them until one would look his way and yell, "What the hell you lookin at, fat boy?" creating a joke that ran unchecked all the way from one end of the hall to the other. It had happened so long ago that he wondered why he still thought of it at all and why he still flinched and blushed when the thought made its appearance. It was as if the embarrassment was so permanently fixed in his brain that it had a nuclear half-life and would be there even when the world was blown apart and all that was left to run the planet were the cockroaches. So the first time he stuck his pudgy finger into the waistband of Conchita's red satin hot pants and pulled her toward him and she fell off her red glitter high heels and into his arms and squealed like a young schoolgirl, Sonny felt the first shifting of the old high school torment, a relief he wasn't even aware he had been wishing for. He glanced around immediately after he did it, while Conchita's arms were still around his neck and his face was still wet from her hot, sloppy kiss, wishing one or two of those high school big daddies had been standing there watching. And then he took another long hard look at the room he was standing in, and at the girl who was doing the kissing, and thanked his lucky stars that there was no one around who had the foggiest idea who the hell he was.

That had been a half hour earlier. Now he stood pitching stones at the sloping concrete abutment that capped the ditch alongside the Roustabout. Across the way was a wall of greenery so thick and convoluted and overgrown that it was hard to pinpoint the actual forms of trees buried inside, for twisty kudzu vines threatened the place. They had already won over the oaks and crape myrtles and the guide wires to the power poles and a portion of metal guard rail, and now a spindly viridian-colored army had sent lookouts across the broken remnants of asphalt. As soon as they met up with the wall of the club, they would begin their climb. Sonny bent and grunted, scooped up a handful of rocks, and poked through them with a stout finger. Sometimes he got lucky and found silver change this way. Once he found a Timex watch minus its band, running like a charm. He looked at his wrist. It was still running to this day.

He tossed a couple of rocks and listened to them clatter down the side and the eventual plop as they found the murky water. Conchita had said Joe had called her earlier in the day while she was still at home and said for Sonny to meet him at The Place. That's how she said it, with capital letters signifying importance. Leaning on his arm, she had looked up at him and asked what place, and Sonny told her it was none of her business. What *he* wanted to know was how come Joe had called her at home, at that private place where she did her personal business like going to the bathroom and shaving her legs and stepping into clean underwear. Sonny had been called at home regular enough by Joe, so the man sure knew his number. There was not a single reason in God's good world for Joe Benson to be calling Conchita at her private residence. Not when he knew how Sonny felt about her. Not when he knew Sonny had never even kissed her properly. Not when he knew the precarious level of Sonny's loyalty. How all it would take for him to spill the beans on Joe's plan was one phone call to the county sheriff's office.

Sonny walked over to the edge of the property and looked down at the floating cups and empty bottles and the red-tail turtle sitting on a busted milk crate at the center of the brown water. Bugs hovered near his head, and the heat was fierce on the back of his neck. Tossing the rest of his rocks at the turtle and watching it slide off the crate and disappear gave him a bit of satisfaction, but not enough. What else did they talk about? he wondered. How long did they talk? Five minutes? A half hour? One thing about Conchita, the girl liked to run her mouth. So did Joe. Knowing both these things created a knot in Sonny's stomach, and for a brief moment all those good feelings he had been having for weeks disappeared, and he felt as ravaged and abandoned and humiliated as he had years ago in high school when the jocks called him fat boy and threatened to break his face if he kept staring at their girlfriends.

"There you are," Conchita said, and he jumped and had to catch himself on the metal guardrail that kept cars and trucks from driving full tilt into the holding pond.

"What's the matter?" she asked him, and he looked down at her. She was already flushed in the heat, and a small sprinkling of sweat dotted her nose and forehead, and the unbreathable material of her nylon shirt was stuck to her chest, and he could see an outline of cleavage. Her protruding teeth had grown on him, and he was beginning to believe she looked a little like that Lamb Chop puppet gal, Shari Lewis.

"Nothin's the matter."

"You was fine ten minutes ago. Next thing I know, you're walking out. You didn't even finish your beer. And it was on the house."

"I gotta go meet Joe," he said, peeved with her for not realizing what was wrong and for being so desirable-looking in the hellish humidity while Sonny felt near smothered by it. His black T-shirt held the heat like a desert highway and was soaked midway down his chest, the rear of his pants damp as one of his mama's kitchen rags, his socks like leather ankle irons. Even his wristwatch was beginning to feel like a wool-covered handcuff. And there she stood smiling up at him, a tendril of her dark hair catching on one of her false eyelashes.

An old trailer had been reconfigured and taken off its tires and set on a slab back a ways from the Roustabout, and the sun was reflecting off its foiled windows, and Sonny stood staring at them until he saw squares of silver before his eyes and had to rub the vision away. "Who lives back there?" he asked.

"Nobody lives there. That's where we go in between shows."

"I seen Joe come out of there once," he said. It was a lie, but at moments he was inspired and knew intuitively when to set a lie in place in order to gain information, and this was one of those moments.

Conchita shrugged. "He uses the place to do it with Floreen," she said, fiddling with the narrow bracelet on her arm. "That's where they go, 'cause he's such a cheapskate, he won't spend money on nothin."

"That old gal in there?"

"She ain't but twenty-eight."

"If she's twenty-eight, I'm a hunderd."

Conchita reached out and rubbed at his arm. She seemed to be grappling with something of serious weight, trying to decide whether or not to tell him some vital fact.

"So that's what y'all do between shows," he said.

"That's what some do. I don't."

"You sure?"

"Okay. He's tried to get me to," she said finally.

"Joe?"

"Yeah, Joe."

"Tried to get you to what?" he asked, though he already knew the answer.

"Do it with him."

"I'll have to kill the bastard."

"Now, Sonny."

"Don't 'now, Sonny' me." He looked across the way, realizing he had suddenly begun to sound like his mother, of all people.

"Listen. He used to bother me all the time for it. Then he left off for a while and wouldn't give me the time a day. And then when me and you got started, he come after me again. Started calling and showing up here late at night and offering me a ride home."

"Did you take it?"

She looked at him, and because she knew Joe and his great big mouth and how prone he was to run it, said, "Just once." A slight pause. "It didn't mean nothin, though."

"The ride home didn't mean nothin, or what you two did on the ride home didn't mean nothin?"

Conchita debated on telling him the whole truth, how it had been one last time for old time's sake, but the childlike expectation on his face held her back. She had never run across a man able to convince himself that the stripper he was dating was still a virgin, and now that she had met one, she wanted to keep him.

"Baby, we didn't do nothin." She rubbed his arm. "He tried real hard, but I wouldn't."

Sonny knew better than to believe her, but he couldn't help it. She could have told him she was the Virgin Mary, and he would have asked her how far he needed to go to buy her a mule to set her pregnant ass on, no questions asked. He looked at his watch. "I tell you what. I'll be back in an hour to pick you up."

"But I'm tending bar," she said.

"Not tonight, you ain't. Tell them you got sick all of a sudden. Tell them your granny died or your mother run her car off the road or some other nonsense. Tell them whatever you have to, but be ready for me by the time I pull up in the car. And tell them this, too: they better be lookin real hard for somebody to fill your shoes, 'cause your dancing days are just about over."

"Where we goin to, Sonny?"

"A place we ought to a gone to weeks ago. It's time for me to meet your mama," he said.

"But I ain't met yours."

"Yeah, well, I guess it's time for that, too."

She had bought him a black T-shirt from Smokey's Bar and Grill in downtown Purvis. On the front of it was a small pig dancing a jig on top of a smoking campfire, and on the back, in large print, SMELL OUR BUTTS. She watched the words as he walked away from her toward his car, the way they stretched all the way across his wide back. His arms below the short sleeves were hairless and pink, and the black jeans were low riders, and when he climbed into his car, she saw exactly how low they rode and looked away.

→←

The creek ran gold, and there was something about it that puzzled Ben.

"How come they call it the Baby Black?" he asked his brother. The two of them were standing side by side, the wind lifting the identical hair from off their sweating foreheads. "It ain't black."

"Don't know," Joe said. "Maybe the person who named it didn't know his colors. It sure is purdy, though."

When they first got there, picnickers were packing their coolers and folding up their blankets and lifting their baskets off the sand, and the two of them had been shy about it, hanging back against the cedar trees with their kites in their hands. Their father said get on out there and show them how it's done, but neither boy had any idea how it was done, so they stood on the low ridge of mossy ground and watched as, one by one, the swimmers left the area and climbed into their cars and drove away. Once they had the place to themselves, they pulled off their shoes and walked out onto the sand and stood there looking up into the sky as though there might be instructions written somewhere concerning the business of flying a kite. Even as they held them, they could feel the wind trying to lift the stretched paper and were encouraged by it. A half hour later, a small track had been laid in the sand from running back and forth, and while he was ready enough with criticism, their father seemed reluctant to get his feet dirty and stayed in the shade smoking cigarettes and watching. They were yet to get their kites up in the air.

"These things ain't ever gonna fly. They're too heavy or something," Ben said as he examined his kite. His was the one made from the funny papers, and he saw Dagwood and Blondie and how their story was stopped short by the thin strip of balsa wood his mother had used. He turned his kite around to see if the story contined on the back, but it didn't.

"Will, too." Joe believed he had stumbled onto the trick of it and ran harder and lifted his kite as he ran and gave out a little play in the line and felt the wind catch the kite and pull it away from him. The trick was not to look at it but to keep running, twisting the stick to the side and letting the string feed away from it. It made a zinging noise. "See?"

Ben came and stood by him and put his kite on the ground and watched in wonder. "How'd you do that?"

"Don't know," Joe said. He was breathless and scared, for the kite was up higher than the trees now, a gray shape with its white tail dancing and darting, missing the limbs and sailing up and higher up until it seemed to touch the clouds. While his one goal had been to get it up there, now that it was flying, he was afraid for it, since distance was being demonstrated in a way that made his stomach feel funny.

"Jeepers. Look how high it is," he said as his arm was pulled away from him, straight up over his head.

"Can I hold it?"

"Yeah. But let me get it goin good first," Joe said.

Ben sat down on the sand and watched it. He was unaware that what he was feeling was similar to what his brother felt; all he knew was that he had turned dizzy from watching the kite and was suddenly afraid, as though he were up in the air looking down at himself, as though he were a square paper-thin bird trapped inside the wind, which might or might not continue to hold him up. He put his fingers to his eyes to try and make himself stop watching, but it didn't help. As soon as he moved his fingers, he was drawn to the kite, and it seemed he was sailing away in the sky, disappearing into the distance.

"Looka there!" their father yelled, and Ben looked over and waved. Joe kept his eyes on the kite.

"Daddy sees it," Ben said.

"I heard him, but I cain't look right now. I gotta watch the kite."

Ben looked across the narrow band of water toward the trees, which were the color of his mother's long velvet coat, the one she wore to church in the wintertime, the coat that didn't seem green at all but black as the inside of a well. The water next to the tree bank was the same color as his mother's thin gold bracelet, and down farther, near the widest bank of sand, the water was the color of the ends of his mother's hair, where the sun got to it and lightened it. Everywhere Ben looked, he saw his mother, and suddenly he missed her and wanted to go home. Their father had never taken them anywhere, and Ben had been excited at first, but now he wished they had gone to a place where his mother was so he wouldn't feel so scared. A louder place where there were people walking the sidewalks. People who might know his mother or him, should his father decide to up and leave them on the sand while they were busy watching a kite sail near a cloud.

"I wanna go home."

He expected Joe to tease him and call him a baby, but he said, "Me, too."

"Can we tell him, then?"

"No."

"Why?"

"'Cause he brung us out here."

"That don't mean nothin."

"Yes, it does."

"How come?"

"'Cause he ain't never took us nowhere."

"Oh," Ben said. It made sense, somehow. "What if he leaves us, though?" Now that the worry was there, it stayed with him and turned more menacing, like the harsh triangles and prisms one sees in a kaleidoscope, a toy that had always frightened him. "What if he sneaks away to his car while we ain't lookin?"

"He's our daddy. He wouldn't do that," Joe said, but he didn't look so sure about it and turned his head to where their father was sitting on top of the picnic table, with his legs crossed like a lady's. "He don't look to me like he's leavin."

"He could, though." Ben dug his heels in the sand and wrapped his arms around his knees. "Mama wouldn't never leave us."

"I know."

"But Mama ain't here. But if she was here, she'd make Daddy stand where we could see him. I know she would." Ben put his thumb in his mouth.

"I know." Joe tugged on the string, but the kite seemed to have a mind of its own. "I'll wind this thing up and we'll go sit with him." He looked at his brother, who had put his head down on his knees. "You wanna hold it before I bring it down?"

Ben shook his head.

"What's the matter with you?"

Ben didn't answer him.

"You ain't gonna cry, are you?"

Ben was already crying.

"Hey, quit that."

Ben shook his head. He wasn't sure what was wrong, he just felt small and unprotected, the way he felt sometimes when he was out in the ditch by the road and a truck was heading their way and his brother didn't seem to notice it. And he wanted his mother there with him. He really liked the way her neck smelled and the way her arms felt, and he was overwhelmed by the sensation that she was gone forever. He wiped his nose on his sleeve and slid a little closer to his brother, to a spot where his shoulder was touching his brother's leg.

All was quiet but for the birds in the tops of the trees and the gurgling sound of the water as it rushed over logs and large stones, and the quiet seemed prolonged and somewhat unnatural to them both, and the darker the sky got, the deeper the silence seemed. It stayed that way for a while, and they didn't speak, and then the quiet was interrupted by the noise of a car, and they both turned to see, half expecting their father to be in it and backing away from them. But it was another car, and it had pulled up next to their father's, and both boys were relieved because now it would be harder for him to sneak away with someone watching.

A large man dressed in a black T-shirt and pants climbed out and walked over to the picnic bench.

Ben removed his thumb from his mouth and said, "Who's that?"

"I don't know."

"Daddy seems to know him."

Ben watched the two of them, the way they were talking. "He's as big as Santa Claus."

Joe chanced a look and said, "Santa's got a beard. That man don't have one."

"But if he did, he'd look like Santa Claus."

"You thought that stray dog we found looked like Lassie, too."

"It could a been Lassie."

"Lassie lives in Hollywood."

"Maybe she got lost or fell off a truck."

"Lassie's famous. She don't ride in no trucks."

"Maybe somebody drove off and left her."

"She's too famous for somebody to leave," Joe said. He was lowering the kite, and while the resistance was strong, he was making steady progress, though wind gusts were doing a job on it, knocking it every which way, sending it close to the tops of the trees, which were in full dark now and stood like waving spears. The sun had fallen and a red band of fierce light was glowing close to the ground, like a fire might be burning from a point far away.

"Maybe Santa shaves off his beard in the summertime," Ben said, in love with the possibility that the man could be Santa.

Joe thought about fussing at him for being stupid and then saw his brother's face and held back. In a few more minutes the kite would be within reaching distance, its tail already dipping into the water. "Maybe," he said.

"You boys!" their father yelled, and Joe was so startled he lost his grip and the kite soared away from him, zinging through his fingers until the wooden grip flew free. While both boys watched, the kite climbed and then dipped, climbed and then dipped, dodging the treetops for a breath-stealing moment before its luck ran out and it landed impaled and stark gray, the color of a ghost, its tail tangled in the limbs. There was no way in the world they would be able to rescue it.

"He didn't have to go and yell," Joe said to his brother as they trudged across the sand, stopping at the cedar trees to reach for their shoes.

"We was right here, he didn't have to yell," Ben said.

"That's what I just said."

"He still didn't have to."

"But at least we're goin home."

Ben thought it was a good thing, for night was almost there, and he'd never ridden with his father after dark, and he wasn't sure he would be as careful as his mother always was, remembering to turn on the lights and drive slow as she watched out for traffic, always looking in the mirror to make sure the two of them were sitting still and not horsing around in back. All those things that good mothers do.

{CHAPTER 22}

"I want you to turn around and go right back through that door!"

Willem was furious, not to mention wet, his morning shower ruined by the presence of the cleaning woman, who either: 1) couldn't read the DO NOT DISTURB sign on the door, or 2) could read it but chose to ignore it. She stood before him in her stained white uniform, her hands folded calmly across her wide stomach, a stale smirk on her face. He was beginning to suspect the second scenario, since this was the third time she had managed to catch him in the shower, each time earlier than the time before. Soap was still on his shoulders and in his hair; Willem could feel the slickness of it sliding down his back. *And dear Lord, would someone please buy Alyce Benson some new towels! Some that would actually wrap all the way around the waist!* He held the rough terry cloth in his hand while he pointed toward the front door, through which he could see Alyce's two kids decked out in their yellow slickers and red boots, hovering around the backside of his truck while rain fell nonstop. The old television in the corner was tuned to WLOX of Biloxi, and a man inside a grainy tubal glow was giving his dire prediction of rain and more rain and still more rain.

Dolores lifted her hand and pointed to the bed.

"Don't you do it! Don't you say it!" Willem waved his hand at her as though hailing a taxi. If he heard the word "sheeets," again, he might just take a razor to her throat.

"Sheeets," she said.

"Jesus Christ, woman!" Willem lifted his necessary clothing from the bed and walked into the small compartment where the tub and shower and toilet were, stepping into his underwear and trousers as quickly as possible. When he came out, the bed was stripped and Dolores was wadding the linens up to a small ball.

"She cain't understand you, mister," Joe said to him. The boy was standing in the doorway, his brother beside him.

"I believe she can."

"Dolores, you cain't understand English, can you?" Joe asked her, looking up at the woman, who was violently shoving the sheets into a white cloth bag. She shook her head negatively. "See?" Joe said to him.

"You two run on." Willem put two fingers to his neck and felt his pulse. He would not be the one to point out the obvious to the kid: that Dolores understood what she had been asked well enough to provide an answer. Bursting the kid's bubble was his mother's job. And speaking of his mother, it was about time Willem paid her a little visit. Lifting a shirt off a hanger, he slid into it and felt overcome by the wrongness of the situation. Routine was his savior, and the immediacy of the situation had robbed him of the necessary redemptive steps. There had been no proper toweling off. No sitting on the bed and putting on his socks. No moment of standing before the mirror to make sure his buttons were all buttoned properly. No time to align his wallet and handkerchief before sliding them in his back pocket.

"Where you goin?" Joe asked.

"I believe it's time I spoke with your mother."

"But she's fryin herself a egg," Ben said. He held a strange tool in his hand.

For almost a week Willem had watched them trudge across the parking lot, one holding a pale stick of wood, the other a piece of metal. What they did with the stick and the rod was a mystery. But whatever it was, they seemed prone to attempt it at least a dozen times a day at various spots in the yard: squatting here and there as they drove the stob into the ground and then stroking the top of it with the thin band of metal as though it were a primitive musical instrument. A minimalist's harp of some sort. The piece of wood was lighter than most and looked like hickory. The metal seemed nondescript, just bluish gray, as though it had been oiled.

"*¡Dios mío!*" Dolores said, picking up Willem's soiled shirt from the floor.

"She just said 'my God,'" Joe explained to him.

"I realize that," Willem said, turning to see the woman holding the shirt stained with barbecue sauce. A stain that had turned dark like dried blood.

"*¡La sangre!*" Dolores said, horrified.

"She says that's blood," Joe said to Willem, his eyes large and questioning.

"Well, she's wrong. It's barbecue sauce."

"*No,* Dolores. *Es la salsa de barbecue,*" Joe told her.

"*¡Este hombre es un criminal!*" Dolores hissed, glaring at Willem.

"She says you're a—"

"I understood her. But she's wrong. I'm not a criminal. It's not blood. It's sauce," Willem told them as he removed the letter from the small table in front of the window and slid it into his shirt pocket. The woman was still chattering to the boys as Willem walked out the door and put a hand to his thick hair and smoothed it down. He had not even had time to take a comb to it. As he went down the short walkway, he stumbled on one of Alyce's large pots and fell into the wall, more embarrassed than hurt. Joe stuck his head out the door and yelled to him, "Mister. Dolores says we ought to call the police."

Willem shrugged and pushed his way through the door to the office, the bell jingling, summoning Alyce from the kitchen, he supposed, since the boy had mentioned eggs. She came through the hallway, wiping her hands on a dish towel, a smile plastered on her face.

"What can I do for you, Mr. Fremont?"

"Alyce, it's about Dolores," he began, and then remembered his manners. "Good morning," he said, taking a deep breath and letting it out slowly, trying to calm down.

"I bet you done run out of fresh towels."

"No, that's not it. I've got all the towels I need."

"Okay, then." She smiled at him.

"I really need . . ."

There was such a good-humored look to her face, such a willingness to please, that Willem couldn't continue. Glancing around the room, he fished for an idea, any idea. "A phone book. Is there one I might borrow?"

"Right there on the desk." She pointed to it.

"Thank you." Willem went to it and opened it to the back and ran a finger down the listings of lawyers. There were none in Purvis and only three in Hattiesburg. He wasn't really sure a lawyer would be required for what he planned to do. All he really needed was a notary public. But any lawyer worth his salt should be able to point him in the right direction. After jotting down the phone numbers on a piece of paper, he was turning to leave the office and saw Alyce standing by the front door in the ribbed light of the open venetian blinds, sun striking her face with horizontal patterns. The illumination was such that she seemed a slatted portrait of a woman who had spent her entire life waiting for something that had never arrived.

"Alyce?"

"Oh," she said, composing her face. "I just cooked too many eggs." She forced brightness to her voice. "The boys done eat what they wanted. There's leftover bacon, too. I could make you some toast."

Willem sat on the corner of the desk and folded his arms and sighed.

"Of course, you don't have to eat if you don't want to. It was just a offer." Flipping her hair behind her ear, she looked at him and caught him glancing at his watch. "Never mind. I'm sure you got places to go and things to do."

"I'm in no hurry," he said, though he was.

"Mr. Fremont?"

"Yes?"

"If you was to walk in here off the street, what would you think?"

He hadn't walked in off the street, but he *had* driven in, and he looked at his hands, wondering over her question. She must have sensed his bewilderment, for she began an attempt at an explanation.

"I mean. If you was a stranger . . . Well, I guess you *were* a stranger."

"At one time I was."

"I guess what I'm tryin to say is that things ain't exactly normal around here, are they? I mean, with my husband gone the way he is."

"I haven't really thought of it like that," he said, swinging his leg forward, noticing with alarm that his socks didn't match. He was wearing one black sock and one blue sock. Shaking his head, he said, "I'm not too familiar with 'normal.' I've always felt more abnormal than normal."

"Really?"

"Really."

"But you were normal enough to run your own business."

"True. But so are you. Look what you've done with this place."

"I ain't done nothin." She picked at the cord to the blinds and wrapped it around her finger.

"I know one thing," Willem said. "You seem to try awful hard."

Her bottom lip began to quiver. "Sometimes tryin ain't enough."

"I realize that. But then again, sometimes that's all we can do."

"You don't even know what I'm talkin about, do you?"

No. He didn't. But part of his disorder, or whatever one might want to call it, was the accompanying net of empathy that got thrown over those in his immediate circle. An uncanny awareness of what others were feeling.

"You see them out yonder?" Alyce pointed out the window, and he went and stood beside her and looked out onto the yard where the rain was still falling, filling the broken oyster shells. A sea of winking eyes was the overall appearance the shells gave, and Willem looked away from them toward the guide wire of the telephone pole, the creosote-covered post connected to the Mississippi earth by a lone clinging vine of kudzu, her two boys crouched beside it.

"You know what they're out there doin?"

"What?"

"It's called worm baitin."

"Worm baiting?"

"It's what their grandpa used to do. You call the worms."

Willem watched as Joe hammered the stob in the ground and Ben began to stroke the top of it with the piece of metal.

"He's lettin Ben try it this time." Alyce picked up the corner of her shirt and dabbed at her eyes, turning away from Willem to do so.

Willem pulled out his handkerchief and handed it to her. "Here you go."

"Thank you. Don't know what's wrong with me this mornin. I ain't bein a very good hostess, I guess."

"You're just fine, Alyce," he said, meaning every single word.

"When you rub that metal across the wood, it sends a vibration down through into the dirt, and earthworms is supposed to come up."

"Does it work?"

"They ain't been able to get it to yet. But they keep tryin."

Willem watched them as the rain began to slack up, pockets of sun breaking through the dark clouds, the glistening sight of wet greenery so plain it was beautiful.

"What kind a life is it when all it would take would be one worm comin up out of the ground to make somebody happy?" she asked, turning to him and pressing his handkerchief to her eyes. Willem didn't know what to do, so he just stood next to her and watched the boys in their endeavors.

"Look at me. Here I am goin on and on." She stood back from him and rubbed her hands over her eyes. "It ain't right. You're a payin guest."

"It's no bother."

"Listen. Don't feel like you have to stay here and baby-sit me. I'm okay. Sometimes it just gets to me—"

He needed to find a lawyer and he needed to take his clothes to the cleaners and he needed a haircut, but what he said was, "I wouldn't mind a cup of coffee."

"Really?"

"Really."

"Well, you come on, then. Right back here to my kitchen."

And while he sat at her table and took note of the rust stain across the porcelain bridge of her sink, her cast-iron skillet, her mismatched chairs, he drank coffee and watched as she buttered toast for him. And then she sat and drank her coffee, and it was the first time Willem ever remembered feeling at ease without the benefit of small talk. The first time he had ever felt that small talk would be terribly inappropriate, for the rain had ended and the sun was out and her hummingbird feeder hanging over the kitchen window winked red and orange and blue, turning slowly in the breeze. While he watched, a tiny emerald-green bird flew up to place its long beak in an opening and then zipped away.

"I've never seen one of them this close," he said to her.

She glanced out the window. "They're always around this time of the year."

"There's not too many of them where I come from."

"Colorado?"

"Yep."

"That's where your business was at?"

"Yep." He drank from his cup. "I spent most of my life building furniture."

"Real furniture?"

As opposed to what? he wondered. "Real furniture. Reproductions, mainly. Queen Anne. Shaker. Some American Federal."

"You reckon you'll ever do that again?"

He looked at his hands, his bulging arthritic knuckles. "I doubt it. You do something long enough, you begin to hate it."

She nodded slowly and listened to him talk about a slipper-foot tea table and bowfront chest of drawers he said he was fond of, her mood lifting as she leaned on the table and watched him sketch the design of each on a paper napkin, and while he talked, prisms of reflected light speckled his hands as the hummingbird feeder rocked back and forth and back and forth in the breeze.

{CHAPTER 23}

The law office of Silverman, Leiman, and Silverman was on Hardy Street in downtown Hattiesburg, next to the old library and directly across from the huge Methodist church that had been standing longer than Eilene had been living. The placement of the office seemed strange, in her opinion, and as she looked at the one-story glass-facade building, she couldn't help but notice how odd it seemed next to the others surrounding it. The library seemed right, with its curving steps and brown bricks. And the church seemed right, with its tall pillars and towering steeple. But the law office, with its ultra-modern look, seemed like a building straight out of *The Jetsons*, that space-age cartoon that Sonny liked to watch. Positioned as it was, it seemed terribly out of place and jarring to look at, but then again, Eilene supposed the spot made it handy for those not satisfied with the judicial system, seeing how they could go next door and read up on their legal rights in the old library, or walk across the street into the church and appeal to God Almighty to plead the case. She didn't intend to do either of those things. Not at this point. The situation was not yet that desperate. Or so she hoped.

Eilene cut the wheels and parallel-parked expertly underneath the limbs of an old oak tree. Turning off the engine, she rolled down the window slightly, so that the heat could leave the vehicle and she'd not be smothered once she returned. Reaching up to the rearview mirror, she rotated it slightly and checked her lipstick. She had not worn lipstick in almost twenty years, and something about the new tube she had picked up in the drugstore still seemed horribly wrong.

The purchase had been a last-minute decision, one she made during the drive from Purvis to Hattiesburg, but once it was fixed in her mind that she was looking old these days and a new lipstick would make her look not so old, the thought became a compulsive need that she couldn't set aside. The drugstore was on the outskirts of town, near the university, where young people were congregating on the street corners, sitting on the low curbs smoking and talking and lounging about as though wasting their parents' college-fund money was a proper thing to do. It took her forever to find a place to park, but once she managed to fit the Pontiac in between the Burger King and Southern Dry Cleaning, she got out and locked it and headed toward the store, overly conscious of the looks she got as she wound her way through the throng of youngsters who had the bad manners to stop and stare at her as though she had no business being there or, worse, might be wearing something that *labeled* her as not belonging there.

Is there anyone in the world besides a tax-paying geriatric citizen who has more business going into a drugstore? She would have liked to poke each of them on the shoulder and ask that. Regardless of her rallying point, once she was out of view of the most tenacious of the teenage starers, she glanced down at her neat loafers and white socks and tan slacks and brushed her hand across the buttons of her starched white shirt. Nothing was unzipped or unbuttoned. All was well. At least with Eilene, who felt properly attired and in command of all her sensibilities. Unlike the lazy loungers, one of whom was sitting on a stool and playing a guitar in front of the dry cleaner. *Since when is that a common occurrence?* she wondered, noticing his shoulder-length hair and the open guitar case near his feet. If she had had change for a dollar, she would have tossed it to him, for he certainly could have used a pair of shoes and a haircut.

The drugstore was so cool that the windows were raining condensation. The whole place smelled of candy and antiseptic, a noxious blend that made her eyes water. Strolling down to the cosmetic section, she was dismayed by the selection. There were just so many of them. Maybelline. Clairol. Pond's. Revlon. More Maybelline. A girl with long black hair drifted up on her open-toed sandals and stood by Eilene's elbow and asked if she could help.

"I'm just looking, dear," Eilene told her. The words seemed to bounce off the girl, who stood there smiling. Eilene wondered if she might be deaf or something and pointed to the display case closest to her. "Lipstick. I'm just looking. I'm perfectly able to look on my own without assistance."

"Ma'am, I was just trying to be helpful," the girl said.

"Well, sugar, why don't you go and try to be helpful somewhere else."

The girl sauntered away, looking, Eilene was sure, for some other elderly lady to torment.

Checking both ways up the aisle to make sure no one was watching, Eilene opened seven tubes of Maybelline Luscious Lip Lacquer and tested each on the back of her hand. Settling on the least offensive color, Peach Dreamsicle, she paid and made her way back through the milling youngsters, who had gathered around the hippie songster, cheering him on. A tambourine player with hair even longer than the guitar player's had joined in the mix, and if Eilene had had the money, she would have paid them all to get off the street and back into class where they belonged.

Left with peach-colored strips across the top of her hand, she rubbed at them with a Kleenex; rubbed so hard that the Kleenex shredded into tiny rolls of almost-nothingness, and still the marks were there. Sitting in the hot car, she calculated how many times she was likely to use her left hand while in the lawyer's office and came up with a number that was less than ten but more than five. If she kept her purse clutched in her left hand, she would be forced to use her right one and would get away without the lawyer's wondering if she was marking herself up with waxy war paint. This settled, she opened the tube and applied it to her lips.

It didn't even come close to being Peach Dreamsicle. It was so far from being Peach Dreamsicle, it was positively laughable.

Going back into the store, Eilene tried to get a refund, but the cashier took exception to Eilene's logic and failed to see the obvious proof that the color was wrong. In a blur of annoyance, she bent her head to the microphone and called for assistance. The noise was so loud, Eilene was sure the hippies out on the street could hear it.

"Is this really necessary?" Eilene asked her.

"Ma'am, you want a refund, don't you?"

"Well, yes."

"Then this is necessary."

The same girl who had tried to help her before wandered up with a gleam in her eye, a thirst for justice in the fullness of her lips.

"This is not the right color," Eilene stammered, holding it out. "I just bought it, and it's the wrong color. It's not even *close* to the color. See? Look at the tube."

The girl took it from Eilene, who had made the faulty judgment of extending the lipstick with her marked-up hand. Tossing her hair over her shoulder, the girl glanced toward the cosmetics end of the store, and Eilene could almost see her calculating a hoard of opened tubes for which Eilene would soon have to account.

"Ma'am, we can't take this back," the girl finally said, handing it to Eilene.

"Why not?"

"Because it's been opened and used."

"Of course it's been opened and used. I wouldn't be standing in here complaining about it if it hadn't been opened and used. If it hadn't been used, there would be nothing to complain about. I'd be on my way downtown to the lawyer's office instead of tryin to reason with you."

"Listen—"

"I am listenin. I'm doin nothin *but* listenin."

"If the product was defective, we could take it back."

"How would you determine if something was defective?"

"Oh, I don't know. If maybe the lipstick was broken in half or the tube wouldn't crank up. Something like that."

Eilene took the lipstick and cranked it all the way up and broke it in two. "It's broke. Now can I have my money back?"

"You want me to call the manager?" the cashier asked in a worried-sounding voice.

"No, I certainly don't want you to call the manager," Eilene said.

"I wasn't talking to you. I was talking to the cosmetic technician."

The long-haired girl shook her head. "Ma'am, we can't give you your money back, and that's all there is to it."

Eilene could be stubborn, too, and she proved it by digging in her heels and refusing to move out of the line, blocking customers who were displaying their discontent with loud sighs and shuffling feet, keeping them from purchasing their Preparation H and candy bars and home-permanent kits.

The girl had the nerve to put a hand on Eilene's elbow and attempt to guide her over to the fluorescent lights shining down over the display cases that held mascara and fingernail polish. Eilene allowed herself to be led, not because she wanted to be, but because any other reaction would have made her look even more foolish.

"Now, stand here and let's have a look at you," the girl said, holding a mirror out to Eilene.

The girl was so obviously patronizing that Eilene refused to look in the mirror, choosing to look at the boxes of hair coloring instead, as she listened to the girl go on and on about pigmentation and the color-matching skills of the Maybelline chemists and how there might be something about Eilene's lips, some collagen abnormality, that *warred* with the basic compounds in the lipstick. She had seen it before, she said. That could be it. Or maybe Eilene just needed new glasses.

"I wasn't trying to buy a weapon, dear. And I certainly don't need new glasses. All I wanted was a tube of lipstick that delivers what it promises."

The girl showed her true colors by rolling her eyes at Eilene. "Most folks realize that none of the colors look *exactly* like the colors on the box."

"Then why in the world do you sell them?" Eilene wanted to know.

"Because people keep buying them," the girl said, and Eilene snatched open her purse and shoved the purchase inside and stomped out of the store.

Blotting her lips on a Kleenex, Eilene thought perhaps the problem might rest in the name. The actual color as it appeared on Eilene's lips seemed more like the raw flesh of a salmon. But who in the world would want to purchase a tube of lipstick labeled "Salmon Skin"? Nobody, she was sure.

Done with thinking about her lipstick, she climbed out of the car and debated over locking it. The wide glass office windows were directly parallel with the car, and on the other side of those windows was a dark-haired woman who looked decidedly Jewish. Would it convey a sense of mistrust if that girl saw her lock her door? Yes, it absolutely would, so Eilene made a point of leaving the car door unlocked and hoped the girl had noticed her cavalier attitude when she slammed it shut. She couldn't understand Jews; they were so serious and full of deep thoughts and quick on the financial uptake of business deals. Not only that, they seemed to want the whole world to know they were God's chosen people, a standing that irritated Eilene, who couldn't understand why God would make a point of telling one group of people they were chosen and labeling the other, innumerable groups of people who had never even heard of a synagogue as second-rate. If she were God, *she* certainly wouldn't do that. Hadn't she tried her best to be fair with her two sons? Didn't Sonny get the same amount and quality of attention as Bruno?

The girl behind the window had glanced Eilene's way before going back to her typewriter, and Eilene figured it was time to start walking. *There. I didn't lock my door. I even rolled down my window a bit.* Satisfied her presentation was appropriate, she made her way past the manicured shrubbery and the brass plaque bearing the firm's name to the front, where the doors were automated and swished open before she had even stretched out her hand, startling her into a loss of composure, a not so rare condition these days.

"He's waiting for you in the conference room," the girl said, standing and swishing around the desk. Mediterranean, that's how she looked. All singular bushy eyebrow and large nose. Not Jewish at all. Unless she was a Mediterranean Jew. Eilene looked up at the ceiling and wondered if Israel was considered Mediterranean, and then she blamed the swishing doors for getting her mind headed down this ridiculous track of nationalities and geography. The entire office swished. The air-conditioning. The automated doors. The girl's nylon skirt. Even the water fountain made swishing sounds.

"I hope the potty's near by," Eilene said, having to walk at a hurried pace just to keep up with this no-nonsense Mediterranean office girl who was already three feet ahead of her.

"I beg your pardon?" The girl turned and looked over her shoulder at Eilene.

Eilene waved her hands in the air. "All this water noise is what I'm talking about."

"Water noise?"

"Yes. This swishy, watery sound. Don't tell me you cain't hear it," Eilene told the back of her nylon shirt.

The girl waved her neatly manicured fingers at the air. "Oh, that. You grow used to it after a while."

"Where's the bathroom, dear? I'm not quite used to it yet and would like to powder my nose."

"It's right over there." The girl pointed to a pair of mahogany doors with a tall metal ashtray in between. "I'll wait for you."

"That would be nice," Eilene said, standing momentarily before the door as though expecting it to swish open for her.

"Just push on it," the girl said. Eilene stared at her, searching for a trace of humor or ridicule. None was there. Not a big surprise, seeing how the girl was ethnic and everybody knew how humorless ethnic people were.

After taking care of her business, Eilene stood before the framed mirror and took a Kleenex out of her purse and rubbed the lipstick off her lips.

There, she told herself. *That's more like it.* It was bad enough being in a strange building with strange swishy noises circling one's head and trying to keep pace with a strange girl with no sense of humor, but to not even feel like yourself because of thick waxy goo on the lips? This had been the strangest sensation of all. She washed her hands and wadded up the tissue and placed it in the tall metal trash can with its lid that popped open at the touch of a foot.

"If you'll follow me, please."

"Why, of course I will, dear."

The two of them made their way down a plush hallway of the type in big city hotels. Wonderful paintings were hanging on the walls, and everything seemed to match. Not an off note anywhere. Salmon-colored upholstered chairs sitting on salmon-colored rugs that matched the salmon-colored walls. Eilene was immeasurably glad she had removed her lipstick, for the color she had picked would have blended amazingly well.

Too well. So well, in fact, she would have seemed a piece of decor, an ornamental walking vase, perhaps.

The girl tapped on the door, and a voice called out for them to come in, and Eilene walked into the room and stood near a chair. It was a test she gave every man she came in contact with. This one passed, standing and moving around the desk and offering her a chair. Once there, she leaned back and put her purse in her lap and folded her right hand over her left one so that he'd not see the lipstick marks.

The office was spacious, and the man seemed to belong there, and Eilene felt immediately out of place and unsure of herself. It had been years since she had been inside her lawyer's office, and the last time the office had not been in this new *fringe* downtown, but in the *real* downtown in a brownstone building next to the old Saenger Theater. And that lawyer, the old Mr. Silverman, had been portly and good-natured, not particularly Jewish-acting, and able to make small talk that put Eilene at ease, so different from this mortician-like figure sitting behind his hard shiny desk.

"How can Silverman, Leiman, and Silverman be of service to you, Mrs. Till?" he asked.

"Which one are you?"

"Excuse me?"

"Which lawyer am I speaking to? I remember the old Mr. Silverman, and you're not him. And you don't look at all like the old Mr. Silverman, so I'm guessing you're not his son, either. Are you Mr. Leiman?"

"I'm sorry. I thought you made the appointment yourself. I'm Ernst Leiman." She extended her hand to him, and he leaned across the desk and shook it, and she began to relax a bit. "If you prefer one of the other associates, I'll certainly understand."

She barely stopped herself from informing him that all lawyers looked and acted the same to her. In the nick of time, she said, "No. You'll do just fine. I just want to make some adjustments to my will."

"Did our firm draw up the will?"

"Somebody here did. Not here in this actual building. But at the old place. Downtown. About twelve years ago."

He began shuffling papers on his desk. "Would the records be in your name? Or your husband's?"

"My husband's dead. He was dead when I had it drawn up, and he's not been resurrected as far as I can tell. So the file should be in my name. I have the original right here." She pulled the blue-backed sheaf of papers out of its thick envelope and handed it across the desk.

He studied it as he leaned back in his large leather chair. "I gather you've had some changes you want considered?"

"A few."

He read silently and nodded, pursing his lips a bit, and then he lifted out a sheet of white paper. "What's this letter in with it?"

"Tell me this, am I paying you by the hour?"

"Yes, I believe you are."

"So I can talk to you about more than one thing?"

"If you'd like."

"Okay. That piece of paper there's the other thing I want to talk to you about. It's a letter."

He read it quickly and then handed it over to her. "Seems an offer to buy a parcel of your land."

"That's what it is. An offer to buy exactly one point six acres. It came registered mail last week, and I wondered if you could tell me a little about it."

"It seems fairly simple," he said. "As far as most purchase offers go. Is the price close to what you were originally asking?"

"That's just it. I didn't have it up for sell. I don't even know where it is or how this person knew about it."

"Why would he want it?"

"That's what I thought you could tell me. There's not even a buyer listed. At least not a buyer's name. There's that proxy person and the notary seal." She opened the letter and pointed to it. "I have no way of knowing who wants to buy it or why."

"Did you contact the title officer listed?"

"I did."

"And?"

"They said the offer stands as is and should be taken at face value. All they were permitted to do, he said, was act on this person's behalf as some sort of liaison. You know, give him my answer and negotiate terms."

"Do you want to sell it?"

"It's not a matter of whether or not I want to sell. I'm just a little mystified by this letter coming out of the blue like it did. I just wondered if you had ever seen anything like this before."

"All the time."

"Is it legal?"

"Of course it's legal."

"Why would a person not want to list his name as the interested party, then?"

"Oh, there could be a thousand reasons."

"Since I'm paying you by the hour, how about listing just one or two of them."

"One thought that comes to mind is that the person may be a public figure and needs to maintain his privacy."

"Then why would he want a place out in the middle of nowhere?"

He shook his head. "I can't really say. Maybe he wants a hunting camp. Or some type of retreat. Here. Let me see that letter again." She handed it to him. "It says you keep the mineral rights. The buyer would be willing to leave those as they stand, in your name."

Eilene looked around the room, noticing the antique duck decoys set on top of glass-doored bookcases, and the prints of mallard ducks in flight over cattailed swamps, and the brass hunting horn fastened to the wall. A man's room. *Of course he would think the person might want a hunting lodge. He probably wants one of those himself.*

"Sometimes people are wanting the right-of-way to other property. You say you don't know exactly where this is?"

"We've got over a hundred acres. It's kinda hard to know it all."

"Well, it's hard to say if a right of way is what the interested party is looking for, since you don't know what this parcel is next to. This being the case, I would recommend contacting the person and simply telling him you want to know more. There's certainly no harm in demanding more information. If the person really wants to buy it, he or she should be willing to do this."

"So you've had offers like this before?"

"Not personally. But I've seen offers like this one. They're commonplace." Leiman pressed a button on his phone and a girl's voice said, "Yes, Mr. Leiman?"

"How about bringing in the file for Eilene Till of Four-seventy Sussex Road." He looked at Eilene. "Would you care for some water or a glass of tea?"

"Tea would be nice."

"And bring us each a glass of tea."

"Yessir."

He pressed the button again. "Sugar and mint, please."

"Right away."

He opened his desk drawer and lifted out a yellow legal pad and leaned forward and waited for Eilene to speak. When she didn't, he said, "What changes would you like to discuss?"

"As you can see by my copy, I've listed my sons as equal beneficiaries in the event of my death. With my older son, Bruno, acting as executor." Eilene looked out the wide expanse of windows and saw the small birdhouses set on the lawn and the slow traffic moving past and the overmanicured bushes, so well defined and orderly that even manufactored chaos wouldn't stand a chance. "I would like to change the beneficiaries listed."

Leiman was quiet, watching her with his serious, myopic eyes.

"I would like to exclude my sons and the sole beneficiary to be my grandchild."

"This is quite a change, Mrs. Till."

"I realize this."

"How old is the grandchild?"

"Oh, there's not one yet."

He leaned back in his chair and folded his hands across his chest. "So you want the land to go to this unborn child?"

"Should there be one, yes."

"And if there's not?"

"Then I want the land turned over to a charity organization."

"Do you have a particular one in mind?"

No, she didn't have one in mind, because she was sure it wouldn't come to that. As soon as she made a point of leaving a copy of the will out for Bruno to see, he would snap out of his insanity and get on with the business of being married. "Not at the moment. But there's seventy-five acres of nothing but pine trees that could be sold off. The rest of it we use for leasing purposes. Oh, we raise a few head of cattle, but our yearly income is a result of what we've leased out and money I've invested. I think there's a copy right there of last year's revenues." She pointed to where she knew the assets were listed and watched as he spread open the papers and read down the list.

"The houses and all are to go to this yet-unborn grandchild?"

"Yessir. Upon my death." Which she knew wouldn't be for years and years.

"What if there is more than one grandchild? Say, three or four?"

Oh, wouldn't that be a wonderful thing! she thought, trying to imagine not one miraculous child but two or three running around the place, digging in her garden, clamoring about the house, racing one another up the hill. "Then it's to be divided equally among them."

"A child won't be able to take full possession of all this—"

"I realize that. That's why I want a trustee listed. I don't have one in mind, but I'm sure you can set it up so that a responsible one is found. Someone who will manage the property for the child and make all the right decisions."

"Someone other than the child's parents?"

"Exactly."

"Now, Mrs. Till, I don't know what's happened to bring about this change, but you might want to think about this for a while. I've seen situations like this come up, and they can create serious problems. I have to warn you, I think your sons will fight this. There might be the question of mental state and possible undue influence. I guarantee they won't sit still for this. A long probate battle's not a lot of fun for anybody."

She looked at the lawyer and shook her head. "Now, who in the world would expect a funeral to result in fun, Mr. Leiman?" She had one more question for him. "Could you please call me at this number and let me know when I need to come back in and finalize the paperwork?" She handed him Bruno's telephone number, printed out on a recipe card.

"Of course."

The girl tapped on the office door and came in bearing two tall glasses on a silver tray and walked over to the desk and set down the tray.

"So, what fun plans do you have for the Fourth?" Leiman asked Eilene, stirring his tea, the spoon pinging against the glass.

"Lots of stuff. Family coming down in the morning from Meridian. Enough smoked pork to send us all to Weight Watchers permanently. I just hope we get some rain today. This heat is a killer."

Leiman nodded and sipped his tea and made no attempt to develop the small talk he had cultivated moments earlier.

Eilene drank quickly and silently and remembered to wipe her mouth with her right hand and not her left, and then she stood up, ready to go. "Well, thank you for the tea and your time. When do you think I'll be hearing from you?"

"Let's see. Today's the third of July. I would expect we'll have the paperwork ready by the end of the month."

"Oh, goody. And you'll call when I need to come in?"

"Yes. We'll be sure and call for an appointment."

And with that, Eilene left his office, walking down the long plush hallway, listening to her shoes swish on the carpet, watching the glass front doors waiting for her, and her car, fully in the shade.

Willem sat at the library table, all alone except for a stack of books piled up near his elbow, a stack yet to be touched. He ran his finger down their spines and wondered what had possessed him to pick so many of them when all he was going for was one fellow who had thought himself a poet.

One thing he could say about Thomas Hood was this: he was a hard fellow to track down. Willem had been at the library since early morning, thumbing through the card catalogs in the waist-high maple cabinet, listing during that first half hour close to twenty books written by more than a dozen Thomas Hoods. There was Thomas Hood the children's writer, who wrote about a little boy hitching a ride in a railroad car with an owl; and an autobiographical Thomas Hood, a Nordic shipmaker who had the sorry luck to wreck on an uncharted South Pacific island, a land so foreign to him he came close to dying of starvation before he recognized a coconut as a food and water source; and Thomas Hood the biographer, who penned a tome about William Schwenck Gilbert, the sheer size and weight enough to guarantee the book would remain forever on the shelf; and finally, Thomas Hood the mystery writer, who was apparently popular with the town's readership, since all sixteen of his books were checked out. It was not until he wandered into the library's reference section housing encyclopedias and textbooks, that he found volume two of *The Literature of England* and struck gold. He found the poem by checking the index, and now that the book was open in front of him and he was ready to copy down all the words to the poem called "Silence," he was dismayed to realize he had used up all his blank pages on book titles and reference numbers, and there was no space left to write down what he had come looking for in the first place.

The window across from him faced the east, and the morning sun was shining through the leaves of the trees, and he saw one or two pedestrians wandering along, shadows falling on their shoulders, while a gardener on his knees clipped the shrubs in front of the large Methodist church. Willem watched him crawl along, hedge clippers in his hand, bending and picking up pieces of greenery and placing them in a wheelbarrow at his side. It was truly a tranquil scene, and Willem felt calmed by the sight, as well as by the cloistered interior of the library, the smell of the books, and the *clickityclickclick* of a distant typewriter somewhere on the second floor. Even the occasional stamping of a library pad carried a pulsing comfort, like placing one's hand on a gyrating washing machine or watching clothes tumble in a pay-by-the-load washateria.

Turning back to the book, he read the poem, glancing once at the notation underneath the poet's name: "Poet and humorist born in London in 1799." He scanned a few lines of another poem by the man, "The Song of the Shirt."

With fingers weary and worn
With eyelids heavy and red,
A woman sat, in unwomanly rags,
Plying her needle and thread—

Willem didn't see one humorous element in the lines, or any that followed, and wondered what the man did in his spare time that branded him as funny. Did he read the poetry while drunk? Make fun of his own words? He turned the pages. "The Bridge of Sighs" was even more grim than "The Song of the Shirt." He kept turning pages, looking for some hint of hilarity and finding none, stumbling through William Wordsworth and Charles Lamb, shutting his eyes and inserting a finger into the thickness of the book as one might stick a finger into a slab of cheese, flopping the pages open and then peering down to see what name or phrase his finger landed on; reading a bit of Virginia Woolf and fanning back to Oscar Wilde's *The Importance of Being Earnest.*

The play was a long one, and he hadn't intended to actually read it, just breeze through as a means of killing time, but he found himself completely captivated by the farce. *Now, this one's a humorist,* he thought to himself, glancing up to see a woman who looked uncomfortably familiar to him standing in front of the librarian's desk to return a book and, once that was done, asking directions to the card-catalog section.

Now would be a good time to find the facilities, he thought, and rose to his feet and wandered through the corridor, stopping at the water fountain and holding his hand over his shirt as he bent and drank, going on down the hall to the men's room and, after a few moments, coming back out and wandering through the periodical room, where newspapers were spread-eagled across maple rods and various news magazines wore fancy plastic covers. Willem bent and read the headlines of all the newspapers he could see, as well as the covers of *Time, Newsweek,* and *Life.* The news seemed to be the same everywhere. Business about Nixon's incredible blunder, the "smoking gun," his weirdness, and the mounting pressure for impeachment. Sitting in a soft leather chair that reminded him of a large baseball glove and made him instantly woozy, Willem picked up a copy of *Consumer Digest* and dangled it in the air, hoping a spare piece of paper would fall out. Glancing over to the copy of *The New York Times,* he read its headline: EDITED TAPE TRANSCRIPTS RELEASED and, in lower-size type: *Nixon claims only expletives were deleted.* Sick of being reminded about the obvious stupidity of a man he had endured a panic attack to vote for, Willem left the small reading room and made a quick dash into the men's room, where he unspooled some toilet paper from a roll and folded it inside his shirt pocket. *Prisoners write on it all the time,* he figured. *All I have to do is be careful about bearing down with the pen.*

Back in the main room, he came to a skidding stop next to a rolling book cart, for the same woman who had been standing near the librarian's desk minutes earlier was sitting at his table, turning toward her the spines of the books stacked there so that she might read the titles. Not that Willem had given serious thought to reading any of them, and it was true, the books weren't literally his, but he had wandered all over the five-thousand-square-foot expanse of the library, pulling them off the shelves, and thought it outlandish that some bystander had the nerve to put her hands on them, to possibly be considering claiming them as her own.

As he pulled out his chair, he saw her loafers and white socks and remembered where he had seen her before. She was the same one who'd had the nerve to call him "sugar" down in the green basement of the Lamar County courthouse. He cleared his throat as he sat, looking at her once before going back to his reading, which hadn't really been reading at all but was more like concentrated skimming. Before, it had been pleasurable skimming, though, something he'd had a measure of fun doing. Now, as he sat and pretended to skim through *The Literature of England*, volume two, it was like sitting in a dentist's chair having a needle stuck in the roof of his mouth.

She folded her hands on the table and sighed. Loudly.

He looked up. Briefly. Was it rude to ignore a woman's sighs? He supposed it was, but it was also rude of her to take over his table.

"Excuse me, but have we met?"

He looked at her and debated the merits of denial. He could pretend to be from another country, burst forth in clicking guttural tongues, but he dismissed the idea as poorly thought out and ridiculous. "Could be," he said.

"I know we have. You have the type of face that's hard to forget."

He looked at her, wondering if her words should be considered complimentary or insulting; after all, the Elephant Man had a face one would not be prone to forget.

"Not many men your age have that much hair," she said, pointing to his head.

"My age?" he said.

"I'm guessing late sixties."

His icy regard of her was beginning to thaw a little. He was starting to forgive her for fondling his books.

She sighed again. Louder than before. "Most men your age have either no hair at all, or hair so thin they would be better served to have the barber whack it all off. At least that's what I think. Women have thinning hair, too. Old women, I mean. It's not widely broadcast, since most nearly bald women would be too embarrassed to step forward and admit it."

"You have nice hair," he said, the words popping out of his mouth before he had time to think.

She patted it. "Thank you. Now, I know we've met. Sometime recent, I think." She reached for her purse and removed a tissue and rubbed it in an abstracted manner across the top of her left hand, where clay-colored marks were lined up like sergeant stripes.

Willem was seriously considering total disclosure. The episode at Smokey's Bar and Grill had set him to thinking about the course of his disease (he was fully convinced now that it was an actual disease; one without a name, but a disease, nevertheless). Maybe he *did* need a bell around his neck, or a warning label, or a little card like deaf folks carried that he could hand to folks to inform them of the risks involved in talking to him.

WILLEM FREMONT
Fit-prone, nervous, and jumpy,
"Able to faint at the drop of a hat!"
Enter into conversations at own risk

This way folks would know what to expect. Diabetics were accepted by society. So were alcoholics. Hell, there were more location listings in the phone book for twelve-step programs than there were for churches. So what if he had some type of emotional meltdown at the least provocation? Would one laugh at someone going into a diabetic coma, or someone locked in the rigors of the DTs?

"I believe we met in the basement of the courthouse," he said. "A couple of weeks ago. Near the end of May." There. He had released all the required information. She should leave him, and his books, alone.

"You're right. Oh, yes. I do remember. You were holding one of those strange, hard-looking safari hats."

"A pith helmet. And I don't believe they're all that strange-looking," he said, still defensive of his purchase. "What I do believe was strange was the way you called me 'sugar.'"

She glanced off toward the balcony as though trying to recall fully. "I did?"

"Yes, I believe you did." He licked his finger and turned the page, pretended to scan the poem "Church Going," by Philip Larkin. "It was the first time in my life I ever recall being addressed as 'sugar.'"

"You were offended I called you that, weren't you? I seem to remember that you took quite an exception to it."

He shrugged.

"Listen, we call everyone 'sugar' down here. But you don't sound southern," she said. "If you were southern, you'd understand that when someone calls you 'sugar,' you should not be insulted."

"Perhaps."

"No, it's the truth. Now, if I wanted to insult someone, I'd make a point of omitting the 'sugar.' I'd simply call them by their first name. Or simply not address them in any specific way at all. Maybe just say 'hey, you.'" This part was not exactly true. Eilene had called the rude cosmetic technician "sugar," and she hadn't meant it as a term of endearment; she had meant to put the girl in her place, and she was confident she had done just that. But she had never been one to take criticism well, and now this man, this stranger (a really handsome stranger, she reminded herself, but that was beside the point), had the nerve to question her conversation skills? Who did he think he was, anyhow?

Willem thought momentarily about offering a reply, but he couldn't come up with one, so he went back to Philip Larkin, his eyes scanning the words "A serious house on serious earth it is, / In whose blent air all our compulsions meet . . ."

Eilene cut her eyes to him, noticing his stillness and seriousness, or was it plain old wariness? Whatever it was, it annoyed her. Life was not being exactly kind to Eilene at the moment. The lawyer's disapproval, which she couldn't believe she cared about, but realized she did. And those boys of hers. Those silly boys! Just look at the mess they continued to stir up. And now this total stranger had the nerve to be offended by something she had said in passing! She glared at him, more irritated than she had been with anyone in a long while, even more irritated than she stayed with Sonny, who managed to push her buttons so far down in their control panel they completely disappeared. How dare this man, this stranger, for God's sake, take offense at her innocent pleasantries? The rage was building, and she felt herself trembling. "Well, I'll be," she said, pretending to pick lint off the front of her blouse. "To think that you've been walking around town for weeks with a great big chip on your shoulder—"

"Excuse me?" Willem put his hand protectively to his chest. He could not believe it.

"It's true. You've got a chip on your shoulder."

"Ma'am, I have *not* been walkin around with a chip on my shoulder."

"I've raised two boys all by myself, and believe me, I know a chip on the shoulder when I see one, and you've got a great big one. Sitting right about there." She leaned across the table and tried to touch his shoulder, and he leaned away from her, a look of horror on his face. Enough was enough. Shutting his book, he began to gather all of them together in a neat stack, with all the spines facing him.

"I'd really like to say that this has been a pleasant conversation, but—"

"Sugar, you don't have to say a word." She wiggled her fingers at him and grinned, watching his color drain completely away.

It was a first, the way Willem kept his eyes on her and waited for her to look away. He never did this, never tested his limits by staring at someone, but he felt there was a lot at stake here. His pride, for one thing. After what seemed an eternity, she looked away first, but it wasn't in defeat, it was a subtle dismissal, and Willem felt banished to the corner of her mind, where he supposed bad little boys with chips on their shoulders were standing with their pants down around their ankles, waiting to be thrashed. He was incredibly irritated by her. Angry, even. He had spent his entire life trying to behave circumspectly, weighing situations and avoiding entanglements, going out of his way to keep from offending people, and this woman, this *tiny,* nervy woman with her little-girl socks and her pointed little chin, had the audacity to bait him!

Another sigh. The loudest one yet.

"Excuse me, lady," Willem said. "But I feel I need to tell you something."

"Please. Go right ahead." She looked directly at him and lifted her eyebrows, her lips curving slightly upward.

"You'd be cute if you weren't so obvious," he said, measuring his words.

"I beg your pardon?"

He waved his hand at her. "That nonsense you do. All these dramatic sighs. Do they work with those sons of yours?"

She leaned forward. "Yes. As a matter of fact, they do."

Willem shook his head. "My God, and you're willin to admit this?"

An unreadable expression was on her face, the look of a woman poised for any possibility, which was good, since the needle on Willem's alarm meter was twitching toward the red-light zone, where anything at all might happen.

Eilene's only friends, Bea and Velma, were not available to offer her consolation, but away on a senior-citizen bus tour of Vicksburg's historic homes and not due back until the early morning hours, and there were so many recent developments that she needed to complain about. (Needed to *shout* about, was more like it.) Her only companion was this man, whom she had just tormented excessively and probably alienated to a point beyond remedy, thus eliminating forever her chance to complain even a tiny little bit about her sons and how determined they were to ruin her life. She ran her striped hand through her hair and attempted a last-ditch effort. "Listen. I'm being rude here, and I know it. Terribly rude. I've had a really awful day, and I was taking it out on you. And I didn't mean to do that. Put your books back." She patted the top one. The *Norton Anthology*. "I'll be good and leave you alone."

The command, and surely it was a command, forced him to look at her, and he noticed again her clear blue eyes and the glasses hanging by a chain around her neck. "You don't seem inclined to do that." "Church Going." Philip Larkin. *Read the words,* he ordered himself. He tried to obey, but she was talking again.

"I don't seem inclined to do what?"

"Leave a person alone."

"Oh, I can leave a person alone if I try." Eilene smiled at him. "Used to be, people wanted me to mess with them a little. More than one said they couldn't wait to see what I might do next." She studied her hands, saw how really old and knobby they were.

"I can believe that."

She nodded and smiled a little more. "Now, this is better, isn't it?" she said as she opened her purse and peeled open a roll of LifeSavers and offered him one.

He took it, noticing the trembling of his hands, a definite warning sign.

"Better than getting all huffy over the word 'sugar.'"

"I refuse to discuss it," he said, but he grinned and raised his eyebrows, which he thought made him look a bit more like Gary Cooper. Then he looked at his watch. It really was time to go.

"Would you tell me one thing before you leave?" she asked.

"I'll try."

"What comes to mind when you hear the words 'undue influence'?"

He folded his arms across his chest and looked at her. Where in the hell did this woman come from? "Influence that one does not feel is due him or her? Maybe?"

"I was afraid of that."

He was silent but watching her. She seemed genuinely perplexed.

"Is that not what you think of?" he asked.

She shook her head and placed her right hand over her left one and shifted in her chair. "Not really. Well, I guess I was thinkin of the words more like 'undo.' D-o, instead of d-u-e. 'Undo influence,' as in the effort required in trying to undo something."

"I suppose it might be open to interpretation."

"No. No, it's not." She rubbed at her forehead. "Either it means a certain thing or it doesn't."

Willem looked around and wondered what to do next, and the lapse in activity flipped the automated switch on his internal alarm button, and without being completely aware that he was doing this, he began to tap his fingers along the arms of the chair, calculating when the head librarian was going to stamp a book and timing his taps to coordinate with the movements of her hands. His eyes took on a distant drugged look. And then he felt himself lifted up to a safer place absent of barbecue sandwiches or Hispanic cleaning ladies or women wearing socks, a place where voices disappeared and all he heard were all the other sounds issuing forth inside the library. The *clickityclicks* of the typewriter. The muffled thuds of shoes moving up and down the stairs. The out-of-rhythm whacking of the loose wheel on a book cart. He even imagined he could hear the zinging of the gardener's shears as he knelt on a lawn across the street. A magical cacophony of *kathunk*s and *kawhok*s and *clickityclick-click*s. An inviting percussion that was pulling him in and demanding he fill the gaps in noise, a space only Willem recognized as being vacant and needful of filling. *Kathunk-kawhok-clickityclickclick. Kathunk-kawhok-clickityclickclick.* Willem shut his eyes. It was wonderful, this noise. And his fingers were tapping with an increased tempo, and he leaned back against the chair, his mouth ajar and his eyes moving underneath their old-man lids in a type of waking REM-sleep manifestation, unaware that the woman was watching him with her mouth open, the almost melted LifeSaver visible on the tip of her tongue, genuine concern and pity on her face.

When he once again became aware of his surroundings, Willem realized the woman had gone, leaving behind no trace of herself other than a single LifeSaver set out on the open pages of the book. Reaching for it, he wondered how badly he had behaved, if he had done something that would make the pages of the next morning's newspaper. Seeing no obvious alarm or even disgust from any of the library's patrons, he settled into his chair, the feeling of exhaustion not so heavy as it had been after previous attacks. The hour was growing late, and there was no trace of the gardener across the street, either, other than neatly clipped hedges and a lawn so smooth and green it seemed more bed than lawn.

Thumbing back through the book, he found the poem and waited until the librarian was about to stamp her pad, and then he tore it out, freezing momentarily to see if anyone had noticed. No one had. Feeling better about the whole situation now that he had managed to find what he had come looking for, he folded the paper and put it in his pocket and, without glancing at anyone, made his way to the front door, realizing he would have to hurry to make it to the sunken house and back again before dark.

{CHAPTER 24}

Though every other element seemed constant, the fields, the red-capped silo standing like a misplaced cold-war missile, the cat on its milk-crate bed licking itself all over, the woman who stood inside the morning shadows of the back porch was a different woman these days. Leah put a hand low to her stomach and rubbed, the cramping worse today than it was yesterday, though the doctor had said it was not to be considered abnormal, that women her age went through it all the time. Her age. *Now, there's a rude category,* she thought, frowning a bit. The ligaments are stretching, the kind doctor had said, placing a finger on her low stomach to show her where those ligaments were. We raise cattle. I'm well acquainted with ligaments, she had told him. Oh? Well, then, he had said, tipping his head to the side as though trying hard to come up with some other area of enlightenment. So you know the uterus is expanding? I do, she had said. Well, then. I guess you know why you're cramping. Cramping is to be expected, because everything is changing down there. In fact, if there were no cramping, I'd be worried. He had gone to the cabinet in the small cubicle and pulled out packets of reading material and handed them over to her and then he had scribbled out a prescription for prenatal vitamins and told her no more lifting for the next two months and no more hot baths for the next nine weeks and absolutely, positively, no more cigarettes. He failed to say no more marijuana, but she supposed that was a given.

It was early morning, and Bruno was moving about the barn, throwing hay bales on the back of the wagon, and Leah stood watching him as she sipped her cup of hot lemon water sprinkled with salt, a peculiar drink she had begun to crave since the mere thought of coffee brought on a gag reflex that made her shut her eyes and reach for the door frame.

Bruno looked good, leaner than he had been back in May, and he had taken to wearing his T-shirts underneath the brace, a wise choice, since the July heat was awful, and his hair was longer, curling up along the back of his neck in a flip that she was sure had to be bothering him. He was back to what he had worn before the injury, his old blue jeans and cowboy boots, but the mustache was new. A subtle change in a man she was still married to but no longer lived with; where he lived and with whom was such a large hole inside her that she held to her low stomach as a way of shielding or protecting herself, believing wholeheartedly in the peanut-size talisman as a means of warding off the pain.

She watched as he disappeared into the shadows of the barn, and she heard the sound of the fuel can banging around and watched as he came out and went to the fifty-gallon drum and worked the hand pump on its side and filled the red container with diesel, then disappeared again. She knew he was filling the tractor. She saw him every morning and every evening, and she had built these brief appearances into a type of Shakespearean play. A play she titled "Much Ado About a Vacuum Cleaner":

ACT 1

Expanse of scorched grass stretching across the fields. Maximum of simplicity and symmetry. Gray morning light. Trompe l'oeil backcloth to represent unbroken plain and sky receding to meet in far distance. Standing on dark back porch, Leah, *arms and shoulders tense as she watches her husband,* Bruno, *emerge from the barn. Long pause. A cat meows forlornly for a time, say five seconds, stops. Leah does not move. Pause. Cat meows more piercingly, say for seven seconds. Leah steps forward to the steps of the porch, throws back her head, and glances at the sky directly overhead . . .*

BRUNO: *(gazing at Leah, calls out from his position near the door to the truck)* Leah?

LEAH: *(stirring from her reverie to turn toward barn)* Yes?

BRUNO: I'll be back in an hour or so, and I'll get on with the bush-hogging. Leah? What's the matter with you? Are you okay? Leah. *(puts his fingers in his mouth and whistles like a cattleman)*

LEAH: *(jumping)* . . .

She heard the whistle and came to herself and lifted a hand to him, for he had been talking to her. She nodded, embarrassed. "I'll have your clothes ready by the time you're done," she told him.

Bruno ducked his head and seemed to be studying the dirt in front of him, and then he looked up at her again and held out his hands in appeasement. "Listen. I don't expect you to do my laundry. All I wanted to do was use the washer. I never meant for you to do it."

"I know. But I will anyway," she told him, and then she went back into the kitchen and sat at the table with her cup of hot lemon water and watched the sky lighten in small degrees, trees and fence line making their gradual appearance. Setting down her cup, she leaned her head down next to the ribbed sugar dispenser. A wave of nausea rocked her, and she tried to make her breathing light and shallow, to place it away from her low stomach and not bother it, so the sickness would stay put and not rise up her throat like all the other mornings of the past two weeks. Reaching out a hand, she shoved Bruno's plate of toast as far from her nose as possible.

With her cheek resting on the surface of the table, she watched sideways as the truck headed out to the fields. The vehicle bounced across the uneven ground, the grass summer-thick and high, crushed under the forward movement of truck tires. She shut her eyes; watching the rolling wheels was making her feel even sicker than the smell of the toast.

Bruno didn't know about the baby, and the way things were going, he probably never would. The news was still fresh to her, so raw it stood separate from actual reality. A bicycle in a box as opposed to a bicycle fully assembled. It was not yet a baby, she told herself, and this was good, since she still hadn't decided what to do about it. Either way, it was her decision, and she would come to it the same way she had come to countless other decisions since the last of May: she would simply set aside her proactive stance and wait and see what turned up. *I've become my father,* she thought. *A classic relativist wallowing in the belief that truth and morality are not absolute but relative to my current situation.* The thought of her father made her want to call him again, but she had already called him three times during the week, and while he always sounded glad to hear from her, she knew he had to be growing suspicious. Why would a daughter who barely managed to phone once a month suddenly strike up an almost daily communication? The current state of the weather and the plans for the Fourth had already been discussed, and he had already reminded her to put green olives and not black ones in her potato salad; the question about whether or not she had a blender had already been asked and answered (yes, she did have a blender), and Leah's spur-of-the-moment invitation to have them sleep over had already been extended and, much to her dismay, accepted. Of all the possible topics of conversation, there was only one that had been avoided: Bruno.

She placed a hand on her stomach and rubbed, trying to imagine what was there, this peanut-size something or other whose fate she held in her hands. There were moments when she really wanted it; needed it, in fact. Like earlier, when she had watched Bruno walk across the backyard, and even though he was fully clothed, she had been with him long enough to know his body by heart, how he had a birthmark on his left ass cheek, how his leg hair grew silky near his upper thighs, how flat his stomach was, and she had a vision of him in the dark, naked, stretched out beside the young woman who ran the motel. Leah had needed the peanut then, and just putting her hand on her stomach had made the vision of the two writhing naked in a motel bed fade away and the aloneness seem not so absolute. But there were other moments when the practical side of her nature kicked in and her thoughts and visions became colored by full autonomy, and she saw herself working downtown in an office, doing research or handling some company's payroll, anything at all besides standing on a back porch in early morning light. A baby had no claim on her then. For those brief periods of time, the baby was not really a baby, the same way a box holding bicycle parts was not yet a bicycle.

Going to the cabinet, she got out the bottle holding extra-strength Sinutab, for she felt the beginnings of a sinus headache, a bad one, too. Lifting Bruno's piece of toast off his saucer, she bit into it and made herself chew. The reading material for new mothers, with its warm and fuzzy promotional packaging on which every single person depicted was smiling her fool head off, had informed Leah that food would help the nausea go away. She was yet to prove this, but she was willing to try anything. She looked at the bottle and wondered what five hundred milligrams of acetaminophen would do to the small peanut, if it might give it a soft shell or interfere with the development of its nut. Caffeine was in this, too. And something else: diphenhydramine citrate, thirty-eight milligrams. It all sounded potentially deadly. Not to her, but to the small whatever-it-was she was now having to consider.

Vetoing the medicine, she left it sitting on the counter and went to the freezer and pulled out a tray of ice and cracked it on the counter and picked out four of the cubes and wrapped them in a wet dishcloth. Opening the front door to let in a breeze, but pulling the draperies behind the couch all the way shut, she arranged the pillows up near one end of the long sofa and lay down, stretching out her legs. While the peanut was so small there was no need to do this, she unzipped her jeans a little for comfort's sake and put the cool cloth over her eyes. Bruno's blue plastic clothes hamper full of dirty clothes was in the kitchen next to the table. The hamper was new (he had left the price sticker on the side), and she wished she had thought to throw the clothes into the washer before she stretched out, because the couch felt wonderful, too wonderful to leave at the moment. Maybe later, when her head was better, she would do the laundry, and while his clothes wouldn't be dry enough for him to take with him, he could pick them up tonight. With that thought, she drifted off to sleep, her arm curled over her head, the inside of her elbow pressing the wet rag down on her head and her feet falling open at the ankles, the way a child sleeps.

Bruno stood in the bed of the trailer and kicked the last of the hay onto the ground. Cows were moiling and bawling, bumping off the side of the truck, nudging for something other than hay; the week had been a dry one, and dust was knee-high in the air all around them. He could see the salt block worn down on two of its sides, like a hard moldy plastic thing melted by the heat. He took off his hat and wiped his forehead with his arm. Lord, he had forgotten how hot the fucking job was, how dusty and gnat-plagued, how good it felt to be doing something that had a purpose. The pond was at its lowest level in years, and the pipe that ran from the artesian well his grandfather had tapped into fifty years back was barely trickling. Bruno went to the truck and lifted out the plumber's snake and dragged it over to the pipe and shoved the hooked end of it up into the moldy pipe. Shove and pull, shove and pull. Slimy weeds the consistency of soggy spinach piled up at his feet. No wonder the pond level was so low. Why in the hell hadn't Leah done this before now? he wondered, and then he shook his head. The old excuses were no longer applicable. He should have seen to it himself, and that's all there was to it.

Sitting by the pipe and watching the flow increase, he dipped his handkerchief in the water and wiped at his face, pushing away the slimy residue he had pulled out of the pipe. The sight of it was awful, and the sun was already hitting it, turning it brown. Bruno cupped his fist and burped into it, last night's dinner still disagreeing with him. Down at the Rocky Creek Inn, Alyce had taken to feeding Willem and Bruno nightly, putting into practice her plan to turn the whole place into a boardinghouse for senior citizens. It had been Willem's idea, and thanks to him, Alyce now had a blueprint of how to expand the operation, double its size. Not only that, but she had already begun to investigate what the state required for running such a place. Getting rid of her deadbeat husband wasn't on the to-do list, but Bruno figured that once a social worker took one look at Joe Benson's green pimpmobile, there would be no way in hell Alyce would ever qualify for any kind of state licensing. Another aspect of the expansion involved Dolores Corrales. The Mexican hellbitch maid had been given the new job description of nutritionist, and the nightly meals were placed in her hands, a type of consumer test-marketing with Bruno and Willem as guinea pigs. Bruno couldn't speak for Willem Fremont, but he for one was sick to death of Mexican food and had begun to crave fried bologna and mashed potatoes and good buttermilk corn bread; he had even gone so far as to consider buying a hot plate so he might do some cooking in his room. He hadn't done it, though. Buying a hot plate seemed too large a step in the direction of living single, and he was already too far down that unhappy trail. So he suffered through tacos and enchiladas and creamy black beans (he actually liked those) and helped Alyce clean out the dining room and haul in some used chairs she bought at a flea market and sat there night after night alongside Willem, making small talk, trying to dodge the surveillance under which Alyce's older boy seemed to feel the need to place him. Sometimes the husband was there and sometimes he wasn't. And on the nights that he was there, his failure to show surprise or even concern that Alyce had taken to feeding and housing two grown men, at least one of whom was still viable and horny as hell, failed to surface. The only time Joe Benson showed any interest whatsoever was when the news of a retirement home was brought up, and Bruno was sure the only reason he had begun asking questions was because he was already trying to figure out a way to steal some unsuspecting retiree's social security check. Bruno shook his head. He was tired of the entanglements, of the way Alyce had begun to seek his advice, of having to watch his swearing around the small boys, of not being able to scratch his balls or his ass, of having to hold in his burps and farts. He was tired of all those things. He was also tired of waiting for Leah to ask him to come home again. But until she did, it was something he simply couldn't make himself do.

Christalmighty but Leah looked great. The color was back in her face and her hair was longer and thicker and there was a clear, wide-open look to her eyes now, a look of startled innocence, a look similar to what he had first noticed about her that day long ago at a stockyard when he'd been sitting waiting to bid on a cow and felt a weight settle on his back. It was like a curtain had been lifted off his memories, and instead of a collection of ill-formed ugliness, so many of Bruno's memories were good and sweet. While cutting into his enchiladas the night before and listening to Alyce go on and on about the installation of stainless-steel handholds for all the bathtubs in what would soon be the twelve efficiency apartments of the Rocky Creek Inn, he had suddenly remembered that Leah's ears were *not* pierced. He was so thrilled by the memory that he almost dropped his fork and couldn't wait to get to the farm to check it out for himself, rising at four-thirty instead of five, and then sitting out in the driveway drumming his fingers along the steering wheel of Leah's old Rambler, waiting for the kitchen light to come on. He had been correct. Not a single hole in either ear. And something about the smooth, unpierced skin made him feel like he was looking at a feature approaching the preciousness of a virgin's hymen. At the breakfast table that morning, she had been fully dressed, but all he could remember was the way she had stomped through the house in one of his old T-shirts, how naked she had been underneath, and even that memory seemed pure and untouched. It was all he could do to regulate his breathing as he drank his coffee.

He knew she believed he was involved with Alyce. It was not so much in what she said, since she never talked about it, or asked where he was, or anything of the sort, and it was her quiet acceptance of this erroneous presumption that hurt him. She should know better. And since she didn't, he came to his own erroneous presumption: the conclusion that Leah didn't know him at all and never had. And of all the reasons for not coming home, this seemed to be the most substantial.

Standing up, he brushed himself off and headed back to the truck, watching the cows begin to wade into the pond, dipping their square pink noses into the water. Looking at his watch, he realized he was later than he had thought, and as he drove across the fields, he pushed the truck a little, cutting east instead of southeast and approaching the backside of his mother's house first, seeing a dark formless something or other out near the silo chute. He slowed to see what exactly it might be, and then he felt like kicking himself in the ass, for it was Sonny's large rear end, and as Bruno watched, the rear end began to back across the grass until Sonny, whole and complete and covered with grain dust, began to emerge from the interior, finally climbing to his feet. "Hiding beer cans in the silo, I bet," Bruno said. Then: "Well, shit!" for Sonny was waving his arms at him, making his ponderous way over to the fence closest to the truck, where he hiked up a leg on the low board and leaned his arms on a rail. A dandruff of grain dross had powdered Sonny's hair and shoulders, but he didn't seem aware of it.

"What?" Bruno asked, hating to look at Sonny, trying to force his irritation back down, since it had collided with his thoughts of Leah and what she might be doing. He could see his house and the barn and the distance in between, and it seemed to be moving away from him, a mirage of hope disappearing from his vision.

"When you gonna run that bush hog?"

"Right now." Bruno squeezed the steering wheel to keep from hitting it.

"Today's gonna be a hot one. You ought to a done it yesterday when it was cooler."

"The tractor ain't got my name on it. You could a done it your own self."

Sonny's mouth turned ugly, and he seemed to be trying to think of a fitting remark.

"Where's Mama going to?" Bruno asked.

"Town. Fourth of July shit to get."

Bruno looked at Sonny, noticed his hair was shorter and his beard was gone. Or did he even have a beard before? He shook his head. Whatever, something looked different. "Why the hell did you flag me down?"

"You gonna be using your truck?"

"Not while I bush-hog I ain't."

"You mind if I use it to run to town a minute?"

Bruno looked at the boat, at the generalized messiness of it, and then he looked at the truck, at the trash stowed on its dash, the empty cans and farming tools, the stuffing that was spilling out of a tear in the seat, the case of liniment turned to its side on the floorboard. Somehow his truck seemed at risk. "How long you gonna be?"

"Not long."

"How come you cain't ride to town with her?"

"Hell, Bruno. She cain't drive over forty miles an hour without scaring her and me both to death."

Bruno sighed, "I guess."

Sonny turned to walk away, and Bruno whistled at him, and Sonny turned and said, "What?"

"You're approaching middle age. Don't you think it's high time to sell that worthless toy out there in the middle of the yard and get yourself a car?" He pointed to the boat.

At first the look on Sonny's face was amazingly blank, and then it changed to one of disbelief and hard-core anger. The nerve Bruno so carefully aimed for had been fully struck.

Sonny said, "Keep your fuckin truck to yourself, then. See if I give a good damn."

"Hey, I said you could use it, didn't I?"

Sonny said, "Screw you and the horse you rode in on," as he began to lumber toward the house.

"Shit, what in the world's crawled up his ass," Bruno said, putting the truck in gear and steering along the fence line, glancing once in his rearview mirror, where he watched his mother leave the house, her purse on her arm. Bruno waved at her, unsure if she saw it or not, and then he drove the truck through the gates and on down to the barn, where he parked to the side of the tractor. He had bush-hogging to do, but first he needed something to drink, and while he had shot himself in the foot by making Sonny refuse the generous offer of his truck, which would have kept Bruno at the farm all afternoon, he could still drag ass while bush-hogging, and maybe the two of them could have an early supper. Maybe the two of them could even drive into Hattiesburg and catch a movie at the Beverly Drive-in. Bruno smiled to himself. He felt good. Hopeful, even.

{CHAPTER 25}

Conchita followed the map that Sonny had drawn for her and finally found the place and pulled her mother's sputtering old Pinto up the long, graveled drive and parked it in the shade of a sweet gum tree next to a scuppernong trellis and two concrete birdbaths. Shit, nobody told her they had so much land! And that it was so far away from the center of Purvis (where Conchita lived in a crowded, run-down house with her mother and four bratty brothers). Shit, there wasn't even a supermarket nearby (where friends were likely to see her pushing a shopping cart next to her big fat husband). Shit, she was totally excited by this.

Opening her purse, she fished for her compact and took one last look at her lips and quickly rubbed at the lipstick that had collected on her teeth before opening the door to the car. The curtains moved in the window nearest her, and she could see her husband's hand, pointing toward the rear of the house, like one of those king-size foam-rubber hands people carry to football games. Those great big hands belonging to that great big man. There were still moments when she felt the terror of the situation descending on her in spite of his large hands and large everything else, and she wasn't talking about his large girth, though he was horribly overweight. It was just so *ridiculous* to be married and not be able to tell anyone. Marriages were supposed to be public affairs, not sweaty romps in the back of a Pontiac. And the days were flying by, and here it was six weeks later and she was yet to meet the mother-in-law, and it all added up to a reality that seemed too ugly to face. There was only one reason he was keeping it a secret, and it was the same reason why Conchita had found herself taking off her clothes in a strip club: she wasn't good enough. The terror of the truth was so large now that it took her breath away, and while Sonny had tried to placate her by telling her it was all right with him to go on and tell her mother, what good would that do Conchita? The only marriage Dolores Corrales would accept would be the one officiated by Father Russ over at Sacred Heart in Hattiesburg. A marriage that was sanctioned, blessed, tied up with a Mexican lasso of rosary beads, complete with mariachis as part of the recessional. Dolores would faint dead away at the sight of a marriage license stamped by a clerk; she would pull her hair out at the mere suggestion that the marriage was legitimate. But Sonny had pleaded with her to trust him on this. Wasn't that what he had kept telling her? Trust me, darlin. *P-u-le-e-ese* trust me, I know what I'm doin. For going on weeks and weeks, she had done just that, and each time she demanded some type of time line, some guesstimation about their future plans (when, for example, did he intend to tell his mother? When, for God's sake!), Sonny's face would drain of its normal ruddy color and take on a dead-fish look and his eyes would seem to shrink down to the size of sun-parched raisins and he would open his mouth and say the one word Conchita was beginning to hate with a passion: "Soon."

She reached under the seat and took the box of Trojans and opened it and took out four of them and crammed them in her purse. Not that they were necessary or would actually do what people buying them expected them to do, but Sonny was still insisting on putting one on, and Conchita was still complying, her acquiescence easier to maintain now that a tiny pinprinck had been punctured in each of them with a needle she pulled from her mother's tomato-shaped pincushion. In one sense, it was a way to be a good Catholic, nothing more, but that wasn't the whole truth, and even Conchita was too old to lie to herself for very long. Until the mother-in-law knew, Conchita was not beyond playing dirty, for she didn't feel permanent yet and sensed she was in the trial stage, still a new employee functioning in the uneasy territory of being on probation, so to speak. Once she was absolutely on the payroll and stamping her time card inside the large kitchen of this great big farmhouse, she'd stop putting holes in the rubbers. Until then, she was hedging her bets, dealing aces off the bottom of the deck, soliciting possible future teamwork by playing a biological Russian roulette. *I mean, what kind of heartless bitch would kick out a woman carrying her grandchild?* she wondered.

Swinging her legs out of the car, she tried to make a point of walking casually, as though she were strolling through an upscale department store, nothing on her mind but finding that marked-down push-up bra. She tried to imagine salesclerks who smelled nice falling all over themselves with a willingness to help her find not just one marked-down bra but three or four of them. She tried to imagine one particular salesclerk asking to see her wedding band and *ooh*ing and *ahh*ing over it, though it was a simple twenty-eight-dollar two-millimeter band like millions of other women all over the United States had on their fingers. She tried to imagine all these gift-wrapped, soft-lit consumer-tinged scenarios as she walked, but none of them worked, and she wished she had told him the truth about her shoe size, for her shoes were slicing into her skin like razors, and her toes were curled up and felt like they were being shoved into a meat grinder. But by God, her new husband had gone to the trouble of buying her a pair of size-seven black strappy pumps, and gone to the further trouble of putting metal tap plates on the bottoms of the soles, and since it was her own fault for lying about the size of her feet, it was too late to do anything other than suffer through and hope he came quick and was satisfied enough never to ask that she wear them again.

She had been with men before who wanted such things, and she wasn't a bit surprised. Cheerleader pom-poms. Baby bottles. Oscar Mayer wieners stuck in all available orifices. Wearing homemade tap shoes was not so odd. Applauding herself for being worldly-wise and intuitive, she had caught on to Sonny's obvious fantasy and gone to town and bought some black stretch pants that came with a tiny gold patent-leather belt, and a sleeveless white boatneck sweater that fit her like a glove, exposing ample amounts of her brown midriff. A wide stretchy headband against her forehead made her feel like Natalie Wood in *West Side Story,* and since her middle name just so happened to be Maria, it was one of those moments that seemed cosmically orchestrated. Sonny wanted a dancer, and by God he was about to get himself a dancer!

"'I like to be in Ah-mare-rica. Okay by me in Ah-mare-rica! Everything free in Ah-mare-rica. For a small fee in Ah-mare-rica.'"

She stopped singing when she saw how shocked he seemed (even though he had been the one who phoned and begged her to come over) and commenced waving brightly, bending forward and shaking her tits at him, topping the whole greeting off by blowing him a Marilyn Monroe–type kiss. His head disappeared from the window, and instead of those carefree I'm-a-shopper-with-money steps, she began to limp along, taking tiny baby steps now that he wasn't watching her. Humming the song, she turned the corner of the house, noticing everything around her and measuring the differences between the crowded parking lot at her mother's house and this quiet place of birdbaths and rambling rosebushes.

Holy shit, he really *did* have a boat. She stopped humming to stare at it, noticing the space it stole from what used to be a manicured back lawn. The steel booms rose above it like giant radio antennae, and a white cowbird was perched on one of the dangling hinged boards. Walking around it, she noticed the space on the hull where he had promised her name would go and how it hadn't even been penciled in there yet, much less painted, and she patted her purse, saying good-bye to the last of the guilt she had been feeling for poking holes in every single one of the rubbers her husband probably couldn't wait to tear open.

The back door opened, and an obviously distressed Sonny motioned for her, saying, "Connie, git on in here," a terribly urgent sound to his voice.

"Comin, baby doll," she told him, stepping over paint cans and a curled-up hound dog and a stack of coiled yellow rope.

"Goodgodamighty, what are you wearin?" He turned her by the shoulders like she was a doll, and she held out her arms and said, "You like?"

Of *course* he liked. That was the durn problem. What *he* liked, his mother absolutely *wouldn't* like, and since it had been his bright idea for Conchita to come over so that she might finally meet his mother, an idea that, as soon as it was broached, developed an alarming weight of regret, regret so heavy he found himself unable to put the phone back in the cradle and instead dropped it to the floor, where it twirled and twirled on its coily black cord, and now that she was standing in his mother's kitchen looking not at all like a ten-dollar hooker but more like a two-dollar one, Sonny felt gut-shot, or maybe run over by a bus.

Cash flow was his problem or, more precisely, his *lack* of cash flow, and it was a problem of such severity that he felt like banging his head against the stove just to get a little relief from worrying about it. To make matters worse, he couldn't drown the worry in a gallon of Kool-Aid, or smother it in a bag of potato chips, tactics he had always resorted to before. Now he had this one here to think about, and he felt like weeping, it was so unfair. So yes, it was time to tell his mother the news. Not because he needed to take responsibility for a decision he had made while drunk, but because he thought the presence of a flesh-and-blood responsibility walking around the place would loosen the purse strings and the old gal would finally see that he deserved more than the stipend she handed out to him once a month. Knowing her, she'd probably be so cruel as to suggest he go out and get a job.

"Darlin. I thought you was gonna wear that nice black skirt of yours. The one you wore when we went to the courthouse."

Her face fell. The light in her eyes dulled a little. She tried to pull her lips over her teeth in a pout but couldn't. *Poor little baby,* he thought. What an idiot he was for expecting her to read his mind. Hell, he couldn't even read his own mind half the time.

"You don't like it." She clicked over to the table in her retrofitted shoes and turned her back to him and looked at the space on the wall where thumbtacks were stuck in the wallpaper.

"Darlin, you are the best-lookin gal I ever seen."

She shook her head and folded her arms together.

Oh my God she was likely to begin crying, and it was likely to break his heart. "Come here and give us a kiss," he said as she turned to him.

"Do you really like how I look?" A tear was collecting underneath her false eyelash as she clicked her way over to him.

Unacquainted yet with the art of it, he crushed her to him and breathed her hair, feeling the magic of his hard-on, still such a new experience he had no choice but to release her and stare down at it like an unexpected guest showing up at his house, a separate entity, a completely focused, pleasure-bearing salesman whose product definitely would deliver. Just the sight of the bulge in his pants cleared his head. He would tell his mother that Conchita was in costume and had just come from dress rehearsal. He would tell his mother she was part of a musical about . . . he leaned back to take one more look. Jesus, she looked like a trashy Hispanic who just got laid in an alley. He couldn't think of a single dance that might accompany such a comparison.

Conchita brightened and looked around the kitchen. Everything was so warm-toned and comfy-looking, so American. Olive-green countertops and an olive-green stove and refrigerator. Olive-green canisters and green-and-yellow curtains hanging from the windows. A wooden bowl holding yellow wax apples on the table. "What's that thing?" she said, pointing to the steel tubing that ran across the black-and-white linoleum and disappeared down the hall.

His eyes were hooded, and he was having trouble speaking. How could he have thought her outfit unacceptable? Hell, dancers were wild as mustangs. Hellfire, dancers were expected to dress this way. "Something I invented," he muttered against her hair, running a hand across her bare stomach. "It turns on them fans out in the backyard so I keep cool while I work."

"Where the boat is?"

"Yeah," he breathed, not caring a bit about the boat. He slid a hand up under her tight top, and his eyes rolled back in his head.

"I seen the boat. It sure is big."

He looked around the kitchen and wondered where he could do it with her. He didn't want to wait for the bed, though it was only fourteen steps down the hall. He looked at the country table and remembered how he'd had his breakfast there and wondered how Conchita would look with her legs propped up on two of the wooden chairs while he knelt on the floor between them. She moved away from him and went to the sink and leaned back against it lasciviously, one leg hiked to the side, opening and closing, opening and closing. He could hear the shoes *schlink-schlink*ing against the linoleum.

"You like them shoes?"

She did a little shuffle that almost sounded real and said, "I sure do, big boy."

"That's sheet metal on the bottom of them." God, he couldn't wait. "I bought the shoes first and drew me a pattern on butcher paper and cut the metal out there in the shed. Once they was cut, I knocked the slick off the backside of them with my grinder and glued them on the shoes with contact cement." He cleared his throat. "They're your dancin shoes," he said.

"I really like them, Sonny."

"You wear them to dance in."

"Whatever you say." She lifted one side of her sweater and exposed a tit, and he lunged for it like a starving calf, dropping to his knees and suckling while she peered around the kitchen and evaluated her surroundings. It was better than she had imagined. She could positively see herself sitting at that table over there and carrying on a conversation with her husband and mother-in-law. She could even see herself washing the dishes just to be helpful.

"Ouch, that hurts." She whacked him on his head. "Don't do it so hard."

"Sorry," he said, and went to palpating her breasts as if they were his own personal tennis balls. "Darlin, dance a little for me," he said, one eye peering up at her.

Even though she would rather walk through the house and take a good look at the rest of it, she guessed there was no pulling off the shoes until she got the dancing business over with, so she pointed to the floor space by the table, and Sonny backed up on his knees and rested his fat hands on his fat thighs and watched. Conchita called up resources drawn from watching *West Side Story* more than a dozen times and did her best. She even sang a little of the "America" song. The effort was not wasted on Sonny, who seemed near to collapsing in a paroxysm of joy, clapping his hands, telling her over and over again how great she was.

"You're a dancer with a troupe," he said as he reached for her and jerked her close to him, rubbing his face on her stomach and giving her a big smacky kiss next to her belly button.

"A what?" She tried to pull his head away and make him look at her.

His eyes shifted away and he said, “A dancing troupe. One that travels around.”

“Whatever you say.”

“No, it’s true. Listen to me, now, ’cause this is real important. You been dancin for over ten years.”

In her mind, “dancing” translated to “screwing” and she had absolutely not been screwing since she was thirteen! “But I’m *only* twenty-three.”

“Okay, forget the ten-years part. Let’s say you’ve been dancin for five years.”

“I started dancin when I was seventeen?”

“Four years, then.”

“Okay.”

Sonny tried to slide his hands into the back of her pants, but it was like trying to shove a canned ham into a sock. Try as he might, his large fingers seemed unable to slip over an inch into the waistband of her oh-so-tight pants.

“Here, let me. You’re gonna break the belt.”

While she unfastened it, he tutored her in the essentials. Unfortunately, Conchita thought he was playing a game and had no idea she was in a class.

Sonny said, “So, you’ve been dancin for a while now. All over the South. Mainly in Alabama and Florida.”

“Where in Alabama?”

“Name a place. It don’t matter where.”

“Birmingham?”

“Birmingham’s perfect. Now, tell me this: what’s your favorite dance?”

Enough of this shit, she was thinking. “Personally, I like the Cockadoodiedoo,” she said, jerking the tiny belt free and slinging it across the room, where it landed next to the refrigerator. She reached for him, pressing her hand on the front of his pants.

“Come on, now. This is important. Be serious.” He took her hands and held them in front of him. “Don’t you love *The Nutcracker*?”

“Nutcracker?” She scrambled for some memory of a dance demonstrating a mean guy who went around cracking other guys’ nuts, and drew a blank. She shook her head. “Don’t know it.”

“How about *Romeo and Juliet*?”

She thought for a moment and then said, "Oh. Them two that died?"

Sonny nodded his big serious face, which was gleaming with sweat and carnal expectation, the potential length of said carnal activity suffering a reduction with each minute it took Conchita to cram for her test.

She shrugged. "I guess they're okay. I could make up the steps, I guess."

He patted her on the rear. "Good girl. You had me worried for a minute there."

Outside in the hellish heat, traveling in a widening path around the two houses, Bruno sat on the tractor. Sonny heard the *phut-phut-phut* of the motor and the sluicing, slicing sound of field grass being slaughtered. *Poor Bruno,* Sonny thought. *So bad in bed his wife had to run him off.* The thought made Sonny giggle, and he leaned forward and licked Conchita's belly button, noticing the slightly musty smell of her and immediately turned on by it. He put his hands on her hips and studied her midriff and felt a strange pulling at his insides, for he could see the worn-out band of her panties and the slight dusting of hairs that ran across her stomach. Underneath her perfume was her slightly metallic body odor, a hygiene deficiency he planned on correcting as soon as she was living underneath his roof and sleeping nightly in his bed.

"You want me to dance again? Pretend I'm Juliet and maybe about to die?"

Good Lord, he loved the almost buried clicks and rolled R's of her Americanized Spanish. The way she looked and acted southern but wasn't. "No. I want you to do somethin else."

"What?"

"I think you know what. But come on and I'll show you."

He began the series of moves that would bring him to his feet, moves he had hoped would be fluid but were far from it, for his backside bumped into the table and knocked over the sugar bowl, and square lumps of white bounced across the table, one or two of them falling to the floor. He thought about how he ate one first thing in the morning, right before he shook his mother's hand, and he began to shake his head, thumping the closest sugar cube away with his thumb, whereupon it skittered under the stove. He didn't want to think of Eilene now. If he thought of her now, the salesman in his pants would hightail it out of there. Once upright, he took Conchita by the hand, fully intending to toss her on his own personal bed and pull off her clothes and try by God to last longer than five minutes. But as he walked down the hall with Conchita in tow, he saw into the living room where his mother's chair sat, her knitting by its side, the curtains opened a bit so that a sliver of daylight speared into the room and Sonny could see Bruno making brief appearances every few minutes. *Goddawg. What better place?* he wondered, remembering how much he hated the chair and the way his mother sat in it, torturing him with her breast-heaving sighs. *Time to purge the old gal once and for all,* he thought, pulling his wife by the hand into the living room, pushing the door until it was almost shut, directing her on the specifics of how he wanted it done. The floor was wood, and her shoes sounded like real tap shoes, and the ceilings were high, which made the room echo with thick wooden percussions that reminded him of large solid things belonging only to men: hand-carved mantels over huge stone fireplaces, the clacking horns of a stag in full rut, a wooden box of marbles all his own that he never had to share.

Conchita *loved* the living room. The soft yellow sofa against the far wall, with its four persimmon-colored pillows; the real piano; the vase of plastic flowers on the coffee table; the corner console television set with the pictures on top of a man and woman she supposed were Sonny's parents. She even loved the stiff-looking draperies and their yellow ball fringe. Never in her life had she seen anything so elegant. And best of all, not a single crucifix hanging anywhere.

"Hang on. Let me put this in the chair," he said, reaching for the hideous sweater the color of his eyes. While he intended to do it with his wife (more than once) as he sat in his mother's chair, he was not so struck by passion that he failed to see the need to protect the fabric. His mother would have an absolute fit if he stained her flowery chintz.

"But what if she comes home?" Conchita wanted to know, her hands on her hips, a little worried now. First impressions mattered. A lot.

"She won't. It takes her forever to make up her mind to leave the house, but once she does, she stays gone for hours. She ain't been gone but an hour and a half." He unbuckled his belt and unzipped his jeans and lowered himself into the chair. "Now, pull off them pants and let me see what you got underneath."

"You seen it yesterday."

"That long ago?" He reached to help her, but she slapped his hands away.

"I ain't gettin naked if you don't."

"I'll get there soon enough. Let me see you first." He put his hands on the chair and heaved up a bit so that it was turned a little more toward the window. This way he could watch Bruno as he circled the yard.

{CHAPTER 26}

Fences, cattle, long rows of pines planted thick as the stars. Willem passed them all and headed up the old logging road with its far-reaching shade, already familiar with the road's twists and turns, the familiarity a steadily growing comfort, like an old shirt pulled on to guard against a chill. The tops of the trees were interlocked, and what light fell through was spangled and moved as though it were music and not light. *These woods have seen it all,* he thought to himself. *All the living. All the dying, both vegetative and fleshly. And still they stand.* It seemed a message of sorts. A remedial lesson Willem needed in this late hour of his life. Climbing out of the truck, he jerked the chain and its hook dislodged from the post and the chain fell to the road. He drove on through, not bothering to stop and reattach the chain this time. No one was there to see him but for the trees and an occasional possum or raccoon, and besides, it was growing late. Barely enough time to climb down and back up again before the woods turned dark and his way out would be shrouded by night.

Catching hold of the crossed limbs, he lowered himself down, noticing the dirt crumbling away from what had seemed permanent just a week earlier. There would be only so many times his descent would be allowed.

He looked up at the giant pine, standing stalwart yet grim. Maybe this was the lesson it was trying to teach him: nothing lasts forever, and once it's gone, it's gone. Like the land.

There was really no mystery or intrigue to it. It had been in his family for years. Fremont land passed down from a French Canadian who had settled in El Dorado, Arkansas. Land no one lived on that was worked for the crops. A hundred acres of it deeded out to Willem Fremont once he turned eighteen, his daddy dying the next year and leaving Willem to make his way on his own. And make his way, he had. Building the house out of logs he cured and shaped and fitted together to form a cabin meant to be the first of many buildings, he had lived there and grown cotton and corn for a year before the sinkhole ate the place. Barely escaping with his life, he had done a stupid thing: he had run from it, disappeared into the wide-flung arms of the Midwest, leaving the land to be swallowed up in more ways than one. The neighbor to the west, Reinhold Till, picked it up by paying the lapsed taxes, and it became a part of Eilene Till's holdings. Gone as cleanly from the Fremont family as though they had never owned it at all. Sometimes there was no way to correct a mistake. Willem was beginning to realize this. And while he had the money to buy all the land back, he had questioned Bruno enough to know the family would never be willing to part with it. Besides, it was only this particular parcel he wanted. He had not yet heard from the agent as to his inquiry. All he had found out was that the letter had been sent by registered mail.

Light as it approached the evening hours was the prettiest, he thought. Purified and intense, it forced a second look at trees and trunks and limbs and sky and, by color alone, painted tumbled stones cerulean and plain Mississippi clay, lapis lazuli. The hole was to the east and caught the dark first, and Willem was full in the shade as he looked to the house, its low roof settled on one end like a sitting dog, the front door agape to the setting sun, as though its mouth were open and it was drinking in the light. Just like he had planned it. Even when he was young, he had felt a strange kinship with the evening hours, and he attributed the fellowship to his belief in reincarnation. His knowledge that everything recycled. Plants fall and then die and rot away before eventually shooting back up through the earth. At odd times and in unlikely places—city streets, the pew of a church (he was Methodist, even though his beliefs were renegade)—a type of emotional shudder would strike him and whisper in his ear that people go on as well. Not the same as before. Certainly not fully aware of the before. But regardless of what was known or unknown, people popped up again somewhere. *So at one point in a past life, I died at sunset,* he reasoned. While watching the evening light make its brittle sweep of a mountain, probably, since west was where he had run when the house had fallen.

He walked to the pool and stuck a hand underneath the falling water, the wall behind it lime-shanked and hard, the color of ice. Drinking deeply from his cupped hand, he thought it the best water in all of the world, in spite of its sulfuric smell. A smell that reminded him of his father, whose face he could no longer see, the only thing left to Willem: the memory of his father's clothes washed in this water.

The woman's note was still stuck down in the bottle, still floating along, the top of it curling a bit from exposure to morning dew. Willem reached for it and almost fell in the pool before catching it and lifting it out. Unrolling her note, he compared the words to the page he had torn from the book in the library, reading over them again to make sure he had been correct.

There is a silence where hath been no sound,
There is a silence where no sound may be,
In the cold grave—under the deep, deep sea,
Or in wide desert where no life is found,
Which hath been mute, and still must sleep profound . . .

After he had set her note back in its bottle, he opened up his shirt and pulled out the empty Coca-Cola bottle and held it between his knees while he rolled up the book page. Then he slid it down into the mouth of the bottle and set it adrift beside the other one. The two bobbing together, a tiny clink of glass meeting glass.

"At least she'll be able to read the rest of it," he said, his voice causing the cicadas to turn quiet.

Walking away from the house, he found a seasoned limb and pressed it to the ground to test for strength and, once reassured, used it to poke through the weeds growing thick around the trees, trying to remember the way the place had been before the fall, how his field had stretched as far as the eye could see and what fence lines there were never seemed restrictive, for they belonged to him as well. Seasons of working the place alongside his daddy, and then that solitary year of working it alone. There had been a permanence to his life that he thought was eternal, as flat and unmovable as the fields surrounding him. A permanence that proved transitory, for the field itself had sunk beneath his feet. Bending beneath a low limb, he came to a small clearing and found the sad remains of a cow, half burned and moldy now, a terrible funk still coming off it while beetle bugs scuttled through the rotting hide and in and out of the cracked bones. There was a fuel can set to the side of it, and a section of rope; the woman had had the good sense to clear the brush in a circular path around the cow, and Willem walked it, noticing the black tendrils of grass, signs the fire had tried to spread but couldn't. Good thing, too. A brisk wind and there would have been no trace of the house or anything else. The pit would hold the heat and cook everything in sight. He immediately became alarmed at the vision of it and thanked his lucky stars he had never taken to the habit of smoking. He looked up at the deepening color of the sky. The woman smoked. He remembered seeing that, and the memory ionized and projected itself into the frenzy of preemptive worrying he was famous for, and he suddenly saw a tossed cigarette landing on the dead palm of a sycamore leaf and spreading to dried limbs and fallen trees until the whole pit ignited with a resounding explosion of cured kindling. The tingling at the back of his neck began, and he shut his eyes against it.

"Stop it," he told himself. "Stop it now." He put a hand to his chest and rubbed. The last thing he needed at this point was to have an attack and be stuck down here overnight at the mercy of some nocturnal scavenger.

"Think of something else. Notice something else."

He looked to the far wall and saw her way of entering the pit. Those precarious handholds that made the descent seem a thing of wonder. How in the world did she do it? As far as Willem was concerned, a gifted trapeze artist would hesitate to attempt it.

Shaking his head, he turned back the way he had come. Though it was four o'clock up there in the real world, the sun had already traveled down low in the gully, and it seemed more like six o'clock. Trees and logs were fast becoming gauzy shapes hard to distinguish. An old rusted can was near his feet and he stumbled on it, seeing the jagged edge and all the dangers the vision implied. Infected cut spreading to gangrenous leg leading to the teeth of a saw cutting into the bone. "Rust is to leg what cattle truck is to crown," he said, his voice low and thoughtful. The comment a private joke he felt like indulging in.

Like it or not, he was beginning to understand some things. A firm believer in cause and effect, he realized he was beginning to backslide a little. Behavior was not always set in motion by some previous trauma. Sure, the house sank with him in it, but as he thought about it, he recognized that he'd always felt a heightened state of anxiety. Even when he was a child. Always worrying about whether or not the next storm on the horizon was going to be the one holding the tornado. Always afraid the train would be late and he would miss it. Always hurrying in from the fields for fear his father would be facedown in his bed. The house sinking was not the beginning of his fears; more like a halfway mark in a long list. Not willing yet to downplay the sensation of waking to a house falling down around his ass, he couldn't help but place the biggest weight of blame (if "blame" was the proper word, and he wasn't sure it was) with his own physical being, the way his brain routed electrical impulses, cataloged reactions, issued out degrees of reasoning ability. He looked up at the narrow square of darkening sky and figured that in some lost life, he would be more suited to life as a hermit, or maybe a religious contemplative. Instead he had found himself living in a world that moved along at an alarming pace.

The house was in the full dark now, and he stared at it, the open slot of a doorway, the collapsing roof, the surrounding ridgeline of leaning trees. He had thought before leaving Colorado and his one or two friends left there that finding the house would cure him, and he saw now he had been mistaken. Shrugging and walking on, he thought to himself: *There's still time to go back. Still time to go.* The first step would be to get up out of the hole and head back to the motel and pack his bags. He felt suddenly buoyed by the possibility. And suddenly thirsty.

More lighthearted than he'd been in fifteen years, he headed back toward the artesian pool, leaning on the limb as he pushed his way through sweetleaf and privet, honeysuckle vines and wild fern. The cicadas and tree frogs were used to him and singing with an urgency Willem had long since forgotten. He bent by the pool and saw his reflection, the pattern that slipped and slewed away from him, distorting his face to the one of his imagination. The way he saw himself most of the time. Done with it, he stood and was reaching to put his hand on the limestone wall when he slipped and fell into the pool headfirst, hearing the sound of a cracked bone a split second before he felt the pain blaze up his left leg and into his hip and finally his low stomach, where it seemed to hook into his gut like a fiery claw. And even while he screamed into the black world of fading consciousness, the cicadas kept singing.

{CHAPTER 27}

Bruno sat on the back porch reading the brochure as the old Maytag went through its final spin cycle, and thanks to the printed words in front of him and the washer's repercussions, it was as though the temporary reconciliatory scaffolding inside his mind was being knocked loose and allowed to fall, section by section.

He looked across the field toward his mother's house. It was now approaching four o'clock, and the old exhaust-smudged Pinto he assumed belonged to Sonny's girlfriend was still parked in his mother's drive, and there had been no movement from the house. The absoluteness of the quiet made Bruno's imagination fire up to new levels of inventiveness, and since each lurid image involved his obese brother and close to twelve inches of exposed butt crack, he felt near to being sick. He had no clue as to what course of action Eilene would take once she finally made it home, but this much he could hope for: that she would make sure the gun was loaded and the safety off before she pointed it at his brother's head. He shouldn't feel this way, or even think this way, and he knew it, and a part of him cringed at the upbeat in his heart's rhythm at the *realness* of the wish, at the way he could almost see Sonny dead and resting in some piano case (since a regular coffin would be much too small), and what

Bruno would wear to the funeral (the same suit he wore to his wedding), and how many minutes (five at the most) he would wait before he broke out the Jack Daniel's and lifted a toast to his wife. Leah was the only one who seemed to share not so much his hatred but at least an understanding of his hatred, and it was a type of almost spiritual communion the two of them grazed on—his simmering hatred of Sonny and Leah's red-hot irritation with her mother. Unknowing targets against which either of them could hurl their pent-up wrath. And while Bruno was sure a marriage therapist would shake his head at the fragile thread of communication between the two, there were moments, stretched out beside his wife on their cold connubial bed as each in turn vented about real or imagined wrongs done to them, or out-and-out stupidity they each were forced to witness, that the talk felt almost like a form of intercourse. A sloppy stroking of genitalia. The weak and sniveling sigh of orgasm. He looked at the brochure again, a coldness flooding him at a point directly below his brace, where he supposed his heart must be.

Leah had been sleeping when he first came in off the tractor, the interior of the living room all dim light and almost perfect stillness, and while he had waited for her to wake, he had begun to experience the disgruntled curiosity of the recently and, as far as he was concerned, unjustifiably ousted. He wondered what she did with her mornings now that he was working the cows. When she took her daily shower. What radio stations she listened to. What she ate. While he had no clue as to the first three, he had already peered into the refrigerator under the pretense of looking for a beer and seen nothing but a square of cheese, four apples, a quart of orange juice, two wrinkled wieners and a jar of mayonnaise, so whatever meals she was eating seemed unhealthy (with the possible exception of the apples and orange juice), and he began to wonder if his mother might be feeding her. And that random thought, combined with the proclivity toward suspicion that most recently ousted individuals—heads of state; soon-to-be-impeached presidents; misunderstood husbands—experience, led him to wonder if some type of conspiracy might exist between his mother and Leah. He hadn't talked to Eilene since the day before he left. This was not so strange. He had gone months without speaking to her, but always before, he had known she was across the expanse of yard maintaining her vigil of frustration against Sonny, and she had known he was sitting in his chair rereading *National Geographics*, and this in itself seemed a form of silent communiqué, a quiet but constant signal light, maybe even a perverse type of caring, so to speak. Her distance bewildered Bruno. There were moments while, strolling across the parking lot of the Rocky Creek Inn, when he half expected ("hoped" was more like it) to see Eilene's gray Pontiac nose itself over the nearest hill in search of him, and it hadn't happened. Eilene's complete removal from the situation led Bruno to believe that yes, of course! Leah was eating over at Eilene's. There *had* to be a conspiracy between the two women. Some type of game in play where Bruno was the opposing team and all the home team had to do was link arms and wait for him to wear himself out running around like a fool. Convinced he was on to something ominous, he walked over to the back door and squatted to examine the lock. Changing the locks was definitely an Eilene Till thing to do. An in-your-face act of reprisal, a smug "Oh, so you think this is your house and you can just come and go as you please? Well, we'll show you, mister!" game-board move. He had put a finger to the brushed stainless steel. The lock didn't look changed, but that didn't mean it hadn't been. Bruno pulled his key out of his pocket and was within a half inch of inserting it before he chickened out. His failure to follow through made him mad. Going back to the sink, he drank water from the tap, irritated that Leah was still asleep and he couldn't crack a tray of ice for fear of disturbing her. While leaning there, weighing the odds of whether Leah and Eilene really were wearing identical game-club jerseys, he had seen his basket of clothes resting exactly where he had left it, and this irritated him even more than his growing suspicion that yes, by God, they were on the same team, and yes, by God, the locks most definitely had been changed. Whether he wanted to admit it or not, Leah's promise to wash his clothes had been a type of "she loves me, she loves me not" played out with dirty briefs and sweat-stained undershirts. Well, the last metaphorical petal had fallen, and he guessed he had his answer. He suddenly didn't care if he woke her, and his footfalls were heavy as he walked across the room and jerked up the basket. It was then that he saw the rag on her head and felt the wallop of remorse. *Shit.* She was sick. What a jackass he was, what a jackass he had always been, what a class-A jackass he would forever be. But even a jackass needs clean clothes and a cup of coffee, so once he had the Maytag churning up an abundance of suds, he tiptoed back into the kitchen (careful not to let the screen door slam) and measured coffee grounds and leaned against the counter listening to the burp of the percolator. It was when he reached for his favorite coffee cup and found the brochures stacked on their side that the playing field changed immeasureably.

He unfolded the pamphlet and stared at it.

The woman didn't look at all like Leah, and he wondered why he had expected her to. THE FIRST NINE MONTHS. A NEW MOTHER'S GUIDE. And in smaller print: *Gift Pack Courtesy of Vorham Pharmaceuticals, the New Mother's Best Friend.* When he first picked it up, he thought it was junk mail she had shoved aside for later perusal. But there was more. The recently filled prescription bottle holding what smelled like vitamins. Coupons for Pampers. Coupons for Tucks. A small packet of Ivory Snow washing powder. "Because what's next to your new baby's skin counts!" He had taken the topmost brochure and left the rest inside the cabinet, and now he sat out on the back porch studying it.

It was beginning to add up. He couldn't remember Leah's ever taking a nap during the day. He couldn't remember her ever putting a wet rag on her head. He leaned around and looked through the screen door. The cloth had soaked into the couch, leaving a half-moon arc that fanned behind her face like a semipermanent shadow. With what sounded like a violent, final convulsion, the washing machine finished its cycle on a loud clack from some hidden gear. A similar noise sounded from inside the house, and Bruno watched as Leah jumped to her feet and pounded her way across the living room and disappeared from sight. As he folded the brochure and placed it in his shirt pocket, he figured now was the time to investigate.

Leah had been sick only once that he could recall. Right before he left for Vietnam, the two of them had driven down to New Orleans for the weekend, where she consumed too many Tequila Sunrises, which resulted in her doing a type of mock flamenco in the middle of Tío Pepe's in the Quarter. The dance was immediately followed by a rush outdoors, where she stood on the steamy pavement and, for reasons Bruno never understood and Leah was too drunk to even remember doing, much less explain, she reared back and threw her purse in a line drive toward the iron lightpost across the street. By the time Bruno retrieved it, she was huddled next to a '56 Chevrolet, holding her hair in one hand as she vomited against the car's chrome bumpers. Trying not to be sick himself, he had released her hand from her hair and taken over the job of shielding it from the spew.

Bruno walked into the bathroom and saw her kneeling on the floor, in a pose so similar to that of the young girl on a smelly New Orleans street, he felt terribly sad.

He wet a cloth and squeezed it out and stood behind her so she could lean back on his legs. "Here," he said, wiping her face as he gathered up her hair and held it away from the toilet bowl. He could see the rust stains from the well water and noticed that whatever she had been eating was yellow. He held back a gag and said, "What the hell made you sick?"

Now would be the time for her to come clean and tell him. Now, while he was being nice and helping her vomit properly.

"Headache," she said, removing the cloth and wiping at her mouth.

Bruno felt the first blow and sighed; even though it was a small blow, he felt a weariness begin to invade his muscles and bones.

"You take anything for it?"

She hesitated and then nodded. "Sinutab."

"Is it a sinus headache?" *Come on, Leah, say it,* he thought. *The words are right there. Say it.*

"I thought so. Now I'm beginning to believe it's a migraine." She pulled away from him, and her hair swung free. He was unaware he had been holding it clasped so tightly in his hand. She wouldn't look at him, just seemed happy to study the small crystalized obloid of deodorizer attached to the side of the toilet by a bent wire. "Did you make coffee?"

"Yeah. You want some?"

She couldn't even answer him. If she answered him, the vision of coffee would stay with her and she would throw up again. She began to push her way to her feet.

Bruno put his hands under her arms and helped her up. Leah flushed the toilet and he refused to look at it. He looked at her profile instead, seeing dark circles underneath her eyes and her pale, pale lips.

The room felt small, but neither one seemed ready to leave it. He could smell her skin and the shampoo she had used on her hair. While he watched and waited for her to tell him he was soon to be a father and how sorry she was for saying all those hateful things that day, she reached for the Pepsodent and smeared a worm of it across her toothbrush and began to freshen her mouth. He looked away when she spat.

"You still got a headache?"

"It's better now."

"You ever been sick with a headache before?"

She shrugged.

"I remember one time." He grinned at her, and she cut her eyes away from his and dropped her toothbrush in the glass. "That time in New Orleans when you thought the lightpost was the football goal."

"Don't remind me."

It was a good memory to Bruno. One that summoned to mind his better days, his days of taking care of her, racing across a busy street to claim her fake alligator bag, holding her hair away from her face while she threw up all her tacos. The news that she didn't want to remember it stung like a slap across the face.

Having nothing to say but wanting to keep talking to her because he had missed talking to her, and also because he wanted her to notice the new and improved Bruno Till, he said, "I went on and did my laundry." The announcement was meant to be nothing more than an innocent bridge suspended over the quiet awkwardness.

She didn't see it as a bridge at all; more like a registered complaint. "I said I would do it."

"Yeah, I know. But it was getting late, and you were resting."

"So you just assumed I was too lazy to do what I promised?" *What in the world was the matter with her?* she thought. *Why was she attacking him?* She remembered the other times she had been sick to the point of throwing up. There were two of them. Once when she got drunk in New Orleans. The other time up in Jackson, when she had first walked into the room and found him encased in plaster from his chin down to his waist. That time didn't really count, since she had been alone in the moment. But the other time, Bruno had been as careful with her as he had just been. Holding her hair, leading her safely to the hotel room, where he put ice in a cloth and held it to her head and pulled the drapes and stretched out beside her, minimizing his moves for fear of making her hangover worse. She remembered waking the next morning and fucking him with a desperation that frightened her.

"Hey. I never meant to imply that you were lazy. Hell, Leah. All I'm saying is that I went on and did the laundry myself." He held out his hands to her. "It wasn't meant as a criticism."

"That's funny, 'cause it sure felt like one." She wanted to slap herself to make herself shut up. *Tell him,* she thought. *Tell him now while he's standing here dirty from field work, his blue eyes soft and puzzled, his face grizzled by afternoon stubble.* Stubble she loved. Stubble that reminded her of his better days. But a more current desire was with her that had nothing to do with their life before Vietnam. More than anything else, she wanted to lean her head on his brace and have him touch her hair, to yield up the weight of the fight to him. To say, *Okay, so you think you love someone else, well, let's talk about it. Let's see where we each turned down the wrong path and try to find our way back again.* Instead she said, "You always were good at buried criticism."

He shook his head, bewildered. There were fresh towels hanging on the rod, and the trapped moisture of what he guessed had been her morning shower was still present in the room. He was suddenly aware of how dirty he was. How terribly he needed to be clean. "Explain to me how it sounded like criticism," he said to her back as she stomped out of the room and made a right turn into their bedroom. He heard the springs squeak as she threw herself across the bed. Her reply was mumbled, inaudible.

"What one single word I said sounded like criticism?" He leaned in the doorway, saw how her jeans were still undone and how her hand was resting on the small white triangle of exposed panties.

"Never mind."

"Never mind what?"

"Just never mind. Forget it."

"What if I don't want to forget it?"

"Bruno, please. My head hurts," she said as she lifted her arm and rested it across her eyes.

The space next to the door frame felt like his, a spatial time warp his recent separation couldn't touch. He had lain on that bed, walked around the room, gone to the closet, and dressed as well as undressed, and for a brief second, he could still see himself doing those things.

"Are you ready for tomorrow?" Another attempt at harmless conversation.

"As ready as I'm gonna get."

"Do you need me to do anything?"

"You mean you're gonna be here?" She raised her head to look at him, and he noticed the fierceness behind the hazel eyes and something else he couldn't distinguish.

"Why wouldn't I be here?"

"You mean you don't have plans with your girlfriend?"

His face turned the color of her lips. All he could manage was a simple shake of his head.

"Come, then. We'll pretend we still care about each other in front of Mom and Dad. Certainly will save me the pain of answering questions."

"Leah, I'm not involved with Alyce."

"Oh. Alyce. So that's her name. I'd forgotten."

"I'm not involved."

"Then why are you still there?"

"Do you want me to come home?"

"I'd say that's up to you."

"I disagree."

"I never asked you to leave."

"I know that."

"So?"

"So it just seemed the right thing to do at the time."

"And now?"

"And now it seems we're getting nowhere. Same as usual."

She looked at him. "Don't do this to me. Not now. Do you realize you've said more to me since you've been gone than in three years of living here?"

"You're willing to keep it this way just to have a chance at conversation?"

He had meant it as a joke. She didn't take it as one.

"I'm sure she's worried by now. You've never been this late before."

He leaned down over the bed, one hand on either side of her legs. "Nobody's waiting for me, and you know it. And I'll tell you something else I know: I think you're the one who's having doubts, who can't decide yet if this might just be the out you've been waiting for."

Crossing the room to the windows, he pulled the curtains together to block the afternoon sun and then left the room, walking back through the house, noticing that the spare bedroom had been freshened and turned back into a sewing room. No trace of his brief sojourn there.

Standing in the kitchen, he looked at the coffeepot. She never said whether or not she had wanted coffee, and she used to love iced coffee late in the afternoon. Cracking open the ice tray, he filled a tall glass with it and poured the coffee over it and stirred in a teaspoon of sugar and put it on a small tray and carried it to her. He saw that she had rolled to her side.

"Try drinking this," he said, the tension making his voice crack. She rolled over and saw the brown liquid and put her hand to her mouth and propelled herself up off the bed like a tiger, racing to the bathroom, where she began to vomit.

Okay, so she doesn't want any coffee, he thought. He set the tray on the end of the bed and went to the bathroom. "Do I need to call the doctor?"

"No. You just need to quit bringing me things to drink."

She retched into the toilet bowl. This time he stood away from her and let her hold her own hair. He waited until the wave passed and said quietly, "Leah."

She shook her head. "Bruno, please."

"Leah." He said it again, and she looked at him, and he forced the question out into the open. "Is something else going on here?"

Leaning on her hand, she thought how similar to her father Bruno sounded, remembering one episode in particular when Merle had come into her room, Leah's own personal daisy-covered diary in his hand, her mother peeping over his shoulder, the smoldering gleam of satisfaction in her eyes. You've got no right! she had screamed at both of them, recalling with absolute accuracy what she had written the night before. The business about how good it had felt for Clyde Stroh's fingers to invade her underwear. You've got no right! she had screamed again, shoving them out the door and locking it, listening to the twittering of her mother haranguing her father for not being more firm, more appalled at the absolute proof he was holding in his hands. Leah hadn't liked being questioned then, and she didn't like it now. She looked up at Bruno and said, "What do you mean?"

He squatted so that he was eye level with her, a clumsy move that annoyed him to no end. He chose his words carefully, determined to keep his eyes on her eyes. "I mean, is there something wrong with you that I need to know about?"

Being pregnant was not exactly a negative condition, so she felt somewhat truthful in saying no.

"Are you sure?" he said, willing her to tell him.

"I've got a headache is all." She was looking away from him, or she would have noticed the way his face changed, the measure of coldness that hardened his eyes and stiffened his mouth.

He grunted when he stood, and before he turned to leave, he said, "I'm sorry for the mess I made of things. For hurting you. For shutting you out. For being such an asshole. I'm sorry you've worn yourself out working in the fields. I'm sorry for it all."

He walked down the hall and stood before the kitchen table and took the brochure out of his pocket and put it underneath his coffee cup and then he went out the back door to the side yard where the Rambler was parked and climbed in, staring out across the fields where sunlight seemed distilled, purified, something other than light.

Reversing down the drive, he pulled out onto the main road and headed toward town, toward the motel.

He'd never been very good at timing, and this day proved no exception. He saw his mother's gray Pontiac approaching and slammed his hand on the steering wheel. To borrow Leah's phrase: he didn't need this. Not now. Thinking he could pass her and maybe, for hospitality's sake, throw up a hand as he zipped by, Bruno watched in disbelief as Eilene swerved like a drunk into his lane, forcing him to practically stand on the brakes to keep from hitting her head-on. The Rambler fishtailed across the asphalt.

"Are you fuckin crazy?" he shouted, banging on the steering wheel one more time for good measure.

Once she saw that he intended to stop, she smiled and pulled up alongside, happy as a clam, rolling down the window as though nothing in the world was wrong.

"What a treat," she said, reaching her fingers toward him.

"Have you lost your mind?"

"Not that I know of."

"How come you steered into my lane?"

"Silly. I knew you'd stop."

"Okay, I've stopped. What do you want?"

"That's no way to talk to your mother, Bruno." Her smile faltered. She had no idea what had happened, but she had never seen him look so dark, so unyielding to any of her motherly charms, so like she imagined Jonathan Ferrier had looked in *Testimony of Two Men* when he discovered the full extent of his really sweet mother's betrayal.

He refused to say anything, but he wanted to, she could see the muscle along his jawline jumping like a fish.

"Can you come back for a visit?"

"No."

She swallowed hard, and the corners of her mouth drooped. "Not for a moment?"

"You know, Mother, 'no' is considered by many to be a complete sentence."

"You have never in your life talked to me this way. What in the hell is the matter?"

She *was* upset. He had never heard her use the word "hell." But instead of answering, he eased the Rambler forward. Eilene put the car in reverse and backed up so that she was still even with him. "I asked you a question. Can you please show me the courtesy of answering?"

"Mother, please."

"Please what?" She smiled at him.

"Are you gonna stalk me all the way to the motel?"

"Is that where you're staying?"

"You know good and well where I'm staying."

"Are you having an affair?"

"I'm done talking to you for the day."

"Come on back. I'm sure Sonny would like some company."

"He's already got company." Bruno nodded behind him, in the direction of the house.

"Who?"

"His girlfriend."

Eilene looked frightened, in his opinion.

"Forget about Sonny. You're the one I'd like to talk to—"

"Mother, I've got to go. Now, you can reverse the car all the way to town if you want to, but it won't stop me from leaving."

"Will you call me?"

"What for? What good would it do?"

"I'm your mother, Bruno. Just because you've walked out on your wife doesn't mean you have to walk—"

He waved at her and pulled away, leaving her sentence hanging in the air between them. Adjusting the rearview mirror, he saw her approach her driveway and pull in and then the car disappeared behind the thick hedge.

{CHAPTER 28}

Sonny felt as though he were in seventh heaven, wallowing on a chintz-covered cloud, as Conchita sat on his lap and pushed the rocker back and forth with her shoes, and since his thoughts had turned heavenly, he found himself filled with thanksgiving at the magnitude of his good fortune. He thanked God for the man who bought the cinder-bricked building from a debt-ridden groceryman and turned it into the Li'l Miss Roustabout, and he thanked God for allowing men to crave the sight of a naked female body so that business stayed good and the place stayed open, and he thanked God that females everywhere recognized the craving and took it upon themselves to learn the breast-thrusting, ass-wiggling moves this one here was demonstrating fully. As he felt something near his toes, his gratitude turned south, and he took a moment to thank God for Levi Strauss, who had created a company that realized even fat men needed jeans. He was still wearing his black T-shirt, but his pants were on the floor in a wad next to his great big feet, while Conchita's clothing had been flung to the far reaches of the living room: her white sweater tossed to the piano, her tight black pants thrown over his shoulder, her panties somewhere under the draperies (he thought). All the gal was wearing were her retrofitted tap shoes, and the *schlink-schlink* of metal on the heart-of-pine floors was driving him wild. He began to trace the smattering of moles on her back, linking them until they spelled out the words "bad girl." The game of skin Scrabble was making him hard again, for there were thousands of ways of being bad, all of them good.

"Shit, Sonny, are you gone come or not?"

"Darlin, it just feels so good."

"You been feeling good for two hours. I need you to come."

"But once I come, it's over."

"That's the point, big boy."

He had already come twice and wanted to prolong the moment. He thanked God for the sensory-depriving thickness of the Trojans that aided in his quest.

"You know what this is like?" she said with exasperation, leaning around to look at him, putting her hands on her thighs.

"Heaven?"

And since she couldn't quite get her mind off shopping, she said, "No. It's like going into a shoe store and trying on a pair of shoes and walking around in them for two or three hours and then refusing to buy them. I'm getting sore. I'm ready for you to come."

Sonny was confused by the verbal example and, as with most things that confused him, he shoved it to the back of his mind. "Just a few more minutes and I will."

He rocked back in the chair and put his hands to her waist and rested his arms on the chintz, thankful even in this moment of sweat-dampened ecstasy for his mother's decorating taste, that she—

The back door into the kitchen slammed shut, and Sonny froze like a zoo lion that's suddenly had its side of raw goat jerked away.

"What was that?" Conchita whispered.

"Shhh. Be still."

"Shit, Sonny. I heard something. I thought you told me you were watching for the car!"

He had tried to, but it just felt so damn good, he kept shutting his eyes. "Relax. She can't hear us. She's stone-cold deaf."

"Well, I hope she's blind, too, 'cause if she's not, she's about to see me in the—"

In many ways, it was like an unexpected bounce on a trampoline, the way Sonny pushed Conchita up off his lap and away from him, sending her sliding across the floor in her homemade tap shoes. The floor was slick and the shoes ill equipped for feet that were running as a result of a body being shoved, and her arms pinwheeled by her sides in search of balance, and she looked for all the world like Bambi on ice. She landed facedown on the sofa and turned to stare at him in disbelief. The look of scorn was wasted on him, for he was heaving up his jeans and scrambling into his shoes, leaving Conchita to search for her panties on her own.

Eilene needed some good news. Some bright spot in an otherwise dismal day that had started on a low note and fallen even further. First the snippy gal in the drugstore and then the obvious disapproval of the lawyer and then the goading she had taken from a complete stranger in the library and now Bruno, who she supposed really was serious about leaving. So, yes. She needed some good news. A splash of hope the color of a daffodil, perhaps. Some bright yellow beacon of light to lead her forward and help her find her way out of the confusing miasma of depressing circumstances. Believing it just might arrive in the form of Sonny's girlfriend, she felt optimistic as she walked past the girl's Pinto, noticing that in spite of its road-worn appearance, the interior of the car was neat as a pin. Only one thing seemed amiss: the blue box with the letters "T" and "R" peeping out from underneath the car seat. A rosary was hanging off the rearview mirror, but Eilene would worry about religious affiliations at some later date.

The afternoon light reflecting off the panes of the kitchen window winked at her and made her think once again of daffodils. She was hung up on the color yellow, seeing it everywhere, or wanting to see it everywhere, wishing she could sweep into the room and find it filled with yellow flowers of all makes and models. She had always thought yellow flowers the prettiest ones to use at weddings. Red seemed too glum, white too rigid. Yellow seemed perfect. Believing she might be able to offer the suggestion of yellow flowers to Sonny's girlfriend at some future date made her feel not quite so old as she had in the drugstore, or later, in the library. Eilene ran a hand down her slacks and smoothed her shirt, hoping to ease in through the back door and sneak a peek at herself in the bathroom off the kitchen. First impressions mattered. A lot. She wanted to look her best. She had already checked to see if Sonny and his girlfriend were in the kitchen, and they weren't, so once the door was opened as quietly as possible and shut in an equally quiet manner, she tiptoed across the room and put her purse on the table and was turning to go to the bathroom when she heard the noise.

Piano, she thought. *I bet they're in there sitting at the piano.* Well, she hoped only one of them was sitting on the bench. There was no way in hell it would hold the two of them. She heard the sound of her chair being rocked and a curious metallic sound and Sonny's voice saying "heaven." *They're studying my* Broadman Hymnal, she was foolish enough to think. Then the girl's voice. Something about wearing shoes and not paying for them. *How strange,* thought Eilene, unable to merge the two conversations into a sensible one. Seeing the door cracked a bit and remarking to herself that the kitchen was dark and there was no way she would be seen, she moved to the doorway and peered in through the slight opening.

The vision would be there long after they quit whatever hideous act they were doing. The vision would be there clean into the next election year. *Shoot, let's be honest,* she thought to herself. The scene she had just witnessed would be there until Jesus came swooping down from heaven to carry Eilene up into eternal life. Sonny naked from the waist down while some female writhed on his lap like a strumpet.

"Oh my Lord," she whispered, searching the kitchen for help. At a loss as to the proper way to handle the act of fornication taking place in her very own living room in her very own chair, she did the only thing she knew how to do: she retraced her steps to the back door and opened it and then slammed it as loudly as possible. Moving to the sink, she lifted her hair net off the sill and popped it on her head so that she might feel helmeted and safe. Once those two things were done, she took the frying pan out of the oven and banged it on the stove and moved to the fridge and, still holding on to her dream of yellow, got out all the squash she could find and threw them in the sink and turned the water on full force and watched it hit the yellow pebbled skin, the gourds rolling around in the surf and sending the water up into a spray on her face.

Enraged, she picked up the closest one and hurled it at the fridge, loving the way it splattered into tiny bits of yellow pulp in front of the Hotpoint.

"Easy, Eilene. Easy, now," she told herself, wiping her face dry on a dish towel and pressing her hands on the countertop. Out the window of the kitchen, she could see Leah standing on the back porch, pulling laundry out of the washing machine, and with the exception of the late hour, it was like that morning a month and a half ago, Eilene leaning up on her toes to watch Leah move around like a ghost.

Sonny cleared his throat and said, "Mama, I'd like you to meet someone."

Let him talk. She was deaf. And since she was pretending to be deaf, she was afforded the ten or fifteen seconds necessary to steady her breathing. So what if she had thrown a squash at her refrigerator? She could always pretend she found a millipede crawling across it.

"Mama!"

Eilene pushed her glasses up on her nose and plastered a grin on her face and turned. The girl was leaning on one leg with her arms behind her. She looked like a twelve-year-old practicing to be a streetwalker. A dancer this girl was not.

"This here is Conchita Corrales Ti—" Sonny was red in the face, with so many emotions engaged, it seemed he was about to explode.

Eilene moved across the room with an extended hand. She'd take care of this trailer trash in short fashion. "Chiquita. Like the banana. How cute. I'm so pleased to meet you."

The girl opened her mouth and refused to take Eilene's hand, glancing at Sonny with her overly mascaraed eyes. Eilene glanced down and saw why: she had extended a squash in the girl's direction. Whirling, she fired it toward the sink, where it exploded.

"Holy Mother of God," Conchita said, fear in her voice, all thoughts of shopping erased from her mind.

"Not quite," Sonny said, believing he had just hurdled the first obstacle, relieved to still be living and breathing and not stabbed or hit over the head with a frying pan. He studied his mother with his small eyes and began to get mad. He wasn't sure what clue he had stumbled over, but stumbled he had. He had begun to believe that Bruno was right, that their mother wasn't deaf at all. "Her name's not Chiquita, it's—"

"I love those bananas, myself. I never buy the other ones. I always look for the little blue label." The girl seemed poised for flight. Good.

And then Sonny, this great hulk of a man Eilene had pushed around for years, turned on her, held out a finger, and said, "You can cut this shit out right now."

It stopped Eilene in her tracks.

"Her name's Conchita. Connie for short. Connie T-I-L-L. She's my wife."

Eilene, never one to let a person see how she was feeling until she had a chance to check those feelings out and shuffle them around until they lined up with her mental guideline of how a mother should be, dropped the mental cards and reached like a cripple for the chair, her age settling on her face. "Your wife?"

"That's what I said. My wife. We got married a month ago."

Now that the words were out, he didn't seem to know what to do with them, so he stood looking from one to the other, doing an unbidden comparison. Conchita failed to measure up in every single way, and her many deficits hollowed out his heart, fixing a place for her there that would never be challenged.

Encouraged by the show of confidence from her husband, Conchita glanced around the room and saw her tiny gold belt over by the fridge, and reminding herself that she had paid for it with her hard-earned money, she clicked her way over and lifted it off the floor, sliding her fingers down it to remove the speckling of squash seeds. Recognizing Sonny's stand as his one surge of manhood that would probably never again make an appearance, she decided to make the most of it. A hard tenure spent in the household of her own mother had not been for nothing. This one here, speckled with water and squash, would be a piece of cake. Smiling brightly, she buckled her belt around her waist and turned to her husband, who was fiddling with the handle of the frying pan as though he might be entertaining the thought of matricide.

"My stuff is in the trunk of my car," she said, walking toward the door. "As soon as Sonny brings it in, I'll help you get ready for tomorrow."

"Tomorrow?" Eilene said, bewildered.

"The Fourth. Don't tell me you folks don't celebrate the Fourth of July." Hands on her hips, she looked at Sonny, who was as pale as white flour, and said the three words he was waiting to hear: "You coming, Sonny?"

"I'm right behind you," he said, lumbering across the room, taking special care to steer clear of his mother, who was sitting and staring straight ahead, quiet but for her breast-heaving sighs.

{CHAPTER 29}

Without a doubt, the manhole cover, not over fifty feet from Russo's Jewelry, was just the ticket.

Joe Benson walked up the dark street, keeping close to the exterior walls of the empty stores, where the dark seemed more opaque, the soft pooling of yellow light off the one or two power poles not strong enough to illuminate him, for a low fog was rolling in and even the fire hydrants seemed a mystery. Every few minutes, cars roared past loaded down with young people who cruised the main drag for hours on end. What was illegal and banned over in Hattiesburg, kids in Purvis engaged in with abandon. Joe counted four pristine hopped-up Fords and three Impalas with throat-rumbling headers. Four motorcycles shrieked by, outfitted like the guy's in *Easy Rider*. The noise was contagious, and he suddenly missed those days and wished for them again and wondered why in the world he had been so determined to marry Alyce. A crowd was inside Smokey's Bar and Grill, and the parking lot to the side of it was full, and motorcycles and trucks were parked alongside the curb, and three people waiting for a seat were lounging there, leaning and smoking and watching the teenagers cruise by, their voices too low to make out the words. Joe stood watching them, waiting to see if he'd be noticed, and once he was reassured that his presence was overlooked, he walked on. He heard the muted noise of camaraderie and wagered with himself that, come the morning, he would have enough money to buy and sell every single one of the country yokels sitting on bar stools and slurping stale beer. He had left his own personal car, the souped-up Impala, parked at the Li'l Miss Roustabout, and while he hated to say good-bye to such a cherry, it was necessary to everyone concerned that people believe he had been there all night still engaged in the activity he was best known for: ogling the dancers and dealing cards off the bottom of the deck. The plan was to get in and out and then crawl half a mile through the new pipe system to its outlet fifty yards from the Li'l Miss. Once there, he would saunter in and order a beer like he'd been there all night. If Sonny would get where he was supposed to be, he would be set.

Walking down an alleyway between Russo's Jewelry and the row of abandoned houses the county couldn't decide what to do with, Joe kicked a rock at a cat and listened to it hiss as it scampered away. The month before, he had climbed to the roof of one those houses and tried to wedge himself down between it and its neighbor and failed, losing a shoe in the process. Pressing his face to the narrow opening, Joe could see the shoe resting on a window ledge, inside a space so small it would be impassable, even for a pencil-thin child. The shoes were wing tips, and he liked them, and he had entertained the idea of bringing along a rod and reel and seeing if he couldn't fish the shoe back up before he dismissed the notion as pure foolishness. Come the morning, he'd have enough money to buy as many pairs of shoes as he wanted. His size eight could just rest where it was.

He'd not seen Alyce since the day before, and while he'd thought he might feel some inkling of regret over leaving her and the boys, he didn't. Cold was cold, and the bitch was cold. Seven years he'd spent trying to warm that coochie up, and still he wagered that should a slab of hamburger be put on it, it would freeze in two seconds flat. Warm was what he needed. Warm and wet. He could almost see himself stretched out on a beach in the Yucatán, having his feet rubbed by some dark-skinned native gal.

Going behind the row of houses, he found the one he wanted and stopped to check out his tools, lifting the wrapped cloth from inside his shirt and opening it and looking. Unless the fool had set a steel wall in place, the break-in would be a piece of cake. Smoking a cigarette while he waited for the moon to hide itself behind a wall of clouds, he calculated his success, and even with the crowd across the street at Smokey's and the cars traveling up and down the street, the odds still seemed to lean in his direction. Snuffing out the butt against the wall, he figured now was as good a time to find out as any.

The abandoned house had a chimney that had gone askew and leaned out toward the back lot, pulling away from the roof in precarious fashion. Two windows flanked it: one boarded up, the other, for the most part, busted out. Joe put a foot to the outcropping of brick and pushed his way up. Using a stout stick, he knocked at the remaining shards of glass and heard them shatter to the floor of the room. Once this was done, he pulled himself in and somersaulted across the floor. "Double-oh-seven couldn't a done it any better," he said, brushing off his pants.

Working his way through the empty rooms, each strewn with bums' leftovers, Joe found the small room housing the bathroom. The toilet and sink and tub had been removed by whatever loan company had foreclosed on the house. Wallpaper fell off the wall in strips that looked like wide, wilted leaves of corn. Tapping on the wall, he went to the space where the pedestal sink used to be and opened his shirt and pulled out the cloth and unwrapped the tools. After finding a saber saw he went to work. Two sections of plaster later, he hit the bricks, which he'd expected, and took the long screwdriver and hammer and began to work them.

A year earlier Joe had approached old man Russo about a security system for the jewelry store, and the old man had laughed at him, saying, "Any sumbitch who thinks he's gonna steal from me better make sure he's right with God." *Well, we'll see about that,* Joe had thought at the time, noticing that the building had been built flush to the old house next door and how the wall behind the counter was absent of cabinetry. Without a doubt, just sitting there waiting for someone with know-how to bust on through.

In truth, he hadn't expected it to be so easy, and once the bricks were lifted out and the store's Sheetrock sliced through, Joe sat back on his heels and thought, *Wait a minute, this is too easy, way too easy,* wondering momentarily if Sonny had squealed on him and cops were waiting inside.

He stuck his hand through first and waited to see if it got shot off, but all he heard was the noise from the place across the street. Putting the penlight in his mouth, he squeezed through the opening and birthed himself onto the floor of Russo's Jewelry like a plaster-covered baby.

"Shit, it worked. It really worked!" Joe had the jewelry in three different bags. Rings in one. Necklaces in another. And the last bag held the watches. He had even taken some of the silver cups people bought as gifts for newborn babies. "Shit. I cain't believe it!" he said, hurrying down the backside of the alley, the jangling of his loot sounding against his chest. After he made the corner, he glanced once behind him, still expecting the cops to be there. Slowing his pace a little, he approached LeClede Street and looked at his watch and timed the cars as they passed. It took two minutes for them to make the turn at School Street and begin to circle back. Across the way was the high school, with its empty swings and monkey bars, the row of windows with the shades pulled low, and beyond it, the railroad tracks where poor old Sparechange had nearly lost his life. A lone figure was standing there, arms hanging down at its sides, and Joe wondered who it was and if it was a cop disguised as a vagrant. The figure was so still that it seemed a piece of the landscape, and as Joe stopped and lit a cigarette and smoked, the figure refused to move. Whatever or whoever it was seemed of little consequence, and as the last of the cars passed and he moved toward the manhole cover, Joe forgot all about it, failing to notice that as soon as he squatted down, the figure moved toward him, a distant shadow in defiance of night, a slight specter watching all his moves.

Joe used the big screwdriver to work the manhole cover loose. When it was ajar, he sat back on his rear and pulled the plastic garbage bags he had brought along over his shoes and tied them around his ankles with shoelaces. He could hear the cars as they shifted gears and began to make their U-turn, but there were rats down there, and while the vision of Mexico was firmly planted in his mind, there was still half a mile of shit to crawl through before he could actually begin to head in that direction. Swinging over the side, he put his feet on the metal ladder and lowered himself down, the smell of mold and wet all around him. He jammed the screwdriver against the metal ridge and pushed on the manhole cover until it clanked back into place. "Holy cow!" he said, his voice echoing into the void. "It really is gonna work!" This thought in mind, he climbed down to where the pipe intersected with two others and took out his penlight and looked at the map again. The one he wanted was the newer one, and while they all seemed slick and grimed, he found it and got down on his hands and knees and began to crawl, not stopping to realize that the fog had rolled in so completely, he could have walked the distance and not been seen. Not aware that Sparechange Dinkins had left his post by the railroad tracks and sauntered across and was kneeling over the cover, one eye pressed down to the small coin-size opening, seeing the fading wand of yellow light play against pipe walls before disappearing into the dark. "Without a doubt, he's in a world of trouble," he whispered. " 'Cause concrete don't never cure."

→←

"I cain't believe you're gonna leave me here with her," Conchita said, watching as Sonny slapped his Australian bush hat against his leg.

"I ain't gonna be long."

"How long?"

"Maybe an hour or two."

"How come you're all dressed up?"

"I ain't dressed up."

"You look dressed up to me."

He took the hat and slung it across the room. "That make you feel better?"

"Not much."

"I gotta meet Joe, and then I'm coming right back."

"What you gotta meet Joe for?"

"Now, baby doll, I ain't got the time for all these questions. I'm late already."

"What in the cryinoutloud does Joe need you for this late at night?"

It was a genuine question, and he stopped and looked at her. She had showered and was wearing her long T-shirt pajamas that said PARTY ANIMAL across the chest. Wet hair and all, the sight of a woman sitting on his bed made his head swim, and he looked at the closed door, aggravated to be stuck wrapping up details he couldn't care less about.

"I have no idea."

"Can I go with you?"

"No."

Sliding back to the head of the bed, she rearranged the pillows, punching at them until they were comfortable. The room was a mess, and as soon as he left, she was going to haul most of it outdoors. The table where the television sat was a good one, and she couldn't believe Sonny's mother had tolerated the boat propeller being placed on it. Through the walls, she could hear his mother in the kitchen banging pots around. "She gonna do that all night?"

"She's boiling the ribs. They ought to be done in a little while."

"You gonna barbecue them tonight?"

"No. They'll soak in beer overnight in the fridge, and me and Bruno'll do them in the morning," he said, his irritation at all the questions barely held in check. Looking at his watch, he saw how late he was.

"I hate to stay here by myself," she said.

"You ain't by yourself. She's in there."

"She hates me."

Walking over to her, he rubbed her leg. "She hates me, too. The trick is to not let it bother you."

"You're her son. How come she hates you?"

Christ, he had to get out of there. In many ways, it was like slipping away from his mother, pretending he had a make-believe lodge to go to. "Listen. I'll be back in an hour or so."

Conchita was quietly studying her fingernails. "I guess I could do my nails."

"That sounds like a good idea."

"Get ready for tomorrow."

"Get yourself all dolled up, why don't you?"

"Who all's coming?"

"Just Leah's folks."

"I ain't met her yet. She ain't mean like your mama, is she?"

"She's sweet. Nothing to be afraid of." He felt momentarily sorry for his mother, who, in spite of being a sometimes hateful hag, was being judged unfairly.

"Okay, then," she said.

Sonny opened the door and headed down the hall, one of his worst fears slowly making an appearance. If Conchita kept up this foolish talking, day and night, he might be forced to get a job just to get away from her.

⟡

The woman was poking at the boiling meat with a long fork, the only light in the kitchen the small utility bulb over the stove, and to Conchita's way of thinking, Eilene looked like a witch stirring at her brew.

Conchita set the bottles of fingernail polish down on the table and asked, "You mind if I turn on the overhead light?"

Eilene looked at her, too tired even for sarcasm. "It's over there. Next to the switches." She nodded at the wall.

"Sonny told me how he rigged up them fans out there to turn on just by flipping a switch," Conchita bubbled.

"Yes. He did at that."

Eilene was off kilter, her routine (and yes, admit it) boring life blown to smithereens inside the space of two hours. Taking the spoon and scooping off the layer of rolling fat and dumping it in an empty coffee can, she found herself short of breath at the sheer magnitude of her feelings. Number one was the sense of diminishing. Number two was the fear of disappearing entirely. Number three was the anger that her plan had gone awry. Number four was the rage at being beaten. Number five was the disbelief that she had been outsmarted by a man barely able to tie his own shoelaces. And number six (a part of her added all them up and came to the sum that matched the number of letters she had received years ago from the school board) was the fatigue that saturated her at the thought of living with this mistake. The girl was oblivious to what Eilene was feeling and continued to rattle on about how she wanted to rearrange Sonny's bedroom so the light wouldn't shine in her eyes first thing in the morning. *I'm in deep trouble here,* Eilene thought. *Stuck with two who like to sleep all day long.*

"—goin to start a fishin business. He said he's been workin on gettin it ready for over a year."

Eilene turned to her. "Dear, do you mind telling me how old you are?"

"Twenty-three."

Eilene turned back to the stove. *How in the world does a hugely fat, nonworking male manage it?* she wondered. In a strange way, the girl's incredible overbite made her look even younger. Eilene had a feeling that high-priced orthodontics were in her near future.

Flipping on the light, Conchita walked to the sink and peered out the kitchen window, leaning on her elbows to see the field between the two houses. *Shit. So much land. Such a great big house.* A bottle of Joy was there, and she took it and went to opening cabinets in search of a bowl.

"Where you keep your small bowls at?" she asked.

Eilene pointed with the long fork to the pie safe next to the Hotpoint, and Conchita went to it and opened the doors, smelling the odor of candle wax and figs, a strange combination that made her think of Christmas. Plunking down a bowl, she squirted the bottom of it with dishwashing liquid and dunked her fingers in, working the liquid against her cuticles with her thumbs.

Eilene was silent, poking at the meat, hating the gray clots of fat that were rolling around on the surface of the water. The Sonny Situation had turned one of her favorite meals into something ghastly. She supposed there was a good chance she would never eat ribs (or squash) again, for the rib of a cow had become Conchita's leg folded over the arm of a chair, and the yellow squash, the girl's breasts underneath Sonny's large hands. Eilene shuddered at the virtuosity of this imagery.

"I like to do my nails at night," Conchita was saying.

Eilene said nothing. She had played at being deaf for over a year. Time to add a new ailment to her arsenal: the suffering entitled the recent mute.

Oh, the prattle of the nervous and desperate, she thought, listening to the girl go on and on about cuticles and the best way to remove them. A Popsicle stick was the method the girl liked the best. Kill two birds with one stone, she was saying, for you ate the Popsicle while soaking each hand and then used the stick once the icy treat had been devoured. "Save money this way," she commented, and Eilene stopped stirring and turned her head in the girl's direction. It wasn't a yellow daffodil, but its color was similar to hope. She continued to scoop off the fat and drop it in the can. There was more. "Get a good job that pays more and has regular decent hours," the girl was saying. "This way we can move out sooner." Eilene almost dropped her utensil at this.

"You do your own nails?" Conchita asked her.

Eilene turned and really saw her. Oh, such an eagerness to please. Such desire to find some type of level ground. The bottle-opener mouth with teeth never covered by the inner softness of a lip. Teeth unusually bright because of exposure to the sun. "I keep my hands in water so much, my nails are shameful," Eilene said. A half lie thrown out to the girl like a life ring. She watched as the girl reached for it like one destined to be eternally foundering.

"I got some capsules I take to harden mine," the girl said in a shy voice. "I brung 'em all with me, too. This way Sonny don't have to buy me none."

Eilene nodded and turned back to her ribs.

"Got the same stuff that Jell-O has in it. And horse's hooves. Cain't remember what it's called right now."

"Gelatin."

"That's it."

Eilene was remembering *Testimony of Two Men* and how seduced she'd been by it, how she had come to forgive Taylor Caldwell for clogging it up with historical medical commentary once she read the last chapter and the whole family was again intact. Happily intact. Willing to spend the rest of their days completely entwined in one another's happy, happy lives. Eilene had actually shed a tear or two at the striking scene where the mother's wisdom had finally been recognized by her sons. Three times she read it, from start to finish. Looking toward the ceiling, she wondered briefly if fiction was addictive and if she needed to find some twelve-step program—Readers Anonymous—to help her break its spell.

"I'm good at doin nails," the girl was saying. "I wouldn't mind doin yours sometime." Her head was lowered, and she was screwing the lids back on, gathering up her means of manicure.

"That would be nice," Eilene said.

"Okay, then." The girl stood and pushed the chair back under the table and walked down the hall, her wet hair swinging behind her.

Eilene sighed. Oh, the fatigue a surrender brings. The bitterness that comes from folding a winning hand to a bluff. Testing the meat and judging it ready, she took the padded mittens and lifted the pot off the burner so it could cool.

The phone rang and Eilene stared at it, insulted by the noise. Was there anything more intrusive than that sound? All was quiet but for the shrill insistent ringing. Moving to it, she lifted it off its hook, the weight of the day spilling over to her hand, which was trembling. *What now?* she was thinking. *Is Sonny on top of the water tower spray-painting graffiti? Has Bruno been arrested for public drunkenness?* All her thoughts were grim, and the pressure of dealing with them was making her head hurt.

"Ahh, Eilene? Is this Eilene?"

"Speaking."

"Merle Maxwell here," he said, and Eilene fished for a chair and sat. She would be okay as long as he didn't put Dora on the line and force Eilene to discuss perverse cocktails. She listened to the natural reticence in his voice.

"I hate to call so late. What time is it, Dora?" he asked his wife, who Eilene supposed was standing next to his elbow.

"It's not but eight o'clock," Eilene said, stifling a yawn.

"Yes, well. Eight's still late for me."

"But not for me!" came Dora's background chirp.

"How are you, Merle? Don't tell me you have to cancel on tomorrow."

"Oh, no. Nothing like that. I was just wondering if something might be going on there that I need to know about. If you folks were okay."

"Oh, Merle," Eilene began, and then couldn't continue. Her throat tightening to the point where all she could squeeze out were squeaky little words that made her sound like an idiot on helium.

"Eilene? You all right?"

"No. No, I'm not all right," she told him, clearing her throat, recalling *Testimony of Two Men* and the calm coolheadedness of Margorie Ferrier, and how brave she had been even though she had fallen half off the bed with a heart attack. "There's been some developments here that, ah, frankly, I'm ashamed to have to mention."

"Developments?"

"Well, you could call it something other than that, but frankly, I'm at a loss for words." *Obviously,* she thought, *since I've used the word "frankly" twice in a row.*

"Can you fill me in? I've had a feeling for a month now that something's amiss, and I've never liked being the last one to know."

"Oh, something's amiss, all right."

"Yes?"

"Merle, dear. I'm afraid I don't know where to begin."

"Perhaps at the beginning?"

"No, I'm afraid it would take too long."

Heaven help me, she thought. *I've come down with the repetitive-word disease.* Sighing, she pinched her upper nose between her fingers.

"Is someone sick?"

"No."

"Is it Leah?" Eilene heard Dora's voice in the background and Merle covering the mouthpiece to muffle his response, which sounded somewhat impatient.

"They've separated." Eilene decided to be blunt about it. "Bruno's left her. Or at least that's the way it looks. He's there every day tending to the cows. But he only stays long enough to feed."

Conchita was coming up the hall, something in her arms. Sonny's rusty boat propeller. "Never seen such a load of crap. This don't belong on that good table in there," she said, and then she saw Eilene on the phone and said, "Oh, 'scuse me."

Eilene covered the mouthpiece. "Just put it outside."

Merle was asking her if she could talk. Eilene said, "No. Not really. I mean, I could talk if I had something to say . . . but"—do *not* use the word "frankly," she warned herself—"obviously I've been kept in the dark, same as you. You have been kept in the dark, haven't you? I mean, you don't know something I need to know, do you?"

Merle was silent. Dora was not. Eilene could hear the woman clamoring for details. Merle said, "Dora, for God's sake, give me a minute here," and then he cleared his throat. "No. I don't know anything. I've just had a feeling. We've talked back and forth through the month, and each time I've asked Leah if something was wrong, and each time she denied it. Well, well. Frankly, I don't know what to say."

Eilene was frankly relieved to hear someone else using the word "frankly."

"I called her tonight, but the line was busy. For two hours it's been busy. I wonder if we should still come down."

"Merle, if she'd not wanted you here, she would have said so. I know Leah. She's never been anything less than totally honest."

"She invited us to stay over," he said, his voice subdued.

"Then plan on it."

"Eilene, I hope you don't take offense at this, but is Bruno . . ." He stumbled on the question, and even though she knew what the question was ("Is Bruno involved with another woman?"), she refused to help him. Lifting the lid to the sugar jar, she put a cube in her mouth and winced. She would need to go to the dentist soon.

"Merle. I'm not offended." But she was. Just a little bit. He could have as easily asked if Leah was involved with another man. "I don't know the reason."

"Like I mentioned earlier. I had a feeling . . ." There was the interruption of Dora's voice again, saying, "Tell me what she said! Tell me!" and Merle hissing at her to wait a damn minute.

"What time should we expect you?" Eilene asked as Conchita came in the back door, brushing off her *party animal* pajamas now imprinted with a rusty shape like that of propeller.

"Early. 'Round nine o'clock."

And because she was a country woman and proud of it, and the man she was talking to was a city man who had practically accused Bruno of being at fault, Eilene said, "You call that early?"

"Well, it's early for us."

"Merle, dear. I'm just picking at you," she said, remembering when she had baited the poor stranger in the library. Was this to be her new role as she waited for grandchildren to sprout up out of genetic bedlam? A look of belated recall crossed her face. She needed to cancel those changes in her will. Immediately.

"Listen. I hate to be on this side of it. I've always considered Bruno part of the family. But—"

"Say no more. I understand." Eilene rubbed her head.

"Well, I guess there's nothing more to do other than go to sleep," he said.

"Sleep would be nice. Seems like I've not slept good for the past month."

"Eilene, those two love each other. I know it."

"I know it, Merle. But sometimes love isn't enough."

Hanging up the phone, Eilene watched as Conchita came stomping out of the room, a trash bag in her hand.

"I cain't believe he eats all this shit and then just leaves it back there in the room, like he was raised in a barn or somethin. A kitchen's where a person ought to eat. Not the middle of the bed. And I tell you somethin else." Conchita pointed her finger. "He'd not be so fat if he'd stay away from all them potato chips and cookies."

Well, well, Eilene thought, pulling the hair net off and holding it in her hand. It seemed she could retire her arsenal permanently. She smiled at the thought of all Sonny had in store for him as she tucked it away in the back of the kitchen drawer.

→←

Joe Benson was lost. Crawling on his belly through a swirling gray funk of stagnant water and tangled limbs and rotting leaves and God only knew what else.

"Well, I'll be GOD*DAMN*!" he screamed, his voice trapped and high-pitched, like a woman's. He unfolded the map again and studied it by the weakening shine of his penlight. "But I *turned* south back there," he said, as if the piece of paper were arguing with him. Either he was growing larger or the pipes were getting smaller, this latest one cramping his shoulders so that he had been forced to stretch his arms out in front of him in order to move. He tried to wipe his face on his sleeve but couldn't. The map was shit. Wet and mushy. Totally worthless. The inked lines all smeared and merging to an unreadable calligraphy. "I turned right. I just know it." Wadding up the map, he let it fall as he eased himself forward, his forearms against the concrete, one after the other. The concrete still smelled wet and new, and he was confident he was in the right area. "Screw the map. This is the right way and I know it." He listened to the bags of jewelry clank against the small of his back. Occasionally he heard the rumble of automobiles traveling down the road, and he would cock his head and try to determine which way they were going, but the sounds were convoluted, and he had no way of knowing if they were heading into town or away. *A drain's a drain,* he thought. *It wouldn't be a drain if stuff weren't meant to drain out of it,* and logic decreed all he had to do was keep moving and he would find daylight sooner or later, be it tomorrow or clean into next week. He was feeling more optimistic and relaxed a bit and eased his neck against his shoulder blades. He would have a hell of a headache come the morning, but he'd be far away from Purvis by the time the aspirin started working, and inside this brief blaze of optimism, his flashlight sputtered and then winked and finally shut its eye, and he was left completely in the dark.

"I cain't fuckin believe this!" he shouted, banging it against the wall surrounding him, hearing pieces of metal and glass and small batteries ricochet against the concrete and disappear into the nothingness of pitch black. Joe was becoming afraid for the first time since he crawled down the hole. Rolling up his sleeves, he scratched at his arm, which was itchy in a burning sort of way. His other arm was suffering the same, and he spent long minutes servicing both of them with his fingernails. His belly was burning, too, but there was no way he could get to it to scratch.

"Okay. So I ain't got a light," he said, shutting his eyes and refusing to look at the dark. *Moles are blind, and they get from one place to the other,* he thought, trying to remember if he had ever actually seen a mole and deciding he hadn't. He had seen proof of them, though, in the small raised humps of grass they left in their wake. Sections of grass he had (more than once) taken great pleasure in chopping down on with the shovel. "So I killed a few moles," he whispered. "That don't make me a bad guy."

He began moving the same way he had before, pulling himself forward with his forearms. Satisfied he was making progress, he told himself it was just like when he was out in the broad daylight, crawling along on his belly to squirrel-hunt. He would come to the end of it eventually. So what if his light was gone? So what if the space he was crawling through seemed to be getting tighter, and his arms and legs were itching like he'd spent time wallowing in poison ivy? He still had air to breathe and the jewelry on his back. In fact, now that he thought about it, the air seemed a little fresher, and he opened his eyes and made himself very still and tried to focus. And what was that up there he saw? The smallish circle that seemed not so dark as the rest. By God, he *had* turned down the right rabbit hole after all! Relieved to the point of total exhaustion, he laid his face on the concrete and breathed deeply. Somebody ought to have told him crawling through pipes was such an asskicker of a job. He was slap worn out and ready for the bed. His vision of Mexico faded somewhat, replaced by the memory of the way Alyce's sheets felt up around his face. *I'll just rest a minute and then finish crawling,* he thought, and with that, he drifted off to sleep.

Sonny turned down the dirt road, no need to look at the map. The huge earthmoving equipment formed giant silhouettes in the moonlight on the adjacent field, their buckets hoisted up like legs of a giant orthopteran, bent and frozen in place. Caterpillar bulldozers and a crawler-loader. A Hitachi excavator with its thirty-six-inch double grouser and its seventy-eight-inch bucket with teeth. There was even a Cat log skidder with an enclosed cab. The stuff of Sonny's dreams. He looked at his watch and wondered if he'd have time to get closer and take himself a look.

"I always wanted to drive one a them," he said to himself, putting the Pontiac in park and turning off the motor.

The drain was about fifty feet in front of him; he could see the orange cones set out by it and the surplus pipes lined up like Tootsie Rolls. His appetite lunged forward ten degrees at the thought of something chocolate, and he wished he'd taken the time to eat some supper. His relief that it had gone as good as it had with his mama had made him relax, and the relaxation had released gastric juices that reminded him he was close to starving.

Walking over to the mouth of the pipe, he got down on all fours and looked inside and saw nothing. He'd had his doubts about Joe's actually going through with it, and the empty pipe seemed to suggest his original opinion had been correct. The fool had come to his senses and realized the scheme was stupid. Or it could be that Joe had already left the pipe and started walking. Sonny *was* late, after all. Hating the thought of going back home right then and there, he stood up and brushed off his knees and made his way to the excavator and walked around it three times, wondering how in the hell a fella was supposed to climb up into it to set the thing in motion. Once he finally found the small yellow steps, he hoisted himself up onto the cracked black seat and sat staring at all the knobs extending in his direction on rods that looked like spider arms. There was a small radio on the floor and he lifted it up and turned it on. "Get your motor runnin . . . head out on the highway . . ." vavoomed into the empty moonlit night, charging it with possibility. There was even a hard hat resting on a lunch box. Sonny put that on his head.

"I was born to be wild, too," he said, wishing he had some chewing tobacco to complete the picture forming in his mind. "Hoy there, mates!" he shouted. "The big boss up in Jackson done called me in to finish the job. Now, git your lazy asses in gear or I'll run you down!" He began fondling the knobs as though he knew their business, and bouncing on the seat as though the big diesel engine were running. Imaginary workers stood around him, their faces shaping up like those belonging to the old high school tormenters. The tormenters' cheerleader girlfriends were there, too. Even his mother was there. All of them reduced to worker bees or, better yet, Negro ditchdiggers. He swept the hat off his head and brandished it at them before putting it back on again. "What's that you say?" He cupped a hand to his ear. "Shout it up to me, 'cause I cain't hear shit over this here sumbitch engine! You say you pissed the day away and ain't ready yet? Well, I done give you a week to get ready, boys! You best step aside and let me show you how it's done. Huh? What's that you say? You're afraid of this here excavator?"

Sonny bounced and played, the hour slipping by and his obligation to Joe almost forgotten as he pretended he was in various places. The sweltering savannas of Africa, where he killed wild elephants with the bucket of the excavator, then on to the steamy jungles of South America, where he rescued an entire village from a devastating mudslide. His final stop was near the craggy mountains of Guatemala, and here he paused and looked up to the moon and realized he didn't know much about that place and figured it was time to head back to Purvis. By the time he climbed down and walked back to his mother's car, there was still no sign of Joe. Sonny shrugged, determined to check on him sometime tomorrow, and set the task on the back-burner portion of his brain, where he could pull it up and use it should he need a place to get away from Conchita's running mouth.

{CHAPTER 30}

His body was half out of the water, for Willem had pulled himself along as far as he could before the pain swallowed him up and he disappeared inside it, delirious. The pain in his leg was a post to hold on to, an excruciating post he refused to reach for. So he ignored it as best he could and drifted back down to the waiting arms of semiconsciousness, to that tiny cramped place where he saw himself curled on his side and conversing with the moles.

The genus *Scalopus aquaticus* was busy at work. Calling to Willem from their private chamber of crumbling earth, where light filtered through a sieve created by an earthworm's industry. Tiny portholes of light everywhere. Diameters the size of small pencils. The gaseous expanse of the sun somewhere so far removed from the man buried underneath the earth that it seemed the very idea of a sun was a vague theory not yet put to the test. Its yet to be explored evidence was everywhere, though. Light prickling the arms and calves and the cleft of Willem's chin. His young man's hands. The bridge of his nose. He was marked by a pox of light, while a sleek vespiary of small furry creatures shuttled by. Velvety fur reigned supreme down here, and even though he was buried underneath three tons of dirt, Willem was finally at peace.

"This is what it would have looked like if I'd been buried when the house fell," he imagined he said to one of them. "This is what I would have seen." He felt a sense of wonder at the thought of it. Moles scurried near his face, staging fits of remorse, for they recognized that he was one with them. They had seen the soles of his shoes as he walked the outside world, and watched his huge shadow play across their entry holes. He was their fallen god. And because he was fallen (and trapped), the genus *Scalopus aquaticus* mourned his demise with tiny puffs of breath licked silver by grief. Like an army, they used their fossorial forelimbs to save his flesh from being crushed; winking, sightless eyes blinked back tears. They mewed with a pathos made famous by dead Greeks and abandoned women. Without hesitation, they formed a bucket brigade, using acorn shells and serrated leaves in order to free his mouth. Willem spat out dirt and tasted their sorry, and tried to reassure them, tell them not to bother. "I'm gonna die, fellas. Rest yourselves. But before I go, come here and listen to me . . ." He wanted to explain the situation to them, tell them how years and years ago he had woken at first shuddering movement and made his way to the door and peered out and seen a shrinking sky, all that dark slipping shut as though held inside a velvet bag, its mouth drawn tight by some incalculable force. The mole brigade slowed and gathered around him in a huddled mass of mink-colored fur. Some dropped their acorn shells by their side. Others turned them over and sat. They had never heard such a tale. They bowed their heads to listen. "This whole life of mine disappeared then," he told them, and his voice broke. "Imagine all of this as it was before. When it stood as a wide-open field. I realize it's hard. But try." They were puzzled and began to look at one another as though Willem were crazy. "No. Listen to me. I'm not lying to you. It's true. It was like a mountain had just been birthed. Pine trees shooting toward the sky. I was a hopeless captive in what looked like a world full of spears," he told them, his throat closing at the words. A nurturing mole came forward and licked the salt from his eyes. "And then?" she mewed in his ear. He thought about it a moment. "I never seen anything like it in my life. Of course, I hadn't seen much up to that point. I was only nineteen." The moles looked at one another. The years were too large for them to reconcile. Too godlike in length. "The next shift of earth threw me to the floor, and I scrambled like a rat for my life." "Ahhh," said his audience, nodding, well acquainted with the wickedness of rats. "I did manage to grab my shoes, and I tied the laces together and draped them across my shoulders." The smallest of the moles giggled and was instantly shushed by the others. "The house was disappearing before my eyes," he told them. "The earth was eating it. And it was a good house, too." He wanted to point to the ceiling, where the handhewn crown beam held up the roof; he wanted to make them see how carefully he had constructed the place, how the sinkhole had carelessly destroyed his best effort to date. He pointed to the four walls of his entombment, marveling at his handiwork, the delicate hand-carved scrolling above the fireplace: "I am the vine and ye are the branches." The moles followed his pointing finger and said "Ahhhh" and clapped their fossorial forelimbs in applause. Willem listened to it and tears came to his eyes and fell down his old-man cheeks as he blinked into the night. *How many die trapped inside a dream?* he wondered. *How many view the inside of their own splendid sarcophagus? How many pharaohs can dance on the head of a pin . . .*

→←

Leah could see one edge of the bookcase sticking out from behind the projector screen in the living room. The *National Geographic*s lined up there in consecutive order. On the screen the men moved silently, grinning as they walked in self-consious strides before the handheld camera, hitting one another in the shoulder, clowning around with manic expressions and broad exaggerations. Everything—palm trees, Quonset huts, the large helicopters—was slightly yellow due to the processing, and the film jumped in places, and huge watermarks would fill the screen, and it would take sometimes thirty seconds before the scene returned to what it was earlier—men, her husband included, standing around a large helicopter, showing off for the camera.

Leah sat curled on the couch and watched for the first time. For years the cans had been in the bottom of the hall closet, but she'd not had the heart to pull out the film and thread it through the machine, since she was reluctant to see him as he was then, whole and complete.

The T-shirts seem so white, she thought. *And the trousers so baggy. And the boots so hot. And the men so young.* They were boys, really. She leaned forward on the couch and rested her elbows on her knees. There was Bruno. Thin and tan, walking out a doorway, his sunglasses on. His sleeves were rolled up around a pack of cigarettes, and she felt the same soft blow to her stomach that she had felt when she lifted the bent harmonica out of the truck ashtray and came to the conclusion that Bruno had played it at an early age. That feeling of being left out and, at the same time, the fresh curiosity of intrigue. *So, he smoked over there,* she thought, and smiled a little bit, remembering how he had made her promise to at least try and cut back to half a pack while he was away. Leah saw his lopsided grin and the way he had pointed to the cigarettes and shrugged. A secret exposed. A Valentine signed but never mailed. She watched as he waved at the camera, and she lifted her hand to him and waved back, unaware that she did this. The images flashed on the screen while, on the bookcase behind it, like a waiting dirge, the spines of Bruno's reading material caught the glare of the projector bulb, and it was like seeing two lives at once. The before and the after. A complex image she would never have the words to explain to anyone. Not her father. Not Bruno. Not even God. And the brief omniscience was like a fixed band around her heart.

She wished she could see the inside of the helicopter where he was standing. She wished she could see what he was doing with his hands, for his back was to her and his head bent forward, and she froze, the sight of his neck so forgotten. The dark hairline. The beginning of a muscle. The small hump of a bone. Leah looked away, and when she glanced back, the men had all stepped away and were pointing to the sky, and the camera turned toward the helicopters lifting off the distant field. Ten of them. Ten soldiers in each, with four crewmen besides. A hundred and forty individuals headed for some landing zone somewhere. A landing zone Bruno would reach early the next morning and return from wounded and changed. The helicopters were hovering and hovering, and Leah could see some of the men crouched near the wide bay doors, and then the nauseating pan as the camera came back to the men on the ground. Bruno laughing and clapping, and the one next to him pulling off his T-shirt and pretending to strip, while behind the triple-strand concertina wire, Vietnamese women waded through the rice paddies, the squares of water like great sheets of mirrored glass, the mountains behind them all so beautiful that even the sight of helicopters flying by couldn't diminish it. Leah watched Bruno put on a grass hat and bend at the waist in a solemn bow. The boy next to him knocked the hat off his head, and the two pretended to scuffle over it in a session of phony boxing, with Bruno looking over his shoulder at the camera. The two of them laughing and slinging each other around inside a yellow world full of light. Bruno throwing his head back and laughing, his neck arched and sweet, his dog tags hanging on his chest. Leah felt her throat tighten and her mouth crimp to one side. *Oh my*, she thought. *Just look at you. Just look at you.* And now the camera had singled him out, and she realized there was a purpose for the footage. Bruno waved for the camera to come closer as he went to the open door of the helicopter and lifted something out and hid it behind his back. His strides quick as he approached the camera, his smile wide open and wonderful. Once he was in the correct place, he pushed his sunglasses up on his head and pulled the card from behind his back: *Leah, babe. I love you. I'll see you soon,* he had written. The last image on the film was a close-up of his face as he watched her with his blue, blue eyes.

→←

Willem woke to light rain on his face. He opened his mouth and let it fall on his tongue and roll down his chin. It was nearing dawn and a faint pink was spreading in the sky and it was incredible. Veins as translucent as those found in marble spread out before him, while a gauzy sheet of clouds gathered in what seemed to be a huge lasso near the center of the sky. He had survived the night, and though it had been full of bizarre dreams he couldn't remember, the one thing he could recall was the way he had willed himself into unconsciousness. It seemed permissible at night. But now that it was day, he felt obligated to try to keep his senses about him.

To his left was the house, quiet as a tombstone, its wall of vines winking with the new wet of rain, the greenery lifted on the soft breeze and then falling back again, like wavy veridian hair. When he had stumbled, he had rolled to his back, and he could feel the wall behind him, and if he looked straight up, he became dizzy, for it seemed to speak of the grave. Which was exactly what it was. Turning his head to one side, he looked at his leg and the way it headed off in a new direction beginning at his thigh.

That's where the break was, and possibly his hip was broken, too. A simmering heat radiated off him, and he felt his chest with his hand, the fresh tightness there, and figured the night spent half in and half out of the pool had brought on what would eventually kill him. Pneumonia.

There is a strange tranquillity experienced by the dying, he thought to himself, somewhat amazed by the unexpected passivity. He supposed it had to do with standing at the doorway to Life's Great Mystery. Whatever answer had been sought concerning whether or not one goes on inside some spirit realm was there, only moments away. Perhaps some feared this transfiguration, but Willem had spent his life afraid of so many things that death almost seemed a relief.

Doves flew overhead, and he decided that the attributes assigned to doves were misplaced. Whether it was the figure of the Holy Spirit or not, he'd never seen a clumsier bird. No direction whatsoever. Four or five of them flapped and dodged like pigeons in the thick bracken and seemed to land by accident on whatever limb turned up in front of them. Three of them were pecking in the gravel. A fourth was intent on tormenting the other three. Willem thought the dove sounds were nice, the low cooing. If he had to lie there and spend the day listening to bird sounds, he'd choose the doves over bluejays any day of the year.

The rain quit, and the sun came out from behind the clouds, and high up in the square of sky, a flock of ducks flew by in formation. Their wavy line looked for all the world like a snake flying through the sky. Trying to follow the pattern for as long as he could, Willem cocked his head back and shifted his body slightly. The movement made him scream, and doves as well as cicadas and tree frogs were startled into silence. "Jesus God. Nooo!" A habitual urge accompanied the pain, and he felt his bowels release, felt the heat and the liquidity of it. Short of breath, he glanced down and saw that he had soiled the water. "I'm a dead man," he whispered, slowly moving his hand as he tried to reach the water where it was falling down the wall, but couldn't.

Regrets visited him, and he was surprised that there were only two of them. Number one was that Alyce would worry over him and probably never be granted the satisfaction of knowing what had happened. She would think he had left without thanking her, without paying his bill, without collecting his things, and her worry would be replaced by irritation and then anger. She would think him a bum, a user, a man who, in no stretch of the imagination, remotely resembled Gary Cooper.

Willem's second regret was that he had left the truck windows rolled down. He imagined pine straw and leaves filling his truck, and the eventual arrival of raccoons and squirrels that would, over a period of time, develop a taste for plaid upholstery.

"Two regrets. Not a bad way to go," he said as he tried to heave himself up away from his own murky shit. He screamed again and fell into the blackness of not knowing, while the doves soared away on the wind in search of some quieter place to feed.

{CHAPTER 31}

"As long as you understand I'm in total disagreement with you, Merle."

"Believe me. I understand," he said.

"No. I don't think you do. I think you believe I'll simply fold, like I always do. Like that time you didn't want to go to Disneyland. And no matter how long or how hard I begged—Leah begged, too, you need to remember that—you just waited and smoked your cigars and knew that I would get sick and tired of talking about it . . ."

Dora's voice droned on. Merle refused to answer her. They had been arguing since pulling out of Meridian at seven that morning. No (he corrected himself), they had been arguing since the phone call to Eilene the night before. He refused to travel any further back down memory's corridor for fear he would see his life with Dora laid out in a series of military operations. Suburbia-influenced advances and retreats. The planting of a flag in the name of a certain ideal or request, and then the later jerking out of that flag from the sheer weariness that came from hearing her voice go on and on. Petty surrenders, Leah called them.

"This is not at all like Disneyland," he said finally.

"Tell me this. Did we go to Disneyland?"

"No we did not, and I don't regret it to this day. All that artificiality. All that molded plastic. Those ridiculous costumes. The fawning of an insincere conglomerate whose goal is to strong-arm money from the public." He looked at her. "You have any idea how much the public spends in such a place?"

"I wish you had never started reading those magazines of yours," she said.

"Information is not the bogeyman, Dora."

"I never said it was the bogeyman."

"Every time I try to explain something to you, you roll your eyes and act like I'm about to dose you up with castor oil."

"Maybe I'm sick and tired of having things explained to me, Merle. Maybe I'm sick and tired of you treating me like I only have half a brain."

"That's ridiculous. I don't treat you that way."

The car they were in was a Corvette convertible. Merle's one weakness.

"This car's what's ridiculous," she said, crossing her legs.

"Funny. Your opinion seems a little different whenever Mavis Stroh is around. Seems I remember you driving her out to the club a couple of Sundays in a row. In this very car." He smiled at her.

"That's different."

"How's it different?" He glanced at her as he downshifted at an intersection.

"A Corvette is not Disneyland."

Maybe not to you, he thought. *But it sure is to me.* "I'd be willing to bet you've already forgotten what we were arguing about." He pulled a cigar out of his pocket and stuck it in his mouth.

Dora was momentarily confused. And then she remembered. "It's about pretending." She glanced at him. At times of disagreement, she hated his profile, his sharp nose and gray hair, the way he looked like an angry eagle. She would much prefer a loose-necked turkey. One could eat a turkey. She paused. Well, technically, one *could* eat an eagle if one were out in the wilderness and starving. But who in the world would want to?

"I think 'pretending' is the wrong word," he said, lighting his cigar. The Tone back in his voice.

Dora hated The Tone. Unfortunately, Leah had it, too. Registering somewhere between the nasal configuration of a confident square-dance caller and a clear ringing bell, The Tone made one's head hurt. And on certain occasions, The Tone could make one cry.

Dora adjusted her sunglasses, still miffed at all the secret conversations taking place between father and daughter. The giddiness in his step as he projected himself up out of the easy chair and toward that ridiculous amplified phone was not lost on her.

Earlier in the week, while changing frantically in and out of clothes, trying to find something (anything!) that would make her look skinnier (not that there was any chance of her ever looking skinny; Leah was the president, as well as vice president, of Skinny World), she had remembered a shopping trip she took with her daughter before Leah had ever met Bruno Till. It was to be a treat, this shopping trip. A Karmel-Korn-eating, afternoon-coffee-sipping, dessert-slurping TREAT. Leah was in her second year at college and had come home somewhat down-in-the-mouth, her usual dourness kicked a couple of notches above normal, and (as usual) had chosen not to talk about what might be bothering her. "Nothing's wrong," she had insisted at dinner, slicing into her veal. "Nothing. Nothing. Nothing."

"Come on, silly," Dora had said the next morning, tossing her purse to her in a spontaneous mood of flippancy, fishing Merle's car keys out of the hall table drawer.

"Mom, I'm tired," Leah had said.

"Nonsense," Dora replied. "You're much too young to be tired. I simply will not allow it!" She had ushered Leah out onto the yard where Merle's new red Corvette was parked next to the curb, willow branches brushing the shiny chrome rear bumper like green feather dusters. "You want to drive it? Make your old dad worry?" She had held the keys up in front of her face and dangled them toward Leah, and the resulting shrug almost did Dora in. The shrug that said *Either way is fine with me, because this is all silly, silly, silly.* The shrug that indicated Leah didn't give a hoot about a red-hot car.

Keeping in mind that the outing was for Leah's benefit and not her own—though she secretly hoped the lunch crowd at Bernardo's outdoor café would all have their glasses on when she roared down the square, especially Mavis, who had just been elected president of SLAG for her fouth consecutive term—Dora refused to be crestfallen.

"I'll do it, then." She beamed. "But no complaining, young lady, about how fast I'll be driving!" The weight of false exuberance wearing her out. Her constant searching of Leah's face for any sign of pleasure, making her wish for one insane moment that she had been born blind.

Once on the road, now that the appeal of the car had been dismissed, Dora flipped through the many radio stations in a gathering panic, trying to find one that Leah might like. Settling on a station playing Nancy Sinatra's boot song, immediately followed by somebody's "Is this all there is, my friend" song, Dora tried to hum along. A part of her believing that *she* was the reason Leah wouldn't talk. *She thinks I'm too old. A fuddy-duddy. Someone whose finger has never been on the switch of a record player.* The "Is this all there is" song was unfamiliar to her, though, and Dora yodeled up when she should have yodeled down, and blushed profusely at the entrapment. *Hoisted by my own petard,* she thought to herself. The saying landed in the part of her mind where sexual-sounding words and phrases took up temporary housing for later examination.

Leah looked at her and smiled. And Dora became enraged at the undiluted pity she saw there. "Who needs the radio anyhow?" she said, snapping it off.

The lunch was nice, even though Bernardo's was barren as a desert. The only other people there an ancient couple both attached to oxygen canisters on wheels. The two were busy making sure their spoons stayed clear of the tubes fastened underneath their noses.

"Probably smokers," Dora said in what she thought was a reasonably soft voice. Expediency demanded she insert a warning about smoking into the conversation.

"Mom, don't."

"All I said was—"

"I heard you. I'm sure they did, too."

Dora looked over and didn't believe it. The table was too far away. They were outdoors, and the grinding sound of the bar's blender cranking out daiquiris would have prevented it.

The meal was finished in silence, and Dora began to wish she had never mentioned shopping. Not only was she being forced to eat a salad garnished with oil and plain old vinegar when she would much prefer shrimp alfredo heaped high with fresh Parmesan, she was also forced to endure the scorn of her daughter. And to pour salt into the wound, come the next hour or two, she would be spending money on this tall and slender ingrate.

Once the meal was finished and paid for (by Dora) and Leah had moseyed her way through fourteen small dress shops and picked out two shirts and one pair of bell-bottom jeans (again paid for by Dora), the two of them walked up the wide sidewalk, Dora swinging her purse and Leah swinging her packages. Their shadows were out in front of them, Leah's tall and effortlessly graceful, Dora's resembling, to her frame of mind, a small hopping toad.

"What fun," Dora mumbled, ready at this point for a scrap of gratitude from her daughter.

"It was nice, Mom," Leah said, looking at her and smiling (down at her, Dora noticed, alarmed that Leah was still growing taller, while Dora had topped off at five foot two and now felt visibly shorter in spite of three-inch heels).

It wasn't really as bad as Dora thought. She knew she was still a reasonably striking woman in her own middle-forty Tupperware-ish way. But she felt ugly and unwanted, like a balding geriatric poodle out for a stroll, the leash held in the hand of someone who didn't really care about the dog, who had never even *liked* it in the first place, who probably couldn't *wait* until it was buried in the backyard underneath the magnolia tree. The thought made her sad, and she suffered a momentary clutchy feeling and reached out to slide her arm through her daughter's.

Big mistake, she thought a moment later. Oh, Leah allowed it, but the moment's hesitation, her flash of pained expression, escaped before she could haul them back in. After a couple of minutes, Dora removed her hand and looked away and pretended to read the parking meters, expressing concern over who would be the first to be ticketed. Leah nodded and laughed, and she reached out to hug her mother, but Dora was too hurt to warm to it. The dry ice of rejection had already cracked her heart.

"This was a really nice day, Mom," Leah told her as they approached the car. But The Tone bracketed the words and carved off any genuineness that might have been there and Dora unlocked the Corvette and climbed inside and spent the next twenty minutes trying to act as though she'd had the time of her life, when in truth all she wanted to do was go inside her closet and squat down next to her Bass Weejun loafers and cry.

"If 'pretending' is the wrong word, what would your holiness suggest as the right word?" Dora asked Merle.

"I can see right now how the day's going to go," he said, sliding away from her in his seat, if that was possible, which, considering the bucket seats, was not.

"I'm serious, Merle. You're asking me to *pretend* that you didn't talk to Eilene last night. You want me to *pretend* that I don't know Bruno's walked out on our only child! Please, for goodness' sake, give me another word."

They passed the sign indicating Purvis, and Merle slowed behind a tractor that was creeping along. The smell of manure and turned-over soil and chemical dusting was everywhere, and Dora felt as though she might sneeze any minute.

"Can we please put the top up?" she said, coughing into her hand.

"We're almost there."

"See? See what I mean?"

"What is it I'm supposed to see?"

"It's just like Disneyland. I ask you to do something and you won't budge."

With that, Merle swerved into the parking lot of a small motel where two little blond-headed boys were shoveling at the graveled dirt with bright red shovels. He slammed the gearshift into neutral and pressed the button. The top hummed and rose over their heads, and once it was where it needed to be, he leaned (rather roughly) over Dora to snap it in place, his elbow, either accidentally or on purpose, digging into her thigh. Once this was done, he pulled back out onto the road, spraying gravel and then laying rubber.

"Happy now?"

"Well, yes. Thank you," Dora said, reaching for her purse and digging around for her lipstick. "Now, since you don't like the word 'pretend,' if you'll just give me another word to use."

"Do what you want, Dora. Say what you want. Attack Bruno with a broom. Swing from the tree and scream. I don't care anymore. You've worn me down," he said, mentally seeing the flag he'd so proudly placed jerked up out of his territorial claim.

{CHAPTER 32}

It was early morning, and their mother had told them that come the evening, they would go across to the field and shoot off firecrackers if they were very good, and the two boys believed her, for she had always told them the truth.

The big earthmoving machines were sitting in the field where they had been for a long time now. Since before summer began. Only the machines were quiet on this day, hunkered down like huge dinosaurs sleeping. But not colored like dinosaurs; the machines were colored orange, like tangerines and persimmons. The field was quiet, too. No men there today, and the red earth that had been scooped up and dumped looked like anthills from where the boys stood. At night, if the moon was full, they could see the faraway blinking lights of the loud place where the music played, but it was day, and what they saw was another quiet square building the size of a matchbox and, beyond it, a ridgeline of trees and one or two cars driving by and nothing else of interest. They would go out into that very field come the night, if they were good, and their mother would let them light their sizzle sparklers and Black Cats and maybe even a firecracker or two. And if the big machines were still there, and if the boys had been very, very good, maybe their mother would let them climb up on one of them.

Ben looked at them and looked at them and wondered how it would feel to be on top of something so large.

"She's makin pancakes," Joe said, sniffing the air.

"I know." Ben took his red shovel and put his foot to it and pushed. They were pretending they were construction workers. Like the men they saw every day over in that field. Men who wore bandannas tied around their heads and drank water out of the ribbed metal barrel fastened to the side of the boss man's truck. A new elementary school was going to be built there. Not for two or three years, but once the pipes were fixed and the red earth was smoothed and the piles that looked like anthills had all gone away.

"I got more than you," Joe said, looking at the small wagon they were slowly filling.

"That's 'cause you're older," Ben said, the logic reasonable.

The parking lot was empty. Mr. Willem's truck was not in its usual place, and Joe wondered where the man might be. They had shucked corn with their mother the evening before, while sitting in chairs out under the tree, and the truck was gone then, and his mother had looked toward the space where it usually was and said, "Good, maybe the poor man's found himself some friends."

Joe looked over at his brother, who was lifting the largest shovel load yet. "I go to school soon," he said.

Ben looked at him and looked across the field, for it seemed a long time away. "Will you come back?"

"Yeah."

"Okay, then."

They heard a car approaching, and it sounded different from all the other cars that traveled up and down the road, and both boys looked and saw it slow, each stepping away from it as it turned into the drive.

"Jeepers," Joe said.

Ben was silent, the sight of it stealing his words.

Joe put his arm to his brother's shoulder. The car was bright red like their shovels, and there were two people sitting in it, not looking at Ben or Joe, but out toward the small hill where the oak trees grew. While both boys watched, the roof came up out of a slot and began to rise like a bent black wing, unfolding and stretching and then falling over the windshield, like magic. Their shovels were hanging in loose fingers by their sides, forgotten, for the boys had never seen anything like it in their lives and stood watching the car as it moved loud and angry-sounding down the highway. And even after it had gone over the hill, they could still feel the noise of it in their chests.

"I think that was a racin car," Joe said.

"There weren't no numbers on it."

"It might be, though."

"It sure was loud," Ben said, running his hand under his nose. He had a stuffy head, and his chest still smelled of VapoRub.

"Have you ever seen a red car?" Joe said.

"No."

"Me, neither. But now we have."

A jingle of a bell sounded and they turned and saw their mother standing at the door. "You boys come eat," she said.

"Come on, Ben," Joe said.

They dropped their shovels in the wagon and walked her way. "We seen a red car, Mama," Ben said.

"I think it was a race car," Joe said.

"But he don't know for sure," Ben said.

Their mother rubbed the tops of their heads and said, "Go wash your hands," and then she stepped out into the parking lot and looked down the row where there were no cars. Not Mr. Bruno's nor Mr. Willem's, and when Joe looked at her face, he thought it looked the same as when dark afternoon clouds rolled in and thunder boomed and she made them turn off the TV and stay away from the windows. Joe looked up at the sky and saw how clear it was, and looked back at his mother's face, but her eyes still seemed the same.

→←

Bruno sat at the kitchen table drinking his coffee and watching Leah as she sipped her hot lemon water.

"Is that good for you?" he asked, noticing the stillness to her hands and the way her eyes were soft and sleepy-looking.

The brochure was still folded underneath his coffee cup. She had removed it and stood staring at it the night before, while the moon shone full on the field between the houses, and realized that he knew. She hadn't felt free to put it back in the cabinet (removing it seemed too much like she was still trying to hide it from him) until she explained to him, and so she set it back where he had put it, unaware that the brochure was now upside down, facing the wrong way, and he noticed this and knew that she knew that he knew. So without asking the question, or waiting for the words to come out of her mouth, he had just let it go and accepted it and refused to carry the fight any further. The fight had gone long enough, in his opinion.

"I don't see why it would hurt."

"All that salt," he said.

"I've cut back on it some."

He sipped his coffee and played with his toast, turning the triangle various ways as though it were rolling across his saucer.

"The smell of this botherin you?" he asked her, lifting his cup.

She looked at him. The house was clean and the sink was full of potatoes that he had insisting on peeling. Her throat tightened. The smell was making her a little sick, but that was not what she wanted to talk about. She was in her robe and her clothes were hanging in the closet and she needed to get dressed, but first there was something she needed to say. "Listen. The reason I didn't tell you yesterday is I didn't want it to be the reason . . ." (*you came back,* she thought).

He was quiet, not sure what to say, and though he knew what she meant, he fell into his old habit of playing dumb and said, "You didn't want it to be the reason for what?"

Leah sighed, feeling tired suddenly. She set her cup down in its saucer.

Bruno reached out and covered her hand and said, "Never mind. I know what you meant by it. I just—" And then he quit talking, unsure of the terrain as well as the climate of this new country he was living in.

In so many ways, it was like operating inside a tantalizing blind spot, a placement on the road that was uncomfortable but necessary to get to the ultimate destination, and Bruno remembered feeling this same exact way on the night they had their first date. He had known absolutely zilch about her (other than the weight of her head on his back and the smell of her hair and the color of her eyes) and had tried to find a place that might interest her and settled on Lou's Wild West Country Tavern, remembering how she had first showed up at a stock auction, and this in itself seemed to suggest she liked things country-western in theme. So they had sat at a table made from a wagon wheel covered with glass and listened to a really horrible steel-guitar band, and after long minutes of surveying a menu filled with such delicacies as Rangler's Rack of Roast and Cowpoke's Pork Supreme, Bruno had said to her, "You hate this place, don't you?"

Her hair was falling over her shoulder, and she had on a white blouse rolled up at the sleeves, and the cloth was such that he could see the faint outline of her bra. Her hands were laced together, and he noticed the thin gold bracelet on her arm and the slight wristbones.

"You mean you're not dying for"—she leaned over the menu—"three pounds of savory smoked roast beef?" she asked him, smiling. *God, her eyes are beautiful,* he thought. Not large and blue like the eyes belonging to every other girl he had ever dated, but oval-shaped and slightly turned up at the ends. And best of all, full of colors found in the heart of a forest.

"I'm only hungry for one thing," he said, shocked at the disclosure, believing she would think him crude and unbelievably forward.

God, she loved the cowboy in him. His discomfort with cloth napkins and more than one fork. The sky-blue color of his eyes. And best of all, the frown line between them. *This one here will never be easy, because he's never learned to be false,* she thought, and the thought made her dizzy with possibilities.

"Me, too," she said, and stood up and reached for her purse and walked toward the door, leaving him to explain to the waitress dressed like Dale Evans that the table they'd waited forty-five minutes for was free now.

The night was starlit and cool, and she held to her arms as she walked toward his truck, her long hair swinging down her back. The truck was newer then, and he'd removed all the artifacts of farm life from the seat and floor; he'd even oiled the door so it wouldn't howl when he opened it for her. He was wearing jeans and a clean blue shirt and cowboy boots that were worn but polished. He smelled of soap and starch and Mitchum deodorant, smells so absent of pretenses and presentation that once she was on the seat, she swung her legs out and captured his with both of hers and put her arms around him and said, "We've got to do this first. If it's good, the rest will be, too."

It was not that he was new to it. He'd been familiar with it since he was fifteen years old and rolling around on the football field with Debbie Drysdale, not to mention the rolling around he had done with the number of girls who followed Debbie, sometimes on the football field and then in more exotic places like dens and spare bedrooms and the backseat of cars and later his own house. But in spite of the fact that this was not a new thing he was doing, it was the first time he'd ever felt the immediate sensation of perfect sychronization. Of some well-oiled gear sliding into place, a first taste of hard-to-define rightness. They kissed for so long, his hands nearly froze and Leah was shaking all over, and still they kissed, his hands working their way over her, beginning with his finger down between the cleft of her breasts, taking care not to pull on the buttons, perfectly happy to just leave his finger there, the rest of his hand freezing while his forefinger probed.

"What in the world did I ever do to deserve this?" he had asked her, already sure they would be together, unable to imagine one single minute of his life without Leah in it.

"You waited for me," she had said, and for a brief second of time, he believed there might be a God after all. "You've got to promise me one thing, though," she said.

"What's that?" he answered, lifting her hair and kissing the side of her neck.

"You've got to promise me you'll never, *ever* bring me to this place again." She pointed to the neon lasso spelling out LOU'S.

"You've got yourself a deal," he had told her, tucking her in and shutting the door and driving toward Hattiesburg, pulling her over next to him and putting his hand between her legs. Pulling into the first motel he came to, one out on Highway 49. La Quinta, he thought it was. "Is this better?" he said.

"Immeasurably," she had said, squeezing his hand.

Bruno had thought that rare feeling was gone forever. But now he felt it again, and since he had witnessed personally just how quickly it could disappear on him, he was afraid to move forward or back or even sideways. If he had to sit there inside a blind spot and play with his dry toast forever, he would.

Leah reached for the brochure and opened it up. "It took me by surprise," she said. "I spent the first day or two wondering how I would explain his conception to him."

Bruno blushed, remembering it all. He put a hand to where he'd been cut on the head when she pushed him into the refrigerator. All was healed. A small strip of hair had refused to grow back, and as he crossed his legs, he felt the blush of embarrassment spread, for he realized that every time he looked in the mirror, he would remember the night he planted this child.

"You think a child needs to know about its own conception? Do you wonder about your own? Where Merle and Dora were?"

Leah smiled. "Fuck, no." She looked at the potatoes in the sink and then the clock on the wall.

"I'll do them in a minute," he told her. "Let's talk first."

"Are you sure you want to?"

No, he was not sure he wanted to. Talking things out was right up there with going to the dentist. But talk was necessary if the two of them were ever going to move forward, and he knew it.

He said, "Leah, my things are in the car out there. I don't plan on going back to the motel. But I have to hear it from you that you want me back."

She nodded. "I want you back. But I have to know about her first."

His first impulse was to play dumb again. He shoved it aside and said, "I told you. I'm not involved with her."

"Then why did you end up going to her motel when the Valley Inn was right up the road?"

It was a risk, but he decided on the truth. "Because I was mad at you. Because a part of me wanted to hurt you."

She pulled her hand away from his and said, "Why were you mad at me?"

He took her hand again, even though he could tell she didn't really want him to. "Because some of what you said was true."

She looked at him. "I've spent the past month sitting here at night and trying to imagine your routine. Where you go to eat supper. What you're watching on television. If you hang out at bars. And in all those scenarios, the girl is with you. Cooking. Drinking. Being with you."

"She wasn't." He *had* spent a lot of time around Alyce's dining room table but didn't believe that mattered.

"So you aren't involved with her? She's not the reason you've stayed so long?"

"She has nothing to do with it."

"Will you think it awful of me if I tell you I'm still not quite sure you're telling me the truth?"

Bruno sighed. "I'm telling you the truth."

"So she's not gonna show up here looking for you? Needing help with her truck or her kids?"

"She won't."

Leah picked up her cup and sipped and set it down again. "Feels a bit anticlimactic, doesn't it? The way the fight has ended?"

"I could pick up a chair and throw it through that window, if it'd make you feel better." He smiled at her.

"No, there's only one thing you need to do for me."

"What's that?"

"Will you change out of those clothes and back into your other ones?"

He laughed. "What? You mean you hate this tropical-print shirt I'm wearing?" He picked the front of the shirt up off his brace. "Hell. Had to go all the way over to Hattiesburg to get it, seeing how I drove off and left every clean thing I owned over here."

"They're dry now. And folded back on the bed."

"Then I'll change." He stood and pushed the chair in, and it was all he could do to keep from touching her hair. Instead he put his hand on her shoulder and rubbed her shoulder blade, and she stood and put her arms around his neck. Something she had not done since the brace. Pulling him to her and running her hand through his hair, the feel of the structure around his neck pressing on her breasts, which were sore. He kissed her and then he did more, behaving like he used to out in the field where the sun was hot and the space between them hotter, fondling her, finding himself unable to breathe, his hand running down the curve of her waist and then the front of her, her low stomach, and then lower, to her pubic hair, and then between as she repositioned her legs so that they were farther apart.

→←

Eilene was standing in front of the kitchen sink peeling boiled eggs and wishing she were a better person. A better person (or more precisely: a *better mother*) would not be crushing the eggshells beneath a flattened palm with barely checked anger. A better person would have seen this coming and opened the mail earlier. Her recent mistake in judgment where Sonny was concerned traveled all the way back to that moment when she had tucked those letters from the school board behind the wire bread basket. If she had only opened them and read them, she might have seen what was in store, and all the mistakes could possibly have been avoided. Enlightenment had been offered to her, and what did she do? She stuck it behind a wire bread basket. So it was no wonder she suffered the consequences. Eilene lifted off a portion of shell and smashed it between her thumb and forefinger. *There,* she thought, the weight of her failures eased somewhat. She was not so old that a U-turn could not be tried. There was still time to change. Time to improve. She could start going to church again. Endure the noncommital platitudes of whatever Methodist preacher was standing behind the pulpit; start sending money to overseas missionaries digging wells for thirsty Africans; volunteer to take meals to shut-ins; sign up for county cleanup and drag her black Hefty bag along the shoulder of the highway, picking up trash. . . *Stop it! Stop it now!* she admonished, sick to death of thinking about herself. Determined to make a go at having a good day, she scooped up all the eggshells and dumped them in the trash. Turning on the water, she rinsed the slippery eggs and then put them on a plate and sliced them in half with a paring knife. Twenty-four halves later, Eilene was still beating herself up, this time for throwing away the eggshells when she desperately needed something to squash.

Across the way, Bruno was standing in the back portion of his yard, near the clotheslines, smoking, and Eilene leaned on the counter and watched him. She couldn't be sure, but she thought he was wearing different clothes from when he first pulled up at five that morning. Eilene had seen the lights of the car trace through her living room draperies and gone to the kitchen and spied on him, watching him appear from the side of the house and move to the back porch and fumble with his keys. Even though the light was new-morning faint, she had seen a printed shirt and casual pants, she was almost sure of it. But now he was wearing jeans and a blue shirt, looking like the old Bruno. A sudden thought charged through her, and she stopped hating herself for a moment, all her self-recrimination reduced to rubble in light of the oldest proof of cohabitation: if he changed his clothes, then he had done it inside the house, inside one of the rooms, maybe the bathroom, or hopefully his own bedroom. The changing of clothes while within the possible presence of a wife nudged the small needle on Eilene's hope barometer up a couple of degrees. She watched him, the casualness of his pose, the seeming absence of any type of stress around his shoulders, the refreshed look about him, as though he'd just crawled out from between the covers. She smiled as she dumped pickle relish in a bowl and mixed it with mayonnaise and was reaching for the paprika when she heard Sonny coming down the hall.

He sat down in a kitchen chair with a great, breast-heaving sigh.

Eilene mixed the glob together and began to slather it into the open holes in the eggs.

"Flitter Brain and Merle here yet?" Sonny asked, emitting another sigh.

"Not yet. I'm sure we'll know it when they arrive."

"You ready for me to put the ribs on?"

"Heavens, no. You cook them now, we'll be done way too soon." For Eilene, timing was everything. She wanted the meal to begin in the middle of the afternoon. That way, by the time the homemade ice cream was done, it would be time for fireworks, which left the barest minimum of time for painful conversation.

Another sigh.

"I wish you'd quit that," she said, covering the deviled eggs with Saran Wrap and putting them in the refrigerator.

"Quit what?" he said.

"You know good and well what I mean."

"Funny how you all of a sudden got over bein deaf." He put a toothpick in his mouth and dug around his gums.

"Seeing one's son violating a favorite chair will do that. Shock can be a healer, I've heard. I was never one to believe in it, but I must admit that it's not too late to be a convert to new types of therapy."

"Yeah, right. Bruno told me months ago that you were foolin about that."

She turned to him, her hands on her hips. The sugar bowl was between them, and she saw it and remembered their routine and walked over to him and stuck out her hand. "Good mornin, Sonny," she said.

He took her hand, somewhat grudgingly, she noted, and said, "Good mornin, Mama."

"There. That's better." And it was, though it would take some getting used to the new noise around the place. Conchita was not a car, but she came equipped with certain standard features. A portable cassette player was one. A tape was playing. Some noisy musical with the volume turned up as loud as it could go.

"How's your wife this fine morning?" Eilene asked.

"She's a light sleeper," Sonny said, leaning on his hand.

"And this is a bad condition?"

"It is for me. Once she wakes up, she don't go back to sleep, and she expects everybody else to get up with her."

"That's not bad, Sonny. That's smart."

Sonny shook his head, hating the way his shirt fit him. "And she hid my overalls from me."

"She did not. They're out there waiting to be washed." Eilene turned to him. "And you know what else she said to me? She wants to do them herself. Wash your clothes. Sounds like the girl's making an effort."

"Hellfire, they weren't even dirty."

"She thought they were. You know, Sonny, not everbody wears their clothes for a week before throwing them in the wash."

"Tell me this!" he shouted, banging his hand down on the table and watching the silverware jump. "Was I so goddamn bad?"

Eilene put down her knife and went to the table and pulled out a chair. "Now. The number one thing you need to remember is I didn't marry her. You've got yourself to thank for this."

"I know, but—"

"But what?"

In a way, it *was* her fault he had made up the girlfriend lie in the first place, a lie that had somehow morphed into an actual girlfriend who had mutated into an actual wife. He wasn't clear on the exact method of blame yet, but he was sure once the damn music was turned down a notch or two and he could think properly, he would figure it out.

Music from *West Side Story* blasted out of the bedroom at the end of the hall and into the kitchen.

"Shit, Mama. This ain't gonna work. She ain't even *heard* of Johnny Cash."

"Sonny, this situation is of your own making." Eilene set the squash and onions in foil and rolled them up. "There's no more silver to sell to buy you a ticket home." Going to the icebox, she took out the corn and began to shuck it into the sink.

"What in the world are you talkin about?"

"Just forget it."

"Did I ask you to sell anything? Have I asked you for one durn thing this morning? I ain't even asked you for breakfast, and here you go!"

"Quit actin like this. It's the Fourth of July. We have guests coming. By the way, what's she plannin on wearin for the party?"

"How the hell should I know? I didn't take her to raise."

Eilene listened to Conchita singing along with the music, all bright noise and nasal twang; her voice a tad off-key, but for the most part contagious in its enthusiasm.

"Whatever it is, she apparently feels pretty in it. What I wouldn't give for a good old dose of self-confidence." Eilene leaned down and looked at her jeans, still uncomfortable in them. Her shirt was made of bandanna material, and she had a white scarf around her neck. The clothes were new and festive, and while she would have fainted dead away if Sonny had paid her a compliment, it didn't stop her from wishing for one.

"I had to change to the other side of the bed, too."

"Why's that?"

"Conchita cain't breathe through but one side of her nose, and it seems she cain't sleep but on one side of her face, and it seems that side just so happens to belong to me."

"Sonny, I'm sure there are benefits to having a wife in bed. Benefits that make up for small sacrifices."

He blinked his tiny eyes at her. She was not supposed to be talking about IT. She was not supposed to even know what IT was. She was supposed to make him some oatmeal and a plateful of toast and that was all. "I, ah . . ."

"Oh, you silly boys. Did you think you sprung up from out of my garden?"

Well, Sonny's head did resemble a cabbage, but that was beside the point, and then she felt the weight of self-hatred descend on her. What kind of mother would stoop so low as to compare her child to a vegetable?

Eilene heard Conchita coming up the hall and braced herself for the worst.

Turned out it wasn't that bad. The girl was wearing white bell-bottom sailor pants and a cute nautical shirt that showed off her midriff and white thong sandals. Her curly hair was pulled back in a headband.

"Shit, Eilene, don't you look cute," Conchita said, studying her from the doorway. "I ain't never seen you in jeans before."

"You only met her yesterday," Sonny said. "You ain't known her but a day. How the hell could you have seen her in more than one outfit?"

Conchita looked from mother to son and shrugged. "She still looks cute."

"Thank you, dear," Eilene said. "And you look adorable. Seems Sonny's cranky this morning," she said, nodding toward her hulking son, who was leaning on his elbows staring at the fridge.

"Sonny, what do you think about tattoos?" Conchita asked. She was holding a *Biker Babe* magazine in her hand.

He opened his mouth in fear. There was no way in hell he was going to be branded with needles. "Why?"

"I was thinking I might get your name tattooed right here." She pulled her shirt collar away and pointed to her upper left breast.

"That way you won't forget who you are," Eilene said to him and turned back to the corn in the sink. The sky had been beautiful a half hour earlier but was clouding up. Low clouds were on the horizon, and the bottoms of those clouds were copper-colored. Should a storm set in, there would be people forced to sit in the living room and talk. A thought that made her shudder. "Sonny, you could both go at the same time. Get Conchita's name tattooed on your chest. Good thing you've got more space than she does, seeing how her name's got more letters in it. Goodness, you could even put her last name there, maybe even an address and phone number." (*Gosh, this is much more fun than banging pots around the kitchen,* Eilene was thinking.)

"Can we, Sonny?"

"No."

"Why not?"

" 'Cause I don't want no tattoo on me."

Eilene got the big steamer pot from the bottom cabinet and began putting the corn in it.

"But it would be fun."

"It would not be fun, and I ain't gonna do it."

"But—"

Sonny stood. "I'm lighting the grills. I don't care if it's sooner than you'd like. I'm doin it, and that's all there is to it!"

Eilene and Conchita watched out the kitchen window as he walked across to the barn and opened the doors and dragged out the fifty-gallon barrels he had outfitted as barbecue grills. Behind him in the sky, a silver streak of lightning jettisoned from a cloud, and a few seconds later, they heard the low rumble of thunder.

"I had no idea he was so sensitive about stuff," Conchita said.

"You'll get used to him, dear. It just takes some time."

→←

Bruno saw them from the big window in the living room. "Your folks are here."

Leah came and stood by him and slid her arm through his. "I wish I could figure it out," she said, watching her mother climb out of the Corvette, the way she had to lean back and heave herself forward and grab hold of the door frame to lift herself up, movements that branded her as too old to be sitting in a sports car.

"Figure what out?"

"Why she drives me crazy. I tell myself not to be irritated with her. To act like a decent human being. To not take her bait, but somehow . . ."

"Let's just get through today," he said, patting her hand.

"What in the world is she wearing?" The subdued sheen labeled Dora's slacks as belonging to the polyester family, and the blouse was so unwrinkled that it had to be a nylon blend. Leah bent forward and stared at Dora's sandals in disbelief. Panty hose! Where was the woman who had taught Leah to love linen? Where was the woman who tested the limits of etiquette by wearing it all the way up through the end of November? Dora Maxwell had apparently taken leave of her senses. She would be pouring sweat in less than thirty seconds.

Bruno could hear the steady whirring of the attic fan and watched as the curtains fanned out in gentle movements. It was going to be a hot day, and he was sure there would be a comment about the lack of air-conditioning. "How long before she complains about the heat?" he said.

"One minute," Leah said, noticing her father was favoring his hip and that he was stooped a little.

"I say five minutes, tops. Loser has to tend to the cows."

"You got yourself a deal."

He suddenly felt as nervous as he had that first time he had been introduced to them, and he supposed at the heart of all the nervousness was the appalling feature of sexual guilt. He had felt it then and he felt it now. Luckily, Merle didn't know how Bruno had chased his beloved child down the hall and captured her foot in his hand and pulled her body toward him to make it more available for an almost-rape, but it seemed to Bruno that he might deduce it somehow: read backward in time to that moment, give him the same piercing stare as the one he'd given him years ago at that first miserable dinner together. The look that said to him, *You can be as polite as you want to be, but I know what you two did in that motel room, and since you're the one with the outdoor plumbing, I hold you responsible.* Bruno blinked away the memory, recalling Leah's preemptive warnings and how they had been ignored. Remember, Mother will want to know your intentions right off the bat, she had told him. Would it be considered rude if I tell her I intend to fuck the living daylights out of you every day of your life? he had asked, uncomfortable in his white shirt and dress pants. Leah said, Listen, you can joke if you want to, but don't say you weren't properly warned. Five minutes after the introduction, under the scrutiny of Merle Maxwell's penetrating gaze, Bruno had wondered what ever possessed him to act so flippant about it.

Leah pushed the screen door open and squared her shoulders. Because she loved her father the best, she ignored him and offered her greeting to the lesser object of her affection: Dora. A brief hug was all she could stand because of her mother's perfume. Willing herself not to gag, she kissed Dora on the cheek and then stepped back and let her enter the house.

"Oh, Leah! It's been so long. Let me look at you!" Dora seemed unwilling to take what she had been given and moved toward her daughter and put a stranglehold on her, squeezing and squeezing, fumigating Leah's shirt and hair, as well as the room, with Chanel No. Five.

"Mom. Please." Leah patted her mother's arms and tried to pull away from her. "Dad, help me out here, will ya?"

"Dora, for God's sake, back up. Give her some room to breathe."

Dora moved away and stood there as Merle hugged his daughter, noticing with pleasure the brevity of the hug, its simple one-armed embrace.

Bruno was standing beside them, being ignored. Leah noticed it and looked to her father, and then her mother, and wondered what to make of it.

"Merle. That's some car you got out there," Bruno said, nodding to the Corvette plainly visible through the living room window, willing to offer up a little male vehicle worship even though his extended hand had been refused.

"Yeah. Well," Merle said, studying Leah's face.

"You sell the other one?"

"Yep."

He was yet to look at Bruno, who was beginning to sweat. The tension was such that he felt the gravitational pull of the sun might just be threatened. It reminded him, in an irrelevant way, of the way they had all seemed when he'd first come up out of the fog of anesthesia. He had been the outsider then, the dolt who didn't know.

"Oh my Lord," Dora said, fanning at her face. "I don't see how you stand this un-air-conditioned house."

Bruno looked at Leah and winked. "Time to go take care of the cows," he said, glad to have a reason to leave the room.

"Nice of you to take that load off my daughter," Dora said with a sniff.

"Dora," Merle said, exercising The Tone.

"What? What did I say that was so wrong? What!" Dora screeched.

Leah looked at Bruno, who seemed bewildered but remarkably unscathed. In the past, a remark like that would have sent him into a rage. She fanned back through memory, wondering if she had ever told her parents how unevenly the work had been distributed. She hadn't.

Bruno went to the fridge and called out, "Anybody need anything before I go?"

"I assure you, we're just fine!" Dora said.

Merle lowered his head and put his hands in his pockets.

"Tom Waite may bring some of his barbecue sauce over for us," Bruno told Leah. "He might show up while I'm out in the field."

"Okay."

"Money for it's back there on the dresser." He sipped his beer and gave her a look of empathy.

"You want me to invite him to stay?"

He shrugged. "Yeah. I doubt if he will. But, who knows, he might."

Silently, the three of them watched as he left the house, the beer in his hand.

"It's really much, much too early to be drinking," Dora said.

"I'll remember that in the morning when you start begging for a Bloody Mary," Merle muttered. "He need any help?" he asked Leah.

"He manages just fine."

"That's not what a little birdy told us," Dora said.

"Dora."

But her two Bloody Marys had made her brave, and she found herself imbued with a strange confidence enabling her to ignore The Tone. "What? If you're going to spend the whole day saying my name over and over again, please do me the courtesy of explaining what I'm doing so wrong. I've not said a word about you-know-what, and I'm not going to. So hush."

"This trip was a mistake. A huge mistake."

"Dad, what's going on?"

"See? I told you she'd know," Dora said.

"The only reason she knows, or even suspects, is because you're too stupid to keep your mouth shut."

"Merle Maxwell! How dare you talk to me this way!"

Leah was shocked as well. And, in a strange way, she felt protective of her mother, which was crazy. "Listen, you two—"

"No, *you* listen," Dora said. "Now you'll see how he's treated me all these years. There's a word for it. A word I've heard over and over, and never in a million years would I think it applied to your father. Never! I listen to other women talk about their husbands, and do I jump in with any complaint of my own?"

"That's because you don't have anything to complain about," Merle said.

"Oh, I wouldn't be so sure about that. Women are different these days, Merle. Women don't let men walk all over them. But do I feel sorry for myself because you're still stuck somewhere in the age of Donna Reed and Robert Young? No. Never. I've always defended you to my friends—"

"What's there to defend?" Merle wanted to know.

Leah watched him, the stillness of his hands, the clenching of his jaw.

"Do I say bad things about you? No, I certainly do not. And that word. That nasty word women sling around these days. Shovenist"—she pronounced it "shove"—"it breaks my heart, but that's what you are. A male shovenist."

"What in the world would you have to defend about me?" Merle asked, shaking his head.

"You're not as perfect as you like to believe."

"Tell me specifics, Dora. Not this vague nonsense."

He was remembering what a gentleman he had been around her friends; how he had taken it upon himself to remember their favorite drinks and answer their questions, however silly, with seriousness; how he had gone out of his way to help Mavis find a good attorney for her son, who had come back from Europe with a heroin habit that landed him in jail up in Memphis; how he proved his concern by driving up there to check on the son and ended up having a little late dinner with an old friend of his, who just so happened to be a circuit court judge; how once he had driven back home and phoned Mavis with the good news, he had stemmed her profuse thanks with the verbal assurance that it was nothing, really, nothing at all that any red-blooded southern gentleman wouldn't do; how she had shown up the next day at his office, reeking of heavy perfume and disappointment (a secret theory of his: the heavier the perfume, the sadder the woman) and fiddled with the window shades and studied his bird-stamp prints hanging on the wall; how he had toyed with the idea of it even moments before she impulsively threw her arms around his neck and kissed him, breathing into his face the faint whiff of bacterial decay so like shit on the bottom of a shoe; how the breath of this woman whose social success his wife pined for had driven out what little sputter of flame there might have been; how he had gone to bed that night and thanked his lucky stars that Mavis Stroh had never been one to drop dental floss into her Piggly Wiggly grocery cart and how subsequently she had appeared to Merle Maxwell as hopelessly flawed, which was a grace, since to appear any other way would have led him to some cheap motel, where he would have been forced into the pathetic position of watching a middle-aged woman who was friends with his wife wrestle with her girdle; how even as he steered clear of the Mavis Stroh Disaster, and all other middle-aged temptations that followed him like sputtering flames, there was no sense of accomplishment, no satisfaction at traveling the moral high road, for however he appeared to his golf and fishing buddies and the friends of his wife, in his heart he saw himself as no more than a well-behaved dog, a Labrador retriever that had learned fear before it opened its eyes to the world, a beloved pet with enough terror of a rolled-up newspaper to ignore damp, pungent female smells, a creature of habitual obedience who had never, *ever* humped a leg. He looked at his wife and said again, "What in the world are you talking about?"

"Stuff. People say things. Word gets around. And while I *never* would have thought of you as a shovenist—"

"Chauvinist, Mother. That's the word you mean."

"What difference does it make?"

"Well, 'shovenist' is not a word."

"What do you mean it's not a word? You just said it. How can it not be a word?"

Leah leaned on her hands and peered through her fingers out the back door, watching her husband's back underneath his shirt, the way he moved as he lifted bales of hay onto the wagon. She wanted to lick that back. Run her tongue over every muscled ridgeline and buried bone.

"What the hell nonsense are people saying?" Normally, Merle would have been able to ignore Dora, but the day was hot and he was tired and he felt foolish and ridiculous. He hated his trousers and his polo shirt. Hated his loafers and socks. He even momentarily hated the woman who was his wife, even though, in all fairness, she was no different now than she had been at eighteen. But most of all, he hated the thought of being talked about when he had done nothing, absolutely *nothing*, wrong. "You can't name anything concrete because you're making it all up."

"Are you so sure of that, Merle? Are you?"

"This is a pattern, Dora. You communicate through disagreement."

"That is not true!"

"You pick fights just to have someone to talk to. It doesn't matter what the issue is, all that matters is that you're leading the conversation around by the nose."

"How dare you!"

"Then tell me this: why are we fighting? What's it about?"

He's got you this time, Leah thought, feeling a surprising wallop of pity. Her mother had never been able to remember the trigger point of an argument.

Dora looked at the two of them, noticing Leah's uncommon tranquillity, the way she was covered in the slick film of composure, pointing out to Dora all of her daughter's planes and angles of superiority. Shaking her head, she was close to giving up and calling it quits, and then she remembered. "It was about pretending," she said.

"No. No, it wasn't."

"I think it was."

Merle said, "It was about a promise we made."

"Jesus. You two are driving me crazy," Leah said, holding a hand over her belly. Her lone argument in favor of abortion would be sparing said baby from these two potential grandparents.

"You wanted me to pretend that you didn't talk to Eilene last night—"

"Don't you do it." Merle pointed a finger at his wife.

"Don't you dare point at me like I'm a child!" Dora stood, the friction of her polyester pants against the sofa creating a blue crackle of electricity, an actual visible spark. "Don't you dare! You wanted me to act like we don't know these two here are separated. If that's not about pretending, I don't know what is."

Merle looked at his wife and then his daughter, ducked his head, and walked out the front door. Leah watched him jerk open the car door and climb in. A plume of dust followed his erratic reversal down the drive, and even though the road was a safe distance from the house, they clearly heard the sound of tires laying rubber.

Dora picked up a magazine and began to fan her face. "Silly man. He doesn't know where in the world he's going," she said. "So typical. Just get in a car and leave."

Leah had lost her patience with men who leave, as well as women who provoke departures. "You enjoyed that. Admit it," Leah said to her.

"I refuse to comment," Dora said, though she *had* enjoyed it, enjoyed it immensely. "Good Lord, it's hot," she said, fanning her face.

"Mom, you're burning up," Leah said, moving into the kitchen and getting her mother a glass of ice water. "I've got some linen slacks back there, and a roomy cotton shirt. You'd be lots cooler," Leah said.

"They wouldn't fit me," Dora said, exhausted and depressed. "I've gained weight, as you can clearly see." She sighed. It had been months since Mavis Stroh got drunk celebrating her reelection as SLAG vice president and spilled her guts to Dora in the bathroom of the country club, falling on her shoulder and apologizing over and over again for kissing Merle, crying and begging with the fervor of an evangelical for Dora's forgiveness. Months. And while Dora knew in her heart that Merle had taken the high road and not done anything, and probably would not have done anything, he *had* done irreparable damage to their marriage by not mentioning it.

"At the risk of making you mad, I need to tell you the pants are too big on me. They'll fit you. Go on. Try them on."

Standing up, Dora walked with as much dignity as she could muster, keeping her head held high. Leah followed behind her and found the slacks and put them on the bed alongside a cotton shirt. Before she shut the door, she said to her mother, "We were separated. We're not anymore. And before you ask, I remembered to put the green olives in the potato salad."

{CHAPTER 33}

Merle Maxwell drove through a landscape that seemed as beaten and tired as he was. Or perhaps what he was seeing was merely a reflection of his own tiredness, a state that was settling into a new role of permanence these days. While the repair of his own mental state would be left up to him, there seemed to be an effort under way to relieve the county of its tiredness. Red earth, raw and exposed, was piled in heaps along the road, and concrete pipes that looked like gray tubes of industrial bowel were lined up, ready for placement. A series of manholes was draped with the orange utility tents belonging to the phone company, while round smudge pots smoked and wobbled in the wind. A sign was painted with fresh paint: YOUR TAX DOLLARS AT WORK; the names of all the county commissioners were listed in two neat rows and in the lower corner, the star-framed logo of the local bank. The sight of progress should have made him feel better, as an engineer, but it didn't, for an army of kudzu was marching across the landscape, climbing power poles, running in tendrils up guide wires, strangling trees, fondling bulldozers. It seemed more than a tenacious plant growing excessively. The kudzu seemed an indicator of unstoppable failure. *You can work all the tax dollars you want,* it seemed to be saying, *but they won't change a thing.* Merle drove on down the road.

Past fallen fence posts and houses that leaned in precarious empathy. Chimneys that had pulled away from their moorings. Clothes draped to dry over pump houses. Burn cans with foul-smelling smoke rising on the wind. He passed an area were people were congregating around an artesian well and saw not one white face among them. The Negroes were standing around the bubbling water with buckets in their hands, filling the containers quietly, almost abstractedly, as though hauling water for personal use was an involuntary act their bodies engaged in with little or no awareness, like a breathing lung or a beating heart. Merle passed a junkyard and saw a child beating a dog with a stick, and he saw how the child stopped the hatefulness to stare at Merle's car. Farther down the road, he passed a house where men were sitting on the porch, staring out into the nothingness of space, shirtless, obese, a haze of gray smoke hanging over their heads, a Confederate flag stretched over the trunk of a car up on blocks. One stood up as Merle passed and put a hand to his eyes, walking out near the fence to watch the car on down the road. The topography of tragedy. A lost world where education beyond the twelfth grade would seem excessive. Where pregnancy before the age of sixteen was the norm. Where trucks were the standard and a late-model Corvette was as rare as a two-headed calf.

"Where in the world am I?" he said, turning off the radio. It was offensive to him, with its Hot One Hundred Hits, its "Cat's in the Cradle" and "Hooked on a Feeling," its Jim Croce and Eric Clapton, its Aretha and Gladys and Joni, its One Nation Under the Groove, music he hated but thought he ought to listen to because listening to what he really wanted (Andy Williams's "Moon River," Tony Bennett's "I Left My Heart in San Francisco") would prove to him that he actually *had* become old. And now that he was buried in the ass end of the county, the car seemed just a little offensive, too. How does one reconcile a Corvette flashing down the road against outhouses still in use? One can't. All one can do is turn around and head back to where one came from and try to pretend the dismal scenes were not actually places where people lived but a careful staging for a Tennessee Williams movie set. He was a southerner, but not *this* kind of southerner, and he wondered what it was in his daughter that made her choose this place over Meridian, or Jackson, or Atlanta, or even Memphis; what she found appealing about sour pigpens and swaybacked horses; what topics of conversation she found available with teenagers toting a second child on a hip. Frustrated that he wasn't doing much more than adding mileage to his new car as a result of a grown-up temper tantrum—mileage that he would guard and measure to maintain its optimum resale value—he turned in at a gas station that seemed more up-to-date than the shacks surrounding it, and climbed out. *Gas the car up,* he was thinking. *This way I won't seem so foolish for having stormed out of my daughter's house. This way there will be a Merle Maxwell Reason for behaving like a horse's ass.* Merle thought the place looked an awful lot like a flat faded cigar box. He thought he had never seen such a sorry set of ramshackle gas pumps. He thought that if he ever got out of Purvis, he would never—

"Hey, mister. That ain't no Poor-Old-Nigger-Thinks-It's-a-Cadillac car, is it?" a voice said.

The fellow was squatted in the dirt, his body between his legs, his knees high up near his cheeks in a pose like that of a grasshopper. Merle took note of the khaki pants and oversize khaki shirt that was open and flapping around the waist. A look of vacancy was on the man's face, as though only his eyes were animate, and even then, the type of animation was questionable. He was next to the gas pumps, and Merle's first thought was *Damn, it's a miracle I didn't hit him.* Even though he liked Burt Reynolds, Merle had been offended by the movie *Deliverance*, finding it exploitative, demeaning, and most of all, untrue, but now it seemed he might be looking at someone who would be right at home on the Cahulawassee River, a boy who had grown up listening to trapped city men squeal like pigs.

"What kind a car is that?" the man asked, hopping forward and scratching at the dirt to look for something.

Watching the poor creature's fingers work in the dirt, Merle realized he was picking up loose change.

"It's a Corvette. You work here?" Merle asked, reaching into the water-filled bin and lifting out a squeegee to cleane the windshield.

"Here, in this place? Are you kiddin me? They ain't no way they'd let me work here. They let me pick up pennies and such, though." The man hopped two little hops and picked up a coin, and then he stood to his feet and shuffled toward Merle and stuck out his hand. "Sparechange Dinkins, here," he said, catching hold of Merle's hand and pumping it vigorously. "Pleased to meet you, I'm sure."

"Likewise," Merle said, dropping the squeegee back into its water.

"How much one a them there cars cost?"

Merle never had liked to give out personal information and was offended at the threat to his privacy. "I can't really say."

"Oh. You must a stole it."

"No, I did not steal it."

"Then you forgot how much it cost you?"

"No, that's not it."

Sparechange touched the hood with his finger. "You reckon if I save up all the loose change I find, I might could get me one?"

A peculiar sadness fastened itself around Merle's head, and he felt dizzy and out of place, more than a little ashamed. "Could be."

"Without a doubt."

"Are these pumps operational?" Merle pointed to the closest one. He'd prefer premium high octane, but there didn't seem to be much demand for it.

"Dawg. Ain't it a beautiful day?" the man said, ignoring Merle's question, looking up to the sky with a certain childlike exuberance on his face.

"Yeah, it is. But there's a storm building over there." Merle pointed to the west, with its gunmetal clouds. "I'd like to fill up the car. You know the owner?"

"Of the car?" Sparechange looked at him. "Ain't you the owner?"

"The owner of the gas station."

"Him? He's in there eating his lunch." Sparechange looked at the sky again. "Without a doubt, I believe you're right. It's gonna rain."

"So. I guess—"

"Hey, mister. You ever seen a frog caught in a drainpipe?"

Merle sighed, exasperated. "Not recently."

"You wanna see one?"

"Listen, buddy. I really am pushed for time."

"So is he. He ain't got long now."

Merle began backing up, his hand stretching out behind him. *Ahh, there's the fender. Now here comes the door.*

"I seen him last night, and he's all swole up. Green as a toad."

"That's too bad."

"You familiar with concrete?" The man was standing in front of Merle, his arms flapping at his sides, his eyes burning with curiosity. There were smells attached to him: cheap wine and urine and car grease and roasted peanuts.

"In what way?"

"You ever rolled around in it right after it's been poured?"

"No."

"Shit. I guess I'm the only one." The man scratched his nose with his dirty fingernails.

Standard pleasantries would be wasted, Merle realized that, but still he said in a casual voice, "I'll be seein you," opening the door and lowering himself into the cradle of his leather bucket seat, the wonderful cradle of cowhide that carried with it suggestions of prosperity and excess, of understanding the value of a high-priced toy, of working hard for a living and enjoying the fruits of it. Above all else, an embossed red leather reminder of just how lucky he was.

The creature looked at him with his dark wet eyes and said, "No, you won't," and then he hunkered down and began digging at the dirt. Merle felt a chill as he pulled back onto the road and headed back toward the house.

⇢⇠

"I think you look nice," Leah told her mother, noticing that the panty hose had been removed, as well as all traces of polyester and nylon. "I bet you're cooler."

"I had to roll them up at the waist. But I guess they'll do."

Dora went to her purse and removed her brush and fluffed her hair. She had always had nice hair, wavy and honey-blond. And her face still was absent of wrinkles, though small pouches of fat were under her eyes, giving her a "just rolled out of bed" look.

"Where's your father?"

"He's still not back."

"I can't believe it! I guess he's going to manage to stay gone until the very last minute."

"Mom, you picked the fight with him, not me."

"I did not pick a fight with him. He pointed his finger at me. You saw it. You left home, so you don't know how he is now. You got to get away from his tire ranny—"

Leah winced.

"He's turned moody and sullen, and so busy! You have no idea what I have to put up with. All he wants to do is fine-tune his car and piddle with stuff around the house. Replace perfectly good windows with storm windows. Replace perfectly good batteries in the smoke detector. Replace the doorbell because he can't hear the old one good enough. Replace the awnings with new polycoated ones. Replace everything."

"He's not going to replace you."

"What do you mean?"

"Isn't that what you're worried about? Being replaced?"

Dora began opening the doors to the kitchen cabinets, peering under the sink and noticing that Leah was terribly disorganized. Furniture polish next to a can of Crisco shortening. Old sponges tossed to the back. Rags piled on top of Johnson's paste wax. Flower vases still stuffed with stiff green florist foam. Two bottles of half-full Windex that should have been combined to make one full one. An old waffle iron with a frayed cord. "Good gracious, Leah, do you *ever* clean out this stuff?"

"What are you looking for, Mom?"

"Don't tell me you don't have a blender."

"Pie safe," Leah said, lifting the bowl of potato salad out of the fridge. "Are you worried Dad's thinking of replacing you?"

Dora found the blender and lifted the lid off and looked inside. While Leah wasn't looking, she sniffed it.

"Guess you don't want to answer me."

"I've thought about it. Worried about it a little. But Merle Maxwell is nothing if not faithful."

"Maybe he's regretting retirement."

"He looked forward to it long enough."

"Maybe it's not all he thought it would be."

"Maybe *you* should ask your father what's bothering him. He always listens to you."

"That's an exaggeration."

"You should see the way he flies up out of his chair every time the phone rings." Dora opened more cabinet doors, looking for liquor. "Don't tell me you don't have any Absolut." Lifting out bottles of Tanqueray and Smirnoff, she set them to the side. "I brought my own. But he left before I could get them out of the trunk. Oh, Leah, if he stays gone too long, it'll ruin everything!"

"He'll be back."

"I wanted cocktails *before* we sat down to eat. Before. Not after." Now that she was opening doors and pulling out drawers, Dora found it intriguing. So much to learn about this daughter of hers. The placement of dish towels was all wrong. They should be in the drawer next to the sink, not in the drawer next to the kitchen utensils. Not only that, but the dish towels hadn't even been folded; they were crammed into the drawer, and none of the drawers (not one of them!) had shelf paper in them. And it looked like it had been years since Leah had reached underneath the stove and scrubbed it with a good degreasing solution. Not that very many women did that sort of thing. But Dora did. Faithfully. The area behind and underneath her stove was as clean as the rest of the kitchen floor. It didn't matter to Merle that it was spotless, and it apparently didn't matter to Leah, but it *mattered* to Dora. When she opened another cabinet door, Dora saw how unorganized the pots and pans were. Boilers underneath frying pans, creating a tottering tower of Revere Ware, and not only that, Leah's cast-iron skillets that had not been coated properly and were rusting away in solitude, and horror of horrors, back along the far wall, a mousetrap (minus the mouse, thank God) still baited with molded cheese. The hidden-from-sight mess was such that Dora, even though she had worked her way up to a size twelve, began to feel better about herself. Leah was not as perfect as her exterior life indicated. So what if she was a size six. Her cabinets were a mess. And there was dirt underneath her stove. Dora stood up and wiped her hands on a dish towel. "Is Eilene making tea?"

"I suppose so."

"Should we make some, just in case?"

"Iced tea is a standard around here. You know good and well no one drinks water south of Meridian."

"Will it be Lipton tea or some off brand?"

"I have no idea." Leah looked for her big basket and thought she remembered seeing it on the back porch.

"Your father says a filtering system will clear out the artesian smell," Dora called to her, watching through the kitchen window as Leah moved across the back porch to retrieve a basket from off the washing machine. "I prefer Lipton. The other brands taste funny."

Lifting a lid off a tea canister, Dora pulled out a plastic sandwich bag full of what looked like oregano and held it to her nose. It didn't smell like oregano. It smelled like Leah's college clothes. The memory as fresh as though it had occurred yesterday. "I think you should talk to him about a filtering system. He needs to feel needed. Important. He would like to be consulted once in a while about improvements in his daughter's house." She held the pack to her nose again, peeling it open to see what it was, and saw the packet of wrapping papers and thought: *Well! Miss Perfect Miss does* this, *too.* Seeing Leah's form flash across the window, Dora stuffed it back into the canister and wiped her hands on her pants.

Leah set the basket on the table. The big salad bowl would fit. "The water tastes fine to us. We're used to it."

"Why don't you just talk to him about it. Ask his advice," Dora whined.

"Because I'm not going to pretend I want something when I don't. I don't believe you have to come up with projects to make a man feel needed."

Oh, just you wait and see, Dora thought. *Just wait until that husband of yours rolls over and goes to sleep without bothering to touch you in six months. Just wait until there's nothing at all between the sheets and you dry up and feel worthless and look in the mirror and begin to believe it's* your *fault he doesn't want you. Just wait until it dawns on you one day that the* real *reason he doesn't want you is because he doesn't want himself. See if you don't start scrambling for projects. Doorbells. Gutters. Anything at all to make him feel needed so he will* like *himself again, so that maybe, just maybe, he'll remember that he likes* you. "If the cat's been out there around that basket, you really ought to wipe it out. Nobody wants cat hairs in their potato salad."

"Thanks for pointing that out."

Dora looked at her watch. "Okay. I've given him enough time. He'll just have to walk over to Eilene's to find us."

As they walked across the yard, Leah saw Sonny keeping watch over the ribs, a white chef's apron tied around him. Dora waved and called out to him, and Sonny sullenly returned the greeting with a hoisted meat fork. "He's really a rude one, isn't he?" Dora said, stepping into a hole and almost dropping the blender. "Have you ever thought about getting a golf cart?"

"What in the world for?"

"So you could hop in and drive over the yard. Save yourself all this walking."

Leah looked at her mother as though she'd lost her mind. And then Eilene was on the back porch waving her dish towel at them and walking down the steps and coming forward to relieve Dora of her blender burden. Finally, Leah had moved outside the reach of the searing heat and was standing inside the cool shade of the boat, thankful for the very first time that Sonny had been foolish enough to park it in the backyard.

⇝⇜

"Where we goin, Mama?"

Alyce lifted the raincoats off the hooks and handed them to Joe and Ben. "Take these just in case." She looked around the kitchen to make sure all was in order, and then she took them each by a hand and led them through the hallway into the motel office.

"Where we goin?"

Alyce went to the drawer in the desk and pulled out the master keys to all the rooms and slid numbers four and six off their rings and walked to the front door. "For a drive."

"Maybe we're goin to look for Santa Claus," Ben whispered to his brother.

"No we ain't. It's too hot for Santa Claus."

"We seen him that day we was flyin our kites."

"That weren't Santa Claus."

"It could a been."

"Come on, boys, quit your dawdlin." Their mother was holding the door open for them and once they were out in the hot sunshine, she pulled it shut and locked it. "Go on and get in the truck. Open up both the doors and roll the windows down so it won't be so hot."

"Where're you goin?" Joe asked her.

"To check on something," Alyce said, heading down the concrete walkway to the room at the end.

"Can we take a Coke with us?" Joe said.

"She ain't gonna let us. Them are the motel's Cokes, not ours."

"She might."

But their mother wasn't answering them. Instead she was unlocking Mr. Willem's room and stepping inside.

Alyce saw that it was neat as a pin. And no thanks to Dolores Corrales. Willem had been adamant about the woman, and Alyce had finally given up trying to force proper motel conveniences on him. She walked into the bathroom, afraid for a moment about what she might find. Nothing but neatly folded towels and washcloths. On the small counter, his leather dop kit was still open, his razor and toothbrush by the side. The bed was made and his clothes were hanging in the closet. His strange safari hat was beside the television set. The clincher was his banded suitcase, upright beside the bed. Wherever he was, he had not meant to stay there, he had meant to come back here.

When Ben was three months old, she had woken in the middle of the night with a pounding heart and a sense of imminent danger, of wrongness, all over her body. Throwing the covers off the bed, she had raced up the hall to his room. There he was, tangled in his covers, the surplus wrapped around his tiny neck. Her baby would have died if she had not been awakened. By what, she never stopped to question, and while Willem Fremont was certainly not her baby, not even her blood kin, she felt the same sense of alarm. Something was wrong. Terribly wrong. Stopping at Bruno's room, she stepped inside, the emptiness making her sad, the depth of the sadness shaming her. The envelope holding a check was on the bed, where he had told her it would be. His duffel bag was gone, and all that was left of him was the smell of his cigarettes. "Okay, then," she said, relocking the room. Across the parking lot, her two boys were standing by the open door of the truck. She noticed their similar height, their sweetness, their little bodies, their complete trust, and realized this was enough for her. More than enough. On the way to the truck, she lifted out two drinks from the Coke box and opened them.

"We goin to town, Mama?" Ben asked.

"We're goin lots of places," she told them, pulling out onto the road.

And they settled back on the seat and drank their Cokes, watching out the window at the cows and the fields and the telephone poles flashing by.

➔➔

With the exception of the time of year and the open hostility radiating off several members of the family, the dining room tableau would have come close to resembling Norman Rockwell's slurpy-sweet picture of Thanksgiving dinner. Leah watched her mother as she jangled her bracelets for Conchita and listened to the girl ooh and ahh over the string of tiny sterling magnolia blossoms. Sonny was next to them, a look of preoccupation on his face.

"What a surprise. Lard-ass found himself a wife," Bruno whispered in his wife's ear as he scooped some potato salad onto his plate.

Bruno really *was* surprised, noting Conchita's extreme packaging, its overall desirability far and above what Sonny deserved. The girl's overbite was all that was wrong with her, and he felt sorry for her, since she seemed aware of it and kept her hand in front of her mouth even when she talked. He couldn't understand the exact reason, but a woman's hair would probably always be a weakness for him, and he noted the red highlights and thickness of the girl's as he listened to her reconstituted southern accent that was decidedly Hispanic-sounding.

Leah leaned on his shoulder and sniffed, loving the smell of hay and sweat, loving to the point of embarrassment every single thing about him. "She's not so bad," she said. "Your mother seems to be adjusting well enough."

"The thing about Mother is that you never really know what she's thinking. She could be sitting there plotting the girl's murder and we'd never know it."

Bruno speared a rib and put it on the plate for her, and all her good feelings went away. "I can't eat this." She nudged the bloody-looking rib to the far side of her plate. "I keep seeing the cow at the bottom of the pit."

"What pit?" He looked at her, noticing the pale, pale ring of skin around her lips.

Tom Waite was across from her, talking to Merle and tearing into his barbecued ribs, enjoying the bachelor's delight of family gatherings.

"What pit?" Bruno asked again.

"That's how I got bruised. I fell off the edge of it."

"When did this happen and where?"

"Out where the big pine tree is. There's a hole. No, it's bigger than a hole. I'm not sure what it is. Maybe some sort of sinkhole. Whatever it is, it's huge. The cow fell off the edge of it, and while I was looking for her, I fell, too." She picked up her napkin and laid it over her plate and said, "Honey, I'm sick."

Bruno put his hand on her thigh and rubbed. Terms of endearment were new to him. He wanted a word for her, just for her, but couldn't think of one. All he could manage was "Jesus. You could have been killed."

"I didn't die. I just got banged up some."

"When was this?"

"In May. It seems like a long time ago."

Bruno ate silently, his eyes on Merle, who was bending over his plate trying his best to pretend to have an appetite. Tom poured some sauce on his baked beans and bread and then scooped the excess off the lip of the bottle and licked his finger. "In our family for over fifty years," he was saying as Merle nodded, his eyes on his wife, who was telling Conchita the ingredients for Singapore Slings.

"You feel like eating anything?" Bruno asked Leah.

"No."

"You want to go lay down?"

"Not really. I might try some crackers. They say crackers will help."

Bruno pushed his chair away from the table. "You sit. I'll go get you some."

"Everything okay?" Eilene asked. She was sitting at the head of the table, at the place where Bruno and Sonny's father used to sit, in the end chair that seemed too large for her. Sonny was next to her, picking at his food, glancing at his watch.

"Everything's fine," Bruno said. "I'll be right back."

The room was large, with windows set across the front, and below the windows there was built-in cabinetry where Eilene kept the good china stored and where she used to keep her grandmother's silver. The box had been there for so long that its imprint was still visible. Looking at where it used to be, Eilene felt the blush of anger building, all the anger from all of the years of fruitless manipulation, of limitless cajoling, of desperate hoping, and of some unknown remorse that defied naming. Conchita's peeping voice was getting on her nerves, and to make matters worse, Dora was going on and on about making cocktails and the latest quick dessert that one made by dumping pistachio pudding into a container of Cool Whip. "Top it with coconut shavings if you want to make it really super special," she was saying. "Shit, where'd you learn all that stuff?" Conchita asked her. Eilene rubbed her eyes, posting a mental note to herself: *See if you can't get the girl to limit her use of the word "shit."* All around her were the sounds of forks and knives on her good china and the slushy tinkling sounds of ice in the tall glasses of tea. Eilene listened to the murmur of courtesy conversation, the words no one really wanted to say addressed to ears that really didn't want to listen. Except for Dora and Conchita. Those two really seemed to be hitting it off, which added to Eilene's sense of outraged sensibilities, while out the wide windows of the dining room, the very sky seemed to reflect her mood as it turned hurricane-ugly.

"Eilene, how in the world did you manage to find a place with two houses on it?" Dora asked. "Are they just alike? Did you build them?"

"Oh, we didn't build them. They were here already. Built by my husband's grandfather. Old Reinhold. This one first, and then the one Bruno and Leah live in the following year."

"It was a large family, then?"

"No. Just the two of them. The old man and his schoolteacher wife."

The table turned quiet, and Leah dabbed at her forehead with her napkin while her father watched her with worried eyes.

"You look sick, Leah," he said, reaching over and patting her hand, which was cold as ice.

"Not sick, just a little bit pregnant," she said in a low voice, giving him a lopsided smile. Before he could respond, she said, "We'll talk later," and turned to Eilene, who was saying, ". . . just couldn't seem to get along. He built her a house and put her over there. They lived apart for forty-seven years."

Conchita said, "Shit, Eilene. How'd they . . . ah . . . I mean how in the world—"

"How did they procreate?"

All heads were turned in her direction. She shrugged. "Who knows. Needless to say, they did. At least three times. There were three boys. My husband's father was one of them."

Leah looked at her father and smiled and shook her head.

"Have you told everyone?" Merle whispered.

"No. Just you and Bruno."

A grandfather, he thought. *A grandfather with a red Corvette.* The two realities seemed at odds. Like oil and water. Like liver and ice cream.

"Who wants a daiquiri?" Dora asked brightly, deciding enough had been said concerning folks who couldn't get along. The last thing she needed at this point was for Merle to get any ideas about building her a house and locking her away. "We've got a full bar. Name your poison!"

"Count me in," Conchita said.

"I want a beer," Sonny said, asserting his demand to his wife, who hopped up and shimmied her way into the kitchen.

"Leah? You want a drink, hon?"

"No thanks, Mom."

"Well, I certainly do. Conchita, let's you and me go fire up the blender. Merle, dear, you want anything?"

It was a peace offering, a sincere one. He noticed the slightly desperate air about her, the fierce glimmer to her eyes that signaled waiting tears, and at first, in spite of the barely visible *pleading* waving to him like a flag, he considered turning it down, but then he realized a grandfather ought to be kind to a future grandmother, especially a woman horrified by aging and sure to take offense at the tag of "grandmother," a woman who would not go kindly into that land of baby-sitting and diaper changing, and so he nodded and forced a smile to his face. "A beer would be nice," he said, leaning back in his chair as he looked across at his daughter, who had suddenly gone pale and sick-looking, her eyes distant and pained. Without a word to anyone, she pushed her chair back and left the room, crossing the hall and disappearing from view.

Eilene was looking out the window as well, and then Tom Waite turned and looked, and finally Sonny, who, upon looking, scrambled to his feet, believing what he had seen could only mean one horrible reality. He'd been caught, and once his mother found out, he would be killed. Slowly. Finally Merle turned around and saw the beat-up truck parked in the driveway and a woman and two small boys in it and Bruno standing next to the rolled-down window carrying on a conversation.

"Who's that?" Merle asked Eilene.

"Trouble," she said, lifting her plate and carrying it into the kitchen.

{CHAPTER 34}

Leah drove across the field, refusing to think about what she was doing, just acting on impulse and the impulse was this: *Go, get away from him, away from his explanations, away from whatever excuses he plans to offer to make this better. Go. Act like Dad, pretend this beat-up truck is a red-hot Corvette and go.* Sadly, she knew of only one place to go. And even though rain threatened, she still had to go there. While she drove, she ducked and parried each approaching thought, forbidding them from entering. It was the way she had always dealt with her mother. Ignoring the unpleasant until the unpleasant got tired and went away. Long years of practice told her that if she stood her ground long enough, the foolish thoughts and impulses would settle down until they became drenched in logic. *These thoughts I'll accept,* she promised herself. *These logical thoughts. And not any of the others.* Looking out the window of the truck, she saw the wind blowing the field grass down in flattened sheets, violently, so that the entire field looked like hair ruled by cowlicks, some sections flattened, others standing on end. Across the field, the cows were all huddled under the largest of the oak trees. She counted them quickly. All were there. Reaching for a rain slicker on the floor, she took her eyes off the field, and the truck plowed into a rough pocket of ground that bounced her in her seat, and her teeth bit through her tongue. Spitting blood out the window, she saw the approach of the tree line, and for one insane moment, she was awash with the impulse to keep on driving, steer through privet and sassafras, bush palmetto and longleaf pine, crush the goddamn mushrooms and dead limbs beneath the truck tires. Drive and drive until she nosed the truck over the rim of the pit. The appeal of it was so overwhelming that she slammed on the brakes and killed the engine by taking her foot off the clutch. The truck rocked to sleep as the engine ticked and hissed. It was beginning to rain. Opening the door, she stood in it, her face up, the drops heavy and falling and striking her skin like pebbles. Back when she was a city girl, she had thought of rain as soft and warm; it was only after working in it that she realized, for the most part, it felt like cold rocks falling from the sky.

Sliding the parka over her head, she went to the woods, stepping over the logs, feeling her way, while the storm increased and rain fell in sheets through the slotted limbs of the trees, limbs that made cracking sounds as the wind snapped them back and forth, scattering pinecones and nests and great sheets of scaly bark. The path she remembered by heart, and she shut her eyes, wiping the rain off her face, everything appearing as a gray wall of wet all around her while a small busted dam of leaves and twigs runneled around her shoes. Clumps of loose greenery slipped by. Sheets of moss like fuzzy skin. Caps of mushrooms like tiny overturned boats. The stuff of chaos. Finding the place, she knelt down and reached over the wall, turning on her stomach and sliding down until her foot touched the first root. It was all so predictably childish, and she knew it. It was like being nine years old and running away from home, clutching a Barbie doll and a jar of peanut butter. It was ridiculous in extreme, foolish beyond belief. But underneath the female melodrama was the female hope that someone would come looking for her.

Clinging to a root, she peered to the side and saw the remains of the cow. The soot had all been washed away, and a sharp angle of a hipbone was evident underneath a soggy tent of rotted skin. Such a sad attempt at a pyre. All wasted effort, it seemed. Dropping the last three feet, she landed hard and put a hand to her stomach. It was the first time she had thought of the baby, what she might be putting it through. *So, you'll be a tough little kid,* she told it. *You'll learn to climb and burn a cow properly. I'll teach you. You'll learn to like artesian water. I'll show you how to hold your nose as you swallow.* She kicked a bottle away from her, and the moment her foot made contact, she felt a peculiar sensation and smelled a strange smell high up in the nether regions of her sinuses, just as the hair on her arms stood on end. Never having experienced it didn't stop her from realizing what it was, and she remembered what Bruno had told her to do and dropped to her knees and covered her head with her hands and prepared to die. The dark gray world turned yellow and blue, and the explosion, which was so loud it moved beyond human comprehension of noise, pressed against her eardrums, and she wondered if she'd been struck. She hadn't. But something had. She smelled it and looked around and saw the leaning pine tree. Fire was snaking up its trunk in defiance of the rain, and then she watched in horror as the tree began to finish what it had started years and years ago. It began to fall.

"Jesus. What have I done," she said as she began to run, headed for the other side of the pit, away from the tree that was so large there didn't seem to be any room for escape. Math had never been her strong point, but she knew distance, and what she saw indicated there wasn't enough of it. Nightmares didn't happen in slow motion, she realized as she stumbled and fell, her mouth filling with mud before she lurched back up and began to run again. Nightmares happen suddenly and without remedy. In preposterous situations and with little forethought. That teenager showing the revolver to his little brother. That college student so intent on pledging that he freezes to death in the trunk of a car. That girl who wants to listen to the radio while bathing and reaches for it. That woman who climbs down in a pit to see if her husband cares enough to come after her.

Clawing through the vines, she turned and watched as the tree fell with a marvelous superiority, slicing across the tops of all the other trees, blazing like one of God's candles, its weight balanced on the fragile wall of clay on the opposing side, the wind whipping it until it ignited all the way up to its crown. Literally a burning bridge. The rain was such that smoke was suspended, but still the tree burned. Wondering how long she might have until the trees underneath caught fire, she shook her head. Not long, she reasoned. Given enough time, it would be like roasting a pig in the ground. "Jesus God, I've done it now," she said, bending at the waist, clutching her knees with her hands. Believing it couldn't get any worse than it already was, she looked over at the artesian pool and saw a dead man lying across it.

→←

"I believe I can help."

Merle said this, and his attitude was one of propriety, and it pissed Bruno off. Tom Waite was out near the truck, trying to answer Alyce's questions about the missing Willem Fremont. Meanwhile, Sonny had left in the Pontiac to buy beer, of all things. Like beer would solve the problem. Out of the corner of his eye, Bruno saw his mother walking across the yard, her hat on her head.

"I'll manage," he said.

"Well, I think you better damn well make sure you do."

"Save it for later," he told Merle, shoving him out of the way.

"Bruno, where are you goin on that tractor. You'll catch your death," Eilene said, holding on to the brim of her hat.

"Do me a favor. Get Alyce inside and fix her and the boys a plate of food. She's been out driving all day looking for Willem."

"Is Willem her husband?"

"No."

"Who is he, then?"

"She'll explain. Listen, talk her through filing a police report. Show how it's done. I'll explain later."

Eilene studied him. "Is it true Leah's expecting?"

"It's true."

"Then you better get a move on." She turned and walked away. Whatever was going on with the girl named Alyce, it was apparently not a threat to Bruno's marriage. Tom Waite seemed to be taking an uncommon interest in Alyce, and Eilene thought she'd sit back and let him handle the situation. Filing a police report sounded like something a man ought to do, not a woman who had a pile of dirty dishes waiting to be washed.

Merle had followed Bruno into the barn. "Why the hell did she run off like this?"

Bruno ignored him.

"It seems a sorry way to maintain a marriage."

"You think?" Bruno climbed up onto the seat and waited for the plug to warm.

"What I think is that you've got some explaining to do."

"Merle, get the hell out of my barn," Bruno said, steering through the double doors, grabbing a rain slicker and sliding it over his head, pushing the tractor forward, the rain so heavy that he could barely make out the fence lines in front of him.

He had forgotton how familiar he was with the land, how it felt like his skin. The terrain that had been faithful to itself, that would always be faithful to what it was. Studying the trees in the distance, he realized something was missing. Something that had always been there. The giant leaning pine was gone. He stood up as he drove, seeing the truck and where Leah had gone in, that small path, and then he did something that surprised him: he steered the tractor east of the truck for a reason he couldn't understand, a reason that just seemed right. Blocked by a fence line, he drove the tractor across it, ducking to avoid the snaking barbed wire, taking down two of the posts and dragging one of them a distance behind him until it gave up the fight. Standing again, he looked at the trees, noticed the way the wind was moving through them, the low smudge of smoke that hovered midway up the trucks. *Fire. Something's burning,* he thought. *Something I can't see but is burning, regardless.* He pulled the tractor up as far as it would go before being stopped by the trees. Climbing off, he began to call for her, hearing his voice made flat by the wind, still calling as he made his way through the dense bracken. He could smell it now, off to the west, where a red glow was building and changing to orange and then yellow and red. Remembering what she had said about the hole, he began to be careful with his steps, as careful as he could be in light of the situation, and when he felt the sudden updraft of wind, he stopped and checked himself, taking one step at a time. Palmetto fanned in front of him, and he walked through it, pierced in the legs and thighs by the sharp blades, and then he saw cattails and smelled the strong water and dropped to his knees and crawled forward, feeling with his hands until the earth dropped away from him.

"Leah!"

"Bruno!"

He stretched out on his stomach and peered over the side and saw her fifty feet down, the giant pine blazing like a bridge directly over her head.

"I can't get out!" she screamed.

He fanned at her with his hand. "Move over there! To the other side! Get away from it!"

"I can't leave him!" she yelled, her hands around her head to protect her skin from flying embers and sparks, her body forming a shield. "He's hurt!"

Bruno saw who it was and couldn't believe it. He abruptly felt detached from the practical and wondered if Willem had somehow managed to fall out of an airplane.

"Bruno!" she screamed.

"Put your hands under his arms and pull him over there!" He pointed to a clearing. "Pull him. I'm going for help!"

"Don't you dare leave me!" she screamed. "Don't you dare!" But he was already heading back, hearing her cry and shout and then scream, "Fuck you, Bruno Till!" over and over as he ran through the palmetto to the tractor and pulled himself up on it, swinging it around and steering it directly through the woods where he thought the truck might be. He saw it in the distance, through the trees, the dull sheen of wet metal, the busted light he never had fixed. Once there, he climbed off the tractor and reached to the gun rack to signal for help and saw the gun wasn't there. Momentarily confused, he wondered where in the hell it was and then forgot about it and scrambled into the truck bed, tossing aside gear until he found the coiled rope. Slinging it over his arm, he jumped back on the tractor and headed into the woods, hoping the rope was long enough and that Leah's knots would hold. Hoping she would remember how to tie a knot. Hoping she would remember what a damn rope was. Standing, he saw the fire had spread, the oily black smoke rising, in spite of the wind and rain.

Willem saw the angel and the fire behind her and realized hell was not as bad as the preachers had warned. With enchanted movements she hovered over him, guarding his face from sparks. "Silence," he croaked. "There is a silence where hath been no sound." He watched her face. She shook her head and said, "Just save your strength," the voice soft and southern-sounding.

He opened his mouth and drank the rain and realized his ears were shutting down, for all he could hear was a soft velvety roaring, the deep-throated purring of his heart, the flood of blood through arteries and veins, and even these elemental gurglings were growing more and more faint, fading like a tide. Like the process of birth in reverse, he realized. That first quickening to the beat of one's own heart. That first awareness of self before the light of the world crowds in and drives the singularity away. But death gave back those elemental sounds, gave back a measure of sanctity, of quietness, even wonder. He looked at her and saw her lips moving around words, and he tried to smile at her, tell her not to work so hard at communication. Over her shoulder, he could see the wall of fire and how it was dipping low in its middle, with blazing arms snaking up into the sky. And then he saw the fear in her eyes, and he squeezed her hand and whispered, "There is a silence where no sound may be," as she bent low over him, protecting him while sparks rained all around. He could smell her hair and her skin, her soaked cotton shirt, the deep warm musk of female. And then she was up and reaching over him and grabbing hold of something and working at it with frantic hands, trying hard to get something right, and the harder she tried, the more she seemed unable to do it. She was crying and looking up to the sky and shaking her head and screaming, "I can't do it! I can't do it!" Some instructions must have come from above, for she calmed down and nodded and fed out a length of rope and made a slipknot and worked it underneath him and then over her back so that the two of them were harnessed together. Looking up, she nodded and shut her eyes and put her arms around him, pressing her head into his neck, and Willem saw over her shoulder the wall of fire crash down on top of the sunken house, spear it thoroughly, until it was crushed. "Hold on, now," she said, and he felt the jerking motion and the alien sensation of being hoisted, and the equally foreign reality of a woman's body leaning in to his and pressing against his broken leg, and then there was nothing, just the grayness of a dismally soggy world and searing pain and flashes of lightning as he traveled upward past the fire, and even as he felt hands pulling on him and a wet plastic jacket being tucked under his chin, it all seemed like the outer edge of a dream. Luminous and exaggerated. Halos of light crowned heads and hands. Dripping angels, all of them.

"Willem Fremont," Bruno said to him, exhaustion on his face. A slash of green streaked across his brace due to a violent encounter with a tree.

"Stay here," Bruno told the woman as he peeled her off Willem. "Stay here. The fire's down there. You're out now. You're okay. Leah?" Bruno took her by the shoulders and shook her. "Snap out of it. You're okay. You're both okay. I'll be back with help."

The woman knelt to the ground and rested her hand on Willem's arm, and they stayed that way, listening to the rain.

Fading in and out of consciousness, he came up out of the mist and noticed with alarm that he was about to be lifted and that there were more people there, a man and a woman he didn't know and Tom Waite; the men were holding what looked like a headboard that had been lashed with a rope.

"No," he told them. "Leave me," and even as he said it, he realized his motivation was pain avoidance. If they lifted him again, he would die.

"We got no choice," Tom said, then: "One. Two. Thr—" and Willem fainted dead away.

His memories were fragmented and surreal, otherworldly. Celtic music would be fitting, he remembered thinking as trees floated by, small green saplings next to towering parent trees, those giant fairy-tale-looking trees thrashing about in the wind. Vibrant waves of chartreuse rippled out in front and beside him as he was pulled along, his fingers trailing the rain-soaked ground. The tractor rattled and sputtered, the flap of its exhaust vent clacking like a castanet. And trapped somewhere in the smell of its diesel exhaust, Willem remembered every bus he'd ever traveled on, every suitcase he'd ever packed, the memory striking up feelings of loneliness and stale smoke-filled depots, memories of his tired eyes scanning departure times, of hours spent staring out a dusty window at the slight variations of changing land, of believing everything looked pretty much the same until he saw the mountains of Colorado. He lingered inside this memory. Smelled the solvents of his trade. Recalled the faces of his workers. And then he woke and found himself back in an open space where the land was flat, and he was confused by the flashing lights and siren sounds and the state-trooper cars. Somewhere between his memory of Colorado and this place, he had forgotten who he was and where he was supposed to be. A young man put a blood-pressure cuff around his arm and asked him who he was, over and over again, and Willem rolled his head from side to side and wondered where the words were, and just at the point when he felt he had fallen into an abstract world where identity and reality were obsolete, a woman climbed into the ambulance and sat down by him and adjusted her straw hat. The hat was familiar, and he studied it, fastened his concentration to it as though it were a lighthouse in the middle of a raging sea.

Patting his arm, she smiled down at him and said the two words that reeled him back to Purvis, Mississippi: "Hello, sugar."

{CHAPTER 35}

Sonny loaded the beer from the convenience store into the back of his mother's car and pulled out onto the road. His heart was beating almost normally again, and he wiped his face and looked at his hand, pleased to notice the sweat was at a moderate level. "It was nothin," he told himself. "Coincidence. Not about me helpin Joe at all."

He had just about convinced himself of it when he passed the Roustabout and saw Joe's lime-green car still parked there. The plan had called for him to get back into the car and head for the border once he climbed out of the pipe. The plan was to hang around just long enough to let folks know where he was.

"Well, shit," Sonny said, his heart hammering again as he pulled into the parking lot and turned off the engine. Once he was sure no one was watching him, he got out and walked around Joe's car, cupping his hands around his face and studying the interior. Cigarettes. Rolled-up newspaper. But no Joe. Scratching his head, he thought about it and then looked through the window one more time. There was no way in the world that Joe would leave behind those big foam rubber dice hanging over his rearview mirror. No way in the world.

Knowing he had no other choice but believing he would feel more up to checking it all out once he had a drink, Sonny walked into the club and climbed on his favorite bar stool and ordered himself a Pabst.

Two beers later, he felt ready for the challenge and left the club, driving as slow as possible toward the construction site for one more look.

All seemed the same as it had the night before. The big machines. The cowbirds out in the field. Walking over to the gray mouth of the pipe, he stared at it a long time, and then he squatted down and stared some more. Dark was funny, he thought. Dark made shapes out of nothing. Dark fooled a person. Looking up, he exhaled, and then he leaned as close to the opening as possible, the smell of mold and decay present, as well as the sour smell of shit.

"Joe?"

"Why, you . . ." A raspy cough. "Fuckin idiot—"

Sonny sat back on his heels. "That ain't no way to greet a fella, Joe."

"I'll show you how to greet a person! Get me outta here! Get me outta here before I kick your fat ass!"

Sonny thought about it, and then he walked back to the car and opened the trunk and rummaged around until he found the flashlight, knocking it against his big hand until it blinked on. And then he thought about it some more. He had not yet *seen* Joe. He had just heard his voice. If asked whether he had seen him, he would be able to say no. No cop in the world ever asked a fella if they'd *heard* somebody. Banging the flashlight against the bumper of the car, he watched the lens shatter. "Oops," he said, tossing what was left of it back in the trunk. On his way back to the pipe, he fished three beers out of the cooler and cradled them against his stomach.

"Sonny?" Joe was whimpering. "Jesus, Sonny. You out there?"

"Yeah, Joe. I'm here," Sonny said, slurping his beer, adding up the circumstances, and seeing how they were finally lining up in his favor.

"Ain't you gonna get me outta here? I'm stuck, Sonny. I cain't move. And my eyes are swole shut. I need help, Sonny. I need a doctor."

"Well, you see, Joe, here's where we got ourselves a little problem—"

"YOU WORTHLESS PIECE OF SHIT! THE ONLY PROBLEM YOU'VE GOT IS ME BASHING YOUR BRAINS OUT!" The tirade ending in a paroxysm of coughing.

Sonny looked at the big Caterpillar across the way. "Screamin like that's gonna make you worse. Yellin at me's not gonna help you one little bit."

He leaned down and tried to peer inside the pipe and thought he saw the tips of Joe's fingers; either that or a quintet of swollen bratwursts, red and split on the ends, beginning to rot. Technically, he had still not *seen* Joe. Technically, all he had seen was something that resembled spoiled German sausages.

"You're in a real pickle, Joe."

"*Pleeese*, Sonny. Oh God. *Pleeese* help me—"

"Now, Joe, I think me and you need to think about this for a minute."

Joe thrashed around violently. "I'LL KILL YOU! I SWEAR TO GOD, I'LL KILL YOU—"

"You see?" Sonny slurped his beer. "The crux of it is this: you ain't really motivatin me to get you out of there. Not with that kind a talk."

Reality seemed to settle on Joe momentarily, and he began to plead in earnest. "Listen. Sonny. You know me. You know I didn't mean nothin by it. Now get me out of here, and I'll forget all about it. I didn't mean a word I said. Go get some help. I ain't gonna say anything. I cain't even move. I cain't even feel my legs no more."

"That's what we need to think about, Joe. You see, if I go get help, they'll know I was in on it. I cain't see me doing that right at this moment, not with me just married and Mama just now gettin used to it all."

"YOU NO-ACCOUNT TURD!"

Sonny opened another can of beer.

"Sonny? Wait. Sonny, get me outta here and I'll give it to you. All of it."

"Give me what?"

"The jewelry. I've got it all tied around my neck. It's here. All of it. It's yours. You can have all of it. You can give Conchita a diamond ring."

At the mention of her name, Sonny crushed the empty beer can and shoved it in the ground. "Let's talk about Conchita, why don't we."

"Who?"

"Now, Joe. Don't go dumb on me." He drank from the can. Christ, there was nothing like a cold beer on a hot day. The humidity was at the terminal level, heavy as a quilt, and the storm clouds were building, and come the next fifteen minutes or so, there would be one hell of a rainstorm. "Conchita. My wife." He leaned down toward the opening. "You thirsty, Joe?"

Joe was panting like a dog, his words little more than strangled barks. "Yeah, I'm thirsty."

"How 'bout you tellin me all about you and Conchita, and I'll get you a beer."

"There ain't nothin to tell."

Relying on his intuition, which told him to lie, Sonny said, "That ain't what Conchita says."

"Sonny. Please. Pul*eeese*. It didn't mean nothin."

Sonny finished his second beer. "What didn't mean nothin?"

"Me and her." Joe coughed again, wet-sounding. "Where's my beer?"

"Comin right up." Sonny popped the tab and turned it on its side and rolled it down the pipe.

The insulting spew revved Joe up a notch, and he began to scream: "YOU DURN IDIOT! YOU CAIN'T DO THIS TO ME!"

"You ought not to have fucked her, Joe."

"Sonny. She's trash. A whore. She begged me for it—"

"I don't think I believe you, Joe."

"SEE IF I DON'T KILL YOU WHEN I GET—"

"I tell you what. You get out of the pipe and we'll talk about it." Sonny stood and brushed off his knees. "You know where I live. Me and Conchita'll be there waitin for you."

Feeling better than he had in ten years, Sonny climbed back into the Pontiac and headed home to his wife, to his boat, to the limitless possibilities of being debt-free, to the feeling of accomplishment in outsmarting Joe, as well as his conscience, by not looking at the man, to the overwhelmingly pleasant reminder that there would be homemade ice cream in the late afternoon and, come the evening, fireworks.

{CHAPTER 36}

The moon was full, and there was a brittle feeling of clarity in the night sky, in the hardness of stars, along the inflexible angles of the constellations. The storm had passed, and in its passing, the heaviness of humidity was lifted and a soft breeze was blowing through the curtains of the bedroom. Bruno rolled to his side and looked at his wife and reached over and put his hand on her stomach. She was not asleep, but her arm was thrown over her face, and he sensed she didn't want to talk. They had been at the hospital until late, and all of them had heard the news that Willem had made it through surgery, and the further discouraging news that in all probability he would not recover.

All the lights had been turned off in the house, and the attic fan was working as hard as it could, but Bruno could hear Dora and Merle complaining about the heat.

"They're burning up in there," Bruno said. "I just heard Dora say she was sweating like a whore in church. I never knew she had such a mouth on her."

"I love you," Leah said, and he looked at her, wondering if she'd heard what he had said.

"I think the only way we're going to get any sleep is to send them to a motel."

"I love you," she said again, a catch in her voice.

"Hey," he said, pulling her to him, lifting a strand of her hair and rolling it between his fingers. "Are you all right?"

"I just wanted to say the words. I just wanted to make sure you knew it."

"I know it." *Now would be the time to return the favor,* he thought. *Say it back to her.* He blushed, wondering why he had always found it so hard. "Me, too," he said.

They both heard the sound of a door opening and then a light tapping on their door. Merle called to them, "Don't get up. Listen. Your mother's having one of her hot flashes and wants to sleep in an air-conditioned room."

"I am *not* having a hot flash!"

"Well, what do you call it, then?" Merle hissed at her. "You said you were having a hot flash, and all I've done is repeat what you said."

"I said I was hot. I did *not* say I was having a hot flash!"

"Jesus Christ," Leah said, swinging her legs off the bed and slipping into a housecoat. Bruno was already up and into his jeans. Opening the door, he saw Merle walking through the living room with the suitcase and Dora tiptoeing behind him.

"I can't believe this," Leah said, her hands on her hips. "You knocked on the door and told us you were leaving and now you're tiptoeing out? I'm trying to make sense of it, but I can't."

Dora turned to her, her eyes on Bruno's brace, which embarrassed her. It was easy to forget it was there most of the time, but he was without his shirt and it looked awful. Awful.

"Well, you didn't say anything after we tapped, and we thought maybe you two didn't hear us."

"Dad, it'll cool off in a little while. All you have to do is give it a chance. You've probably got your window opened too wide. If you lower it a little, the draft is stronger."

"I've slept in harder climates than this," Merle said, uncomfortable in light of his daughter's bathrobe and Bruno's casualness concerning his neck gear. He looked away from them both. "It's your mother who thinks she's going to melt."

"He was hot, too, Leah. He was complaining just as much as I was. Aren't you two hot?"

"We're used to it," Bruno said, grinning.

The old Leah would have turned herself inside out trying to make them happy, trying to make sure they were comfortable. The new Leah gave them each a quick hug and promised to call them the next day to make sure they got home in one piece. "Leah, you really ought to get yourself a window unit. Something to help you keep cool. Going through pregnancy in hot weather is awful. Awful." Dora shuddered dramatically to prove her point.

"Good night, Mom." Leah kissed her on the cheek. "Dad?" She kissed him and hugged him. "Don't try to drive all the way back tonight. The La Quinta Inn is the closest. Out on Highway 49. We could meet for breakfast in the morning?"

"I leave all the planning up to your mother. She runs the show."

Leah and Bruno stood out on the front lawn and watched them leave, and then Bruno sat on the top step and pulled her down so that she was nestled between his legs, and they both looked at the stars. The smell of burning was still in the air, and even though Leah had washed her hair, when he lifted it to his nose, he could still smell the smoke.

"What kind of man was Willem Fremont?" Leah said.

Bruno thought about it and then said, "A quiet man. I didn't really know him that well."

"So, he was a missing person twice."

"Seems that way. He sold his business and then left. Nobody should have thought anything about it."

"Who filed the report?"

"I don't know. Probably a friend he didn't realize he had."

Leah stretched out her legs, rubbed her toes in the wet grass. "Tom Waite seemed quite taken with Alyce."

Bruno ran his hands down her arms. "I refuse to comment."

"You can talk about her if you want to."

"There's something else I'd rather do."

"You can do that in a minute." Leah plucked the grass with her toes, her thoughts still on Willem. "Do you think he'll die?"

"He'd have to be a tough old man not to," Bruno said, lifting a section of her hair and dividing it with his fingers and beginning to braid. Once he was done, he tucked it behind her ear and reached for another section and began to braid it while Leah rested her elbows on his knees and looked out across the fields and upward into the clear night sky, toward Sagittarius and Scorpius, toward the bent arm of Libra, toward whatever was out there. She felt her view of life was as wide open and clear as her large kitchen window. She felt that no matter where she looked, the view would be a good one. Bruno tucked the second braid behind her ear and bent close to her, as close as the brace would allow, and said, "I love you." And she nodded and shut her eyes and enjoyed the feel of his hands in her hair.

{EPILOGUE}

The olive-green truck with the Airstream camper attached pulled to the far side of the parking lot of Ruby's Regal Truck Stop, almost out of view of the wide windows, but not quite, and parked. Sunlight winked off its aluminum sheathing. The waitress noticed it and stuck her order pad in her front pocket and turned to the industrial coffeemaker and flipped the orange toggle and waited until the hot coffee was dripping properly before walking around the counter and sitting on a stool. Pulling a cigarette out of her pack, she turned to the cook, a new know-it-all who didn't know the first thing about scrambling an egg, and said, "My break just started, and I plan on sittin here and smokin a cigarette. I'm nearly 'bout dead on my feet." And then she turned back and watched as the owner of the Airstream climbed out of his truck and walked around to open the door for his wife. Maggie remembered who they were. Even before the old man handed the straw hat to his wife, she remembered.

"Hell, is it already the month of May?" she asked the cook, who looked at her as though the question might be a trick one. Like the time she asked him how much cream he was supposed to put in the scrambled eggs and he said half a cup and she almost had him fired on the spot.

The couple walked slowly across the gravel lot, but not slow like invalids. They walked like people who were taking their time, enjoying the view, what there was of it. The two of them were holding hands like young folks. Maggie saw he was still walking with a cane and couldn't believe another year had already gone by. "Is it really already May?" she asked again.

"Yes, ma'am."

"Shit, Bobby. How many times do I have to tell you not to say 'yes, ma'am' to me?" She knocked the ash off her cigarette. "How old do you think I am, anyhow?"

Too old for me, he thought, and then he blushed violently and fought the temptation to wipe his nose on his sleeve, and since any answer would be the wrong one, he simply shrugged.

The breakfast menu had just been wiped off the board and the lunch menu printed out and it was that in-between hour of ten o'clock, the brief slip of time when a hardworking waitress could sit on a stool and enjoy her Virginia Slim.

"Hand me that water pitcher," she told him.

"I thought you was on break."

"I know these folks. My break just ended," she said, snuffing out her cigarette and going to the table where she knew they would sit and wiping it down with her cleaning rag. With fluid movements, she filled the two glasses and laid out two menus and checked to make sure everything was as it needed to be. When they came through the door, she looked at them and smiled, and her smile was genuine.

"Maggie, you've not changed a bit," Eilene told her, smiling at the girl, noticing she still hadn't learned to brush her teeth properly.

"It's all this steam. Keeps the skin young."

And greasy, Willem thought, warning himself not to say it out loud. Reminding himself that if he suddenly felt the urge to say it, he was to reach over and squeeze Eilene's hand. It was their fourth year of visiting the place, and each time it got a little easier. Through the wide window, he could see the prairie vastness of the field, the nondescript beige color of everything, the wind playing with the plunder of the road. Ten o'clock shadows were barely leaning, and the parking lot was empty but for one or two pickup trucks. It was hard to gauge time and its passage in such a place. It might have been yesterday that the two of them were there last.

"You two headed west again?"

"All the way to Los Angeles," Willem told her. "Eilene's never been there."

"We promised the kids we'd check it out first. See what it has to offer."

Willem slid into the booth and set his cane next to his leg, where it wouldn't trip anyone.

"I'm sure it's better than *this* place," Maggie said, tapping her foot.

Eilene reached for Willem's hand as the girl walked away.

"Coffee?" she said.

He nodded, his blue eyes looking around the room. There was still nothing regal about Ruby's, he noticed. But the lettering on the menu was better, not a misspelled word anywhere to be seen. And the paper crowns had been kept to a minimum. Small improvements that muffled Willem's alarm bell.

"How's your leg?" Eilene asked him.

"Better," he told her.

"How's everything else?"

He could feel the thundering of his heart and tension in his neck, but instead of reaching for his buttons or grabbing hold of the ribbed sugar dispenser, he looked at Eilene, counted the soft wrinkles around her eyes, the smattering of freckles that he had finally convinced her didn't need covering up. Though only three years old, Leah and Bruno's twin girls had the same freckles. Sonny and Conchita were yet to have a child, and while Willem would never admit it to Eilene, he didn't see much hope of that marriage lasting. Of course, he had thought this for years, and they were still together.

More customers came in, and Willem noticed this and shifted in his seat, stretching his leg as he pulled out his pocket watch and snapped it open. It was a gift from Bruno, and Willem had found that the act of pulling it out and opening it had a calming influence on him. The trick was to keep the opening and shutting to a bare minimum.

"We're making good time," he said, willing himself to relax.

While Eilene watched, his long fingers began to play with the chain, and she realized this was one of those moments he had told her about; that he was looking at his watch to avoid seeing something that he found alarming. That he was trying very hard not to let his panic get the best of him. Glancing around the room, she wondered what might be bothering him.

"I'll be right back," she said, slipping out of the seat and walking toward the front door. Reaching up, she jerked down the paper crown and folded it in half and walked back to the booth and handed it to him.

"There," she said to him. "Better?"

"Much better," he said, rubbing her hand.

ABOUT THE AUTHOR

Melinda Haynes lives with her husband, Ray, on a barrier island along the Mississippi Gulf Coast. She is the author of two novels: *Mother of Pearl* and *Chalktown*.